Gc

Lit

Li

Good Little Liars

SARAH CLUTTON

Bookouture

Published by Bookouture in 2019

An imprint of StoryFire Ltd.

Carmelite House
50 Victoria Embankment
London EC4Y 0DZ

www.bookouture.com

ISBN: 978-1-83888-030-9
eBook ISBN: 978-1-83888-029-3

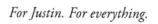

For Justin. For everything.

PROLOGUE

The photograph tumbled across the grass, blown by a short, cool gust of November wind. It slowed for a moment and the girl in the image was flipped onto her face. Across the other side of the oval, behind the old camellia hedge near the north gate, the girl herself lay equally still. Her school uniform had been lifted, well above regulation length, by the playful bend in her left leg. Where her upper body had taken the blow, bone had sheared the fragile nerves of her spinal cord, leaving her neck thrust sideways. Her nose had bled only briefly, the blood trickling like a single tear-drop into the curve of her lip. A shadow loomed over the trench in which she lay. After a moment, it disappeared and all was still again.

The photograph didn't stop moving though. It flipped again as another gust caught the blades of grass, making the girl's image skitter and dance towards the gum trees at the far end of the oval. Inside the hollow of a fallen branch, a tiny pair of marsupial eyes watched as the photograph approached. The branch stretched out like a gnarled road block at the forest edge, and as the wind whipped up again, the girl flew face-first towards it. She was naked in the photograph, and her pert breasts slammed briefly against the smooth wood before she slipped down and fell backwards. A tiny smile played across her lips and her eyes, heavy with promise, stared up at the canopy. Then, with one more small whisper of wind she was tossed into the dark embrace of the forest.

CHAPTER ONE

EMMA

March 2018

There were three distractions that caused the email catastrophe that morning. Unremarkable, ordinary office happenings – only to be expected while sipping coffee and settling into her Friday. But nothing unusual. Nothing that could completely explain the lapse in concentration.

It was only later that week when Emma heard the scientist on the radio talking about the myth of multi-tasking, that she had her answer. Small, insignificant tasks happening at once couldn't be processed simultaneously. They needed her brain to alternate quickly from one thing to the other, then back again. Three small tasks needing quick flicks of attention – the phone ringing just as she remembered she still hadn't booked the dishwasher repairman, which happened at the same time as a junior girl came into the office holding up a coat for lost property.

Three small distractions that each demanded the same response. *Finish the personal email and get back to work.* There was a momentary hesitation as she looked at the email – something grating at the edge of her brain as she pressed 'send' – but her neurotransmitters were on a furious collision course as they changed between tasks and hadn't got the processing order right. The fear though, as she lifted her finger from the mouse was instant.

'No!'

A terrible plummeting knowledge. An immediate, that-can't-have-just-happened shock. Emma stood up with a jerk. Her office chair rolled back and crashed into the wall.

'No!'

She reached down for her mouse and clicked into her sent emails box. The office receded into one black line of text as the oxygen slipped from the room. Hot panic rose in blotchy red patches up her neck as the implications of the email thudded sickly around in her head. It wasn't possible that she'd just emailed those words to the whole group. *It just wasn't possible.*

When her breath returned it came in short bursts. There were more than fifty people on the list. *All over the world.* How had she accidentally pressed 'reply all'? She *never* replied all on large group emails. Only really confident people or self-important idiots did that.

'You've got to be kidding me. Please God – you can't do this to me!'

'I don't think it works like that.' Lena appeared from the back office, stolid as a brick wall, her brow furrowed. 'What's happened, Emma? You'll give old Moira a heart attack if she comes in and hears that sort of talk to the heavenly father.'

'Oh shivers, sorry.' Emma looked back at the photo on her computer screen – the gaudy taffeta, the big hair, the guarded, hopeful smiles. Every one of her 1993 graduating class now seemed to be staring out at her accusingly. Her stomach plummeted further. 'I mean, umm, I'm really sorry Lena. I, err…' She half turned, fumbling blindly for her chair and sank down. 'I think I'm going to be sick.'

Lena dumped her pile of papers on Emma's desk and picked up the waste paper bin in the corner of the room, efficient and purposeful. She held it out. 'Here. Or head to the loos.'

Emma ignored the bin and put her head in her hands. When she un-scrunched her eyes, she noticed Lena's blue lace-up leather walking shoes were topped with garish mustard-coloured socks. Her trousers sat a centimetre too high above her ankles in a practical declaration of Lena's indifference to fashion. Why couldn't Emma be sensible like her? Do her work, go home and walk the dogs, knit squares for charity blankets. Live a sort of life where group email fiascos were as unlikely as the Queen coming to tea.

'Sorry but I'm going to have to go home for a bit. Something's… come up.' She stood and picked up her phone off the desk and slid it into her handbag.

Lena tilted her head and narrowed her eyes. 'Emma, of course you should go if you feel sick but… what's happened?'

'I – It's just a personal thing. Sorry.' Emma brought both her hands to her mouth to mute the scream that was threatening to escape, then she pulled them down and squeezed two tight fists at her sides. 'I've finished the stationery orders and sent the parent email about the Gala Ball. There isn't anything else I needed to do urgently. I'll come back in this afternoon or… make the time up later in the week. Sorry Lena. I…'

Emma looked across at her computer and imagined the responses pinging into her inbox. What would they say? She barely knew most of those girls now. Every year since graduation had removed her a little further from the group. Now, twenty-five years on, there was only the brittle knowledge that she'd never really been like them. Not smart enough or talented enough. Not from the right sort of family – her lack of breeding displayed so obviously in the width of her ankles, her pouchy, undefined knees, her plain face. To make matters worse here she was, now employed at their old school, her staff position a confirmation of where she had really always belonged. A supporting role to their leading ladies – their girls who wandered the park-like grounds of Denham House School in graceful, tittering gaggles.

'I'll call you later.' Emma grabbed her handbag and stumbled outside and down the steps, brushing against the sign on the garden path that announced *Denham House School Administration Office*. She took the quickest path to the staff carpark, through the Wentworth Gardens and over the Great Lawn that sank like lush green carpet as she hurried across. The head gardener had a fetish for perfect blades of grass and the sprinklers were like a constant, guilty presence when everything was so dry.

Emma's hand shook as she unlocked her car. She just needed to get home. Phillip would be completely sensible. He was good in a crisis. He'd know what to say. *Nobody died. Pull yourself together. What's the worst that can happen?* Probably a lot since she'd inferred in the email that she knew something in connection with Tessa's death.

As Emma pulled out of the carpark her phone began buzzing on the passenger seat. She looked down at the lit screen and relief washed over her. *Marlee.* Emma pulled over and took the call, balancing the phone on her lap and putting it on speaker.

'Please don't say anything awful. If I was near a cliff, I might be really close to jumping off.'

'Don't be daft,' said Marlee.

Emma cringed with fresh horror. 'Oh my goodness, I'm such an *idiot*! What have I done?'

'Call it marketing. It'll make the reunion a much hotter ticket now. We might even get Helena and her handbag dogs back from New York if we're really lucky.'

'Oh Marl, be serious! Did it look like I was saying I knew what happened to Tessa? Will everyone guess what I was talking about?'

'Em, stop. It was twenty-five years ago. Nobody gives a toss anymore.'

'Of course they do.' Emma felt a mild burst of irritation. 'If someone sends it on, I could lose my *job*!'

'Would you stop torturing yourself? It's bad for your metabolism.'

'What? I'm not torturing myself… it was just the Year Twelve photo of everyone Selina sent. I was thinking about Tessa and it brought it all back. Now they'll all think I'm a fruitcake.' Emma balanced the phone between her legs, speaker up, and pulled back onto the road.

'Well, you're a very nice fruitcake. And anyway, the only bit about the email they'll remember is that you don't want sex with Phillip because he picks his toenails and flicks the dead bits onto the carpet.'

'Oh *shit*. I can't believe I said that.' Thirty of those women might as well be strangers it was so long since she'd seen them. Now they were laughing about her most private thoughts.

'I love it when you swear. Haven't heard you swear like that since you were pushing Rosie out. Go you!'

'Stop it.'

'Well the toenail thing's disgusting. I'm not surprised you haven't had sex for months. It was funny.'

'Glad you think so,' said Emma, staring bleakly at the wash of autumn colour as she reached the edge of the city and the trees began to thicken. She jumped as a car tooted her from behind, then she stamped on the accelerator to start through the light which must have turned green a while ago.

'Em, really, it'll all be fine.'

Emma felt the pounding of her heart recede as she changed lanes and concentrated on the traffic on the bridge. The truck in front was blowing palls of black smoke that thinned and spread into the blue sky above the Tasman Bridge. She imagined the soot particles floating down onto the pristine waters of the Derwent River below and felt a strange urge to cry.

'What if someone shows that email to Dr Brownley? What if people forward it on?'

'Don't be ridiculous, Em. Brownley's too busy running the school to worry about something that happened when we were kids. How did you manage to press "reply all" anyway?'

'I was distracted,' said Emma. 'I'm not checking my email for a week. I can't bear to think about it.' She tried to ignore the sick throbbing in her head as the truck pulled off to the left at the end of the bridge, giving out one more juddering thick plume of smoke. She flicked on the recycled air button, then reached into the middle compartment of the car and dug out an old packet of mints. The top one was dusty and had something suspiciously like BluTack stuck to it. Today could be the day she cleaned the car. She'd been meaning to do it for months.

'Good idea not to check your email,' said Marlee. 'And if you're tempted just get Rosie to check for you. But she should only tell you about the nice replies.'

'Are you kidding? I'm not letting her near that email! Parents and sex in the same sentence? She'd die of shame.'

'Mmmm. Maybe ask Phillip then, although I'm not sure that school gossip is really his bag. And he might have a problem with the toenail thing.'

'Well that, and the fact that I'd have to do a naked jig to get Phil away from his own computer this week. He's trying to finish the paper he's giving at the World Soil Conference. Submission day looms.'

'He's such a barrel of fun, your fella.'

'Oh, Marl. Leave him alone.' Emma felt a heaviness descend as she thought about Phillip and his constant, distracted grumpiness.

'Well, go and get the cottage ready for your next guests or something. *Do not* check your email. I'll come over tomorrow night early and do it for you, okay? And tell me what I can bring. Salad?'

'No, don't bring anything. Rosie's asked for roast lamb, so I'll just do veggies. I'd better go. Talk to you later.' Emma fumbled with the phone as she disconnected, then she unwrapped the top of the mint packet with her teeth and threw the dirty one into the side pocket of the car door. The next one looked perfect. She squeezed it into her mouth as she took the Cambridge exit off the highway. She looked across at the dry grey-brown paddocks dotted with dirty sheep and wondered if the brief bit of rain yesterday would make a difference to the garden. She needed to water the pots. There was plenty she could do around the garden to stop herself from checking the computer. Maybe the car cleaning could wait.

Emma pulled into their driveway and parked next to the huge jumbled stack of firewood that had been delivered yesterday by weird Wesley, pleased she'd been out when he came. It saved her from hiding in the study to avoid a freaky conversation about the roadkill he collected and buried at his farm to see how fast it would decompose and make his plants grow. Although if she'd been here, she might have convinced him to dump it closer to the shed. She was the one who'd have to stack it. Phillip wouldn't have time, despite being the one who had pushed for them to move out of the city to be closer to nature.

She'd been reluctant to leave the centre of Hobart, but when Phillip had found the gorgeous old timber farmhouse with its high ceilings and picture windows looking out across the endless paddocks, it had entranced them both. It needed a little work, but he had convinced her that they would enjoy the challenge and Phillip was thrilled to have his work life right at the back door. As an environmental scientist studying the effect of microorganisms in different kinds of soil, Phillip was able to set up large-scale experiments and now had three huge greenhouses behind the sheds. She still missed the convenience of living in the city, but over the last year had thrown herself into renovating a small guest cottage that had come with the house, and renting it out to tourists.

She glanced across the paddock. Outside the cottage she could see Pia's old white hatchback. Maybe it was good that she was home early. They could clean the cottage together. Another good distraction. Pia's earnest Germanic nature hid a wicked sense of humour and she was glad Phillip had suggested her for the cleaning job. Some of his other PhD students sounded incredibly boring, but Pia was fun. She would cheer Emma up.

Inside the house, Emma called out to Phillip as she neared the office, but everything was quiet except for the comforting churn of the clothes dryer. Maybe he was in one of the greenhouses.

She changed into her cleaning clothes and headed outside, walking quickly across the paddock. She cringed as the email rolled around and around in her head. *Silly woman. Silly, hopeless person. What a stupid thing to do.*

At the door of the guest cottage, Emma took off her gumboots and opened the door into the kitchen. The only sound was the buzzing of a lone fly, bashing itself repeatedly against the kitchen window in a mad tapping frenzy. Pia must still be doing the bathroom or the beds.

Emma padded through the newly carpeted lounge room. As she reached the hall a murmuring sound made her look up. She felt a flicker of confusion at the sight in front of her. It was Pia, framed by a doorway at the end of the hall, with her back turned. Her bottom glared at Emma – two full white moons cratered with cellulite, split in two by a tiny strip of black lace. She was otherwise naked. Emma's confusion gave way to a sharp cringe of embarrassment – the poor girl was obviously in the middle of getting changed! *But why was she changing her clothes in the cottage?*

The startled, bird-like chirp that escaped through Emma's lips surprised them both.

Emma's hands flew to her mouth as Pia swivelled around and shot her a look of pure alarm. She ducked down to the floor and bent forward, grappling to cover her huge breasts. Crouched over her knees, with her G-string rising up from between her bum cheeks, Pia looked like a terrified white rhino caught in the sight of a hunter's rifle.

'Emma!'

It was Phillip's voice. Behind Pia he stood frozen, stark naked, with a huge, quivering erection.

'Emma! Shit!' His erection began to wilt.

For a moment, the sight of Phillip's failing hard-on struck Emma as both hilarious and completely mortifying for all three of them. She let out a startled choking sound. Her feet were cemented to the spot. She noticed that the scene was bathed in a beautiful incandescent glow as the sun penetrated the room's picture windows – every single, terrible detail was awash with bright, yellow-white light.

The scene seemed to unravel in slow motion, like a dream sequence. From somewhere, Phillip grabbed a towel. Then he hurdled over Pia, who was still squatting in the doorway.

The room was revolving. Then finally, reality hit her with a forceful thud. Emma's knees began to buckle. The blood in her head fell away, like a tide that had turned. She held onto the wall, teetering with sick comprehension. Phillip was coming towards her, wrapping the towel around his waist and saying something she couldn't hear. His mouth looked strange. *She needed to get out.*

Emma spun around and stumbled through the kitchen, then pushed blindly at the cottage door. She ran across the paddock, her feet still in socks, not caring about the rabbit holes or the thistles that bit at her ankles. When she'd covered the fifty metres uphill to the house she was panting. Her hand slid off the door handle as the sweat pooled in her palms. She jerked again at the door and ran down the hall towards the bathroom. Inside, she locked it behind her then clutched at the sink. A noise began rushing in her head. She felt a choking sensation, a spluttering, as she tried to calm her ragged breath. Then, as if from nowhere, wailing erupted, piercing the walls, the floors, splintering the silence of the house.

The noise of her grief grew, taking on a life of its own. It was the sort of crying she hadn't managed since her mother died. Another bitter betrayal that had made her surprised and stupid and had caught her unawares. She quashed the thought as she heard footsteps running down the hall.

'Emma! Emma, let me in.' Phillip was jiggling the door handle. His voice was like a jug of cold water in her face. Her sobs slowed into jagged snorting breaths. She dug her fingernails into the palm of her hand to stop them. Her face was blotchy in the mirror, stricken, strange.

She had an unsettling desire to open the door and apologise to Phillip for embarrassing him, just as she would have if she'd interrupted him in his office on a phone call, asking him if he wanted lunch and he'd point angrily to the earbuds hidden in his ears and mouth at her indignantly – *I'm on the phone!* – and she'd slink away, berating herself for not paying better attention, and wondering if he'd want seeded mustard, or the smoky tomato relish with his ham sandwich, because he seemed to have changed his preferences lately and she never seemed to be able to get it right.

But suddenly fury welled up and burned in her throat. It was unbelievable what she'd seen, and… horrible. She ignored the knocking, noticed her heart pounding, sat heavily on the rim of the bath before sliding down onto the floor and slumping against the toilet. She pulled a towel off the rail and rested her head on it. *Please God, let me wake up. This day cannot be real.*

Phillip knocked again, tentatively this time.

'Emma, can I come in?'

Emma wanted to get up but it was like gravity had condensed around her. An invisible weight pushed down on her shoulders.

'Go away.' The words were raspy.

She unrolled some toilet paper from the wall beside her and pushed it hard against her eyes. *How could he be sleeping with Pia? Was she an idiot? How dare they sully her cottage! She hadn't even had a chance to tell him about the email.*

How silly the email seemed now, and yet she felt another sob rising in her chest. She should be sharing that story with Phillip. The pain was like a tightening noose, making it hard to breathe again.

'Emma? I'll leave you alone… if that's what you want. We can talk later.'

After another minute she heard his footsteps walking away. A prickling rush of sadness made her shiver. *How dare he leave her?*

Her mind and her stomach were spinning. Emma opened her eyes and stared at the pink art deco tiles of the old bathroom, noticed a daddy-long-legs spider and a web, high up in the corner of the ceiling above the shower. She sighed, then looked at her watch, bit her lip. She'd been in the bathroom for half an hour. She shook her head, trying to stop the awful images that seemed to have been branded into her brain. *Maybe this was the end of her marriage.* The idea made her chest pain spike.

What were her options? Did he expect her to want to talk about it? To forgive what he'd done? Could she really be one of those tolerant wives who stayed for the sake of their child? Fury bubbled at the edges of her thoughts. She spat into the toilet and flushed. And then, inexplicably, she began to giggle – the strangeness of the idea that she could be the wronged party who would, from now on, have the upper hand in the relationship.

A flicker of righteous anger gave Emma a surge of energy. Lying, cheating arse! How dare he? How dare he! She would never have believed it if she hadn't seen it for herself. It just wasn't… Phillip.

She unlocked the door and poked her head out into the silence. Suddenly the shadowy high ceilings in the old farmhouse hallway took on an uneasy edge. She felt a strange disconnection from the place, as if it wasn't really her home.

She wondered what Phillip would say to try to justify himself. She'd always thought men who cheated were weak. Pathetic, selfish slaves to their inner caveman. Phillip *knew* her views on this. He'd agreed with her, hadn't he? She distinctly remembered him agreeing with her last Saturday night during *Midsomer Murders*, when she'd said something mean about the wealthy playboy socialite who was having an affair with the pretty librarian. Although,

Phillip was asleep on the couch for a bit of it, so maybe he hadn't been following the plot. Then a terrible thought occurred to her. If this wasn't his first time with Pia, it meant anything he said last Saturday didn't count anyway. He'd been supervising Pia's PhD for two years. What if they'd already been getting their gear off in his office at the university before he recommended her for the cleaning job? *Do not think about it.*

She shuddered and pulled out an overnight case from the hall cupboard. Her head was throbbing a sick, constant beat. She would go to her dad's place for the night. Rosie was going to her friend's place after school for a sleepover so it wouldn't matter. She needed time to think. It all seemed too unreal. Too ridiculous.

She went into the bedroom and threw the suitcase onto the bed she'd made hastily that morning, ignoring the lump under Phillip's side where he'd left the wheat bag she warmed up every night to soothe his sore neck. She tossed in a jumper, a clean pair of knickers, her pyjamas and slippers and zipped it up, then she dropped it onto the floor with a loud bang, extended the handle and pulled it down the hallway. She listened to the clatter of the wheels on Phillip's precious polished floorboards. Hopefully they'd leave a mark.

CHAPTER TWO

HARRIET

Harriet drummed her fingers noiselessly underneath the table, wondering how long she could endure Justin Broderick's incessant nasal whine. Honestly, the man was a wind bag. She looked down at her fidgeting fingers and stilled them. Something suspiciously like a liver spot seemed to have appeared amid the fine wrinkles and veins of her right hand. She sighed with irritation and flicked her robes off her knees, readying herself to interject.

The judge saved her the trouble. 'Mr Broderick, I'm sure the jury understand the distinction. It's not a difficult one. Do you have anything else, or could we perhaps finish on time today?' Justice Sadler looked pointedly at the wall clock over the door. It was ticking around to 4.04 p.m.

'Apologies, Your Honour. If Your Honour pleases, there is one further witness I was hoping to call this afternoon. Perhaps Your Honour might consider…' He paused and raised his eyebrows at the Judge then tilted his head to one side. The courtroom remained perfectly silent as Justice Sadler returned his gaze without speaking.

'No? Of course. Well, I'm sure arrangements could be made to bring her back again on Monday, Your Honour.'

'Very good, Mr Broderick. If we can move through questioning the witnesses a little faster on Monday, we should be in a position for closing statements after lunch wouldn't you say?'

'Certainly, Your Honour. The Jury could expect to retire to consider its verdict well before the end of the day.'

'What do you say, Ms Andrews?'

Harriet stood as Broderick sat back down.

'Yes, Your Honour. I'd say even before lunch if my learned friend can be less loquacious on the points of law that aren't at issue.'

'Quite. Well, I'll see you back here on Monday at 10 a.m. then, Counsel,' said the Judge.

Harriet gathered her papers as the jury was warned about not discussing the case with anyone over the weekend. Then the court clerk's voice boomed across the room. 'All rise!'

There was rustle and scrape of activity as everyone in the courtroom stood. The judge straightened up her wig, picked up her files and left through the back door. The courtroom hummed into life.

Harriet sat back down at the bar table and pulled her phone from her jacket pocket beneath her robes. As she turned it on, half a dozen text messages flitted onto the screen. Jonathan had sent one an hour ago asking her to call when she finished in court. She wondered if it was about the drink they'd arranged to have.

'Your girl's not standing up very well. I don't think the jury like her,' said Broderick, after the last juror had disappeared through the jury room door. His robes fell open, revealing the strain of his generous belly against a well-cut suit. 'Pity you didn't take the manslaughter deal.'

Harriet's smile was more of a grimace. She was tired of the game. She kept her voice low so the defendant, still in the dock across the room, wouldn't hear her. 'It's the cricket bat that gets me, Justin. He used his son's *Christmas* present. And not just once or twice. Fourteen strikes. Was he practicing his cover drive, do you think? Or just a good hook to the boundary? It's all there you know.' Harriet motioned vaguely to the brief of evidence as she picked up her papers. 'It was self-defence and you know it.

I'm just surprised she didn't kill him years ago.' Harriet took no pleasure in her flippant response, but she couldn't help it – thirty years at the bar did something to your soul. She picked up her folders and zipped them into her wheelie case.

Justin Broderick was an old-fashioned chauvinist. In his world view, a bit of wife-beating was a distasteful reality of life, best left behind closed doors. Still, her client *had* been losing the plot on the stand today. The woman was sounding unsure of herself. Unreliable. She was in the throes of major depression and certainly wasn't the same woman who had given her witness account to police straight after she'd fatally stabbed her husband in his sleep and then turned herself in. But Harriet wasn't about to give Broderick the satisfaction of seeing this case had her worried yet.

Harriet turned to the solicitor next to her. 'Better run. Let's meet at my office at seven-thirty on Monday morning to go through the evidence before closing statements.' She leaned down and lowered her voice. 'And… check on her, will you?' Harriet motioned towards their client who sat motionless, staring down at her knees. The young man nodded fervently, making his glasses jiggle on his nose.

Harriet walked out of the courtroom. As she crossed the foyer, she nodded farewell to the clerk behind the glass panel and caught a glimpse of her own small, black-swathed figure in the window as she waited for a large, defeated-looking woman in front of her to exit through the sliding doors. She grimaced, snatched the wig off her head and smoothed her black hair back into its chignon, aware that a firm line of grey regrowth would start to show along her part if she missed her hairdresser's appointment again this week.

Outside, she watched the woman grasp at the balustrade as she made her way heavily down the sandstone steps and turn right towards the enticing waterfront. The late afternoon street noises of the city centre blared and receded and the old buildings threw shadows in the deepening light. Harriet looked briefly down the street towards Salamanca Place with its fringe of pretty tourist shops and restaurants, warehouses and wharves that extended invitingly out into the freezing Southern Ocean. She turned in the opposite direction and pulled her case up towards Davey Street and walked briskly towards her chambers, tallying the list of work to be done before the weekend set in.

It occurred to her that she hadn't returned Ben's call from this morning. Since his announcement six weeks ago that he wanted to separate, neither of them had come up with any sort of idea about how to proceed with dismantling things. Resting heavily between them was the problem of Scarlett. Harriet could barely imagine the tantrum that would follow if Scarlett returned from her gap year job in England to find her childhood home had been sold. Perhaps Ben had been calling about that.

This morning, Harriet had spotted him from inside the main house as he came out from their garden flat to go for his run. She'd spent the next half hour fighting the urge to go and check the mailbox or prune the roses so she could be there at the gate when he came back, sweaty and endorphin-happy. She longed to inhale the musky scent of him. Instead she had sat back down at the table and finished a complex insurance law advice and sent four more emails.

Her phone buzzed, jolting her back into Friday afternoon. *Jon Brownley*. The beautiful face of her brother on her phone screen made Harriet's heart lift. She swiped her finger.

'Jon, I was about to call you. Are we still on for that drink?'

'Yes, sure, Hat, but I'm about to go into a meeting and was ringing to say I'll be a bit late. Something urgent has come up with a couple of the Year Ten girls. Six-thirty alright instead?'

The extra hour would give her time to send some emails.

'No problem. See you then.' She ended the call, hoping Jon wasn't going to be faced with another student scandal. When you were in charge of a high school, problems were forever springing up without notice. Drugs, sex, social media bullying. But when it was a boarding school that housed the children of Tasmania's oldest and wealthiest families, the newspapers loved to air details of the scandals on the front page. All those moneyed brats and their indulgent parents paying for privileges that most children couldn't even dream of. When they messed up, it was *not* an event to be missed. There would be weeks of head shaking and tut-tutting about how ungrateful the children were and how unfair it was that they got so much government funding. The general public adored a private-school scandal.

As Harriet neared her chambers, her phone began vibrating again in her hand. A photo of her youngest daughter flashed up on the screen. Harriet did a quick calculation – it was about five-thirty on Friday morning in London. Way too early for a social call from Scarlett.

'Hello, darling. You're up with the birds.' Harriet waited for the slight delay of the overseas call to pass, but it continued.

'Scarlett? Are you there?'

'Hi, Mum, I'm… yeah.'

Scarlett's voice sounded coarse and full. There was the faintest hint that she was on the verge of tears. Harriet felt a flicker of annoyance. She wished she could be more tolerant of her daughter's endless little problems, but *Good Lord,* it was hard. The traffic noise and the clicking of the light signals seemed to rise to a loud buzzing distraction. Harriet realised she was standing directly outside her accountant's office. She hesitated, then pulled her suitcase through the rotating doorway and into the quiet sanctuary of the empty foyer. She spoke in her calmest voice.

'Scarlett, what's wrong?'

The silence on the line continued and she prepared herself for another teenage drama. Whatever it was, she had a few minutes to sort it out. Scarlett wasn't particularly *resilient* – a word that seemed to be endlessly bandied around these days in parenting conversations. She'd probably had an argument with her roommate, or another night with her asthma keeping her up. She and Ben had sat Scarlett down before she left for her gap year and had lectured her on the importance of taking control of her asthma when they weren't there to remind her. So far though, she'd blamed her two bad bouts on the terrible London smog. Harriet was certain she just wasn't bothering to take her inhaler.

'I'm being sent home.' Scarlett's words spilled out, and were promptly followed by loud sobs. 'I'm s-sorry Mum.' Then her voice began to rise with barely controlled hysteria. 'I just made a stupid mistake!'

Harriet took a moment to register the words. They were not what she'd been expecting.

'Don't be silly, Scarlett. The school can't send you home for making a mistake at work. What do you mean?'

She steeled herself in readiness for whatever was going to come out next. The sobbing continued, then after a while there was a loaded silence. Harriet could almost feel her daughter drawing up her reserves to force out the next words.

'They found a couple of tablets in my drawer. The form master searched my room without asking. Ollie got them for a party we're going to, and I was keeping them in my room.'

Harriet felt an electric stab of fear. The veneer of her perfect life was coming badly unstuck. Marriage breakdown. Tick. Daughter in trouble with drugs. Tick. Now all she needed was a major health crisis or a scandal at work. *Bad things always happen in threes,* as her mother would so gloomily say at all appropriate opportunities.

Harriet took a deep breath and waited. Her legal training had taught her that silence was often the fastest way to get at the truth. Plus, she needed to think.

'Mum? Mum, I'm really sorry,' said Scarlett miserably.

Harriet felt a flame of unexpected rage.

'Jonathan went out of his way to pull strings to get you that job, Scarlett! It's one of the most prestigious schools in England.

Minor royalty go there, for pity's sake! Are you *really* telling me that you were idiotic enough to keep illicit drugs in the school *boarding house*?'

Harriet had been holding her forehead with one hand, staring at the shiny taupe leather of her shoes against the marble floor. She looked up. A man in a suit was staring at her. *Damn.* Hobart was a small town really, when it came down to it. Gossip spread fast. Luckily, she didn't know him.

'Mum, it was only some caps for a party we were all going to. It wasn't just me!'

The words sent another shot of fury through Harriet's chest. It was the casual undertone of blame-throwing and feigned innocence.

'What are you talking about? What exactly *were* these tablets, Scarlett?'

'MDMA. Just a few pills, Mum. They're not a big deal. Everyone takes them. But the headmaster said last night that he's going to contact the gappie agency and have me sent home.'

Good grief. Harriet wondered briefly if motherly platitudes were required, but her legal head wasn't having it. Gather precise information; undertake swift damage control – that was what she needed to do now. Thankfully they were her forte.

'How many pills, Scarlett? How did you get them? Did you sell any?'

'Only three, Mum. Ollie bought them from some guy. I was just holding them for him and me and Lucy. Mum, I'm meant to go to Ibiza with the others in the term break. I can't be sent home. I *can't* miss that!'

Harriet held her phone away from her ear as the sobs began again. She did a quick tally of the fallout. As a university medallist and the youngest woman to ever take silk at the Tasmanian Bar, she had a plethora of useful skills when it came to assisting her child with a drugs problem from the other side of the world. So far, the tally was not looking great:

- Bringing illicit drugs into a school that housed the children of Britain's richest and most powerful people – *bad* idea.
- Scarlett was eighteen; if the police had been called she would be looking at criminal proceedings in an adult jurisdiction, in a place where Harriet had few friends in positions of influence – *very* bad.
- Scarlett didn't appear to have been involved in dealing the drugs, nor was it a significant quantity – good.
- The headmaster of the famed Baddington College was probably keen to avoid a scandal, so hopefully the police would be kept away – *very* good. (Harriet assumed that getting an errant gap student off his property and back to the Antipodean swamp from which she had come was probably the man's top priority.)
- Scarlett was about to create untold embarrassment to her uncle Jonathan who had personally vouched for her good character (on Harriet's rather insistent requests, but she wasn't ready to think about that yet) – somewhat bad on all fronts, but a peripheral concern for now.

Harriet looked at her watch. She was meeting Jon in two hours. She had time to deal with this. 'Scarlett, your Ibiza trip is the least of your worries. Have the police been called?' Her voice was laced with impatience.

'I don't think so. Mum, what will I do?' Scarlett's sobs had descended into hysteria.

'Scarli, stop that. I can't talk to you right now.' Harriet looked up but the man had gone. Thankfully the foyer was now empty, but she needed to have this conversation properly, in private.

'I will call you in exactly half an hour. Make sure you answer. And Scarlett, do not speak a *word* about any of this to anyone. Do you understand? Not. One. Word. If the police come, insist that you have a solicitor present before you speak. And I mean insist!'

Scarlett whimpered.

Harriet allowed herself to feel motherly for a moment.

'Darling, stop crying and go for a walk or something. I'll ring Aunt Lila – you can go and stay with her. We'll sort this out.'

'Okay.'

'We'll talk in half an hour, darling.' She pressed the screen on her phone to end the call and picked up her briefcase trolley handle from against the wall.

Bugger.

She'd better call Ben.

Harriet walked to her chambers building, three minutes further up the street. The lift door opened and the dreadful mirrored wall reflected every day of her fifty-nine years back at her. She turned away and pressed the button for her floor, just as the new barrister they'd recently taken into chambers flew through the exterior doors and bounded in between the closing lift doors.

'Hello, Harriet!'

The boy was ridiculously enthusiastic. She forced a tight smile and turned slightly to face the lift door. She couldn't, at that precise moment, remember his name.

'I wanted to pick your brain about a little matter I've got coming up in the Resource Management Tribunal. It's a really interesting point of law.' He grinned at her, all fresh-faced and eager. His name was proving elusive.

'Sure. But I'm busy today. I'll be in on Sunday afternoon. Otherwise Monday after court.' Harriet dismissed him as the lift doors opened and she stepped onto their floor. She hoped her lack of name usage hadn't appeared odd. Her exceptional recall of small and insignificant details appeared to have deserted her. She hoped it was a temporary glitch then she wondered if she'd sounded too harsh. Poor kid. He looked about twenty-three. He'd be needing all the help he could get, but right now Harriet needed Ben. She typed a text message.

Need to meet urgently. Will be at your office in ten mins.

Within a few seconds her phone buzzed.

Sorry. In meeting for another hour.

Harriet sighed. Ammunition was needed.

Urgent matter about Scarlett. Can't wait. See you in ten.

Harriet retrieved some papers from her briefcase. On the way out of her office she stopped at the desk of her secretary, a giant of a girl who was usually quite efficient but had been prone to making mistakes lately, as her pregnancy progressed. She was standing at the filing cabinet, but turned and smiled down at Harriet as she approached.

'Sharon, I've made a few notes in court. Please type them up and put them on my desk before you leave. And I need the full extract of these cases printed. Three copies of each please.' Harriet handed her a list.

Sharon took the notes in one hand and rested the other one on her enormous stomach, before lifting it to look at her watch. It was ten minutes to five.

'I'm really am sorry, Sharon, but they're urgent. If you have some sort of pressing need to leave at five, then would you mind asking one of the others to do it? And tell Andrew I'll be back around seven-thirty tonight to talk to him about the chambers meeting on Monday. I need his input before he leaves for Hong Kong.'

'Sure.'

The girl sank down behind her desk, looking pale and exhausted.

'Thank you.' Harriet tried to smile. She supposed she shouldn't work the poor girl so hard, but really, pregnancy wasn't an illness. Harriet had worked fourteen-hour days right up to the day Scarlett was born. She'd studied just as hard when she'd been carrying Clementine. Still, she knew most people didn't have her constitution. She'd give Sharon an early mark next week to make up for it.

Outside the chambers building, the evening was closing in with unusual humidity. The office of Caldwell & Chadston Architects was two blocks from Harriet's chambers, across the waterfront. She strode it out, weaving in and out between a couple of Chinese tourists, a mother with a fancy pram, and a group of high school boys walking in a pack, jostling and laughing and swearing. She felt her heart rate rising as she warmed under the fine wool-cashmere mix of her suit. It pleased her. Today there would be no time for the gym.

When she arrived a few minutes later, Ben was waiting in his glass-fronted office and beckoned her through from the empty reception area. She nodded at two junior architects who sat in the open-plan area towards the back wall, then she closed the door of Ben's office behind her.

'What's the disaster?' Ben tilted his head, the line of his mouth taut.

'Hello, Ben. Nice to see you too,' said Harriet. He could suffer the curiosity a little longer for his rudeness. By the look on his face, she had a discomforting sensation that he thought she'd called this meeting under false pretences.

'Harriet, if it's urgent and about Scarlett, spit it out. I had to leave a new client in the lurch for this.'

Harriet felt the sting of his rebuke and she let out a sigh. 'I've had a call from her. I don't have a lot of detail, but a search of her room by staff at the school turned up three pills of MDMA – an illegal party drug. She says it was for her and two of her friends. The school are dismissing her and they want to send her home. That's all I know.'

Harriet took a breath and looked out the window across the roof of the old art deco building below, to Constitution Dock.

The Antarctic expedition ship sat like an angry orange pillar of righteous judgement alongside the wharf. She allowed the enormity of the situation to settle on her shoulders. Silly, *silly* girl.

Now she was with Ben, it felt real. It was now an official shared parenting catastrophe.

'Bloody hell.' Ben's shoulders sagged.

Harriet felt sorry for him. He hadn't been expecting it. Perhaps she'd been wrong to spring it on him like that.

'I said I'd ring her back. I thought you should know too, before we decide what to do.' What Harriet actually meant was, before *I* decide what to do. They both knew it. Harriet looked out the window again.

'Well it wouldn't seem there is much to do except organise a flight home I expect, unless they decide to give her a second chance,' said Ben. 'I mean… are police involved?'

'Not as far as she knows. If they were going to call them, I assume they'd have done so immediately. They probably want this sort of thing kept quiet. And as for second chances…' Harriet shook her head, allowing her gaze to drift out the window again.

When she looked back, Ben's eyes were wide with questions.

She gave a loud sigh. 'They have a duty of care to keep their students safe and having drugs on school grounds breaches that duty. They also have a duty to prevent any foreseeable injury to students, and if Scarlett is a known risk for potentially supplying their children with drugs, or if at some future time she was found not to be in a fit state to undertake her duties and they had decided not to get rid of her now, knowing what they know, that would open them up to further liability. They'd be mad to give her a second chance.'

Ben's face crumpled. 'How could you even *think* that, Harriet? Scarlett would never do that.'

Harriet felt the injustice of his outburst like a slap.

'I know that, Ben, but at the moment I'm required to think like a school principal and a lawyer! Unfortunately, I don't have the luxury of reacting like a parent because I am yet to sort out the mess that our bloody daughter has got herself into!'

Why was it always up to her to fix things? She was always the bad cop. The one who had to make the hard calls. Ben got to stand by and be generally loving and ineffectual and the vastly more popular parent. Scarlett worshipped him.

Harriet took a deep breath then looked at her watch. She harnessed her anger. It was time to ring Scarlett.

'After this I'll ring Leonard Spanner, Jonathan's friend who runs the boarding house. To smooth things over we should offer to pay the placement fee for another gap student, then I'll ask what the extent of the situation is from their perspective. But let's ring Scarlett first and get the full story.'

'That sounds sensible.' Ben gave her a tired half-smile and his eyes crinkled kindly. They reminded her of the deep blackish-brown of the tea tree-stained stream that ran alongside their favourite bushwalk. Unfathomably lovely. The thought gave her a jolt. How did he remain so even-keeled during disasters? Maybe that's why their marriage had lasted for more than twenty years before he got tired of her. He'd always steered her towards a calmer, nicer version of herself. It was a miracle really, that they'd lasted as long as they did. Harriet was self-aware enough to realise that she was probably quite difficult to live with.

She dialled Scarlett's number and put it on speaker. As it rang, Harriet imagined her daughter hiding away in the vast courtyard of the school behind a sandstone pillar carved with age-blackened gargoyles, shivering as she tried to find somewhere private to have the conversation.

'Mum?'

'Hello, Scarlett, your father and I are both here. Tell us what happened. Be precise please – I need all the details.' Harriet sat on the chair opposite Ben with her pen and a legal pad. She had written the date at the top and underlined the word *Scarlett* twice.

'Daddy?' said Scarlett. There was a strangled sound, then at the end of the distant line came the sound of an exploding well of misery. Scarlett's sobs were so anguished that a wracking silence announced each new one as it built and burst.

Harriet watched Ben's eyes becoming moist.

'Yes, darling. Please… Scarlett. It's alright. We're both here.' He pushed his hand through his hair, Harriet noticed, just as he always did when he felt completely out of his depth. He'd done the same thing at Scarlett's birth when Harriet had refused to take any drugs and the pain kept hitting her with the force of a speeding freight train. Over and over.

Wine. Harriet turned the idea over in her mind as her pen hovered over the page, waiting for the return of calm. She was meeting Jonathan in an hour at The Cables – a smart new bar on the waterfront. She would order a glass of wine. Nobody ever told you when you decided to become a parent that it would be so bloody excruciating. After the birth, the pain was meant to be over. But it was never over. As a rule, Harriet didn't believe in alcohol as a remedy for stress. And with nobody to go home to, now that Ben had left, she wouldn't usually have indulged the idea. She certainly never drank alone. It was, in Harriet's opinion, a slippery slope towards unmitigated disaster – akin to being stupid enough to get off the ski lift at a double-black-diamond run when you were only a green-run skier. There was only one way down the precipice, and it was fast and perilous and would invariably end badly. But today, she decided, a glass of Pinot Gris was definitely on the cards. Perhaps two.

'Scarlett, pull yourself together now,' said Harriet calmly. 'Tell us what happened, starting from the very first time you were offered drugs.'

From: Jemima Langdon-Traves
To: Peta Kallorani
Re: Holidays and reunion and things!

Hi Gorgeous lady,
How are you and your gang? Sitting here thinking about our school days… eek!

Can you believe the email from Emma Parsons (assuming that's Emma Tasker as I can't remember another Emma)!? I can't believe she's bringing up all that stuff! Tessa would never have done it, anyway.

Not sure how anyone presses 'reply all' either, without meaning to. Anyway, I've decided to come back home to the reunion in June. Just trying to train up my new au pair so she can be here for the boys, then I don't have to suffer 23 hours on a plane with them back to Hobart. Could be an impossible job though – she's forever sleeping in after late night skype calls then moaning about missing Melbourne and her boyfriend. She still hasn't worked out how to separate the washing properly and it's been three weeks. Then yesterday I asked her if she'd disinfected the bath toys as per Friday's schedule and she actually rolled her eyes at me. It's like I've got a third child!

Onto more fun topics, we are now definitely thinking Italy for the holidays instead of Finland, maybe Lake Como, so if you can make it over this way in July that would be fab! Must run. Having a lovely girls' lunch today. Lots of bubbles are needed. (My useless au pair would try the patience of a saint!)
Jemima xxx

CHAPTER THREE

MARLEE

Marlee took the gin and tonic from the barman and smiled her thanks. A slice of cucumber floated serenely in the glass. Alone at the bar she was wrapped in the swirl of conversations. She felt unaccountably soothed – the rumble of optimism, the anticipation of alcohol's promise, the hopeful, convivial tinkle of glasses.

She had excused herself from her new workmates to send another text to Emma, but there was still no response. She scrolled through her phone and looked at Emma's accidental group email, cringing as she re-read it.

> **From: Emma Parsons**
> **To: Class of '93 Reunion goddesses**
> **Re: Fabulous formal photo… the countdown is on, girls!**
>
> *Hi Marl,*
> *Had a huge laugh at that formal photo Selina sent. We should have been locked up for crimes against fashion! Can't wait to see what everyone looks like now. Apparently, Larissa Maiden has an interior design business in Sydney these days and did the house of one of the guys from MasterChef! She was so quiet and shy!! Felt like I was in a parallel universe when I heard that.*

Tessa's face in that photo made me teary. So sad to realise she won't be at the reunion. It will be my first time together with everyone since the funeral so I guess it will make the whole thing real again. I can't believe none of us spoke up about what we knew. It's only now I've got Rosie I realise how hard for her parents it must still be and how dumb we were not to admit what she'd planned. Still can't explain it.

Anyway, no point dwelling. Phil gets annoyed if I ever bring up that stuff from the past. 'Oh, that lovely husband of yours', I hear you say. Well, I do admit he's annoying me A LOT at the moment. Last night he was picking his toenails on the couch and flicking the bits towards the fireplace and missing. DISGUSTING. When I complained he stomped off in a huff. I think he might be a bit touchy due to a tiny deficit in his intimate relations with his goddess wife. Well, maybe not tiny exactly. Maybe a medium-sized deficit. It's probably been three months. But who's counting? (apart from Phil, judging by the moods he's in).

Anyway, I'd better go. Lots to do. Envelopes to stuff and letters to file and so on. Complex, important things, obviously. Can't be too careful – wouldn't want to put the wrong letter in the wrong envelope and that sort of thing. Lena is looking super-efficient over in her corner of the office and making me feel guilty.

Em xx

Marlee looked at the slew of group emails that had followed. Emma would be chewing herself up about them. She flicked back to her text message screen and looked down at the last jokey text she'd sent to Emma. She sighed heavily.

'If he stood you up, I'm happy to stand in.' A middle-aged man in a suit was leaning on the bar next to her with an air of inflated confidence. He had a pasty, under-baked softness around his jaw. Maybe an accountant. He nodded towards her phone and gave her a surprisingly genuine smile.

'I'm good. Thanks.' She picked up her gin and pushed her way back through the crowd towards her new workmates.

'Marlee, we were just discussing the Lathe House and deciding whether there was too much concrete. Ben thinks they deserved the Telopia Award but I wonder if the place is too sterile.' Lidia smiled up at Marlee. The questioning, inclusive tilt of her head made Marlee suddenly conscious that she might be looking uninterested.

'I love it,' said Marlee, 'Some timber would have warmed it up though – some ceiling battening maybe?' She looked across at her new boss. Ben had joined them a few minutes ago. She guessed he was in his late forties. He was tall with a strong, pleasant sort of face but after a week of working with him, Marlee decided he was probably more conservative than she'd guessed at in her job interview, despite his impressive swathe of architectural awards for modernist buildings. There was no doubting his brilliance, but there was a diffidence about him. Marlee couldn't decide whether it was introversion, conceit or quiet confidence.

'Perhaps,' said Ben. He smiled absently. Maybe he didn't like noisy bars. The invitation for the evening had come from Finton, the other partner in the firm. He'd put his credit card behind the bar and had booked a table in the adjoining restaurant for later – all to welcome Marlee to her new role in the firm. Usually she'd be having a great time at a party in her honour, but thoughts about Emma's email kept intruding. Still, the booze was working its magic and she allowed herself to relax into the swanky, buzzing vibe of the bar. There was Friday-night fun in the air.

'So, Ben, tell me all about yourself,' said Marlee. He might be boring, but she was prepared to give him the benefit of the doubt since his company's credit card was paying for the pleasant after-effect of her second drink.

'Not much to tell.'

'Oh, c'mon. Kids? Dogs? Art collector? Lycra-clad cyclist with road-sharing issues on the weekend?'

Ben laughed. 'You don't beat around the bush, do you?' He took a deep sip of his drink. 'Well, no dogs I'm afraid. And thankfully no lycra. I do like to go running though. As to the home front, I've, er, recently separated from my wife. I'm a step-father of one daughter who lives in Europe and father of another just out of high school and driving her poor parents insane.' He smiled ruefully. 'How's that for a summary?'

'Oh Ben, I'm so sorry! I didn't realise you and Harriet had separated,' said Lidia. There was a faint thrill of hope in her words.

Marlee watched as she blinked like a startled butterfly and pushed her hair behind her ear, then she reached out and placed her hand on Ben's forearm. Marlee suppressed a smile and made a mental note. Office Politics 101: find out who is secretly in love with whom, then try not to offend anyone by saying the wrong thing.

'Well, it was recent,' said Ben. 'After Scarlett left for London.' A small uncomfortable silence was swallowed by a sudden outburst of laughter by the group of men near the window. They began slapping each other on the backs and clinking their beer glasses together. Marlee scanned her brain for something to say.

'What's your daughter up to that's so maddening?'

'Oh, just testing the limits of her new-found freedom, I guess. She finished high school last year and went off to make her mark in London before she starts uni.' He looked down at his watch, then tilted the glass in his other hand and swirled the remains of his drink. Lidia had been pulled away and was now talking to another two of the architects in the firm, who were pressed up against an exposed brick wall. Marlee wondered if she was delivering the delicious gossip that Ben had separated from his wife. Or maybe she'd nurse the secret to her heart for a bit longer.

Marlee ploughed on. 'Well, that's the job of kids, isn't it? Not that I'd know. I don't have any.'

Ben didn't answer but he continued to hold eye contact and Marlee felt her face getting warm.

'How about another drink?' he said eventually. 'I know I could use one after the day I've had.' He beckoned to a waiter who was coming back through the crowd with an empty tray and a moment later the young man stopped beside them.

'What can I get you?'

'Another…' Ben looked questioningly at her, gesturing to her drink, which was still half full. 'Gin and tonic,' she said to the waiter. 'Mine was Hendricks with a slice of cucumber if you don't mind.'

'Make that two.' Ben nodded and smiled at the waiter.

Marlee noticed his healthy tan and the squareness of his jaw. She watched as he scanned the room, then put two fingers into the top of his collar and tugged at it. She sensed his discomfort amongst the humid crush of well-heeled professionals, then watched him gather himself, remembering his role as host. He looked back at her.

'How are you settling into Hobart? It's a lot quieter than Melbourne. I'm surprised we managed to lure you here.'

'I grew up here and it's definitely not as quiet as it used to be. Dad's not doing too well on his own anymore. Thought I'd better come home. Keep an eye on him. And to be honest, I was getting sick of the big city. I think I might be a country girl at heart, although I suppose Hobart hardly qualifies these days.'

'No. It's gotten busy. Are all your family here?'

'My brother's in San Francisco. My oldest friend lives here though – I'm godmother to her daughter. It's nice to be able to see them a bit more.'

Marlee took a final large sip of gin and handed the glass back to the waiter as he brought the new ones. Her head felt tingly. Polite conversation suddenly felt like an effort. She wanted to get out of the place too, but it wasn't an option before dinner.

'So, how are you enjoying being single again, Ben?'

'I guess I'll get the hang of it. My wife has never been the homebody, so after twenty odd years you manage to build up a few skills. I can turn on the oven and the iron, so I'm pretty well equipped to be honest.'

His self-deprecating smile left Marlee in no doubt that he was well house-trained. She wondered what his wife had been like, what type of woman he preferred.

'Dating's a whole new world these days you know. How's your online profile looking? Any hits?' Marlee tilted her head and narrowed her eyes in mock cross-examination.

She watched his face drop, and wondered if she'd misjudged his sense of humour. To her surprise Ben lowered his voice.

'Well, as a matter of fact, I'm meeting my potential perfect match later tonight. A lady called Barbara. We are ninety-eight per cent compatible, according to the dating agency algorithm.' He looked frankly at Marlee as if she might be able to provide some insight into the likely outcome of such a successful match.

She felt a sting of embarrassment for him. It had probably cost him a lot to reveal information she hadn't actually been seeking. She hadn't *expected* him to be online dating. He'd only just become single after two decades.

Ben continued talking, saving Marlee from having to find her voice.

'She's a few years older than me, but very glamorous from the photos. Used to be an air hostess. Perfect figure, gorgeous face, long blond hair. Maybe she does that Botox thing.' He raised his eyebrows.

'Well, umm, there you go,' said Marlee, looking at the glass in her hand. The cucumber was alarmingly close to the bottom. She looked around for the waiter.

'Her nickname's Barbie,' said Ben thoughtfully. 'She's being dropped off by her ex-boyfriend, Ken, in his convertible red sports car a bit later on. You might get to meet her if you stick around. She's a real doll.' He held her eyes in a solemn stare.

'Oh, well... I...' Marlee shifted uncomfortably, then took a large sip of her almost-empty drink as Lidia edged back towards them.

When she looked back at Ben, the corners of his mouth were turned up and his eyes sparkled gleefully.

Barbie and Ken. *Real dolls*. Marlee felt a rush of embarrassment that it had taken her so long to get the joke. Then she let out a snort. Emma would have called it her pig-laugh and been mortally embarrassed for her.

'She sounds almost perfect,' said Marlee. 'Although, I have heard that excessive Botox treatment can turn your skin into rock-hard plastic, so you might want to watch out for that.'

Lidia had been talking to some of the other architects in the firm, but Marlee could see she was straining to hear their conversation. Lidia turned towards Ben and put her hand on his arm. 'What do you need to watch out for, Ben?'

Ben grinned. 'Marlee was warning me about the dangers of skin contact with toys made from thermoplastic polymers.'

'Oh, ah...' said Lidia. Her eyes darted from Marlee to Ben and back again. 'Well, um, we're all going in to dinner now. Our table is ready.'

The slight furrow of anxiety, the way she'd been following their conversation out of the corner of her eye – Marlee wondered just how deeply Lidia had fallen for him. Poor girl. She was nowhere near perfecting her poker face.

They walked across the bar and into the restaurant together. Lidia took Ben's arm and looked up at him in question as the staff milled around the table wondering where to sit.

'Marlee, why don't you sit in the middle of the table so you get a chance to talk to everyone,' said Ben. He sat down further up the table and Lidia followed him. Marlee felt a stab of disappointment.

Finton sat down opposite her and the other architects and support staff gradually found their seats. Finton was the Caldwell at Caldwell & Chadston Architects. Ben was the Chadston.

Finton leaned across the table and said something as he filled her wine glass from one of the bottles that had magically appeared on the centre of the table. The billowing chatter from the adjoining bar spilled into the room.

'Sorry, Finton, what was that?' asked Marlee.

'I was just saying how nice it is to have another woman in the office to add a bit of bounce and zing,' boomed Finton.

Marlee noticed a ring of damp fabric under his arms from the unusual Hobart evening warmth. Or perhaps it was the large amounts of red wine he'd been drinking. The heat generated by the crowded bar hadn't enhanced his ruddy complexion either. Finton wore heavy, black, square-rimmed glasses which Marlee thought looked a bit ridiculous on him, given that he looked more like one of the 'grotty yachties' who frequented the Hobart pubs around new year after the famous Sydney to Hobart Yacht Race had finished. If he was aiming for an intellectual look with the glasses, it wasn't working.

From the first day on the job Marlee had noticed his habit of standing too close and invading her personal space. All week she'd found herself surreptitiously stepping backwards when they talked, which made it hard to concentrate on what he was saying. His lingering eye contact was equally off-putting. In her regular chats to Emma, she'd already started calling him Smarmy Fint.

'Thanks, Finton. Nice to be here. I've watched the work you guys have been doing for years. It was one of the reasons I decided to move back home to Tasmania.' Marlee gave him a generous grin and the benefit of the doubt. No point being too precious about the comment – there was always the chance that he was referring to the fact that another female architect might bring some kind of unique talent and balance to their office, which was predominantly staffed by males. It might not be a reference to her boobs, per se.

'Brightens the place up to have some colour and sparkle around.' He leaned forward. 'Utzon wouldn't be the only architect who appreciated curves, you know.' Then he attached his eyes to her cleavage.

Marlee suddenly wished she hadn't chosen her low-cut silk top. She rested her elbows on the table and folded her hands in front of her cleavage. 'Oh, I know. I know. Such a shame that curves are so expensive to build. I'd love to design our own little Sydney Opera House project right here in Hobart, but I doubt we'd ever get it funded.'

Without warning Ben leaned over her shoulder. 'An Opera House, or anything else you design would put you in high professional esteem with your colleagues, Marlee. Wouldn't it, Fint?' he said. Ben was staring across the table at his partner as he topped up wine glasses. There was an edge to his voice.

Finton sat back in his seat and beckoned the waiter.

'Yep, it certainly would.'

Finton then turned to one of the new young graduate architects next to him. The girl edged away from him and Marlee wondered if taking the job had been the right decision. The offer of partnership in twelve months if everything worked out well had been a good inducement, but the hurdles might be too great if Finton turned out to be a major sleaze bucket. She turned to the junior architect on her left who had joined the firm a few months earlier. He was fiddling with the menu.

'And what about you, Andrew? Are you enjoying the work so far?'

'Yeah, it's awesome.' He paused and looked across to Finton who was now in an animated conversation with a waitress, before he said, 'Where did you work before, Marlee?'

Marlee glanced up the table and noticed Ben watching her.

'I was at a big firm in Melbourne. Studio Metro. Do you know it?'

'Yeah of course! They have such a cool social responsibility ethic. I'd love to go and work on that sustainable street project they've got going on,' said Andrew.

His reverent Gen-Y appreciation of such things made Marlee feel fraudulent and old. She hadn't had time to work on any of the optional social impact projects for the homeless or the environment at her old firm.

Marlee's phone was sitting on the table and it began buzzing as it lit up with a photo of Emma poking out her tongue at the camera. She wondered if it would be rude to take the call but then she noticed Smarmy Fint was leaning towards her, ready for another chat.

'Sorry, I just need to take this.' Marlee raised her eyes in apology as she stood and headed for the restaurant door and out towards the night-time quiet of the street.

'Hi Em, I've been calling to check you hadn't jumped off that cliff. Everything alright?'

The fresh evening air wrapped itself around her as Marlee looked across the docks at the spectacular Hobart waterfront. Boats of all sizes were docked across its width, casting blue-black shadows beneath the twinkling lights. The looming backdrop of Mount Wellington made it more picturesque than any other place she knew.

'No, it's not. It's not alright, Marl. It's horrible.' Emma's voice had a strange pitch.

'Em?'

'Poor Rosie!' Emma let out a sharp sob and dissolved into breathy tears.

Marlee felt a flicker of confusion. The email hadn't been all that bad. And it didn't really involve Rosie.

'What's wrong, Em?'

'He's a complete bastard!'

The words were slurred and Marlee's concentration slipped as her mind bounced across the various possibilities.

'Who's a bastard? Are you okay?'

'Phillip! I had to see her naked! Every time I close my eyes, I just see her big white bum. Oh my goodness, they ruined my cottage!'

'Phillip? Slow down, Emma. What do you mean?' Marlee walked further away from the front of the converted warehouse that housed the restaurant and into the semi-darkness of the carpark.

'He was having sex. It was horrible. He was naked with our cleaner in the cottage! I can't believe they could do that to me!' Emma began a low, moaning cry.

A cold creeping sensation moved up Marlee's spine. She was pretty sure Emma was drunk and absolutely certain that Emma had just used the word bastard – both pretty unusual events. But mostly, she was disturbed by the thought that Emma's bookish, boring husband was having an affair. The idea was ridiculous. Marlee could pick an adulterer a mile off and Phillip wasn't one of them. He got embarrassed if Marlee turned up showing cleavage or made a lewd joke. She couldn't imagine him looking sideways at another woman, let alone having the balls to seduce one. The idea of him getting his kit off in their guest cottage with the cleaner was way too weird to contemplate. She shook her head, trying to banish the mental image of Phillip naked. Middle-aged paunch, hairy, flabby. *Yuck.*

'Is Phillip there now? Do you want me to come?'

'I'm at my dad's.' Emma voice was high and plaintive.

'Okay, I'll get out of this work thing. I'm coming over there.'

'No, I'm going to bed. I don't want to talk to anyone. Stay at your dinner. Sorry. I'll be okay.'

A sob echoed down the line then it went dead.

Marlee's hand fell to her side. She stared up at the blackening sky, just beginning to show the stars. *Phillip having sex with someone else.* It was unbelievable. It was quite a disgusting thought. But, it was not the end of the world. And on the scale of upsetting things she could have heard today, it wasn't the worst. Phillip was a controlling dickhead and frankly, Emma would be better off without him. And you had to look on the bright side of these things – it had distracted Emma from the email debacle, leaving her with nothing more to worry about than a faithless prat of a husband. So, there was that.

CHAPTER FOUR

EMMA

Emma woke with a dry mouth and a pounding head. She needed water. She tried to sit up but was assaulted by a dizzying wave of nausea. Prickly heat crawled over her face and her stomach churned. There was a distinct possibility she was going to vomit. She slid back down into the softness of the pillow. The curtains of her father's spare room provided a garish floral panorama that did nothing to calm her stomach. Her mother's taste in interior decor had been awful.

She shuddered, remembering the previous night. She had shared a bottle of wine with her dad. But she definitely hadn't told him about Phillip and Pia. She'd made up some story about having an argument with Phillip and her needing to stay the night so she could have some space. Then when he had gone to bed, she'd opened another bottle of wine and drunk another few glasses. Not a fantastic idea for a woman who usually stuck to one drink on the rare occasions she drank anything at all.

She turned her head carefully towards the bedside table and edged her arm towards the phone. There were two missed calls from Rosie and one from Phillip and a text message that he'd sent two hours earlier.

*Should I get Rosie from Ellie's place and take her to softball?
Please call me.*

She looked at the time. *Blast.* She'd forgotten about Rosie's game. It would be half-way through. Hopefully Phillip had taken the initiative for once. She closed her eyes and let the sounds of her father pottering around in the kitchen soothe her.

A few minutes later footsteps sounded in the hall and there was a knock at the door. Her father peered around the door holding out a cup of tea.

'Good morning, sunshine. Looks like you could use this.' He was in his gardening clothes and proffered a steaming mug with a smile.

Shame crawled over Emma's skin. What would her dad be thinking? Had he seen the second near-empty wine bottle?

'Thanks.' Emma pushed herself upright, concentrating hard on looking normal. 'Sorry if I was rabbiting on last night. Phillip's just been annoying me lately.' She tried to smile but her head throbbed viciously.

'Well, he needs to make sure he's not working too much so the three of you can have some family time. Give him a call later and work things out. If he's putting his work first, he doesn't realise the treasure he's got right under his nose.'

'Thanks, Dad. I guess it will all blow over. I'm just a bit stressed, that's all.' Emma tried to smile again.

The last thing she wanted was for her father to find out about Phillip and Pia. Last night she'd decided that she couldn't face the idea of getting a divorce. She wasn't good at being alone. Phillip had been her only lover. She'd only ever kissed a few guys before she had met him at university. The idea of ever being naked with another man made her quite literally feel like throwing up. Although being naked with Phillip again was an equally hideous idea, now that she thought about it. *Later. She would deal with that later.*

Emma knew she was going to have to try to forget what she'd seen in the cottage if she was going to make things work, but her father would never forgive Phillip if he found out. He didn't get worked up about much, but adultery was one thing he didn't tolerate. He'd ended one of his oldest friendships a decade earlier when he found out about his friend's affair with a woman from the tennis club. The irony was that nobody who knew Emma's mother would have blamed her father for finding some joy in a love affair. Her mother been a difficult woman. But her father had, as far as Emma knew, been devoted to her throughout their thirty-eight years of marriage.

'Would you mind if I shut my eyes for a bit longer, Dad? I think I might need another hour if I'm going to make it through the day.'

Her father smiled and shook his head in mock disbelief. 'It's past nine-thirty. The day's almost over! I'll be up at the bee hives, so I might not see you before you go. Shall I still come over for dinner tonight with Roger and Vivien?'

'Oh, gosh. I'd forgotten about that.' Emma closed her eyes and thought about the preparations she was supposed to be making for the arrival of her parents-in-law for Rosie's birthday dinner. She clenched her teeth to stop a hot rush of tears.

'I suppose you'd better since they're making the effort to drive down for it,' she said heavily. 'They would have left Launceston by now.'

'Right-o. See you later, love.'

Her father retreated into the hallway, pulling the door closed behind him and Emma lay back down.

Rosie was turning thirteen on Monday and the birthday dinner with her three grandparents had, until a recent bout of teenage attitude, been the highlight of her year. Now that her godmother, 'Auntie' Marlee, had returned from Melbourne to live in Hobart and could also come, Rosie had been bubbling with excitement again. Marlee gave extravagant presents.

Roger and Vivien were coming to stay for the weekend and Emma felt hollow at the effort she'd have to make to pretend things were all okay. She picked up her phone. She was in no state to cook. Phillip would have to make the effort. It was his fault she felt like this after all.

> *You need to organise roast lamb for dinner tonight and make the spare bed up for your parents. Coming home around lunch time. Also pick up Rosie. Don't call me. I'm too angry and upset.*

Emma tossed and turned, letting the fearful thoughts she'd tried to keep at bay swirl around in her head. She needed to think. What if they really did break up? She'd never find anyone as clever or as stable as Phillip again, if she left him. Her mother had told her that plenty of times before she died. Her mother had worshipped Phillip – he could never put a foot wrong in her eyes. She would have been livid at the very idea that Emma might leave him after one indiscretion. Plus, how would she afford to live? How would she manage on her own? Emma didn't understand their insurance policies or how they managed the bills. She couldn't even work out how to get the television to work properly most days. There were too many remote controls and input buttons. She *liked* having someone to take care of those things. Marriage was more than just loving someone.

Emma dozed, letting the headache engulf her thoughts. An hour later, when she woke and it became obvious that sleep wasn't going to return, she took some paracetamol tablets and hobbled into the shower. She turned on the hot water to full and slumped onto the tiled floor, letting the water pound relentlessly on the back of her head. An image swirled in her mind of working with Pia in the cottage a couple of weeks earlier. Pia had laughed when Emma told her about Phillip's hopeless efforts to vacuum the house after she'd begged him to help before her book club friends turned up. He'd pushed the vacuum cleaner randomly around the room, not picking up the school bag, books or other bits of junk Rosie had dumped on the floor, then after he had announced he'd finished, he'd dropped the vacuum cleaner in the middle of the lounge room floor and slammed his office door. It had been good to share the frustration with such a sympathetic listener.

But Pia must have been planning to steal Phillip from under her nose the whole time. Her stomach flipped ominously. Had Phillip encouraged her? Had he been seeking her out in the common room at the university? Following her around while she cleaned the house, admiring her curvy bottom? Now that she thought of it, Phillip hadn't actually initiated sex for ages. Emma had assumed that he was finally just picking up on her please-don't-reach-over-and-rub-my-back cues, but maybe it was just because he'd been getting enough sex with Pia.

She leaned back and let the water cover her face. If she could just throw up, she'd feel much better. She hadn't been this hungover since her cousin's wedding fifteen years ago.

Emma pulled on her crumpled clothes from yesterday and wandered into the kitchen. She glanced at the recycling bin where the second bottle of wine poked its head out accusingly. She put an old newspaper on top and squashed it down, forcing the lid. It felt like a positive step. She *was* capable of doing something decisive. She could go home and face this.

Half an hour later, in the car, Emma's bravado melted as she thought about the scene that would be waiting at home. The talk. It would feel so tacky and false. How did they even start to talk about going forward? But they'd have to. She didn't think she could bear it if Rosie had to suffer a broken home. Maybe she and Phillip could become different sorts of people. People who faced up to reality and talked about awkward things. One of those annoyingly connected couples who faced some horrible trauma and came out the other side holding hands and fist-pumping the air. Although that was probably unlikely. Phillip was a bit too serious to do fist pumps.

She drove down the driveway, wondering if she was still over the limit. She felt spaced out, distant, as if she was drifting. She would just have to make a careful effort to stay under the speed limit and to concentrate.

Her father lived an hour from her house, on the opposite side of Hobart, out near the D'Entrecasteaux Channel. She focussed on the rough driveway, potted with holes as it weaved through the bush block. A rock wallaby startled her as it jumped out from behind a clump of native pepper bushes and bounded across in front of her. She squeaked and clenched her jaw, slamming on the brakes as it scuttled into the greenery, then she slowly continued down the driveway.

On the main road, her heart rate returned to normal and she began to get glimpses of the stunning black watercourse with dark forest spilling down to its banks. It gave Emma a floaty, sad feeling.

She was driving on autopilot, suspended in a hazy light, skittering images swirling through her head. Pia's bottom kept reappearing. Then random, painful thoughts would occur to her. It had taken her a year to do up that cottage and its little garden so she could rent it out! *Focus on the road.* She drove through small rural hamlets, dotted with farm-gate shops and art galleries, barely noticing the pretty roadside stalls through her headache. How was she going to bake the birthday cake if she felt like this? *Give way at the roundabout. Slow down at the zebra crossing.* Did she even have the ingredients? *Was this a sixty zone?* She was out of food colouring. *Road. Road Emma!* Pia's breasts. Phillip's penis. Ugggh! It was absolutely unbelievable that Phillip had taken off his clothes with Pia. Disgusting! *She needed to focus – the road was so winding and pot-holed.* Also, did she have enough butter? She sped up as the road straightened out and she approached the edge of suburban Hobart. Strips of dowdy road-side houses began to replace the thick, bushy scrub. She would have to check the supplies for the cottage too. The cottage! *Orange light.* They had guests checking in this weekend. What if Pia hadn't finished the cleaning or hadn't left out the key for them? Red light.

Red light!

The sound of screeching tyres seemed to pierce the car, buffeting her from every direction, making her heart stop. Emma jammed her foot hard on the brake, sending her case on the passenger seat crashing into the dashboard. Her car skidded to a halt in the middle of the intersection. She froze, the violent jolt of her seat belt humming against her chest. On the passenger side, the bonnet of the approaching car appeared to hover at the door. Miraculously the cars coming from her left and right had braked, just in time. The three cars all sat idling together in the middle of the intersection, then horns started blaring angrily.

Acid waves of nausea rolled through Emma's stomach. Shaking, she edged the car forward through the intersection and pulled over onto the pebbly verge, the leather of the steering wheel still biting into her hands. She turned off the engine and burst into tears.

CHAPTER FIVE

HARRIET

Harriet's earpiece was talking to her. *You have run five kilometres.* She should run another three, but her muscles felt like lead and her endorphins were failing to cooperate. Sleep had been the same – rolling in then receding all night, like waves lapping at the salty-brown shore of her guilt. The anger at Scarlett was there too – obviously – but it was secondary to the guilt she felt for letting down her little brother.

Last night Harriet had walked into The Cables and spotted Jonathan immediately. He was hard to miss. Every head in the room had probably focussed on him at some point in the evening. After a lifetime of it, she hardly noticed the stares anymore, although it did sometimes occur to her that the thick crop of blond hair that framed Jonathan's beautiful face was startling for a man in his forties. Their mother had once admitted that Jonathan's father had been a 'fair-haired looker'. She'd spat the words at Harriet as if they tasted bitter in her mouth, as if it was somehow Harriet's fault that she'd been seduced by the man's golden charms.

Jonathan had been waiting at a small table in the back corner, drinking a beer. He waved to her, then stood to kiss her cheek and pull out her chair.

'What can I get you, Hat?' he asked, waiving at the waitress who was taking table orders. 'Mineral water?'

'White wine tonight thanks, darling. It's been a trying afternoon.' She forced a smile. The idea of revealing Scarlett's indiscretions irked her, but she wouldn't let it show. He would be thoroughly disappointed. Probably angry. Not to mention embarrassed. Jonathan's friend who headed up the boarding houses at Baddington College had not been a happy man when they'd spoken just a few minutes earlier.

'What's been happening in your world, Jon? Everything okay with those Year Ten girls?' She noticed a new furrow forming in between his eyebrows and a slew of new grey hairs at his temple. Her baby brother was heading into middle age. Was *already* middle-aged. Given that she was twelve years older than him, she found the idea unbearable.

'It's not too bad. A couple of girls caught smoking pot. Parents in uproar. The school's fault, obviously. Lax supervision. *It was only one joint, Dr Brownley. What's the fuss?* You know, the usual. Out of character for one of the girls though. I'm frustrated that she's being led astray.'

Harriet felt a stab of guilt. Drugs. Kids. Disappointment.

'Hmm. So how's the Ledbetter girl going? Still Denham's Year Ten shining star?'

Alexia Ledbetter had been given a full scholarship to the school after Harriet had badgered her brother to give the girl an interview, two years earlier. She was the daughter of one of Harriet's very few criminal clients. Harriet tried hard to stay out of the criminal courts these days, but sometimes her civil matters had to take a back seat if a favour was asked – if somebody's uncle's cousin's daughter had made a terrible error of judgement in getting behind the wheel after their tenth glass of wine. Or if, like her court case today, the principle of the matter was at stake and she decided that the accused person deserved the best justice money could buy. Although in a case like this she would often waive most of her fee.

'Yes, she's a great kid. An incredible mind. She makes the average marks of that cohort look great,' said Jonathan.

'What luck I found her that day.' Harriet felt it only sensible to put the idea at the front of his mind. Balance the scales, as it were, before the topic of Scarlett arose. But she was meant to look after Jonathan's interests too. She'd loved him first after all. Loved him best, she might have conceded if she'd allowed herself to go down that track.

'Absolutely.' Jonathan took a long sip of his beer and settled back in his chair.

'Now, why don't you tell me about your day, Hattie?' he said. 'Anything interesting?'

'A challenging murder trial actually. Well, self-defence if I can manage it. You might have read about it when it happened last year. A woman from out near Lanendale who stabbed her husband.'

'The guy who was sleeping at the time?'

'Yes, which makes it hard to prove self-defence. But the last time she tried to leave him he tracked her down to her mother's place. Put a shotgun to her head and dragged her home by her hair.'

'Oh, Hat, I really don't know how you do it.' He gave her a sad smile and took a sip of his beer. 'Let's change the subject. How's Scarlett getting along?'

Harriet picked up her wine and took a large sip. She wasn't ready. She hadn't processed her own anger and disappointment yet. And somewhere in the mix was guilt too. Perhaps she hadn't been a good enough mother. Not vigilant enough. She thought back to Jonathan's efforts on her behalf to get Scarlett the job at Baddington College. At first, he hadn't been keen. Scarlett could be a spiky creature. She didn't have Harriet's strict approach to following the rules or her father's gentle equanimity. She'd had her fair share of troubles at school. But in her final year she'd knuckled down and studied hard. She'd done well and it felt to all of them as if she turned over a new, more mature leaf. Eventually Jonathan had capitulated in the face of Harriet's requests for help to get a good placement for Scarlett's gap year. He'd called old friends. He'd twisted arms. He'd finally gotten her the most prestigious gap-year placement in the school's history. He'd been a good brother and a good friend to Harriet.

'I've just been talking to her actually. I'm afraid she's blotted her copybook rather badly.'

'Oh? That sounds ominous.'

'They found party pills in her room, Jon. MDMA. I'm absolutely livid. She's lost the position at the College and I know this will reflect badly on you too. I'm so sorry, darling. I really am furious with her.'

Jonathan reached over and put his hand on top of hers. 'Bloody hell.'

'Yes. Well. I may have said something rather more fruity.' Harriet closed her eyes for a moment. 'It's the immaturity of it, Jon. She doesn't seem to understand the magnitude of it. I just got off the phone to her now. She seems to think it isn't that bad!'

'Well, she'd be like a lot of other kids then. When the peer pressure takes hold, they can lose their heads, Hat. I've seen it time and again.'

Harriet let the silence stretch out for a moment before responding. 'I thought you'd be angrier with her, Jon. And with me.'

'Well you didn't do it. Why would I be angry with you?' He shook his head, then continued. 'As for Scarlett, though, she should have known better. I'd sack any gappie who brought drugs into our boarding houses too. And it won't be great for any future students I might want to recommend either.' He sighed, shook his head absently. 'But I guess it's not the end of the world.'

'Well I won't be letting her off the hook that easily. When she comes back, she'll be making it up to you. I don't know how, but we'll think of something. She's lucky the police don't seem to be involved. That's all I can think of at the moment.'

Harriet's Fitbit buzzed, bumping her out of her maudlin recollection of the previous evening. The beeping of the traffic signal began, telling her to cross the road. The crowds were milling around Constitution Dock, enjoying the bright Saturday sunshine. The Salamanca Markets were bustling, as the Hobart waterfront showed its prettiest face. Delicious smells of Indian cooking were coming from one of the colourful tents that lined the footpath. Further down, tents displayed leather bags and colourful handicrafts, and huge crates of fresh apples. Handmade silver jewellery shone next to buckets of fresh locally grown flowers being offered for five dollars a bunch.

The tourists and locals surged and spilled out of the cafés housed inside the row of convict-era sandstone facades that decorated the waterfront. Harriet skirted around them and jogged across the road onto the grass parklands. No amount of loveliness could shift her heavy mood today. Perhaps she needed to do some work this morning instead of having her usual Saturday morning to herself – it would be a good distraction from thinking about her imploding family. It wasn't just Ben and Scarlett who were making her heart heavy. Her eldest daughter, Clementine, had also emailed last night announcing that she was coming back from Prague to stay for three months in the lead up to Harriet's sixtieth birthday.

It will coincide with the Dark Mofo festival and a 25-year school reunion dinner thing, Mumbles. Thought I might pop along and see if I can recognise anyone. Could be a hoot! Hopefully they haven't all turned into boring middle-aged accountants and Stepford wives. Fingers crossed there's a drug addict or porn star in there somewhere! Clem. Xx

Harriet had sighed when reading it. Clementine coming for an extended stay. That just took the cake. She'd felt her blood pressure rise a fraction. Clementine had an appetite for anarchy and took up three times as much space in the house as anyone else with her chaotic presence and artistic paraphernalia. Harriet always felt a tiny bit guilty when she was around Clementine for more than a couple of days. There would invariably be an argument and Harriet would find herself wondering why she hadn't agreed to give her up for adoption all those years ago, when the pressure had been so strong from all fronts. Her mother, her school teachers, the social workers. Then she'd feel guilty for having the thought and would scramble to assuage her guilt by making it up to Clementine in all sorts of silly ways, most of which Clementine found annoying. It was exhausting.

To make matters worse, Clementine's 'sleep and work space' – otherwise known as the granny flat – was currently being used by Ben as his living quarters. This piece of news would not please Clementine. How could she be expected to paint? Though at forty-two, and an internationally acclaimed artist, Clementine could probably afford to buy the entirety of one of the swanky warehouse conversions on Hobart's wharves to sleep in and splash paint around on her canvasses, even with the rising price of real estate. This time, Harriet mused, she just might have to do it.

After sending a suitably happy-sounding response to Clementine, Harriet had spent the rest of the night sorting out short-term accommodation for Scarlett in England. She'd arranged for Scarlett to be despatched to Great Aunt Lila's place in Hertfordshire with her tail between her legs. Harriet had given a sanitised version of the truth to Ben's eccentric aunt – substituting alcohol for drugs in her version of Scarlett's expulsion story – and requesting a bed in the draughty old house for Scarlett for a few days until they all had a chance to consider the next steps.

Lila, an unconventional spinster with a passion for Irish whiskey and repulsively ugly hairless cats, was delighted that a young drinking buddy would soon be arriving on her doorstep to take long rambles in the woods with her. Harriet was equally delighted by her response – such healthy country pastimes would be an excellent punishment for Scarlett, who not only hated cats, but had an aversion to walks of any kind, particularly, Harriet imagined, the rambling variety. And the lack of civilisation and more importantly free WiFi within twenty kilometres of Lila's house would annoy Scarlett no end. That punishment alone was enough to warm the cockles of Harriet's heart. She would deal with arranging Scarlett's return airfare to Hobart next week. Scarlett hadn't wanted to return immediately and Harriet had run out of energy to argue about it. Anyway, she had too much else to do this weekend to worry about it.

CHAPTER SIX

MARLEE

Marlee had never understood the aversion most people had to sleeping with their colleagues. The workplace was often, in her experience, a great source of sex. But there were limits to this approach and sleeping with the boss was one of them – especially when the boss was the managing partner who had agreed to consider partnership with her in the very near future. She opened her eyes again, glad that the blinds were only letting in the barest shards of Saturday morning. Yes. It was definitely Ben. In her bed, apparently naked. Had she lost her *mind*?

She closed her eyes and felt the mild swoop of nausea. It was all coming back to her now. Stumbling through the front door like lust-struck teenagers. Ben fucking her, up against the lounge room wall (quite skilfully) then again, later, on the bed (very skilfully). She sighed. If she stayed very still perhaps the worst of the morning would be over quickly.

She watched him for a while, his deep even breaths providing a distraction from her need for the toilet. In the dim light she could still make out the strong, tanned line of his jaw. Looks weren't enough to account for the judgement lapse though. It must have been the booze. God, she really needed to stop drinking so much.

Her bursting bladder meant she was going to have to move. Marlee slipped as gently as she could from the bed and padded across the room. The full-length mirror on her wardrobe threw her naked reflection back at her. Slim, tall and toned, long red hair, dark circles under her eyes. Her curls had started to frizz and fell in a messy cloud to just below her breasts. She leaned forward and wiped the specks of last night's mascara from under her bottom lashes, then lifted her bathrobe from the back of the door and slid the green silk around her shoulders.

'Good morning.'

Marlee froze, then continued to tie the belt of the robe before she turned back to face him.

'Hi.'

Ben sat up allowing the covers to fall to his waist. He seemed unconcerned that his toned and rather fabulous torso was on display. *Dammit.* Lusting after her new boss's body every day was not going to help her settle seamlessly into office life. Apart from the fact that there was a lovely naked man in her bed, this situation was not ideal.

'I was just about to make some coffee if you'd like some.' She headed for the toilet without waiting for his response.

What the hell had she been thinking? Marlee splashed water on her face in the bathroom and walked downstairs to the kitchen. She put beans into the coffee grinder and pushed the button. The high-pitched metallic scream drowned out her spinning thoughts and she moved through the familiar calming routines of making coffee. Grind, pour, plunge. *For the love of God, now she was thinking of sex again.*

When Ben walked in a few minutes later, his hair was wet and slicked back. The bathroom was a tip, but he'd obviously found a towel. She wondered how he managed to look so fresh in yesterday's pants and shirt, unbuttoned at the collar, sleeves rolled up.

Marlee pushed the coffee pot and a cup towards him and sat down at the table. She crossed her legs and her robe slid apart, baring the pale, toned length of her legs. Her toenails glinted like tangerine jewels, one foot dangling languidly above the other. She watched him notice as she pulled the robe across to cover herself. He stayed standing in uncomfortable silence. After a while Marlee took pity on him and gestured vaguely towards the window. 'Gorgeous morning.'

'Mmm.'

Ben poured himself a cup of coffee and took a sip. The silence hung like a shroud.

'Marlee, I should apologise. It was inappropriate… last night. I should never have…' He took a breath, another sip of his coffee. He looked down at his shoes as if they might provide the right words, or maybe he was hoping that if he clicked his heels together the shoes might send him to Kansas or some other exotic destination where he didn't have to face up to his worst workplace nightmare.

She studied his deliciously serious face and suddenly felt sorry for him. Her earlier discomfort began to fade. It seemed pointless for them both to be beating themselves up about something as mundane as a one-night stand. Puerile even, given how damn good it was. Marlee shrugged off the remaining disquiet and decided to let him be the one to worry.

'Sleeping with a brand-new employee, Ben – never a good move.' She furrowed her eyebrows and tried to parrot his serious tone but, inexplicably, she felt like laughing. Nobody had ever apologised for sleeping with her before. Regrets, in Marlee's opinion, were not something to be shared. They were best accompanied by a good bottle of wine when curled up alone by the fire, to be indulged in only when there was no chance of interruption.

'I had a really nice time, Marlee. But I'm not making sensible decisions at the moment. Things are falling apart a bit on the home front.' He looked down at his coffee.

'Well, splitting with your wife… it must be hard.' Marlee sipped her own coffee.

'Yeah.'

'Is it a permanent split?' Marlee had a sudden vision of an uncomfortable work dinner down the track where partners were included, and she was forced to sit next to his wife.

'As far as I'm concerned it is. But my wife doesn't like to admit defeat, so I'm not sure she's convinced.'

'Right. That must be hard.'

'Actually, it's our daughter who's the problem this week,' said Ben. 'She's been kicked out of her gap year placement at a great school in London for having party drugs.'

'Oh.' That would account for the serious face.

'Yeah. It's…' he seemed to deflate then, as if a little hole had been pricked between his shoulder blades.

'Lots of kids are mucking up at that age, Ben. I know I did after I left school.'

He didn't reply and for some bizarre reason she felt compelled to fill the silence.

'She's lucky to have a dad like you to support her. I'm sure it'll be fine.' Marlee watched him run his fingers through his hair. It was lovely thick hair, she noticed.

'I hope you're right. Anyway, I have to be somewhere in half an hour so I'm afraid I have to go.' He didn't move and Marlee's eyes fell to his hands, both now clenched around the coffee cup. She wondered if he was weighing up whether it was appropriate to kiss her goodbye.

'Marlee, I haven't been in the dating game for a very long time, and I hate to bring it up, but we didn't use a condom last night, so I hope I haven't… put you in any difficulty.'

Christ. This was excruciating.

'Ben, it's fine.' She gave a small laugh as she thought of her withered uterus. Although to be fair, she did usually take precautions against catching a disease even if pregnancy wasn't on the cards. Why hadn't she insisted on a condom last night? Her memories of the night returned in fragments. She remembered him telling her about his twenty-two years of faithful married history. To a woman called... Harriet, who sounded pretty uptight. Marlee must have believed him.

He moved around the table and gave her a quick kiss on the cheek.

'Thanks, Marlee. I had a really nice night. I'll... see you...' He walked to the front door and raised his hand in a half-wave, dropped it again as he pulled his mouth back into a sad sort of smile, then held her gaze. When he finally closed the door, the click was almost soundless.

Marlee let out her breath. *Crapity-crap-crap.* What a shitty twist of fate that he was her boss. He was really quite lovely. She took a head-clearing breath and exhaled loudly. Then she scanned the headlines of the newspaper, enjoying the splash of sunlight and the way it played across the newsprint. She watched it with interest, until a mental image of Ben kissing her collar bone distracted her and she felt a shot of delicious yearning in her groin.

She shifted in her seat and sighed. Men. In a perfect world, they would come with far fewer complications.

CHAPTER SEVEN

EMMA

Vivien and Roger's dark blue Audi was parked in the driveway as Emma pulled up in front of her house. She felt tears threaten again. She fingered her lank hair and brushed frantically at the front of her creased floral shirt attempting to straighten it out. It felt sticky and tainted, having been on her body during yesterday's discovery in the cottage. Emma's mother-in-law was an elegant woman who held an unyielding personal philosophy about appearance. Sloppy, overweight and dowdy were, for Vivien, synonyms for ill-bred, lazy and careless. Emma wondered if she could sneak in through the kitchen without them noticing.

'Emma,' said Phillip, as she pushed open the door. He stood at the sink next to his parents, watching her.

'Hello, Vivien, hi, Roger.' Emma put down her bag of groceries and hugged them both. She waited until she'd stepped away before saying anything else. Her breath probably smelled evil.

Vivien watched her closely, taking a little extra time to bestow a closed-mouthed smile. She was wearing beautiful flowing pants made from charcoal-coloured linen. Her cream silk blouse billowed down one side in effortless, asymmetrical perfection. Emma felt a pang of jealousy looking at her gorgeous earrings, featuring some sort of large yellow stone set in thick silver casing – the expensive kind you could only find in galleries that sold handcrafted artisan pieces. The sort Emma would never find or be brave enough to buy anyway. She'd look ridiculous if she tried to wear anything so arty or glamorous.

'Phillip was just saying you'd been at your father's last night,' said Vivien.

'Yes.'

'How is he?' asked Roger.

'He's well, thanks.' Emma watched as the three of them lined up along the kitchen bench. Phillip was now looking down at the floor, his hands shoved deep in his pockets. They all appeared to be waiting for her to do something.

'I'm not feeling well today actually,' said Emma, speaking to her father-in-law, the only one who was smiling. 'I might lie down for a bit if you don't mind.'

'Of course,' said Vivien. 'You've probably been very busy with your cottage guests and your little job. You have a rest. Phillip has just offered to take us on a tour of the new glass house at the Terribee Flower Farm, and we've almost convinced Rosie to come along too. It'll be a nice change of pace for us.'

Emma's mother-in-law wasn't one for taking things easy. Dr Vivien Allison sat on several boards, consulted to universities and commercial entities about positive management practices and, until her recent semi-retirement, had run a thriving human resources company. Emma had often wondered when the woman slept. She certainly never required a daytime nap due to drinking stupid amounts of wine. Emma's hangover would mean several brownie points being deducted from the already below-zero tally that her mother-in-law probably kept. Her head throbbed just thinking about it.

'Right. I hear the whole five-acre glass house is controlled by computers,' said Emma, as Rosie came into the kitchen wearing dirty tracksuit bottoms and a crop top.

'Hi, Mum.' Rosie threw her hands around Emma's neck and kissed her cheek.

'Hello, darling.' Emma tried not to flinch. Rosie hadn't put her deodorant on and she had a serious bird's nest on the back of her head from lack of a hair brush. Usually Emma would have made sure Rosie looked pristine for a visit from Vivien. One more point deducted.

'Do you think you should change before you go to the flower farm, darling?' Emma pleaded with her eyes.

'Sure.' Rosie bounced off down the hall.

Emma assured her parents-in-law she'd be fine when they got back, then she headed for the bedroom. Strangely, she didn't feel angry at Phillip. She felt an empty, fluttering sort of anticipation – a perverse interest in what was yet to come. It must be the hangover.

Emma pulled the curtains closed. Her headache had ratcheted up to full blast and she'd never be able to sleep until the painkillers kicked in. She took two more tablets and sank onto her bed. Then she picked up her laptop and hesitated for a moment before clicking on her email.

From: Yolanda Stevens
To: Emma Parsons
Re: Fabulous Formal Photo… the countdown is on, girls!

Dear Emma,
So great to hear from you, even if you didn't mean to email me! I'm in Sydney these days, running a dog and cat minding business. Dog-a-roo! (no roos yet, but plenty of other furry friends). Don't worry about the 'reply all' by the way. I did the same thing last year when I suggested my husband come home from work early and join me in the bath to help me shave my lady bits. My husband thought it was an awesome idea. My mother-in-law not so much!

Anyway, what's this about Tessa's death? Has the police investigation been reopened? It wouldn't surprise me. There was definitely something weird about it. I wonder if they still have her clothes to do DNA samples or something. She was sleeping with someone I'm pretty sure. Maybe she snuck out to meet him. Probably a St Marks boy who's now the police minister or in parliament! Ha! Anyway, see you soon at the reunion and we can catch up on it all.

Best,

Yolanda (Stevens nee Montague)

Emma didn't read any of the others. She felt like crying again, but instead she crawled into bed and stared up at the old, water-marked ceiling that was badly in need of paint. She hadn't noticed it before, but the ceiling dipped in one corner and had begun cracking above the window architrave. Their house needed so much work – Philip's dream house that he never had the time to work on. The sadness sank into her and she closed her eyes, but behind the darkness of her lids, her thoughts swarmed like angry bees. Emma let them buzz, until eventually the headache receded, and she fell into a deep, black sleep.

*

The sound of a car door slamming outside the bedroom window jolted Emma from her dream. She scrambled out of bed and saw Marlee getting out of the car, dressed in tight black jeans and an elegant knee-length green coat.

She looked at the bedside clock. It was five-thirty! *Why hadn't they woken her?* She pulled off yesterday's clothes and flicked through the closet, pulling out pink woollen top and teaming it with a clean pair of beige chinos. She pulled the hairbrush through her hair, put on a splash of pink lipstick and stumbled down the hallway and into the kitchen. Phillip was leaning down into the oven checking the potatoes. She felt her stomach do a sick little flip, in the same kind of way it used to do before her school drama performances.

'Hello, darling,' said her dad. He looked up from his chopping board at the table, a carrot in his hand.

'Hi, Dad. I must have slept all afternoon. Sorry.'

'That's alright, pet. Phillip said you were still feeling off colour. Better now?'

'Yes, thanks.'

Phillip kept his back to her as he rustled in the utensil drawer. Then Rosie bounced into the kitchen and gave her a hug. 'Mum, Grandma says to get the good wine glasses because it's a special occasion.'

Emma smiled at her. 'It sure is.'

She sighed and walked into the dining room and spent the next few minutes finishing the table settings, listening as Marlee chatted to her parents-in-law who were relaxing on the couch with their customary scotch and soda in the good crystal tumblers, waiting to be served. She tried to catch Marlee's eye, to warn her not to say anything about Phillip, but Marlee seemed engrossed in a discussion about seventeenth century art with her father-in-law.

Throughout dinner, Emma moved the conversation along with a kind of stilted jollity, hoping that nobody would notice the strange tension in the room. So far, they had made it to dessert without a hitch.

'Can you pass that to Vivien please Phillip?' said Marlee.

Emma watched nervously as Marlee handed the plate to Phillip. The scorn in Marlee's eyes when she glanced at Phillip was barely concealed. Emma could have kicked herself for telling Marlee about Pia. Marlee only just tolerated Phillip at the best of times. She wasn't sure that Marlee would be very supportive of her decision to try to make things work between them.

Phillip passed the plate to his mother, who regarded the melting cake with undisguised disappointment and passed it across to Roger.

'Thank you, dear, but I won't have any. That lamb was wonderful by the way, Phillip. You really are a fabulous cook. Isn't he, Emma?' she looked across at Emma, waiting for confirmation of her son's general excellence.

'Mmmm, it was nice,' mumbled Emma. She looked at the cake melting on her own plate and wondered why she'd thought a psychedelic supermarket ice-cream cake was a good idea when her mother-in-law was coming.

'I wish your father was as handy as you in the kitchen, Phillip.' Vivien smiled up at Phillip then looked across at Rosie who had just slurped the last of her lemonade through the straw. As Vivien watched, Rosie poked her finger into the ice-cream cake and began licking it off. Emma's heart sank. Why couldn't Rosie just make an effort to have good manners occasionally? Just when Vivien visited would be enough. Emma tried to think of something to say to distract her. Phillip was no help. He'd been silent all night apart from filling in his father about a new paper he was co-authoring that looked at soil microbes and crop rotation, until Rosie reminded him it was her birthday party and he was boring everyone.

'After dessert you'll have to show me all the outfits you got for your birthday, Rosie,' said Marlee. 'We can see what goes with the leather jacket. Then we can spend the gift card next weekend. Get some boots maybe?'

'Okay, great!' said Rosie. She launched into a description of her favourite new clothes, filling the air with words that floated around Emma's head like dust.

A hot tension built in her chest as Emma watched her father put down his spoon into the purple pool of melted ice-cream. She needed to get out of the room.

'Phillip, could you help me clear please,' she said. She forced a smile as she piled up the bowls from her side of the table and walked down the hall.

In the kitchen, Emma dumped the bowls on the sink with a clatter and stood still, waiting. The sound of Phillip's footsteps made her stomach clench.

'Close the door.' The catastrophe had to be faced. It had been the elephant in the room all night, but now the elephant had sat down squarely on top of Emma's chest and she was struggling to breathe. She couldn't let the charade go on another minute. Her need to confront Phillip had been tightening like a vice. She needed to hear him say he was sorry, that he still loved her, that it was a terrible, awful mistake. All night she'd forced out light conversation as if Rosie's life depended on it, but she'd explode if she didn't say something. Phillip closed the door with an ominous click.

'How could you do it?'

She spun to face him and he walked across and put the bowls by the sink, avoiding her eyes. The silence hung like a guillotine poised to fall.

'You had an affair in our cottage! *My* cottage, Phillip! Sex with someone else in a part of our own home. Phil…?'

Phillip turned his back to her and poured himself a glass of water. Then he put both hands on the kitchen bench and his shoulders slumped.

Why wasn't he answering her? She couldn't remember what she was meant to say next. She'd sort of planned it in the bathroom before dinner, but now it had gone. It was something about how sick the whole scene had looked to her; how she didn't deserve to be treated so badly; how she thought Pia was almost a friend – a lovely girl who Emma had gone out of her way to help with the endless rounds of paperwork needed for her visa extension. But Phillip didn't look like he was up for a fight. He looked beaten.

A picture of Emma's mother flashed through her mind, angry and bitter. *Put on your sensible shoes, girl! No point being so dramatic. He might have done something stupid, but he's your husband.*

'I think we should do marriage counselling, Phillip. I thought we were okay. I thought—'

'Emma, I'm sorry you had to see that.'

Emma looked at him blankly.

'You should be sorry that you *did* it. Not just that I saw it, Phil! I know you always want more sex than me, but getting together with the first pretty thing that bats her eyelashes at you, well, it's just... *stupid*!' Why couldn't she find a better word when she needed it? Did he really not understand how disgusting it was?

'I want a divorce, Emma. I love Pia.'

Emma felt the words wash over her, but the meaning seemed to slip away. She sat down on the stool and put both hands on the worn timber of the old kitchen table. It was Rosie's birthday on Monday. They'd promised to take her out for pancakes on the way to school. The new curtains had finally arrived for Phillip to hang up in their bedroom. Did he just say *divorce*?

'I'm sorry.' He turned to face her.

'You... you can't be serious, Phillip. You're old enough to be her father. She doesn't even have citizenship!' said Emma, in a rush, as if Pia's visa status was a crucial factor in it all.

Phillip stared at the fridge, unmoving.

'What about Rosie?'

The door opened before he could speak and Marlee walked into the kitchen with some more dishes.

'Everything okay in here?'

An overblown balloon of silence expanded around them. Marlee looked hard at Phillip, then at Emma.

'Phillip... wants a divorce,' said Emma staring into Marlee's glittering green eyes.

Marlee put the dishes down carefully on the bench then closed the door. Phillip turned away and started stacking the plates. There was a long moment, in which they all seemed to focus on the scraping and clattering noises as Phillip placed dirty plates in the dishwasher.

'You selfish, *selfish* prick, Phillip,' hissed Marlee. Her anger was piercing, releasing Emma from the bubble of unreality.

'Stay out of it, Marlee,' said Phillip. He slammed the door of the dishwasher.

'No. I won't! Not when it's my goddaughter's life you're about to screw up.'

'Get down off your high horse, Marlee,' said Phillip.

Marlee turned to Emma, ignoring him.

'It's late. Rosie looks tired. What about I get her to show me her outfits in her bedroom then suggest she goes to bed.' She sounded like an annoyed parent speaking to her naughty children.

Emma spoke. 'I'd better come and say goodnight to her.'

'You should come and say goodnight too, Phillip,' said Marlee. 'It's *Rosie's* party. She needs to be a priority, even if you've decided that your marriage isn't one.' Marlee's glare landed like a javelin and Phillip seemed to deflate.

Marlee walked up the hall leaving the door open. Emma followed her, catching the scent of her anger. It began to boil inside her too.

They walked through to the dining room listening to the last squeaky notes of 'Daisy Bell'. Rosie stood with her violin in one hand and the bow in the other, making little curtsying motions, one foot behind the other. All three grandparents were clapping and smiling.

'Come on, Maestro,' said Marlee. 'You wanted to show me some outfits, didn't you? Let's have a fashion parade in the bedroom. You'd better say goodnight first though. It could take a while.'

'Awesome,' said Rosie, placing the violin on the sideboard. 'Will I come out and show you too, Mum?'

'How about we do another parade tomorrow, darling? I've got a bit of a headache so I might head to bed in a minute.'

'Okay. Thanks for dinner and all the presents.' Rosie walked around the table to kiss everyone before heading off to the other end of the house with Marlee.

'Goodnight, darling,' said Emma, smelling Rosie's freshly washed hair as she leaned in to hug her. She wanted to hold on to her forever. Capture the pubescent smell of musky hormonal innocence and bottle it, before Rosie's world came crashing down.

Emma watched her walk down the hall and felt new anger twisting inside her gut. She sat down across from her father and her parents-in-law. Without the razzle of Marlee's party banter or the guarantee of Phillip's dry academic lecturing disguised as conversation, she felt alone and exposed. Her head hurt. She wasn't up to the tennis match of loaded questions and insincere compliments Vivien would serve out. She might have been the perfect grandmother to Rosie, but she'd never thought that Emma was good enough for her gifted eldest son. Her clever prince.

Phillip walked in to the dining room and looked from his parents across to Emma. There was a warning in his eyes.

'Well, that was a nice night,' said Roger, leaning back in his chair after refilling his wine glass.

'And who'd believe our little Rosie is a teenager?' said Vivien. She looked across to Emma's father. 'She's a darling girl isn't she, Ian?'

'Emma was the same at that age,' said her father proudly. 'The light of our lives.'

Emma's heart began to crumble.

'Well, she certainly takes after Phillip with her musical ability,' said Vivien. 'He was always so dedicated to practising the piano.' She looked up at Phillip. 'We'll give you the baby grand when we move into the villa, Phillip. You really should have it here. You and Rosie could both use it then. It would fit nicely in the living room, or perhaps you'd prefer to put it in here, Emma?' Vivien looked at Emma, expecting gratitude for her largesse; agreement that there was certainly room for the huge, ugly piano in their house, whether Emma wanted it or not.

Emma felt her head getting hot. Her chest expanded with resentment as she watched Vivien wait for the thanks she felt was due.

'I don't think we'll be wanting the piano to be honest, Vivien. Phillip and I are getting a divorce.' The words gave Emma a ping of satisfaction. *Look Vivien, he did do the wrong thing in choosing me. You were right all along!* Emma watched the shock fly across Vivien's face.

Phillip's eyes widened. Then he tensed his jaw and gave a brief shake of his head as if she were a naughty child.

'What? That's ridiculous!' said Vivien. 'Why would you do that, Emma? You can't do that to Rosie.'

Both of the grandfathers remained silent, staring, open-mouthed.

'Well, maybe *Phillip* should tell you why Rosie's going to have to go through this,' said Emma. Her headache ratcheted up a notch, throbbing behind her eyes.

Phillip went to the door and closed it before he spoke. 'Tonight isn't the right time to discuss it, Emma.' He had that imperious look on his face that annoyed her – as if she was just a tiny bit slow and he deserved an award for his forbearance. She tilted her head to the side and waited. Why should *she* be the one to feel guilty?

He looked across to his mother.

'Phillip, darling, this can't be right,' said Vivien.

He shifted from one foot to the other and looked down.

'Is it true, dear?'

'Well… since Emma insists on raising it now… as it happens… Emma and I haven't been getting on for some time,' said Phillip, avoiding Emma's stare.

Emma felt a crack as a volcano began spitting hot grief inside her chest. The lie, the unfairness, the injustice of it. 'What? Are you *kidding* me, Phillip? Are you freaking *kidding* me!'

Vivien's head jerked backwards but Emma was beyond caring. She let her rage boil over.

'Tell them truthfully, Phillip, why *you* have decided that you don't want to remain married to *me* anymore. And make sure you put in the bit where I had absolutely no idea about any of this until yesterday, and I actually thought we were getting along fine. And maybe even share the bit about how I walked in and found you having sex with our cleaner in the cottage, you selfish pig!'

Everyone stared at Emma in slack-jawed silence. Their faces became blurry.

'Keep your voice down. You're being *silly*!' hissed Phillip, 'Do you want Rosie to hear you?'

Emma took her voice down a notch. 'Oh, I'm sorry for upsetting you, Phillip, by telling everyone about your sordid little affair with a girl twenty years your junior. You make me sick!' In the ugly throes of adrenalin, Emma wanted to smack him. She stopped and looked around at the stricken faces of her father and her parents-in-law.

'Dad, I'm really sorry.'

'Oh pet, don't… don't…' Her dad got up shakily from his chair, his face sagging.

'I think I really need to go to bed. Vivien, Roger, I'm…' Emma's mind went blank. She turned her head away from them. 'Sleep somewhere else, Phillip.'

As she said it, she knew that he'd go to Pia tonight.

Emma walked out and down the hallway. She kicked at the suitcase from Phillip's trip to Perth that he'd promised to put up in the loft storage a week ago. It scuttled along the hall and fell over with crash onto the floorboards. Her toe flamed with pain.

CHAPTER EIGHT

HARRIET

Harriet watched the baggage circulate on the carousel and wondered why people crowded so closely together in a huddle around the machine, when it was perfectly easy to identify when your bag was coming out from the seating area. It was then a simple matter of standing to collect it at the end, thereby obviating the need for an unpleasant scrummage with the rest of humanity.

She sat down on the bench – an enormous rugged length of lacquered timber showing off the natural terrain of the tree's delicate edges. One more giant felled from a Tasmanian old-growth forest, she thought dismally. She sighed. She'd been in a bad mood all week, ever since Clementine had announced her arrival date and Ben had refused to move out of their granny flat to accommodate her. He seemed to think that it was reasonable that Clementine could stay in the main house with Harriet, and he would stay out in the garden flat until they sold the house. She couldn't decide if it was the unusual way that he refused to capitulate to her demands, or the fact that she was going to have to live in close quarters with Clementine and her mess that was making her more irritable. It would have been much more pleasant having Ben in the spare room than having Clementine. At least he was tidy and out of the house most of the time.

What exactly he had been doing with his newly busy social life she wasn't sure, but she'd noticed the absence of his car a lot in the preceding weeks. The fact that she found herself so interested in his comings and goings irritated her. She still loved him, but she wasn't about to beg him to return. He probably just needed to 'find himself'. His mid-life crisis was right on time, and if she was honest, she probably should have seen it coming. Should have taken measures to avert it. Bought him a sports car or something.

Harriet took out her phone and clicked onto her calendar, wondering exactly what she might have to move around in her diary to accommodate Clementine in the next few days if she wanted to spend some time catching up. A lot. She put the phone back in her handbag and snapped it shut.

Harriet watched the passengers starting to come into the arrivals hall, hopefully from Clementine's domestic transfer from Melbourne. She stood up, a small flutter of anticipation surprising her. She hadn't seen Clementine for nearly two years, since they'd met in New York for Clem's fortieth birthday weekend.

The crowd thinned as suitcases were plucked off the carousel and Harriet scanned the remaining travellers for Clementine's small blond frame. A woman with baggy pants and chunky lace-up boots was running her fingers through her spiky, dark hair and staring at a quarantine officer. His little beagle was jumping on and off the carousel, sniffing at bags for contraband fruit and other items. The woman's pants had a strange crotch that appeared to hang all the way down to the knees. A most peculiar ensemble. Suddenly the beagle jumped on top of one of the suitcases and began sniffing madly and riding it around the carousel. The handler gave it a treat from his pocket and pulled the bag off, landing it next to the woman's feet. She turned to move out of the way then caught Harriet's eye and smiled. With a start, Harriet realised it was Clementine. She had ruined her beautiful blond hair. Without her wispy bohemian style, Clementine looked like a different person. Harriet suppressed any obvious sign of disapproval. It would make Clementine far too happy.

'Clem, I almost didn't recognise you. How are you, darling?' She leaned forward and gave her daughter a hug. *She's barely there*, thought Harriet, *such a tiny frame for such a potent force.* She closed her eyes and inhaled the scent of her.

'Hello, Mumsy, I'm fine thanks. You look well. Even more corporate than usual.'

Harriet was wearing a navy and cream tailored woollen knee-length skirt and a matching fitted jacket – similar to every other business suit in her cupboard. She was adorned plainly, with a crisp white collared shirt, diamond studs and her usual pearl pendant. Nothing in her appearance was in any way different to how she had always dressed for work. Clementine was up to her old tricks.

'Well, obviously I've come straight from court. I cancelled a few meetings to come and meet you. It was the least I could do. But I have to be back in chambers in an hour for a client so we'd better hurry.'

'No rest for the wicked hey, Mumsy?' Clementine smirked. 'Just drop me at home and I'll be fine.'

They collected the case from the almost empty carousel and walked outside to Harriet's sparkling white BMW. They drove out of the airport in silence, Clementine looking out the window at the rugged hills, a palette of dry greens and browns. Harriet tried to think how many years it had been since Clementine's last visit home. For some reason she couldn't locate the detail in her mind. Years and years. Eight or ten perhaps? As time had passed, her absence had left Harriet feeling hollow, but now that Clementine was actually here, Harriet just felt a mild anxiety. How would they get along? How was she was going to tell her about the new sleeping arrangements?

'So Mumsy – your sixtieth. What sort of party are we having? Something elegant and low-key at a restaurant with all your lawyer buddies?'

Harriet detected a faint thread of derision. She wasn't turning sixty for a couple of months and the idea of a party had completely slipped from her radar when Ben announced he wanted to separate. Unfortunately, Ben had emailed Clementine before Christmas to suggest she return for a party, in the knowledge that Clementine's diary, since she had rocketed to fame amongst the elite art world, was difficult to manage. It had surprised them both when she announced in her most recent email, just a few days ago, that she had cleared her diary so she could come home for three months.

'I think we can just go out for a small dinner. No need to make a fuss. I'm perfectly happy not to mark the occasion actually.'

'Come on, Mumma, that's not going to happen. You know Ben will want to do something big for you. He loves all that birthday palaver. His foxy lady's turning *sixty* after all.'

Harriet pursed her lips and tooted the horn at a driver who indicated late to turn into a driveway in front of them off busy Hamden Road. There was a slight tightening in her chest whenever she thought about having to reveal her marital disintegration to anyone, but it was morphing into an acute pain now that she was faced with telling her eldest daughter. Clementine was fond of reminding Harriet at every available opportunity, how lucky she had been that a young, handsome Ben had come into her life all those years ago and had not been put off by their age difference or by Harriet's obsessive-compulsive issues around general household and bathroom cleanliness.

Harriet made a non-committal sound and indicated to turn left into Lilly Lane, a winding, semi-circular path, barely wide enough for one car. It bustled with tourists and smartly dressed locals loitering outside the new wine bar that had recently been voted as best in Tasmania. She drove past restored fishermen's cottages, sandstone mansions and historic guesthouses that jostled prettily together. Harriet slowed as she approached the huge century-old pin oak tree that marked the entry to her street.

'So tell me about this reunion you're going to, Clem. Twenty-five years seems like a strange sort of time frame. Aren't they usually held each decade?'

'It's an informal one. A dinner organised by one of the girls who lives in Sydney, marking a quarter-century. Should be a bit of fun though, seeing as I missed the last two.'

Harriet pulled into their driveway, and turned to watch Clementine's face. She was looking up at the imposing sandstone façade of the home she'd spent her teenage years in. The hint of a smile played on Clementine's lips and Harriet was about to ask what she was thinking when Ben's car pulled in beside them. *Damn.* Harriet looked at the dashboard clock. It was only four o'clock.

Clementine got out of the car and walked around the back to give an enormous bear hug to her step-father. Seeing them together had always made Harriet feel uncomfortable in a way she didn't care to fully articulate. When she and Ben had met, she was in her mid-thirties and he'd been a handsome, newly-minted architecture graduate a decade younger than her. He was also unaccountably attracted to older women; or, more particularly, Harriet. And he was only seven years older than Clementine.

It had taken Harriet a while to take Ben's passionate devotion to her seriously. She was, after all, a workaholic single mother whose eighteen-year-old daughter was much better suited in age to be his girlfriend. But it was soon obvious that Ben saw no attraction in Clementine's wild youthful antics, and yet he had always accepted her completely as part of the package.

Clementine was dismissive of him at first, teasing him relentlessly about his penchant for older women. But Ben's good nature meant he bore the teasing graciously, and after he commissioned her to paint some large artworks to hang in his office, he and Clementine had become firm friends. Not that it made her easy to live with. When Clementine had headed off to art school in Sydney not long after Ben had entered their lives, it had felt like a relief to both of them.

About a year after that, Harriet had agreed to marry Ben on the basis that he understood there would be no more children. One experience of parenting had been more than enough for Harriet. So it was a shock to them both when, five years later, she had visited the doctor to address the nausea she'd been experiencing for weeks, only to find she was fifteen weeks pregnant with Scarlett. Ben had been over the moon. Harriet, forty-one and in the prime of her career, had enquired about a termination.

Harriet got out of the car and watched Ben pull Clementine's suitcase out of the boot.

'Let me get this inside the house for you, Clem, then we can have a drink and you can tell me all about your latest exhibition. Zurich, wasn't it?'

Ben followed Clementine's career with devoted enthusiasm. He put Harriet to shame.

Clementine reached for the suitcase. 'It's okay, I'll just take it round to the granny flat and meet you in the house in a few minutes.'

Ben gave Harriet a piercing look. She turned away and pretended to be searching her bag for the house keys.

'Umm, Clem, your mother obviously hasn't mentioned it, but I'm afraid the granny flat isn't available at the moment. You'll have to take the spare room.' He gave her an encouraging smile.

Clementine turned to Harriet. 'What? Mum? Who's staying there? If you'd told me you had visitors, I would have got myself an apartment. You know I'm not good at sharing.'

Harriet couldn't believe Ben was putting her in this position. He was the one being difficult about the granny flat, and now Clementine was looking at *her* for an explanation, as if she was some kind of evil witch who was attempting to thwart her holiday plans on purpose. Ben was standing there looking empathetic and pretending it wasn't his fault.

'It's not *me* you should be asking, Clementine,' snapped Harriet, turning to get her coat. Harriet could feel their eyes on her back.

Eventually Ben spoke again. 'Clem, I'm really sorry, but your mother and I have decided to go our separate ways. I'm staying in the granny flat until we sell the house and work out what to do.'

Clementine looked at Harriet and raised one eyebrow. 'Oh. Did that little piece of news just slip your mind in the car, Mum?'

Really, the girl could be so terribly condescending. Like Scarlett, Clementine adored Ben. She would never lay the blame on him for the marital decay. Oh no, it would all be Harriet's fault. Harriet stayed silent. It was generally the best thing to do when Clementine was in a mood.

'Well, I'm sorry that you've split but I can't say I'm surprised.' Clementine looked from Ben to Harriet. 'How's Scarlett going to feel when she comes home from England at Christmas and finds her home gone?'

Harriet flinched as Ben tilted his head to one side and gave her a tight stare. Why would he assume she would have told Clementine everything immediately? Especially since the news was all bad. The poor girl had barely gotten off the plane. He was probably still angry with her about the row they'd had last night about Harriet's criticisms of Scarlett. He hated it if she made judgements about people and he was irritated about her need to repeatedly express her anger at Scarlett out loud.

'Scarlett is actually coming home earlier than Christmas time,' he said neutrally.

'What? Why? Couldn't she cope with all those rich brats in the boarding house?' Clementine seemed to infuse the question with some small amount of glee and Ben's face fell.

Harriet decided to take charge of the conversation. Clementine could be scathing.

'Your sister got into trouble with some party drugs. Nothing serious, but she lost her placement.'

Clementine pondered this for a moment. 'Right.' The hint of a smile played at the corners of her mouth. 'Sooooo… that was pretty dumb.'

'Clementine, that's hardly something for you to make comment about. I recall when you were that age, you had several run-ins with authority! You were just as bad, if not worse,' snapped Harriet.

Clementine laughed bitterly. 'Right. And as I recall, *Mother*, when you were that age, you got yourself up the duff with me and shamed everyone. I'm sure it was a great look for that school you love so much when they gave you a scholarship and you repaid them by sitting your final exams looking like you had a watermelon stuffed up your tunic.'

Harriet felt her lungs deflate like a broken balloon. Her eyes fluttered closed.

Clementine turned to Ben. 'Can you drop me into town please, Ben? I'll find somewhere else to stay.'

Ben spoke quietly. 'Clem, we all know that what Scarlett did was wrong. This argument is not going anywhere. At least stay here tonight, and we can sort something out tomorrow. What about we all go out for dinner?'

Always the peacemaker. Ben's endless patient solutions used to be like flicking off the switch of the kettle for Harriet – an instant balm to soothe her boiling emotions. Now though, she just felt empty. She needed him to stop this nonsense about them divorcing.

Harriet opened her eyes. They were both looking at her. She knew she needed to speak. If she didn't extend the olive branch now, Clementine was just as likely to jump on the next plane out of Hobart. This thought had a certain appeal – it would, in many ways, be the answer to Harriet's immediate problem of having to share her living space with someone who did not respect her need for cleanliness. On the other hand, Clementine provided a welcome distraction to her other problems, and Harriet could not deny that Clementine was, and always had been, the only person who could make her laugh. And now that Clementine was standing right there in front of her, she felt a precarious urge to reach out and clutch at her. Perhaps she *could* mend the frayed threads of her relationship with her zany, antagonistic daughter.

'I have a client meeting. But I'll be home in an hour or so. Clem, please stay. I'd really like to hear all your news when I get back. And we can talk about what's been happening here too. I'm... sorry you had to hear it like that.' Harriet got back into her car and closed the door.

Breathe, Harriet, breathe. That was apparently the solution. She had been reading about the health benefits of meditation. Perhaps this was the time to start. There were classes at the fancy new health retreat next to her chambers. They had tucked a flyer under the office door.

> *Mindfulness and Meditation for Beginners: reduce stress, increase your feeling of wellbeing and self-acceptance; slow down your life and increase focus; just $620 for 8 x 2-hour classes.*

It had sounded like a good investment, except Harriet was very accepting of herself already. She fully accepted that her habit of working on her laptop until 1 a.m. in bed could be annoying – Ben had reiterated that fact when he had left her. And she had no particular problems being focussed or embracing stress – it came with the territory when you dealt with people's legal catastrophes. Plus, she absolutely could not find an extra two hours in her week to devote to lying down and chanting. Her calendar was full up to the very brim for the next six months at least.

Harriet wondered how she had thought that having Clementine home was going to be smooth sailing this time. It was never smooth. Clementine had every right to comment on Scarlett's dumb behaviour, but somehow every criticism she made felt personal to Harriet. *Now your other daughter has screwed up too – that makes you a really terrible mother.* No, deep breathing and self-examination were not going to help with anything. Work was the best place to avoid having to think about it too much.

But she did need to make amends. She *did* want Clementine to stay. And it was only day one. When this meeting was finished, she would have a drink with Clementine and smooth things over. If they were going to be under one roof for a while, she needed to focus on finding some strategies for managing their time together. Perhaps she could ask the cleaner to come in every day before she got home. Yes, that was an excellent strategy. She would warn Clementine about it so she didn't snap at the poor woman for tidying up around her. She sighed. Children were not meant to make you feel like this.

CHAPTER NINE

MARLEE

Marlee took the band off her wrist and pulled her curls up into a ponytail as she looked at the screen. It was not that she was particularly fazed by the difficulty of the project – it was an interesting brief, waterfront location, clients were open to new ideas – it was just that the clients were insistent that Ben, as senior partner, closely oversee the project. He'd been personally requested, and when he'd said he was unavailable to take on the new brief, they were only happy to have the new associate do the work if Marlee would agree to work closely with him. So far, she hadn't had to do more than sit down with Ben in their initial conference with the client, but in the next few days she needed to meet with him to get some substantial input so she could finalise initial concepts to present to the clients on Tuesday.

Marlee looked again at the roof lines on her computer screen and back at the modelling done by the solar expert. The angles weren't right and the pavilions weren't working in harmony either, mostly because the owners wanted to build around some old trees, which was making it difficult to get the orientation of the walls right. She needed Ben's input but couldn't bring herself to schedule a meeting with him. Since their night together a few weeks earlier, he'd been nice and helpful, but they hadn't really been in any one-on-one situations where they might need to acknowledge their drunken fling, which had suited her just fine. She'd been busy furnishing her apartment and getting a handle on the new projects she was going to supervise or take over.

Marlee saw an email ping into her inbox. She clicked on it, looking for a distraction from the house design.

From: Emma Parsons
To: Marlee Maples
Re: Thanks & Bats!

Hi Marl,

I am stuck on reception answering phones as the usual person is sick, which means plenty of time for emailing!

Thank you again for all your help with moving. I can't believe how much stuff we have and now nowhere to put it!

Have to tell you about my night… I was about to go to bed when something started swooping around my lounge room. At first I thought it was a weird miniature bird or a gigantic moth, but as it swooped closer to my head, I spotted its beady eyes and evil little face and realised IT WAS A BAT!!!!

During my desperate escape manoeuvre, I fell back onto a chair which crashed against the fireplace and broke the mantelpiece (whoops)!

Luckily it then swooped straight into my bedroom and I could slam the door and trap it, so I didn't have to call the fire brigade or anyone. Then I googled 'bats' on my phone. Guess what? Basically, if they scratch you, you can die! So then I was forced into a horrible night's sleep on the couch dreaming of flesh-eating birds. This morning I got one of the groundsmen in early to get the evil bat out and he's coming back to fix the mantelpiece I broke. (Yah!)

*Better go and await phone calls and focus on directing
them to the accurate person and also name tags to print
for a parent function. Important, complex tasks that are
now in the hands of an extremely capable chiroptophobic
(the name for my newly discovered bat phobia.)*
Love Em xx

Marlee laughed, picturing the tumble-down staff cottage at
Denham House that Emma had managed to secure after Phillip
had refused to leave their property. It seemed that the cheap rent
should have come with a warning about the bad-mannered wildlife.

Marlee watched Ben come in through the front door of the
office. She wondered why she hadn't mentioned her fling with
him to Emma yet. Probably because Emma had sworn off men
forever. Somehow it didn't feel right talking about a one-night
stand. Or maybe it was because he was her boss and she didn't
want Emma telling her she was crazy. She'd been doing a good
enough job of that herself.

She turned back to her concept diagrams and stared at the
screen blankly. Her creativity seemed to have deserted her. She had
designed a perfectly luxurious and interesting home, but it wasn't
jaw-dropping. Certainly not good enough to prove her worth to
Ben or Finton. She had an overwhelming desire to climb into bed.
She had spent last night with an old family friend. They'd had some
food at a new craft brewery on the docks and had sampled the
beers. The midnight finish wouldn't usually have been a problem,
but today she was feeling unusually tired and mildly nauseous.

She looked up again to see Ben approaching her desk.

He smiled at her. 'Hi, have you got a moment? I just wanted
to discuss a development proposal for some work on a heritage
site down at Port Arthur.'

'Now?'

He nodded. 'Let's use the meeting room.'

Marlee picked up her note pad and pen and watched him walk into their meeting room. It was glass-sided and not at all private. She hit 'print' on her concept plans and walked in the direction of the printer before following him in – she needed his perspective on her design while she had a chance.

'How are you?' Ben smiled and waited for her to choose a seat at the conference table, before he took her lead and sat opposite.

'Not too bad, thanks.' His presence seemed to calm her and, inexplicably, stir up her stomach with butterflies at the same time. Today that was just adding to her general feeling of illness.

'How are things with your daughter?' asked Marlee.

'Oh, well, Scarlett's in Rome. She wanted to hang around for a trip to Ibiza and after that she decided Italy was essential. She had some money saved, so…' He raised his eyebrows and gave her a rueful smile.

'Lucky girl,' said Marlee.

'Well, underneath it all she's a good person. She's very much like Harriet in some ways – kind and intelligent if you can get past the spiky exterior. But she surprises you with how immature she can be in the next breath. I suppose letting her loose on the world, to go and discover who she is without insisting she do one thing or the other, may help her grow up.'

'Wow. I wish I had parents who thought like you when I was eighteen,' said Marlee. A wave of nausea suddenly surprised her and she felt herself getting hot.

'Marlee, are you alright?' asked Ben.

She must look as bad as she felt. 'Sorry.'

She got up unsteadily and walked to the bar fridge to get a bottle of cold water. 'I had a late night catching up with an old friend. We got a bit carried away tasting some beers. I suppose you're the last person I should be telling that to.' She sat down, giving him a sheepish grin. 'Let's discuss this project and just ignore me if I look off-colour. It's self-inflicted.'

Ben showed her the new brief and when he was satisfied that she was able to take on further work, he delegated some of it to her before she unrolled her house design and they pored over it.

'That's looking great. I think the topography of that site's tricky and you've used it well. The glass walls bring those pavilions together nicely and you've maintained privacy with the angles of each bedroom. Nicely done.' Marlee felt herself flushing as Ben went on to give her some suggestions for maximising the passive solar design. With his ideas in the mix, her concept would improve no end.

Ben's phone buzzed on the table and Marlee saw the word 'Clementine' pop up on the screen.

'Sorry, I just need to take this call.'

Marlee nodded as he slid his finger across the screen. She listened to him confirming some arrangements for a time and a place to meet later that day.

She looked out the window and wondered who Clementine might be. A new girlfriend? The sky was grey and rain drops began spitting and swirling on the window panes. Wind swept through the gum trees in the adjoining garden, dragging slices of stringy bark away from the trunks. The bark strips made her feel untethered as they swayed and swung, whipping back and forth onto the half-stripped bareness of the pale trunks. *She'd known a Clementine once. At school. She was famous now.* The nausea began churning in her stomach again. She felt like she needed to lie down.

'Sorry about that,' he said, as he ended the call.

'Ben, I have to run. I promised to deliver some plans to a client before two o'clock and I need to have them done in A3 at the printers.' She forced a smile as she gathered up her paperwork. 'Perhaps we can catch up on all of this next week?' She gestured to the table. She needed to go home to bed, right now. She felt dizzy and weak.

'Sure. You don't look well. Why don't you go home after you drop off the plans?'

Marlee felt a twinge of guilt. Your boss wasn't meant to be solicitous when your hangover was costing him money.

'Thanks. I might go home for lunch and come back later.' She hurried out the door, the salivary glands in the back of her mouth working overtime. Lunch was actually the last thing on her mind. Her reactions seemed to be lagging, as if she was moving and thinking in slow motion. A few seconds after the thought occurred to her that she might throw up, she realised it was urgent. She needed a toilet. Immediately. She hurried down the corridor, dumping her paperwork on the tea bench, then pulling open the back door of the building. The wind and rain hit her with a fierce, cooling welcome but she didn't have time to acknowledge the relief. She hurled herself through the door of the staff toilet and put one hand on the cistern, then with the other she pushed back some stray red curls that had escaped the ponytail. Her faintness solidified into a wave of prickly heat over her face. Then finally the swirling in her stomach gave way to retching convulsions as the vomiting began.

CHAPTER TEN

EMMA

Emma stared through the office window across the sculpture gardens and watched girls hurrying in and out of the new music centre. She could hear the faint tinkling of piano tunes drifting into the office.

She looked back at her computer and saw that a new email had landed in her inbox. She could tell it was a response to her 'reply all' email by the topic line. The name of the sender was familiar, and she took a moment to conjure up the face of the girl she hadn't seen for at least twenty years. She toyed with the idea of ignoring it, but the email taunted her like a ripe pimple that was crying out to be squeezed.

> *From: Lola Bailey*
> *To: Emma Parsons*
> *Re: Fabulous formal photo… the countdown is on, girls!*
>
> *Hello Emma,*
> *I've been wondering whether to write after your email when it clearly wasn't meant for me. But I decided what the heck? I hope you're well and it will be good to catch up at the reunion. I've been thinking about what you said about*

Tessa... do you think her death was suspicious? I know she'd fought with her brother that day on the phone. I was on the phone switch that afternoon in the senior boarding house and I put his call through to the common room opposite which meant I could hear what she was saying. They'd planned to meet after school and she sounded really upset about their fight. It always bothered me. I'm not saying he did anything, but I wonder if the police knew. Is that what you were talking about? Anyway, it always felt like unfinished business, leaving school without her. I never felt like it was an accident, but it sounds so unbelievable to say it out loud, doesn't it? Perhaps we can chat at the reunion. I'd love to hear about how you are and what you've been doing.

See you soon,
Lola

Emma felt fatigue dragging at her limbs. She was so tired of thinking about that day at school. She didn't know much about Tessa's brother, except that he had a reputation as a bit of a bad boy and had ignored her both times she'd been to Tessa's beautiful sprawling farmhouse, an hour outside Hobart. He hadn't been interested in conversation with plump, boring virgins. She wondered again why she had opened this can of worms with the email? But there *was* more to Tessa's death, Emma knew it. And what she had found this morning had confirmed it with a cold certainty.

It was after Lenny the groundsman had come in to remove the bat and inspect the fireplace when Emma had noticed it – a tiny triangular corner of something poking out of the gap between the fireplace and the mantelpiece, where the timber had started to come away from the wall last night. A small card, or piece of paper that had slipped down and at some stage in the history of the little old cottage, become hidden. She coaxed it up the wall with her fingernail, finally getting it up past the lip of the mantelpiece where it had fallen through the crack. She pulled it out with a flourish. It was an old photograph, date stamped in the corner: *24 November 1993.*

The photograph was of a naked girl, reclining on a sofa. Her hands were arranged artfully on her thighs, covering her pubic area. Her brown wavy hair was teased and sat like a soft, puffy cloud around her head before it fell down one side over her shoulder and rested gently across her breast. From beneath her hair, the girl smiled lazily at the camera. Emma must have been focussing on the girl's slim figure, her firm breasts, the curious tilt of her head, as if she hadn't quite been sure whether to show her profile or look directly into the camera, because Emma had held the photo for a long moment before her eyes properly focussed on the familiar terrain of the girl's face. But when she did, she had dropped it and let out a muted cry. The girl in the photograph was Tessa.

What on earth was Tessa doing? Why had a naked photo of her been hidden behind the mantelpiece of the old staff cottage?

Poor, *poor* Tessa. It seemed somehow disrespectful to be looking at her naked photo when it was clearly never meant for Emma's eyes. And if she was honest, there was something unsettling, even a little bit sinister, that Tessa seemed to be everywhere now, when for so many years no one had spoken about her. It was as if Emma had conjured up her naked body by disturbing her ghost with that stupid group email. It made her shiver to think about it. That's why she hadn't said anything to Marlee about the photo yet. She'd upset some sort of karmic balance and she wasn't sure what to do about it.

Emma shook her head and focussed her attention back to the present. She sent a vague reply to Lola and then got back to designing a flyer for the school art show, wishing she could just shut out the niggling, dark thoughts of Tessa and the photograph.

Emma looked up as Jonathan Brownley walked past her office window, more formally dressed than usual today in a well-cut charcoal suit and tie, probably off to charm a gathering of wealthy parents or speak to the Board of Governors. He was walking towards a group of junior girls. One of the girls was wearing an exquisite birthday cape, embroidered in shades of green and blue.

There were about a dozen capes in circulation at Denham House, a special marker to be worn on a student's birthday, tied around her shoulders from the moment she dressed in the morning and entered the dining hall for breakfast, until after she retired to the boarding house at night when homework supervision was finished. Or if she was a day girl who went home after classes, she would wear it the whole time that she was on school grounds. It was considered a privilege. Once each year, the girl in the cape would have special breakfast cooked for her, doors opened and books carried for her by other students. She would often be given a reprieve if her homework wasn't finished or some other issue arose during the day. All of the capes were hand-stitched with the initials of girls who had worn them over the years, and then further decorated with ribbons and beautiful handmade fabric flowers by the students who were artistically inclined – exquisite heirlooms to be worn once each year to mark out a girl as special for the day.

The girls in the group had been laughing and whispering about something, but stopped when Dr Brownley approached. He said something and they all started chattering at once and pointing towards the main office, pigtails and ribbons bouncing with excitement. She wondered what had made them so animated. He had a lovely way with the girls, a lovely way with everyone. It felt like she was the only one who hadn't fallen under his spell.

She looked back at her very long 'to-do' list. Jon Brownley wasn't a distraction she could afford. Emma already had more on her plate than she could manage. For the last few weeks, as a single mother, every day felt like a marathon, even though Phillip had rarely helped with managing the house or with organising things for Rosie when they were together. She closed her eyes at the thought, remembering the moment she'd stood up to Phillip – had stood in the doorway of his office the day after the birthday dinner with her arms crossed.

'When are you going to tell Rosie you're leaving?'

Phillip had looked at her with an expression of puzzled annoyance. He swivelled around on his chair and took off his glasses then rubbed slowly at the bridge of his nose with his thumb and forefinger.

'What?'

She sighed loudly, dropped her arms to her side.

'Just answer me, Phillip. Think of Rosie. The least you can do is tell us when you plan to leave.'

'I'm not planning to, Emma. You know I can't leave. My lab is here.'

'*Sorry?*' She narrowed her eyes. 'You can't be suggesting that Rosie and I should move out instead? You can't seriously be proposing that your thirteen-year-old daughter be uprooted from her home just because you decided to have sex with our cleaner and ruin our lives!'

Phillip shook his head slowly and took his time to answer.

'No, I'm not suggesting that. I can't afford to help you to pay rent on another house anyway. Not if I'm going to have to pay those ridiculous fees for that school that you and my mother are so hell-bent on. You and Rosie can stay in the house. Pia and I will just have to move into the cottage. That way the impact of this breakup is minimised for Rosie with me being around, and I still have access to the greenhouses.'

Emma felt like she had been punched in the stomach. She held onto the windowsill as her legs became weak. The *cottage*? She looked down across the lawn and into the paddock – she could see directly into its kitchen window. Phillip actually thought it was alright to move Pia onto their property? That it would minimise the hurt to Rosie? Had he lost his *mind*? She was so gobsmacked she was unable to speak.

'I've already thought it through,' said Phillip. 'I've told Pia we just need to wait a few weeks until she moves in so that Rosie has time to get used to the idea that we've decided to split.'

Emma let out a guttural sound so monstrous that even she had been shocked.

'You have to be *joking!* You think Rosie and I want to see you with your girlfriend in our garden every day? And this was *you*, Phillip! *You* decided to break up this family. There was no *we*!'

Tears were streaming down her face. Their cottage? It was her cottage really. She was the one who had stripped the boards and painted the walls and sewed the curtains so she could find some joy in moving out of the city when Phillip wanted to follow his dream of having acreage. It was true, their setup in the countryside had helped his career flourish. But it was Emma who had worked on bringing the cottage back to life every weekend for the first year, sanding, tiling, using more tubes of Polyfilla than should rightfully be legal, so she could rent it out for short stays to earn some money to help pay for Rosie's school fees.

The cottage had become their second source of income and Emma had weekend bookings confirmed stretching forward three months. She couldn't just *cancel* them. It was people's holiday plans. They were important.

But more to the point, was he so seriously untethered that he thought that moving Pia into the cottage in their garden would have no impact on their impressionable teenage daughter? Emma slammed the office door as she left.

With Rosie staying at a friend's house for the night, Emma collapsed onto Rosie's bed and sobbed until her eyes were so puffy, she looked as if she'd had a severe allergic reaction.

Eventually she rang Marlee. She would *not* allow her daughter to witness her father's disgraceful behaviour. She told Marlee she wasn't sure how she would finance it, but she would need to move out. Rosie was now at Denham House in Year Seven. It was the most expensive girls' school in Tasmania and without Vivien and Roger's contribution, they could never have afforded it. Emma knew it was the best though – she had gone there herself, with Marlee, and now she worked there.

Marlee had tried to convince her to see a lawyer to force Phillip to move out. And she'd also been adamant that if Rosie had to change to a public high school, she would be absolutely fine. Emma agreed to think about a lawyer, but the thought of pulling Rosie out of Denham House made her feel panicked. Rosie was thriving. Pulling her out of the school so she could afford to pay rent wasn't an option. There had to be another way.

From the moment Rosie was born, Emma had dreamed about seeing her in the gorgeous blue and white uniform with the Peter Pan collar, topped with the navy and red blazer and matching red felt hat. Just because Marlee didn't care about their old school didn't mean that it wasn't a perfect fit for Rosie. Her daughter deserved to have all the privileges that the best school could offer – the exclusive opportunities, the right doors opening for her, the right *circles* open to her. Emma's parents had only been able to afford for Emma to go to Denham House for her final two years. They had scrimped and saved to give her the chance to start in Year Eleven. But by then the friendship groups had all been formed, the special ways of doing things so woven into the fabric of the girls' days that they didn't understand why a newcomer might fall behind, watchful and quiet. Emma had felt constantly bewildered and anxious for nearly her whole two years. Her lifelong friendship with Marlee, forged on the street corner of their childhood homes, had been what had made it tolerable, sometimes fun even, but the feeling of not quite fitting had never gone away. And she had so *wanted* to fit. She wanted that for Rosie too. The women in Phillip's family had all gone to Denham House for generations. His mother was an old girl, so were his cousins and his sister. Rosie was born into a long line of Denham House old girls. Rosie *fitted*.

Marlee fitted too. She carried a kind of casual disregard for privilege that was only evident in the truly privileged. Emma closed her eyes and retreated into her pounding headache. Their daughter still had to come first, even if her marriage was over.

The next morning, Emma took a deep breath and emailed the headmaster about moving into one of the vacant staff cottages ahead of the scheduled renovations next year. They were dilapidated but cheap, and if she got the house, it would be just a two-minute walk to work for her and to school for Rosie. It was the answer. She *needed* that house. Nobody would have told Jon Brownley about her 'reply all' email yet, would they? Anyway, nothing in it pointed to her suspicions of his involvement with Tessa. Hopefully he'd take pity on her and let her rent the house. She and Rosie could manage on their own if he did.

The door of the administration office creaked, distracting Emma from her wild thoughts about the last few weeks. She looked up to see a woman standing there, smiling at her and holding a large, thin, bubble-wrapped parcel. She let it slip down and balance on the top of her shoe. Emma wondered how it was possible that some human beings just popped out perfect. The woman was small with flawless olive skin, short, spiky blackish-brown hair and eyes that were hypnotically dark, almost black and shaded by extremely long lashes. They reminded Emma of Bambi. 'Hello,' said Emma. 'How can I help?'

'Hi, I just need to drop off this painting for the live auction at the art show.' The woman came into the room, leaning the parcel up against the far wall. 'Are you Lena?'

'No, I'm Emma. Lena's popped out. But you can leave it here for her.' Something about this woman was familiar.

'Okay, no worries. Can you just tell her that Clementine dropped in the painting?' She looked intently at Emma as if she was trying to work something out. 'And just pass on that the minimum bid should probably be about twenty thousand.'

'Dollars?' Emma gulped.

'Yeah.'

'Wait, Clementine *Andrews*?' Schoolgirl images of Clementine flashed through her head – a wild sprite in a school uniform, messy blond hair escaping her pony tail. Then a small blond bombshell who was sometimes in the news, as much for her crazy political antics as for her art. Clementine no longer looked like a woman-child without her blond hair, but she was even more striking now. In her black jeans and chunky boots, she looked like a bikie princess.

'Yeah,' said Clementine. 'You look really familiar too.'

'I'm Emma Parsons… I mean I was Emma Tasker, back at school.'

Clementine tilted her head to one side.

'Shit! Emma – wow! Of course,' said Clementine, grinning.

Emma blushed. She came around the desk to take the painting. Her face reddened at Clementine's steady gaze. To her surprise Clementine leaned the painting against the door and came across the room to give her a tight hug. She smelled like lemony-sweet shampoo.

'I… I didn't realise you were donating a painting for the auction,' said Emma, breathless. She wondered whether it was the close brush with fame or Clementine's startling prettiness that was making her stammer. Or maybe it was that being in a room with a celebrity she'd known as a child made her feel a bit ashamed that her achievements in life had amounted to an arts degree and a job helping in a school.

'No, neither did I,' said Clementine, smiling.

'Oh, right, well…' Emma let her hand rest on the painting, not sure whether to take it.

Despite her stature, Clementine was larger than life. Before she left Sydney for Europe a few years earlier, Clementine's face was regularly in the media – and not just for her art. She'd once chained herself to a gigantic tree in the Tasmanian wilderness that was designated for logging, then waved at the cameras as the police cut off the chains and she was arrested and dragged away. Her artwork was just as confrontational – the most recent series of works Emma had seen were detailed paintings of important historical figures showing them morphing into alien creatures surrounded by grotesque images of moral degradation. Clementine had been interviewed on NBC about her work and the violent sexual imagery that had caused a public outcry in America, where she was exhibiting. 'Power corrupts. Don't you think as members of this screwed-up society we should think about that?' she'd said. Emma wasn't sure if it was the disturbing paintings or that Clementine herself – petite and exquisite – didn't conform to an image of an anarchist artist, that had seemed to unnerve the interviewer the most. Clementine still had her long blond hair at that point and had been wearing a simple white dress.

Clementine looked around the office, then picked up the painting and brought it around to the wall at the back of the office where she placed it down carefully.

'My mother talked me into donating it,' said Clementine. 'I couldn't be bothered to argue with her. She's a dragon.' She wore a look of amused exasperation.

'Oh really?' said Emma.

'You obviously haven't met the esteemed Harriet Andrews QC,' said Clementine, rolling her eyes.

Emma had a sudden image of the face of Harriet Andrews. She knew her as the mother of Scarlett – one of the senior girls last year. But of course, now that Clementine said it, she remembered – Harriet was also the mother of one of Denham House's most famous alumni, Clementine Andrews. She would have been at the parent gatherings when Emma was a schoolgirl. How could she have forgotten that? Probably because Harriet demanded attention on her own terms, without reference to her children. On the two occasions Emma had had cause to speak to her when she'd come into the office, she was sure she'd sounded like a stuttering idiot. Harriet's intimidating presence seemed to banish all intelligent thought.

'Besides,' went on Clementine, 'I made them agree that the proceeds could go into the Indigenous scholarship fund. If I'm propping up the coffers of this joint, I'd prefer it goes to someone who needs it.'

Emma smiled. 'That's great. Thanks for bringing it in. I'd love to have a look at it some time.'

'Sure, well you can unwrap it now if you want. Or later. You're probably busy now.' Clementine suddenly looked unsure.

'Well I have to get a document out soon, so if it's okay, I might take a look later today?' Emma regretted it immediately. She felt a sudden need to look at the painting and see the world as Clementine saw it. It might explain why she felt so strange, so off-kilter.

'Sure, sure. I'll let you get back to it.'

Emma watched her walk towards the door and had a sudden longing to stop her. But she knew she couldn't act on the impulse. She was just an office assistant. Clementine was an international celebrity, with an amazing life and important artwork to do. She may not have the willowy, long-legged confidence of the polo set who wore their looks and superior lineage with effortless indifference, but her fame still put her several rungs up the social ladder above Emma.

Clementine stopped suddenly in the doorway and looked back at her.

'Emma, do you want to catch up tonight?'

Emma stared at her, her mind suddenly blank in the face of such an unlikely proposal.

Clementine put her hands in her pockets. 'You know, for old time's sake. We could get a drink at The Emerald, or wherever people get a drink in this town nowadays.' Clementine raised her eyebrows in question, as if she were talking to someone who might know all the best bars in town.

Emma finally found her voice. 'Um, okay, sure,' she said, wondering what on earth she would be able say to Clementine that would be remotely interesting to her and then, more pressingly, how she could organise someone to look after Rosie at such short notice. At thirteen, she may have been legally able to remain at home alone, but Rosie was terrified of the dark. Staying by herself in their creaky old little cottage in what felt like a clearing in the middle of a forest, although still on the edge of the school's grounds, was definitely not something she'd do.

'What time?' asked Emma, mentally scrolling through her wardrobe for something pub-worthy and vaguely un-mumsy.

'Whatever suits,' said Clementine, shrugging again at such a trifling detail. 'Nine?'

Emma suppressed her urge to giggle. Who went out at 9 p.m. on a school night? 'Want me to pick you up?' said Clementine. 'I've still got my old car. She's been locked up in a friend's aircraft hangar. It's fun to drive the old girl around again.'

'Oh. Sure, okay. I'm at number 7 Rondle Road, just on the edge of the school here. You need to slow down at the big willow tree on the bend or you'll miss the driveway. Look out for the old drystone seat, it's not far past that.' Emma knew she was blabbering, but suddenly, she didn't want to miss this opportunity for some fun. She got out her phone. 'Maybe you should take my number, just in case you can't find it or need to cancel or something.'

Clementine laughed. 'Why would I need to cancel? But okay, tell me yours and I'll ring it.'

Emma called out the numbers and watched Clementine thumb them into her phone. She stifled a giggle as a surge of anticipation bubbled – an evening at the pub with a really interesting (*and quite famous!*) person. It was the sort of exciting thing that would happen to Marlee. Clementine looked up as Emma's phone buzzed, then she stopped the call and shoved it into her back pocket.

'See you tonight, little lady!' said Clementine, then she let the door slam behind her.

Emma sat with a dumb grin on her face, then picked up the top letter on her filing pile and opened the cabinet with a flourish. She would wear jeans and something black. Black was just right for a pub. She was sure she had something – there was that top Marlee had bought her a few years ago with three-quarter sleeves. She would have to unpack the last few boxes to see if she could find it.

Now, to sort out Rosie for tonight. She was glad Lena was up at Erinby Hall setting up for parent-teacher interviews, so she could make this phone call to Phillip in peace. Most of their conversations since she moved out had been over email, so she felt a flutter of anxiety in her stomach. As she dialled, she doodled the words 'Clementine' and 'famous' on her page in flowery script.

'Hello?' Phillip answered on the second ring, his voice terse.

'Hi,' said Emma. 'I've got a meeting tonight and I need you to have Rosie. I know you said you're busy until next weekend, but tonight is urgent.'

The silence went on a beat too long.

'I can't,' said Phillip.

'Why not?'

'I have things to do, Emma. I'm not free tonight.'

She scrawled 'THINGS?' on the page in capital letters. 'Right. And these *things* are more important than seeing your daughter who you haven't seen for five days?' she asked. She began making hard, heavy circles around the words with her pen and stopped when it broke through the page and left a mark on her desk. Next to it she began drawing a picture of a hangman on a rope.

'Yes,' said Phillip.

Anger flared in her chest. Why was he being so unreasonable?

'And what exactly might these things be?' asked Emma, barely trying to conceal the irritation in her voice.

Lillian, from the Alumni Office, walked through the door in one of her usual tailored linen dresses, her neat bob all swishy and shiny. She handed Emma the invitations for the art show mail-out she'd been waiting for. Emma mouthed her thanks and hugged the phone to her ear. She walked over to the cupboard to look for a box of envelopes so she could begin slotting them in.

'Emma, I just can't tonight, alright?'

'No, it's not alright, Phillip.'

Lillian raised her eyebrows at Emma in silent camaraderie as she opened the door and walked out again.

'Well, it'll have to be – I've already hired a ute to pick up the rest of Pia's stuff tonight. I can't cancel it. Pia's re-let her room so she has to be out by tomorrow. I can have Rosie any other night, just not tonight. You gave me no notice. Be reasonable!'

Patronising pig. Why couldn't he have just lied? Why couldn't he say, 'I have a meeting with the Head of Department and it's important to my salary for next year', or something like that? Something which Emma would have understood because it had a bearing on her and Rosie's financial future. It was beyond belief that he'd just admitted that a few dollars for ute hire to pick up his lover's stuff was more important than spending some quality time with his daughter. Had she really been with him for twenty-three years and not seen what he was like? She picked up the pen again and began making satisfying little stabs where the hangman's eyes should have been.

'Unreasonable?' She lowered her voice and pressed the phone hard against her ear. 'I'm having to juggle being a single parent because you moved your floozy into our home and forced us out, Phillip. Do *not* talk to me about being unreasonable and stop being such a self-absorbed... arsehole!' She took a quick breath, annoyed that he'd made her swear, but cheered by the thought that it would have shocked him. She looked down the outside path. Luckily it was empty. There was silence on the other end of the phone.

'"I'm too busy" doesn't cut it anymore, Phillip. And "I'm too busy because I have to help my teenage girlfriend move into the family home" is *much* further down the list of being okay.' Emma's heart was pounding. The pain in her chest was like a pulsating hot poker. They should reinstate the law against adultery. It was too gruesome to be legal. The torture was relentless. And poor Rosie too. The whole thing was child abuse.

'Pia's nearly twenty-seven, Emma. She's nowhere near a teenager. Don't be so vile. It doesn't suit you.'

Emma picked up the bundle of invitations and cut savagely at the string that was holding them together as she held the phone to her ear with her shoulder.

'This is what's going to happen, Phillip. I'll drop Rosie to you at six. You'll have a home-cooked meal waiting for her and you'll also help her with her history assignment and help her study for the French test she has tomorrow. Then you'll drop her back to me by seven-thirty tomorrow, so she's got time to get changed for school.' Emma watched some students approaching the office down the path. She held her breath, then let it out as they veered off the path to the back of the dining room.

'For God's sake, Emma.'

'And make sure Pia isn't there tonight, Phillip. If she is, I will ring the Department of Immigration and tell them that she's breaching the conditions of her student visa by working for cash and not declaring it. Believe me, I'll have no problem personally making sure she's kicked out of the country.'

Emma jabbed at the phone to end the call. Then she looked at it in stunned silence. Usually Phillip won any argument they had. No, that wasn't true. Usually they just didn't argue. She felt thrilled and sickened at the same time. She'd never *really* report Pia. Her heart was beating madly. She jumped as a gust of wind slammed shut the casement window. In the office, the only remaining noise was the sound of her jagged breathing.

From: Belinda Stuart
To: Sally Stuart-Pemberton
Re: Of course I have thought about it!!!

Hi Sal,
I've thought a lot about what you said, but I really don't think Issy is ready for the pill. She's too gullible. I know I started at that age, but now I regret it. When I think about those afternoons when I'd meet Tommy Terrano in the clearing near the witch's house, it feels really tawdry. And even then it all felt very one-sided. That email from Emma Tasker has made me think a lot about the afternoon that Tessa died. It was the last day we were together and I remember he was really angry at her. I don't know why I would think this really, but imagine if he was involved somehow?

I used to beat myself up about why he ignored me after that day, and I just can't bear the idea of the same thing happening to Issy if she starts sleeping with some dreadful sleaze (the way Tommy turned out to be!!!) She's just too young. I know maybe I'm being ridiculous, and maybe every other seventeen-year-old is having sex. But I just want Issy to wait a bit longer. Is that so bad?

Anyway, onto better topics… Mum says she's got something sorted for our birthday so you won't have to host this year. Forty-two – bloody hell, we are officially old!

One of the girls says I've just had a call out to deliver a calf, so better go and get my gumboots on. Some new farmer to the area who drives a Range Rover and is nervous about the cow panting too much! Suppose I should be grateful ... gotta pay the school fees somehow.

Love Bel.

CHAPTER ELEVEN

MARLEE

Marlee stood in the middle of the crowd and shrugged off her woollen jacket. Ben had invited everyone to the opening of an art exhibition showcasing the stories of some migrants who now called Tasmania home. Apparently, he was involved in some group that promoted social cohesion through the arts. The man was becoming more surprising every day.

Even so, Marlee hadn't been intending to come – not that she wasn't interested in art, or social cohesion, or Ben for that matter, it was just that she had a heap of work to do and she was having trouble keeping up with it. The move to Tasmania, the new job, checking in on her dad a couple of times a week, it was making her so bloody tired. But Lidia had come around to all of them, wide-eyed and serious.

'Please come, Marlee. Ben works so hard for these causes and it would be a boost for him if there were lots of people there. I know he'd love it if we all showed up for a quick drink.'

Lidia seemed to take it on herself to ensure that Ben's life ran as smoothly as possible. Lucky Ben. Marlee wished she had her own personal Lidia to smooth out her life.

But now that Marlee was here at the exhibition, she wondered why Lidia or Ben had been worried about the turnout. Someone had just whispered that Clementine Andrews was in attendance, so not only was it a full house, but reporters were here, vying for an interview with Clementine about her views on the exhibition. A newspaper photographer walked around clicking away at small groups and writing down their names on a notepad. Marlee grabbed a drink as a bearded guy with a man-bun walked past bearing a tray full of glasses. She took a sip and grimaced. Chardonnay.

Ben's familiar face suddenly appeared through an opening in the crowd and she felt herself relax.

He leaned forward and put his hand on the back of her arm. 'Marlee, thanks so much for coming. Have you seen the art and photography?'

'Can't get to it for the crowd,' said Marlee. 'You throw quite a party.'

'Thanks,' he said. His eyes didn't waver from her face. Outside the constraints of the office and amid the chatter and buzz of the crowd, Marlee allowed herself to feel a warm thrill of connection. It was exciting and disconcerting at the same time. She didn't intend to get involved with Ben. He was too… she couldn't quite put a finger on it. Honourable? Each time she had a conversation with him, she came away thinking about the world a little bit differently. He was so unjudgemental. So interested in differing points of view. Eventually he looked over her shoulder and smiled, lifting his hand towards someone approaching.

'Clem! Thanks for coming. You've really raised the profile of this thing. I'm so grateful.'

Marlee froze. From the corner of her eye, a small recognisable figure had come into view at her shoulder. Ben turned to Marlee to include her in the conversation.

'Clem, I'd like you to meet my colleague, Marlee Maples. Marlee, this is Clementine Andrews.' He looked from one to the other.

Clementine grinned. 'We went to school together. Hi Marleen – I can't believe I'm running in to you too. I saw Emma Parsons yesterday. Feels like I'm in a time warp, except we've all got wrinkles and better fashion sense.'

Marlee looked down at Clementine. She was wearing thick-soled lace-up yellow shoes, royal blue pants and an olive green long-sleeve t-shirt printed with the words *I know I look tired. Fighting the Patriarchy is Exhausting.* Marlee felt her head spinning. How was Ben on such close terms with a celebrity? Why hadn't Emma mentioned catching up with Clementine?

'Hi, Clementine. Wow. Your hair makes you look really different.' Okay, so that was lame – after twenty-five years, the best she could do was comment on the woman's hairstyle? It wasn't as if she didn't have an incredible career or a fascinating public profile to chat about. But it was hard to think of Clementine as anyone except the baby-faced rebel she hadn't seen for twenty-five years.

Clementine laughed. 'Thanks. Nice to see that you're a supporter of the arts.'

Marlee felt a twinge of guilt. She was really only here under duress, pretending to be interested. She had an odd, discomforted sort of feeling. Maybe it was because only the kids you went to school with knew who you really were. There was no hiding behind a veneer of adult success. Clementine would see the truth.

'So, what do you think, Clem?' Ben gestured to the art on the walls.

Clementine was swaying from side to side with her hands in her pockets and a grin on her face. 'Great job. Some of it's pretty decent! Have you seen the art, Marlee?'

'I just got here actually – I'll be interested to see it when the crowd finishes the wine and heads off.'

Ben laughed. 'Well, it will be lovely for you two to reconnect.' He leaned forward, placing his hand on Marlee's upper arm again. Marlee had a sudden urge to put her hand on his neck and pull him into a kiss. Christ. Not even remotely appropriate. Their fling had been accepted as a one-off night of madness, both of them turning up to work the following Monday and acting as if nothing had happened, although Ben had continued to be the perfect gentleman.

Ting Ting Ting. Someone was tapping a spoon on a glass. Ben turned to stand next to Marlee and they faced the direction of the spoon tapper as the silence settled. His arm slid down and rested comfortably in the snug of her back – gently and politely. She shivered.

A little old man in a colourful coat and mustard-coloured pants bounced out of the crowd and up onto a chair. He beamed at the crowd through his long grey beard.

'Hi, everyone. Thanks for coming. I'm Rufus Lennox, one of the committee members of Artists for Peace. Amaya and Mika are talented artists and we're really pleased to have this space to share their stories. It's been a long journey for them both, but there's so much to celebrate in the work that they're doing and the way that this community has embraced them and they have adopted us. Please come and talk to both of them at some stage during the night and feel free to buy or commission some work too!' The man laughed as if he'd made a fantastic joke, and everyone clapped as he gestured towards a couple standing at the front of the room, the man grinning, the woman smiling shyly and looking towards the floor. When the clapping died down the bouncy man continued.

'I'd also like to thank the fabulous Clementine Andrews for agreeing to come along tonight and fitting us into her very busy schedule.' He clapped and the crowd burst into a short round of applause. 'Clementine is working with us to promote the organisation and to get the message out about art as a form of therapeutic expression and community engagement.' He gestured to Clementine, and Marlee saw her nod.

She wondered what work Clementine had been doing for them. She took another sip of her wine and swilled the rich, oaky flavour around her mouth, then realised it wasn't agreeing with her. A flush of heat made her neck and face prickle. The crowd suddenly felt too close. She needed some air and then for a terrible moment, the figures in the room started spinning and became a blurry, hot streak of light. She grabbed at Ben's arm to steady herself. He must have seen something in her face that alarmed him, because Marlee registered the grip of his arm slipping tightly around the waist and the other one sliding along her arm. She closed her eyes but heard his urgent whisper.

'Marlee, you look terrible. Let's get you outside.'

He propelled her towards the door and she forced herself to walk. The hot prickling sensation seemed to spread, then a wave of cold nausea rolled over her and she wasn't sure if she was going to make it to the door. The crowd seemed to part, and Ben pulled her outside into the quiet of the street and sat her down on the window ledge. Her stomach was churning.

He squatted down in front of her and rested his hand across her forehead.

She closed her eyes for another moment and allowed herself to focus on the cooling touch of his hand.

'You're white as a ghost,' he said, almost to himself. 'And clammy.'

A minute passed and Marlee's head began to clear. She tried to breathe deeply to calm her stomach.

The clip-clip of high heels approaching enticed Marlee to open her eyes. In her peripheral vision, she could see the figure of a small woman approaching. Marlee turned her head to look at the woman over Ben's shoulder. Her elegant figure was shown off beautifully in a tailored, very expensive-looking grey dress and matching waisted jacket. She sported a shiny, dark chignon and wore huge dark sunglasses. With her string of oversized pearls, the woman reminded Marlee of an older Audrey Hepburn. A second wave of nausea struck as a cold finger of familiarity tapped at her memory. The woman stopped as she reached them and took off her sunglasses and suddenly Marlee knew. Harriet Andrews. Clementine's mother. Marlee felt herself becoming dizzy again as she registered a look of pure distaste on the woman's face as she regarded Ben, and then looked back again at Marlee.

Ben seemed not to notice her. 'Marlee, you're not well at all. I'll drive you home.' Mrs Andrews was standing directly behind his right shoulder, listening. She watched as Ben took Marlee's hand and gave it a comforting squeeze.

'Um, no, I'll be fine in a sec,' said Marlee, wondering why Clementine's mother was so obviously eavesdropping on their conversation instead of going into the exhibition, or walking on to wherever she was going.

'Hello, Ben. I see you're busy.' Mrs Andrews sniffed. She ignored Marlee's gaze. Ben stood up and turned towards her, surprised, but he didn't let go of Marlee's hand.

'Harriet,' said Ben. 'Clem didn't mention you were coming.'

Mrs Andrews took her time to survey the scene, glancing down and fixing her glare on Marlee's hand in Ben's.

She looked up. 'Artists for Peace is a client of mine. I provide them with pro-bono services – at your behest, if I recall correctly, Ben – hence, I received the invitation.'

There was a cool civility between Mrs Andrews and Ben. Marlee wondered how they knew each other, and why they didn't seem particularly pleased to see each other.

'This is my colleague, Marlee. I'd introduce you properly but she's unwell and I'm about to drop her home,' said Ben.

'I'm fine,' said Marlee, pulling her hand out of his. The dizzy spell had passed. She was feeling at a distinct social disadvantage sitting down. She pushed herself up off the ledge. Some sort of bizarre interaction was going on between the two of them. She needed to be at eye level to read it.

'Alright then,' said Ben. 'Harriet, this is Marlee Maples. Marlee, this is Harriet Andrews, my... ex-wife,' said Ben.

Marlee felt a disorienting slip, as if she'd fallen through a rabbit hole and into an alternate reality. Ben and *Harriet Andrews?* And now the woman had turned up just as Marlee was playing damsel in distress. Well, there was nothing she could do about it now except be a grown-up.

'We've met before actually.' Marlee extended her hand towards Harriet. 'Nice to see you again, Mrs Andrews. I'm afraid I came over a bit faint in the middle of speeches. The wine must have been off.' She said it with a weak laugh. It wasn't a brilliant joke, admittedly, but neither of them even smiled. Mrs Andrews looked down at the hand Marlee was extending, then looked back up at Marlee, keeping both hands by her sides.

'It's Ms Andrews, Marleen, not Mrs,' said Harriet, pointedly using the name Marlee hadn't used since high school. Then she turned to Ben. 'And as far as I'm aware, Ben, we are not yet divorced.' Harriet looked back at Marlee and opened her mouth, then closed it again before walking past them both and opening the door to the bar. Then she turned back, her hand clenched white around the door handle. 'I thought you donated the wine for this event, Ben. How very careless of you to poison the guests.'

She walked into the bar and the door slammed shut behind her.

Marlee slumped back down on the window ledge. The small burst of energy had sapped her.

'Sorry,' said Marlee. 'I didn't mean it about the wine – obviously. And I've, um, met your wife years ago. When I was at school.'

Ben gave a gentle laugh. 'It's fine, Marlee. Don't worry about it. And please forgive her. She's not taking our separation very well.' He sat down on the ledge beside her and sighed. After a moment, he put his hand on top of hers and they sat in silence.

She wondered what to do. She had the strangest desire to take hold of it and bring it up to her cheek, but she couldn't. He was just being solicitous. Besides, the idea of holding his hand made her stomach churn again. She had no desire to get involved with him seriously – not because he was newly separated and came with baggage, or even that he was her boss. It was just that she sensed that there was a potent sort of chemistry between them that might be more than she could manage. It made her chest constrict to think about it.

She glanced sideways at the line of his jaw and his five o'clock stubble, just beginning to show in dappled grey across his upper lip and cheeks. There was something so essentially good about him that she felt like crying.

'I'm just going to grab a cab,' said Marlee, getting up and letting his hand slip away. 'I'm probably coming down with the flu. I've been a bit off-colour all week.'

He stood up quickly. 'Please let me give you a lift, Marlee. You look really pale.'

'You need to stay here with your friends, Ben. You helped organise this. I'm absolutely fine.' She leaned forward and pecked him on the cheek. She breathed in deeply, the musky scent of him unbalancing her momentarily. 'Really. I'll see you tomorrow. And please say goodbye to Clementine for me. I didn't realise she was your step-daughter.'

She turned and walked down the street towards the cab rank, letting out a heavy sigh. He really was the complete package.

CHAPTER TWELVE

EMMA

Emma picked up her glass of wine and took a large sip. It was her new ritual: one glass every night. She was unsure how it had taken her until she was forty-two to realise that a nightly glass of wine could fundamentally improve her life. Actually, it was no surprise she hadn't discovered it earlier. Phillip was teetotal, so it had just been easier not to bother with it before. Still, her liver would thank her for all those years of abstinence. It was in top form to cope with the filtering of a single glass of wine each night. *Sorry liver, but you'll just have to get up to speed. You've had it easy for far too long. If you were Marlee's liver, then you might have something to complain about.*

It had been a strange couple of days. She closed her eyes and let the lovely sensation of the wine running through her veins warm her. Maybe she was becoming addicted. Last night, with Clementine, she'd had three glasses followed by some vodka and for the second time in a month, her inhibitions had gone out the window and she'd ended up in a seriously strange situation.

True to her word, Clementine had picked her up in her bright orange Datsun 120y. She'd had the same car at school twenty-five years ago and even then, it had felt ancient to the other girls.

'Jump in!' Clementine called, leaning over and throwing open the door when she picked her up from the cottage. Emma had already chewed her thumbnail down to the quick, waiting for Clementine to arrive. She'd changed outfits three times and her tiny bedroom resembled a junk shop by the time 9 p.m. rolled around. Emma was just beginning to look longingly at her rabbit pyjamas when she'd heard a horn tooting outside.

She walked to the car, going over the news articles in her head about Clementine's career and the art world in general. She'd spent ages googling 'Clementine Andrews' and 'modern art' and reading the stories behind her bodies of work. She now knew quite a bit more about art than she had this morning – which had been pretty non-existent, in spite of the original artworks by notable Australians that lined the halls and decorated the offices of Denham House. She read up on John Olsen, Brett Whiteley, Margaret Olley – vaguely familiar names that topped her internet searches. She thought she might be able to discuss different styles of painting if the conversation didn't get too in depth. But she was nervous she'd get it wrong. *Gouache, impasto, monochrome.* She recited the words and their meanings in her head.

But Clementine hadn't wanted to talk about painting. Or about herself. Over a bottle of wine, she had wanted to know what Emma had been doing since high school. Emma found herself telling her about Phillip and his affair, and Clementine reached across the table at the pub and held her hand while she cried, declaring Phillip to be a 'complete and utter wanker.'

There was a band playing in the pub – loud 80s music. Clementine and Emma danced in the dark, smoky corner, thrilled when they both remembered the lyrics to old favourites. They swayed and jumped around, losing touch with their surroundings as the alcohol and darkness and pounding music roused in Emma a yearning for her girlhood.

When the band finished, the pub suddenly seemed empty and sad. Clementine promised she was fine to drive, and in the moonlit carpark, the top of Mount Wellington peaked above the city streets.

'Let's drive up there,' said Clementine.

She sounded wistful and Emma dismissed her own niggling doubt. She was hanging out with Clementine Andrews after all – one of the quirky, cool kids. They drove through the quiet outer suburbs in silence. At the base of the mountain, the street lights petered out and gave way to an inky blackness, barely breached by the weak headlights of Clementine's little car. The dark winding road ascended gently at first, but then the climb became steeper and stretched on much further than Emma remembered from her last visit to the mountain, years and years ago. She took no comfort from the tiny guide posts that stood like white toothpicks, warning drivers away from the perilous drop at the road's edge. Emma gripped her seat in silence as Clementine turned the steering wheel of the little car in endless fluid motions, seemingly unconcerned.

As they rose higher, the shadows of the dense forest gave way to shrubs, clinging to boulders in the blackness like gloomy ghosts. The bends in the road became sharper and more frequent but Clementine barely slowed down and Emma felt a tight, sick terror rising inside her. Finally, rectangular shadows loomed in front of them – shelters announcing their arrival at the summit. In the deserted carpark they pulled up near the lookout, the lights of Hobart twinkling ahead and to their left. To their right there was only blackness.

Emma's heart was still pounding as Clementine turned off the engine. They sat in darkness and Emma sent up a silent prayer of thanks that they hadn't tumbled off the mountain's edge.

'Well, that was fun,' said Clementine eventually, fumbling in her bag. The interior lights of the car weren't working and Clementine brought out her mobile phone and turned on the torch. She pointed it towards the back seat, then reached over and pulled out a half-empty bottle of vodka.

Emma let go of her grip on the seat and forced herself to breathe.

Clementine unscrewed the bottle cap and handed it across. Emma took it, staring at the bottle in a kind of glazed wonder, before braving a swig.

'Uggh! That's terrible!' She spluttered as the alcohol hit the back of her throat like a grenade.

Clementine laughed. 'It's bloody fantastic is what you mean.' She took a long gulp. She was so small. She seemed completely unaffected. Emma wondered how it was possible.

Clementine unclipped her seat belt and swivelled, leaning back against the driver's door. She tilted her head to one side and stared at Emma through the dim light thrown by the phone.

Emma squirmed.

'You're beautiful. I'd love to paint you,' said Clementine.

Emma was glad it was shadowy. Her head swam and she felt her face becoming splotchy and hot. How could Clementine, with her elfin face, her velvet eyes, her sweet, perfect features think *Emma* was beautiful? She felt like a huge, clumsy horse next to Clementine.

She reached over and took the bottle out of Clementine's hand and took another swig.

'There was always something about you, Emma. You're so girl-next-door innocent.'

'Am I?'

'Yeah. You were always like that. So sweet, without even knowing it.'

The vodka was making Emma feel like she was floating. What a nice thing for someone to say to her. She looked across at Clementine. Would it be possible to swim inside those huge eyes?

Clementine reached across and put her hand on Emma's cheek. It felt lovely. Emma closed her eyes as Clementine began stroking the side of her face with her thumb. Then, surprisingly, she felt Clementine's lips touch hers. They were soft, gentle. They were kissing her. She tasted like vodka and sweet vanilla. It was the most beautiful sensation. Emma thought how nice it would be to kiss her back. Then she was. It was dizzying; gentle, dream-like, warm. She wanted to dissolve in the feeling forever.

And then without warning, it was as if a cold wind had swept through and Phillip was in the car with her. Emma jerked her head away. What was she *doing*?

'Oh God, Clem, I'm…' Emma felt a cloud envelope her words.

Clementine watched her patiently, a half smile on her lips.

'Clem, I'm not… I don't really think… well, I'm not gay.'

Clementine let out a tinkling laugh. 'Okay.'

It wasn't okay. Emma wanted to experience the perfection of that kiss again. But she couldn't. Everything was wrong.

'I'm sorry.'

'Emma, it's fine. You don't have to *be* anything. You're just you. It was just a kiss.' Clementine looked out over the lights of the city and beyond, to the freezing, endless black of the ocean. Antarctica was the only possibility. A heavy silence settled.

'This place makes everything hard,' said Clementine. 'Nothing feels right when I come home.'

'Tasmania you mean?'

'Yeah. But it's not really my home. It's a graveyard.' Clementine wound down the window and tipped her head towards the void. A freezing blast of wind filled the car.

Emma felt the blackness of the night pour in.

'It's not so bad, is it?'

'No. I suppose it's not. I suppose it's really because of Tessa I don't like being here.' She wound the window back up and stared straight ahead.

'What?' Emma felt a thread of fear.

'You asked me at the pub why I don't come back,' said Clementine. 'I think that might be why.'

'You mean because of Tessa dying?'

Clementine nodded. 'Yeah,' she said slowly. 'It was a shitty time.' She pulled a second smaller bottle of vodka from the bag and took another swig.

Emma turned back to look ahead to the city. The darkness seemed to encourage a tenuous intimacy.

'It was horrible,' said Emma.

'Well yeah. But not just that. I loved her. Not just as a friend.'

'Oh.'

Clementine looked away, staring out at the dark sky sprinkled with stars. 'I told her, the day before she died.'

Emma stared at Clementine's perfect profile through the black shadows.

'Oh,' said Emma again, blank as to what she might be expected to say.

The silence expanded unbearably.

Emma didn't know if she wanted to talk about it anymore either. Had Tessa been attracted to Clementine in return? That would mean she really hadn't known her at all. Tessa was a chapter from a book she'd read long ago. It was a crazy idea that you could take that book off the shelf to read it again and the words would be different.

When she spoke again Clementine sounded distant. 'I was pissed off that she didn't want me. She said she liked boys. I should have just kept my mouth shut.'

Emma's heart hammered unevenly. She kept staring at Clementine's profile. The night had a surreal quality. Nothing felt tangible. She was in the car with a famous painter. She had kissed a girl. Clementine had been in love with Tessa.

'It's good to speak up. It's staying silent that eats you up,' said Emma.

'What do you mean?'

'I saw something just before Tessa died. I didn't tell the police about it.' She noticed that her own voice was breathy, quiet.

Clementine bent her head closer. 'What did you see?'

'Oh…' Emma felt the rattle of emotions clambering for escape. The sickness of the secret, the squirming guilt over her own weakness.

'What?' asked Clementine again.

'She told a couple of us, the morning she died. She said he was in love with her. She was going to seduce him before we finished school. We didn't think she'd go through with it. I mean, she was always so confident, but… he was a *teacher*.' The awful truth that had been confined for years in the tiny dark basement of her mind was picking its lock. Emma felt her chest heating up. Expanding with it. What she'd seen afterwards *had* been related. She knew it. She'd always known it really.

'Who was?'

'Mr Brownley… I mean he's Dr Brownley now. The headmaster.'

'*What?*'

'I saw them. I was in the upstairs store room… I saw her running and then he caught up to her and grabbed her arm. He looked angry.'

'What were they talking about?'

'I don't know. I couldn't hear, but they were definitely arguing. I could see that. Then she shook his hand off her arm.'

Emma was trying to focus. The lights of the town were hazy balls that kept expanding and fading. Clementine's breath came at her in jerky clouds of alcohol.

Clementine turned back to stare out the windscreen. Emma wondered what she was seeing.

'Afterwards they both went behind the hedge near where she was found and I… couldn't see what happened. I didn't… I didn't know what it was all about, so I didn't tell anyone.'

There was silence for a while, then Clementine spoke. 'Maybe it was nothing.'

'Why didn't I tell the police?' asked Emma, as if Clementine could fathom the murky depths of her conscience. 'It could have been important. It's just... I mean, he was such a nice teacher and everything. He was lovely. I didn't want to cause trouble, or say anything bad about Tessa in case it was just her being silly. But if they'd been together it would have been important to the police investigation, wouldn't it?' She turned to Clementine, wanting something she couldn't articulate. Agreement? Absolution? She felt an inkling of nausea mixed with fear. The start of the downer. The vodka was turning tricks.

'I should have said something. I've felt guilty for years, keeping that secret. But I suppose I thought, well, maybe it was nothing. We were all kind of crazy over him, and I thought, well, maybe nothing happened with her plan. I mean she probably backed out! She said she was going to go to his house. But maybe she didn't – that's what I told myself.'

Clementine stared out the window. 'He's my uncle, Emma.'

Emma's stomach lurched. She had forgotten that about Clementine. That Dr Brownley was her uncle. But it didn't matter. Now that she had said the words out loud, she knew it was the truth. Jonathan Brownley had been involved, whether Clementine believed it or not. She felt a lead weight descending on her through the darkness.

'Jon's my uncle,' Clementine repeated, almost to herself. 'He's a good guy. He'd never have hurt Tessa. Even if you did see them together, that doesn't mean anything. Maybe she just ran ahead and fell into the hole. If she was upset, she might not have been looking.'

'There was a barrier around the building site.'

Emma felt a shiver of fear. There were too many puzzles to Tessa's death. Why would Tessa have been in that part of the school so late? It wasn't near anywhere she might have been going to. The nearby gates were always locked. Why would she squeeze inside a building site area that was fenced off? Why was she arguing with Jon Brownley?

Clementine spoke again. Her words didn't seem to follow from the ones before. 'When I left for art school in Sydney, I told Mum I wasn't coming back to this hole. She knew I hated the way this whole town talked about each other, so she didn't tell me much about what went on back here. I guess I was partying and drinking too much and doing lots of other stupid stuff. I managed to push Tessa – the whole thing – out of my head after a while.'

Emma pondered Clementine's words. 'Well, you couldn't help it if you loved her. I've tried to forget it all too. But, Clem, what if he *did* have something to do with it? If he pushed her? Is it ever too late to go to the police?'

Clementine turned to Emma, her eyes huge. 'He'd never have hurt her, Emma. Why would he? I know you're wrong about this and if you say anything, you'll bring him down, even though he's innocent. He's high profile. Respected. What could the police do anyway now? There's no proof. It's just speculation and he's a good guy.' Clementine rested her elbows on the steering wheel, then flopped her face into her hands.

Occasionally, Emma still woke with nightmares about school. Usually it was because she hadn't studied for her maths exam. In her dream, she would look at the scribbled equations on the page taunting her like an ancient unknown screed. Then she'd wake in a sweat, and realise, with supreme relief, that she was a grown-up, with a family and no more maths exams ever again.

But very occasionally, the dreams would be about Tessa – sitting on the circular slatted chair around one of the huge trees in the South Courtyard and she would be calling out to Emma in the drama room. *I'm not going to die. Don't worry, that was just a dream. He loves me.* Then Tessa would run towards where they were digging the foundations of the new building and Emma would be screaming at the very top of her lungs, *STOP!* But the window was closed and her fingers were scrabbling with the catch, pushing it round, jerking at the window rim. *Open. Please just open.* She was always trying to call out as she yanked it up, but Tessa couldn't hear her. Each time she'd wake herself up with the scream – *Stop!* She'd be sweating, heart pounding. She would turn on the light and take a sip of her water, then put it down with a shaky hand and Phillip would mumble, 'What's the matter? Are you alright?' She'd wipe away the tears and pretend she was fine. Tessa was dead, and each time it seemed like the first time she'd heard.

The thing was, she'd always known Jonathan Brownley was there, at the edge of every single dream. His gleaming, blond hair and heavenly face. A perfect shadow. His beauty was a pure counterpoint to Tessa, who hadn't been beautiful at all. Not really. She had a big nose and an ordinary kind of face. Her hair was brown and straight, although she teased some body into it. Her eyes were a lovely dark brown, but they were just a standard sort of size. Tessa had one exquisite feature though – her perfect, olive skin. There was a purity in it that marked her as special, and once you knew her, those other ordinary features suddenly became *something.* If a stranger had said to you 'Who was that girl? You know, the short girl, really plain, serious looking?' You would have said '*Who?*' and you honestly would have been wondering which person he'd been talking about, because nobody nearby fitted that description. In the eyes of people who knew her, Tessa *wasn't* plain or big-nosed. There was something magnetic about her, electric even. You couldn't quite put your finger on it, but you knew it could be shocking and beautiful and dangerous all in one, like a lightning strike.

'Clem, I really think they had something going on between them.' Emma felt a clash of emotions – the urgent desire to make Clementine understand that she'd always thought it was about Jonathan; the need to make her feel okay about having loved Tessa; the guilt that she'd stayed silent and let Jonathan's career blossom.

'No way.'

'Clem, I think it really is possible he was involved in her death.'

'Well – yeah, I get that maybe he upset her about something. But there's no way he was involved in the way you're suggesting, Emma. Jesus, why would he be?'

Emma pondered this for a moment. 'Because I think maybe he had feelings for her. I'd seen her in the hall with him in guitar lessons. They sang these amazing ballads and they'd just be looking at each other so… intensely. We all loved Tessa, Clem. That voice of hers, when she sang… it made every girl in the school want to be her. And he was just a young guy. What… twenty-two? What if he'd been under the same spell as the rest of us. What if they were involved with each other?'

'Emma, he wouldn't hurt a fly! I know it was a lifetime ago but the truth is, I just know Jonno wouldn't hurt anyone. He's one of the good ones.'

They both sat in silence for a while. Emma knew that Clementine was right. If her secret came out – even the little she knew – it would ruin Jonathan Brownley. You couldn't have someone who had withheld evidence from police in a homicide investigation being in charge of hundreds of impressionable young teenagers. Not in the minds of the parent body. Probably not in the minds of anyone.

'That vodka's making me spin. Let's just leave all this shit in the past and drive this baby home.' Clementine patted the steering wheel of the car, then turned and ran her finger tips over Emma's cheek. 'You are so *gorgeous*, Emma. You know that?'

Emma squirmed again and looked out the windscreen.

'You can't drive down the mountain yet, Clem. You're drunk.'

Clementine dropped her hands from the wheel. She stared ahead as if she was thinking hard. 'You might be right.' She opened the car door and the wind blew in, ferocious and cold. She slammed the door shut as she got out.

Emma watched her walk off across the carpark and disappear down the dimly lit path to the visitors' centre. She stared out at the blackness and wondered why she'd let Clementine drink anything at all. The mountain descent was a death trap. She wondered how Rosie would cope without her if they drove off the edge. Tears welled in her eyes. Would anyone miss her? What had she achieved with her life anyway? She thought of Tessa, a box of bones in the cemetery, nobody willing to blow the lid on her death. She hadn't spoken up when it counted. Would anyone believe her now if she accused her boss of killing Tessa? How did you even go about something like that? It didn't matter what Clementine said, he was obviously involved. She couldn't just live in fear of looking stupid or protecting others. She needed to do something about it. If she got off this mountain alive, she *would* do something about it. She made a silent promise to herself.

She wasn't sure how she was going to keep her job at the school when she accused the headmaster of murder. Or maybe it would be manslaughter. Either way, it wouldn't look good for Rosie. But there must be some way forward that didn't jeopardise everything. She would ask Marlee. She'd know what to do. Emma closed her eyes and felt her head spinning sickly. She just wanted to sleep. She let herself dissolve into the feeling, and drifted down into it, losing consciousness for what felt like only moments.

'Boo!'

Emma screamed.

Clementine was spread across the bonnet of the car, her face jammed against the windscreen like a bolt of lightning in the blackness. She gave Emma a loony grin.

'Christ, Clem. You scared the pants off me,' said Emma as Clementine climbed back into the driver's seat.

'Sorry,' said Clementine, giggling. 'That's cleared the cobwebs. All good to go.' She started the car.

'How long was I asleep? Maybe we should wait a bit longer,' said Emma.

Clementine ignored her and patted the steering wheel then turned the key and revved the engine. 'Come on, baby.' They listened to the car's engine purr in response.

Emma knew Clementine was still over the limit. She wondered if she could insist they call a taxi. But no sensible taxi driver would accept a fare to come up the top of a winding deserted mountain summit in pitch darkness, and she didn't have the energy for an argument. Emma clutched the sides of her seat and closed her eyes as Clementine took the first bend. The vodka was making her spin too.

From: Peta Kallorani
To: Jemima Langdon-Traves
Re: Holidays and reunion and things!

Dear J,
I can't get that email from Emma Tasker out of my head. Flashes of memories from the day Tessa died keep popping up at the strangest times – while I was tying Theo's shoelaces this morning and then when I was in the Deli, picking up the fig and prosciutto salad for a tennis lunch today. Weird.

I suppose it's because I knew something wasn't right that day too. Did I ever tell you that I saw Clementine Andrews just before they found Tessa? She was pelting out of the staff cottages, running up towards the far end of school where they found Tessa dead. And then the next day when I asked her about the rumour – about Brownley and Tessa – I remember vividly, she went white. Literally white. She said that Tessa couldn't possibly have been with him, because she was with her. But I know Clementine was lying, because she was alone when I saw her, and running as if her life bloody well depended on it. From exactly the direction of Brownley's cottage too. I couldn't work it out, so I didn't say anything.

I'd quite like to skip this reunion but if you're coming from London I suppose living in Sydney is no excuse! The whole thing is doing my head in though.

Would love us all to catch up during the holidays. Ivan's keen on Positano, so I'm hoping I can persuade him to divert for a few days so we can all meet in Lake Como in early July. Would that work?

P x

CHAPTER THIRTEEN

MARLEE

The waiting room at Dr Anna-Beth Rawson's surgery was soothing. There were magazines about glossy house renovations and lovely relaxing music that made Marlee think she was about to get a massage, rather than waiting nervously to talk to an obstetrician about all the terrible things she'd done to her foetus before she knew she was carrying it.

For the last few weeks, Marlee had presumed that she'd picked up a persistent sort of vomiting bug but had continued to drink alcohol at every opportunity that she could stomach it. Thankfully, this had been less than usual due to her all-day 'morning' sickness. Even so, her baby had probably picked up foetal alcohol syndrome by now.

Marlee could barely believe she was pregnant, despite the two pink lines on the test declaring it to be a certainty. A second test brand had announced it in blue – as if the manufacturer felt the need to address the gender bias. Both brands were in complete agreement though. She was definitely in the family way. *Unbelievable.*

'Marleen Maples.' A tall woman in her sixties was looking around pleasantly for an unfamiliar face.

Marlee got up quickly and placed the magazine back on the pile.

'Hi, yes that's me.' She followed Dr Rawson into her rooms. 'We've met before actually, Doctor, though you might not remember. My friend is Emma Parsons – I came to her daughter's birth about thirteen years ago.'

'Well, doesn't time fly. And call me Anna-Beth. It's lovely to see you again Marleen. Take a seat.' The doctor motioned to the chair across her desk.

'I see from your referral that you're pregnant. Good news?'

'I don't know.' A rush of some unknown emotion welled in Marlee's chest and her eyes became moist. 'I'm single and I didn't expect it. But the first problem is I've been drinking a lot. I was told a long time ago I'd never be able to get pregnant, so I didn't realise that feeling sick for a few weeks meant anything, and now I'm terrified. I've probably given this kid brain damage or liver failure or something, which I wouldn't have done if I'd known about it. Obviously.' She sniffed and looked down, twisting the chunky blue and green resin ring on her finger and plucking a thread of lint off her black pants.

'I understand your concerns. We can do some tests and of course you need to stop drinking completely now,' said Anna-Beth. 'But let's put those worries aside and start from the beginning. When was your last period?'

'Well, I can't remember. It's been a bit on and off for the last couple of years. But I know the exact date of conception. It was eight weeks ago – fifteenth of March.'

'Well it's good to know the date,' said Anna-Beth. 'That helps.'

'Actually, I think my period was a couple of weeks before then – it was the week I was packing up my stuff to move to Hobart. So maybe around the first of March.

Anna-Beth wrote down some notes and consulted a chart.

'Great. Why don't you pop up on the bed and I'll do an ultrasound to confirm the pregnancy.'

'What – now?'

'Well, now's as good a time as any don't you think?' said Anna-Beth.

'Alright, yes, well… it's just that…' Marlee's voice trailed off as she lost her train of thought. She wasn't ready to see whether she had an actual living creature inside her belly. She thought she'd have to go to a specialist ultrasound person for that. It was too soon.

A few minutes later, Anna-Beth squeezed the cold slimy gel onto her stomach and Marlee closed her eyes. She felt the ultrasound nozzle being pushed around on her stomach, pausing, then restarting, pushing, pausing and moving around lower, left, right, then stopping.

'There's your baby,' said Anna-Beth.

Marlee's eyes shot open. A tiny jelly bean-shaped figure with a rapidly beating heart jumped out of the screen at her. She felt an overwhelming sense of something huge. Terror or exhilaration. She wasn't sure.

'Is it healthy? Will the drinking have hurt it?'

'Well, we can't be sure of anything, but often if a foetus is harmed in the early stages it will spontaneously abort. So, it's a good sign that it hasn't. I would try not worry further. As long as you cut out alcohol from now on,' said Anna-Beth calmly. She was pressing some buttons, clicking, tapping her computer screen, pulling a line across the screen to take measurements. 'But your baby looks exactly right. You are ten weeks pregnant, Marleen, and everything looks fine.'

'But I can't be ten weeks!' said Marlee. 'It was eight weeks ago, on the fifteenth of March. I've only had sex with one guy since I came back to Tassie, and nobody before that for a couple of months!'

Anna-Beth gave a small laugh. 'Sure. But we add two weeks at the time of conception when calculating dates – it's from the date that your last period should have come. It's just a method. It means…' she picked up another small moveable chart on the bench next to her and fiddled with it, 'your baby is due on the sixth of December, give or take.'

Tears began to roll down Marlee's face.

'Marleen, if this isn't good news – if you're concerned about having this baby – we should talk about that.'

Marlee wiped her eyes. A huge lump in her throat was constricting her breath.

'I don't know… I never imagined I could, but now it's here I don't know what I want. I hardly know the father!'

'Well, perhaps you need some time to consider it all. It sounds like it's a big shock.'

'It's just that, I was told I couldn't have children because there were issues when I was younger.'

'Could you tell me about the problems you've had previously?'

'Sure, but… do you think you could stop calling me Marleen? I'm Marlee. I stopped being Marleen a long time ago.'

'Of course.'

Marlee paused and stared behind Anna-Beth at the photo of her children and grandchildren, a huge laughing group of people with Anna-Beth and an older-looking man who must have been her husband at its centre. It looked warm, being at the centre.

'I guess it started back in my last term of high school. Some awful… things happened. I went off the rails a bit. Then a few weeks after graduation I found out I was pregnant. My world kind of shattered.'

The phone on Anna-Beth's desk rang and she spoke quickly to her secretary then hung up the phone.

Anna-Beth looked up at her again. 'Sorry, Marlee, please go on.'

Marlee squirmed. In the stark daylight of the doctor's surgery the story felt stale and contrived. But now she had started she didn't feel she had much choice but to finish.

'It was a huge shock to find myself pregnant. But I couldn't have told anyone. My mother was terminally ill and I didn't want to make things worse for her. There were huge expectations that I would go to university and do well. I was dux of the school. It would have been embarrassing for my family if anyone found out – my parents were so proud of me being Head Girl of Denham House. It was like they formed an identity around it.' Marlee stopped and looked down at her fingers.

'I can imagine,' said Anna-Beth. 'I was Head Girl at Ellery. Many years before your time, but the expectations were immense.'

Marlee smiled at her. 'Well, anyway, someone told me about this doctor who could help me terminate the pregnancy. I was going to visit him, but I miscarried and it turned out to be an ectopic pregnancy. Then there were some complications and I just remember them telling me I wouldn't be able to get pregnant again.'

'What a tough time you've had,' said Anna-Beth.

'Yeah, it was. Mainly because I fought with my dad, because he wanted me to keep the truth from Mum. Not long after that, Mum died and I moved to Melbourne and started architecture. I slept with pretty much every attractive man I met and they were right. I couldn't get pregnant. Until now.'

Anna-Beth was looking at her kindly. 'That sounds like a very difficult period of your life.'

'Well, I topped my year at the end of the degree. So that was a small consolation.' Marlee wiped at her eyes with a tissue from the box on the desk.

'Goodness,' said Anna-Beth. 'Well, this pregnancy must have come as a huge surprise. I'd like to schedule another appointment with you in a few days if you're okay with that. We have a few things we should talk about and a few investigations I would recommend we do. I'd also like to see your old medical files from your last pregnancy if you can get them.'

'Okay. I suppose I can,' said Marlee. The tiny beany-baby was bouncing up and down inside her, making her want to heave up the oats and chia she'd had for breakfast. That would teach her for switching to healthy food since those lines on the test had turned pink and blue, just to prove she could be a good mother.

'In the meantime, I've written down a few things that I'd like you to do to encourage the healthiest possible pregnancy, Marlee,' said Anna-Beth, pushing a piece of paper across the desk to her. 'If you could manage those, you'll be covering all bases, and at the next appointment we can explore a few of the issues you've touched on today and decide how you'd like to proceed. I'm afraid that phone call was my receptionist letting me know that I am needed at a delivery, so unfortunately we seem to have run out of time.'

Marlee wondered if it would be inappropriate to ask Anna-Beth to come home with her and tuck her into bed. She didn't want to explore the issues. She just needed to sleep.

CHAPTER FOURTEEN

HARRIET

Harriet watched the young mother at the next table. She had perched the baby on the edge of the table and was jiggling her up and down whilst simultaneously reading something on the screen of her phone. Intermittently the woman would look up and blow faces at the child and make inane, cooing noises. Harriet looked back down at the file she was reading. The case was tedious and there was little chance that the meeting she was about to have with the instructing solicitor would improve her attitude towards it. But still, it would have been nice to be able to read it without having to listen to gibberish. Although it probably wasn't the woman's fault she was in this mood.

She was annoyed that she'd agreed to meet Clementine for lunch at a café. Harriet had moved a meeting to be able to fit in a completely unnecessary thirty-minute lunch date in the busiest part of her day, when she could just as easily have seen Clementine tonight when she returned from work. Although she had been staying at work late in the evenings these past weeks, so they didn't see each other every day. She looked at her watch again. Seven minutes late. Typical.

Harriet ran her eyes over the decor of Clementine's choice of waterfront venue. Paint-stripped recycled brickwork formed two of the walls and there were odd items suspended from the ceiling masquerading, she supposed, as artwork. An old bicycle. Rusty farm implements. Dead tree branches. The effect was somewhat bewildering. The door opened and Clementine weaved her way through the tables.

'Hello, Mumsy, how are you?'

'I'm fine. Did you have something else on at 1.30 p.m. that clashed with our lunch, darling?' Harriet was annoyed with herself for pointing out Clementine's lateness. It made her feel socially uptight. Her usual rule was to not mention someone's lateness unless it had reached the ten-minute mark. That seemed to Harriet to be more than fair and it provided her with a framework that made people think she was actually more flexible than she was.

Clementine laughed. 'I've just been out to MONA again. That museum is mind-blowing.' She took off her jacket and put down the bag she was carrying onto the floor.

'Mmmm,' said Harriet. 'Well it gives me a headache. A whole wall of plaster cast vaginas? I mean *really*.'

'Come on, Mumma-bear. Open your mind. That exhibit shines a light on the dark and saggy bits of life.'

'Well, that's a stretch,' said Harriet, and they both burst into laughter. Harriet recovered her composure and poured them both a glass of water from the bottle on the table. 'They do take some things too far though, Clem. I mean, you have to admit, the exhibit of the chocolate-coated entrails of that suicide bomber – that was just awful. How is that art?'

'Oh, Mum. It's a museum about sex and death. You can't expect sunshine and lollipops. Anyway, I was a tiny bit late because I had to buy some shoes.' She opened the box on the floor and pulled out some bright purple suede boots with a three-inch square rubber heel and green laces. 'You can borrow them next time you need to seduce a grumpy old judge.'

Harriet burst into laughter again. 'They're hideous, you crazy girl! Honestly, I don't know where you get your style.' She shook her head and picked up the menu, burying her grin. There was always something so unsettling about outings with Clementine.

'What looks good?' asked Clementine, picking up her own menu.

'I'm going to have the salmon salad and a mineral water,' said Harriet, trying to wave down the waitress who was now fawning all over the baby at the next table. 'I don't have much time.'

'Well you never seem to get home early enough to see me before I go out at night,' said Clementine cheerily, 'so I thought lunch would give us time to catch up on some mother-daughter stuff,'

'Oh,' said Harriet again, wondering what sort of stuff she could mean. 'Is something wrong?'

'No, Mumma-bear. Not at all. But there is something I wanted to ask you,' said Clementine, putting down the menu.

Harriet was having difficulty getting the waitress' attention. She stood chatting to the mother of the baby and making all sorts of gurgling noises at the child. She was saying things like 'such a little stunner!' and 'she's just way too cute!' The child was actually quite unattractive.

'What do you need to ask?' said Harriet, turning back to Clementine.

'Why has Jonno been single for so long? Seems a bit weird to me.'

Clementine was the only one who called Jonathan, Jonno. It didn't really suit him, in Harriet's opinion. But Clementine liked to do things her own way.

'What sort of question is that?' asked Harriet.

'I just want to know. He's a nice guy. Good looking. I'm just interested.'

Harriet took a few moments to consider the question.

'Yes, he's all those things.'

'And smart,' said Clementine. 'So... why still single?'

'Perhaps he just hasn't met the one,' mused Harriet. She had wondered the same thing herself over the years. Her brother was in many ways an anathema to Harriet. She adored him because he was her little brother, and she'd as good as raised him. Plus, he was one of the few people who didn't make her feel in the least bit uptight. She could tell him anything. She could share her worries about Clementine and Scarlett and he always had sensible advice to share. But sometimes she felt that she didn't really *know* him.

'Why do you ask, darling? Do you have someone in mind for him?'

'No, I'm just being nosey. Has he even been on a casual date since Carol died? I mean, I know he loved her and everything, but they were only together for a few months before her cancer came back. She's been gone twelve years. It just seems bonkers.'

'Well perhaps he didn't want to risk being hurt again. He takes things to heart too much.'

Clementine seemed to ponder this. 'Remember when I was at high school and Tessa Terrano was killed? He seemed to take that really hard.'

Harriet felt herself stiffen. She didn't want to talk about this. It was all so long ago. She would try for the food after all. By some miracle the waitress was walking past.

'Could you bring me the quickest salad the kitchen can muster please? I need to leave in fifteen minutes.'

'I'll have whatever she's having,' said Clementine smiling at the girl.

Clementine spoke again as the girl left. 'I remember, during those school holidays, he was in the kitchen with you and he was crying about it. I always wondered why he would have cared so much. It was weeks afterwards.'

Harriet recalled the time clearly. Her brother had been in his first job out of teachers' college. The girl had been his student – a musical protégé of sorts. After she died, he'd spent the summer moping like a lost dog. Clementine hadn't been any better. Harriet had told them both they needed to snap out of it. Luckily, they had had the long school holidays to do it.

'Well, he's always been soft-hearted. And that accident was a terrible tragedy. You yourself were very affected.'

'He wasn't keen on her, was he?' asked Clementine.

'Don't be ridiculous,' said Harriet.

'I'm not. He was young. He took it hard. And everyone at school had a crush on him, Mum. Tessa would have been no different. I… I just thought there might have been more to it,' said Clementine, fiddling with small packet of sugar she'd removed from the cup in the centre of the table.

She must be wearing mascara, thought Harriet, as she marvelled at Clementine's huge brown eyes. Although she'd never known Clementine to wear make-up. Harriet sighed. 'Leave the past in the past, Clementine. I haven't cancelled meetings this morning to come here and discuss the Terrano girl's accident. It was nothing to do with Jonathan anyway.'

'How do you *know* that, Mum?'

'Clementine, that's enough.'

Clementine sighed and tipped her head to one side. Resigned to defeat, Harriet was pleased to see. She got out her phone and began checking her emails. Her appetite had disappeared.

From the corner of her eye, Harriet saw the baby at the next table drop a small pink teddy bear on the ground. Clementine leaned down and picked it up, then stretched over and handed it to the baby's mother.

'Cute baby, how old is she?' asked Clementine.

'This is Harlequin. She's five months next week,' said the woman, smiling at Clementine then back at the baby and jiggling her up and down.

Good Lord, thought Harriet. What is the world coming to? *Harlequin!* It wasn't even a name. Harriet understood the desire to provide your children with slightly distinctive names – to give them their own special identity. There was no need to be pedestrian about these things. Clementine and Scarlett certainly weren't common choices although both were beautiful, traditional names. But *Harlequin*? The child was sure to be bullied.

'Cool name,' said Clementine.

'Thanks. She named herself really. She had such a great aura when she popped out.' The woman turned back to the baby, 'Didn't you my poppet! You are one wild and wonderful tiny person aren't you, Harley?'

The woman dug her fingers into the baby's stomach and the baby giggled.

Harriet felt a tinge of regret. Parenting seemed like such an enjoyable sport these days. The rules had changed. Parents gave so much more credence to their children. It was as if the woman truly believed that the child had arrived with some sort of colourful calling card that announced itself into the ether and she had miraculously picked up on its vibe. *Ta dah! I bring rainbows and kaleidoscopic brilliance into your life. Name me Harlequin!* It was mystifying.

'Apparently Scarlett has run out of money in Italy,' said Harriet loudly. 'She's asked me to book her flight home in a week.'

'Cool,' said Clementine, turning back to her.

'So, there will be three of us in the house then,' said Harriet, a pang of anxiety striking again at the thought of her two daughters under one roof for more than a couple of nights. It was unprecedented. Scarlett and Clementine were both very strong personalities who should be handled carefully, and in separate locations if possible. It was like adding hydrogen peroxide and sulfuric acid together. One could easily predict a spontaneous detonation – a fact she had been required to research in detail for a recent insurance case. She wondered what she'd done to deserve such challenging children. Some people had lovely, close families who actually didn't mind spending time together. They got along when they gathered for special occasions. Good Lord, some of them even *looked forward* to it.

'You'll manage, Mum. Don't sweat it.'

Their salads arrived and Clementine picked up her fork and started shovelling the salmon salad into her mouth, her fork flying up and down, without a break. It was as if she was deliberately ignoring Harriet's forty-two years of meticulous guidance about the importance of table manners. It was infuriating.

'Your mouth is full, Clementine. Put down that fork!' Harriet controlled the urge to smack Clementine's hand. Why did Clementine always have to drive her towards the worst version of herself? Clementine raised her eyebrows at her mother, eyes twinkling, fully distended cheeks moving up and down with brazen disregard for propriety. It was almost as if she was laughing at Harriet. It felt like an unfair slap after all she had borne – the fight to keep Clementine out of the hands of the government social workers who insisted she be put up for adoption; the shame she'd had to bear before and after Clementine's birth; the lack of respect for all she'd sacrificed. How *could* she be so ungrateful? A tiny snake of buried anger uncoiled itself inside Harriet and lodged its fangs in her throat. It caused her next words to come out in a hiss.

'Clementine, you're eating like a pig!'

CHAPTER FIFTEEN

EMMA

Saturday morning used to be Emma's favourite. She could lie in for a little while – longer if the cottage guests had checked in on Friday night and there were no last-minute preparations to finish for guests coming in during the weekend. Emma would read a novel or catch up on her Facebook feed or go for a long walk. Phillip would be out riding with his cyclist friends, dressed up in lycra that clung mercilessly to his backside and middle-aged belly. Rosie would be doing whatever Rosie did before she turned into a morning-monster who hated getting up. Usually it involved watching something on television or searching the internet for new types of craft to assist in turning her room into a junk pile. It was lovely. Nobody cared what the other was doing.

But now that Rosie was in high school, and now that single motherhood had been forced on her, Saturday was a chore. Rosie's school sport was compulsory and usually early and very often at some location on the other side of the city that didn't respect Rosie's need for sleep.

Emma stood in the doorway of Rosie's bedroom and watched the lump in the bed roll over and tug the blankets up higher over its head.

'Go away, Mum!'

Emma shivered and went to her own bedroom to dig out a second jumper. The cottage had terrible heating. May in Hobart was cold. Some mornings it barely reached eight degrees in the cottage. Emma didn't blame her daughter for not wanting to get out from under the warmth of her bedcovers.

'Dad will be here in twenty minutes, Rosie. You need to hurry.'

Emma retreated to the kitchen and shoved some bread in the toaster. She looked around at the mess. From the corner of her eye, she saw Rosie skitter across the hall to the bathroom.

'Quickly get your gear on and come and eat this toast, darling.' Emma picked up her cup of tea and took a sip. It was cold. She sighed and tipped it down the sink.

'Mum, where are my shin pads?'

'In your shoe cupboard?' she offered. She wondered why she might be expected to know.

'I looked in there, Mum! They won't let me play if I don't have them!' Rosie stood in the doorway of the kitchen, glaring. The hysteria in her voice had a rough edge. She was bordering on tears and she'd only been out of bed for five minutes.

'What did you do after training on Thursday, sweetie? Could they be in the car?'

Rosie looked at Emma as if she had just announced a cure for cancer.

'I think they're in the boot! Can you get them, Mum? I have to find my mouthguard!' Rosie ran back to her bedroom.

Emma felt her gloom spilling out, spreading like a stain across the room. Her parenting book had said that indulging your children by doing things for them made them incapable of becoming independent people. You weren't supposed to give in to their demands. But Phillip would be arriving in a few minutes to take Rosie for the weekend. Nothing was ready. She didn't want him to think she wasn't coping without him. She took the car keys off the hook and walked outside. The cold sucked at her bones. There was ice on her windscreen and crisp white frost on the grass – the first of the year.

She pulled her dressing gown tighter around her neck as she opened the car boot. The offending bright pink shin pads glared at her accusingly. *Bad mother.* She should have checked the boot earlier and now she was compounding her poor mothering by saving Rosie from having to look for them herself. She scooped them up. The crunch of tyres on the driveway behind her made her freeze. Oh no. Why did Phillip have to turn up when she was still in her pyjamas?

She closed the boot with deliberate care and walked back inside without turning around. She handed the shin pads to Rosie.

'Thanks, Mum.'

Rosie was brushing her hair over the dining table and drawing it up into a ponytail. Emma looked at the cold pieces of toast on the board. She buttered them, then put jam on top.

'Rosie, you need to eat something. Come and have this toast. Dad's here already.' She tried to keep the rising panic out of her voice as she put the plate on the table.

'I'm not ready. Who cares if Dad has to wait?' Rosie's face was twisted into a sullen, angry mask.

'Don't be rude about your dad, darling.'

'Why are you sticking up for him, Mum? He's the one who ruined everything.'

'Don't say that, darling. He's still your dad and he still loves you.'

'Mum! No wonder he got a new girlfriend! You don't even care, do you? You don't even care that he's wrecked everything. We could have still been all together if you didn't let him get away with being horrible to you!' Rosie swiped angrily at a tear that had run down her cheek.

Emma thought her heart might break. But she didn't have time to think about it now. She needed to calm her down. Get everything back on an even keel so Rosie would go with her dad.

'Please, sweetheart. Yes, I'm angry at Dad too, but it's not going to get us anywhere by fighting with each other. We have to stick together.' She reached out and put her hand on Rosie's shoulder. Rosie shrugged it off.

'Please have some toast, sweetie. You don't want to be late for hockey.'

Rosie scrunched up her nose and picked a piece up by the corner.

'Gross. The butter's all thick and it's cold.' She dropped the toast back onto the plate and picked the shin pads. 'I'll just get something at the hockey canteen.'

Without saying goodbye, Rosie picked up the overnight bag that Emma had packed for her and walked out the door, leaving it wide open. The freezing air swirled into the corners of the old cottage.

Emma shivered again as she closed the door. She walked across to the window to watch the car retreating down the driveway and noticed a third head in the car. She wondered who it was, then felt herself slipping, panicking as the understanding set in. *Pia.*

The hide of the man! How dare he expect Rosie to accept Pia so quickly? Emma hadn't even really talked through the whole thing with Rosie yet, although she knew that Phillip had talked about Pia to her. For Emma, it was too new. Too horrible. And now Pia was going along to watch Rosie's hockey game, hand in hand with Phillip as if she was part of a perfect family group – two parents watching their child run around the sports ground, leaning idly against the fence, chatting to the other parents. The other mothers would have a field day with such fantastic gossip material. They'd make heartfelt remarks about 'poor Rosie' to their daughters in the car on the way home to show how empathetic they were, when really, they just wanted their children to know how lucky they were that their family wasn't so dysfunctional.

Emma wanted to sit down and sob. Last night she'd woken again at 3 a.m., worrying about Rosie and about the paltry amount of maintenance Phillip had agreed to pay. Then it had spiralled into her worry about Tessa and about her own silence during the crucial police investigation. Admitting what she had seen all those years ago to Clementine had opened up a hairline crack in Emma's conscience. And now there was the photograph.

Emma clenched her fingers around the edge of the sink and forced the thoughts away. What she really wanted to do was climb back into bed, but she had to start setting up the school hall for the art exhibition soon. She'd promised to help Lena. It was going to take a week and the artists were going to start bringing in their works this morning. For some reason the task of setting up an art exhibition right now made her feel weak. Overwhelmed. There was too much to organise.

A knock at the door made Emma freeze. She straightened her bathrobe and smoothed down her hair then rubbed her finger across her teeth. Who would be visiting this early on a Saturday morning? She hoped it wasn't Alan Lenstaat, the new science teacher who had just moved into the next cottage. He was awkwardly shy and seemed to be looking for a new friend.

'Hello, sleepyhead.'

Marlee was standing at the door smiling, sleek and effortlessly glamorous in tight jeans, divine ankle boots and a gorgeous black roll-neck jumper.

'What are you doing here so early? I thought we were meeting at eleven,' said Emma, unaccountably annoyed that Marlee was dressed and out of the house so early. It was unheard of on weekends.

'I've given up alcohol and it turns out that the mornings are much easier to face,' said Marlee walking towards the kettle and flicking it on. She sat herself down at the table and crossed her legs, leaning back to look around the kitchen.

'Oh. Good for you,' said Emma, trying to hide her surprise about Marlee's new stance on alcohol.

'I like what you've done to the place,' said Marlee.

Emma watched as she surveyed the open boxes and the mess scattered in every corner and piling up on the benches.

'It's a work in progress.'

'Is Rosie still asleep?'

'No, Phillip just picked her up and took her to hockey,' said Emma.

'Good.'

'He had Pia in the car,' said Emma miserably.

'Bastard.'

'It should be against the law.'

'Mmmm. Good idea,' said Marlee, distractedly.

'Anyway, why are you here?'

'Just to hang out… and to let you download about the bits of your life that are, you know… kind of shitty.'

'You mean the bit where my little girl is having the innocence of her childhood ruined by her idiot father at this very minute?'

Marlee tilted her head to one side. 'Yeah. Something like that.' Marlee picked up Rosie's cold toast off the plate and bit into it, looking pensive as she chewed. 'Emma… would you have another baby, you know, if you… met another guy?'

'What?'

'Well, it's possible isn't it? At our age… no reason why you wouldn't. I mean lots of people are having babies in their forties, aren't they?' Marlee walked to the cupboards and got out the cups and began making tea for them both.

'Well, some I suppose. But there are so many risks when you're older – Down's Syndrome for a start, and other things too.' Emma took the cup of tea and put it down on the table. She started folding up the basket of washing that was sitting on the kitchen floor.

'But I guess you can test for all those things to set your mind at rest,' said Marlee.

'Well, I'm not sure why you think I will ever be inviting another man into my life. Although… maybe if he was gorgeous… and young. Obviously, I wouldn't be wanting another one like Phillip. But even then… all those sleepless nights and nappies… uuuggh.' She shuddered and stared thoughtfully at the shirt she was folding. 'And with a younger guy, he'd probably be out partying all night anyway and leaving me to do all the hard work. So no, I don't think so. Although I'd make an exception for Prince Harry if he was still single.'

Emma wondered why Marlee was trying to distract her from thinking about Phillip by talking about other men. It wasn't helping. She knew she was probably too old to get another guy now anyway. Plus, she had outgrown all her jeans in the last few weeks by 'comfort eating', despite it making her more depressed and much less comfortable. She needed to buy a bigger pair. She wasn't about to take her clothes off for anyone. Her tummy looked much flabbier than it had a few months ago, and even then, Phillip had been in the habit of poking his finger into her tummy fat and wobbling it around and laughing. He and Pia were probably laughing about her flabby bits at this very moment. Although, they had Rosie in the car, so maybe not.

'Yeah, we'd all like Harry. But seriously, the hard work and sleepless nights bit, that's all temporary,' said Marlee.

'No, it really isn't,' said Emma. 'It just goes on and on.' She shook her head, thinking of the terrible sleep she'd had last night, half of it because of Rosie and their uncertain future. 'I'm not sure why we're even talking about this though, since the likelihood of either of us having a baby is pretty close to zero.'

Marlee didn't say anything. Emma wondered if she'd sounded too insensitive about Marlee's infertility. Although it was an open discussion topic that had never bothered her before. Probably safest to change the subject though. She put two pieces of bread in the toaster and got an avocado out of the fridge.

'Marl, I've been wanting to talk to you about something.'

'Mmmm.'

'Well, I went out a couple of weeks ago with Clementine Andrews. You know, the artist we went to school with.'

'Clementine Andrews. Mmm, she told me she saw you.'

'Did she? Well, anyway, we got a bit tipsy and—'

'Since when do you go out with celebrities and get drunk?'

'I know. We went to the pub and ended up drinking lots of wine and then we went up the mountain and drank quite a lot of vodka.'

'Party animal.'

'Mmmm. Anyway, I told her something. Something I've never told anyone except Phil before.'

'What?'

Emma paused and noticed her mouth had gone dry. Marlee was looking at her expectantly. 'Well… before Tessa was found dead, I saw her having an argument with Jon Brownley – near that building site.'

'What?'

'I saw it from the upstairs drama storeroom.'

'Saw what?'

'Tessa. She was yelling at him and he was saying something to her, holding onto her…'

'What… what was she saying?'

'I couldn't hear. I don't…' Emma trailed off, remembering the moment clearly. Ms Telston had given her the set of keys to the main storeroom. She had remembered the sombrero hats from a play they did a couple of years ago. She thought they might still be there – perfect for their Three Amigos of Denham House skit to be performed on the last day of term.

Emma had the hats in her hand when she saw it through the window – a movement below her. A student was running, her backpack banging heavy blows against her back in time with her steps. She'd come through the sculpture gardens and was running across towards the building site area that was out of bounds. Emma was about to turn away, when from behind the old hedge she saw someone else running. Someone following the girl. As the figure got closer, she was startled to realise it was Mr Brownley. The blond hair and masculine form were unmistakeable. The girl stopped and turned back towards him and as she turned her head, Emma saw clearly that it was Tessa. *Strange.* Tessa had left drama class early, feeling sick, so she should be at sick bay or in the boarding house. Then it occurred to Emma that the illness thing was a ruse. She felt a thrill of fear in her chest. Tessa had implied that it would be today, but they weren't sure whether to believe her. It was a crazy plan. They'd told her so. But you had to admire Tessa. She was nuts, but she was brave too.

Emma watched as Tessa walked back towards Mr Brownley, shaking her head, then she turned away from him to walk on. He reached out and held her arm. She wrenched it out of his grasp, moving her shoulder to block him. They looked like they were arguing. Emma fumbled around looking for the window latch to see if she could open it. *What were they saying?* Mr Brownley reached out for her arm again, obviously wanting Tessa to stay where she was, or to follow him back the other way maybe. Something definitely didn't look right.

Suddenly, Tessa pulled herself from his grip with a force that sent her stumbling backwards and she fell onto her bottom. She looked silly and childish and Emma gasped with shared embarrassment. She watched as Tessa got up, picked up her bag and ran, disappearing behind the tall cypress hedge on the other side of the building. Mr Brownley hesitated briefly, and looked over his shoulder. He made a scooping movement with his arm, twice, as if he was motioning to someone else. Then he turned and ran after Tessa. He rounded the corner and the hedge swallowed him up and then there was nothing else for Emma to see. No more movement below her at all.

Now, as the weight of the old story stained the silence of the kitchen, Emma locked eyes with Marlee. 'It was probably important. Maybe it was related to what Tessa told Linda Perkins and me, remember?'

Marlee suddenly went pale and put her hand to her mouth. Emma wondered if she was going to be sick. She was staring past her, through the window, breathing hard.

'Marl, are you okay?'

'Mmmm? No, not really. I... um, I just wasn't expecting that.'

'No. I know. Sorry. But I don't know what to do.'

'What do you mean? What is there to do? Tessa's death was an accident.'

'I know the police said that. But what if he chased her in? You know... they had a lover's tiff or something.'

Marlee was staring blankly at her.

Emma persisted. 'What would they have been arguing about so badly that he'd grab her like that? He was a teacher. It didn't look right.'

'I don't know.'

'Don't you think we need to find out what happened? I know I should have spoken up at the time. I'm not sure why I didn't. I told Phillip once, years ago when we were first going out, and he said I probably blew things up in my mind to try to make sense of it. That I'd imagined it.'

Marlee was staring out the window again. 'Marlee? What if he pushed her?' Emma couldn't believe how dramatic she sounded. But still. What if he had?

'I'm pretty sure he's not the murdering type, Em. Listen to yourself. He's the headmaster of Tasmania's most prestigious school. *Rosie's* school. Maybe Clementine brings out the drama in you. She's a bit of a lunatic, if you believe the media stories.'

'But she was telling me it *wasn't* him.' Emma picked up the breakfast plate off the bench and began rinsing it. 'He is her uncle though, so of course she'd say that.'

'Em, do you really want to stir up a shit storm over something that might not have happened? What if it *is* a false memory? I read an article in *Time* magazine once about them. They're common. Something to do with the hippocampus area of the brain distorting things that are suggested to us. Tessa suggested she'd be with him, didn't she? So you thought you saw that. But maybe you just dreamed it. Why else wouldn't you have told me before now?'

'I didn't want to upset you. You were so upset already. Plus, with your mum… you know. And with Ms Sharp asking you to make sure everyone else was okay, you just went into overdrive. I know being Head Girl wasn't easy. You had to keep everyone going for those last few days.'

'Mmmm.'

'Marl, what if he lied? Maybe the school kept quiet about it to protect his reputation or something. I don't know.' Emma paused, watching Marlee's disbelieving face. 'And that's not all.'

'What do you mean?'

'I found a photograph.' Emma closed her eyes. The naked picture of Tessa was right there, behind her lids. Then another image of Tessa flitted across her mind, as real as if she'd been in the room – Tessa, flicking her hair out of her eyes as she leaned over her guitar and strummed a ballad during music class, ignoring everyone, intent only on her music, her voice so startlingly soulful that every person in the class was completely still. Mr Brownley, watching, mesmerised.

She opened her eyes and saw Marlee watching her.

'What sort of photograph?'

'Of Tessa. Naked. It was behind the fireplace here. It was date stamped the day before she died.' Emma reached up to the shelf above the kitchen sink and pulled down a box. She opened it and handed the photograph to Marlee.

Marlee stared at it for a full minute, her face not changing. Eventually she spoke quietly. 'She wanted to be a model. Remember?'

'Did she? Well not a playboy model. Don't you think it's strange that she'd even pose for a photo like that? Who took it? And why was it here?'

'Who knows, Em? She probably took it herself with the timer. She was a bit mixed up.' Marlee sounded resigned. She closed her eyes and slumped, as if she was suddenly exhausted. 'I was having my piano lesson after school with Brownley that day, remember? Em, he was in the music block when she died. He had students back-to-back. You must have seen her quite a while before she fell.'

'Yeah, I know. But it's just that maybe the time of death was a bit out or something.'

'Or maybe you're just in a muddle.'

Emma's hands were clenched into tight balls. Why wasn't Marlee worried about this? It was a gigantic, terrible possibility.

'I think I need to tell the police.' Emma felt tears blurring her vision. It was the lack of sleep. Or maybe she just wanted someone to believe her.

'Em, I'm sure it couldn't have been him. You're making yourself sick for nothing. I...' Marlee's face had taken on an ashen pallor. 'I just need a glass of water.' She went to the sink and ran the tap, the gushing hiss of the water breaking into Emma's thoughts. Marlee's head slumped forward and her shoulders sagged.

'There's something I need to tell you,' said Marlee.

'What?'

Marlee turned back to her and leaned against the sink, sipping her water. Around them, shafts of light coming in through the tiny window pierced the cold air as the sun moved up in the sky. The call of a magpie rolled in through the silence.

'I'm pregnant.'

'What? How? You can't be!'

'Well I am. And I'm feeling pretty disgusting.' Marlee moved to the table again and sat down, then leaned down and put her head in her hands on the tabletop.

'Marlee! Oh my goodness. Are you alright?' Emma placed her hand gently on Marlee's back. Her mind skittered. Marlee was pregnant. *Pregnant!* That's why she looked so ill.

'Marl, are you okay? It must be a shock. How far gone are you?'

'Ten weeks.'

'Okay. Well, that's good, isn't it? You'll be a great mum! Who's the father?'

Marlee sat up. 'I don't know what to do, Em. He's just a guy I met, but everything's so messed up. I don't know if I even want to keep it. What would I know about being a mother?'

Emma pulled her chair around to face Marlee and rested a hand on her knee. 'Marl, you'll be a fantastic mum. Look how you are with Rosie. You know all the right things to do. You might have to give up the night life for a bit, that's all.'

Marlee gave a hollow laugh. 'Yeah.' Her face crumpled and some strands of gleaming red hair fell out of the loose pigtail.

'Listen, you're just tired. And sounds like you've got morning sickness. You need some thinking space. Want to come on a yoga retreat I saw advertised today on my Facebook feed? It'll be a perfect opportunity for you to have a think about it all.'

'Jesus, Em. I don't think so. I'm having trouble getting through a work day at the moment, let alone managing bloody downward dog poses. Can't you take Carol?'

Carol was Emma's perpetually cheerful and chatty friend from her old mothers' group. Emma had taken her on a beginner's meditation retreat last year and during the morning of silence Carol had lasted exactly thirty-seven minutes before shattering the peace with a stream of chatter that burst like water from a dam wall. She had ruined Emma's carefully constructed concentration, forcing her to move to the other side of the creek to find space on her own.

'No! Carol is even less the yoga-type than you are. It wouldn't be peaceful. Anyway, Carol doesn't need thinking time like you do.'

'Okay, okay. That woman does have verbal diarrhea, I'll give you that. I'll think about it. I've got a couple of weeks up my sleeve before I need to decide whether to terminate or not.'

'Oh no! Marl, I really think that would be the wrong decision. You've got this one chance. You never thought you'd have it.'

Marlee sighed heavily. 'Maybe.'

'Would the dad want to be involved? Who is this mystery man anyway?'

'Just someone I met through work. Don't think he'd be up for it.'

'Well, even so, it could be the best thing that ever happened to you. Let's just take a couple of days and we can talk it over, okay? When you're sick, everything seems horrible.'

'Yeah, okay.'

Emma smiled at her. 'Want to come up to the school hall and help set up for the art exhibition?'

'Not especially,' said Marlee.

'Come on, it's the school's major fundraiser.'

'Screw the school. They've got loads of cash. Let's go do something fun.'

'Some of the money raised will be for doing up the staff cottages,' said Emma, mildly irritated.

'Well, so it bloody well should be. This place is still as rundown as it was when we were at school.' Marlee peered around the room and Emma was suddenly self-conscious about the mess and the dingy, dark room with its scuffed paintwork. 'Let's go shopping for an outfit for the school reunion. You can't not go to it just because of the group email. Come on, I found a really cute little boutique.'

Emma sighed. 'Okay.'

'And I know it's Saturday, but you might want to think about your choice of outfit.'

Emma looked down at her pink rabbit pyjama pants. She grabbed Rosie's pile of clothes and headed towards the bedrooms, catching a glimpse of Marlee's frown as she looked out the window.

'I'll just jump in the shower. Stop worrying about things.'

'*You* stop worrying about things,' said Marlee.

Emma wondered if that was possible. Could she stop worrying about things? Motherhood made everything so much worse. It was like wearing your heart on the outside of your skin, where everybody could prod at it with a stick. Being responsible for another little human made you so fearful about what could go wrong. Marlee would find this out for herself if she went through with the pregnancy.

From: Linda Perkins
To: Emma Parsons
Re: Fabulous formal photo… the countdown is on, girls!

Dear Emma,

Loved your email! (Obviously not meant for me but who cares!) How funny are you about the toenail thing. My DH is the same! Gross! Can't wait to catch up at the reunion. We obviously have heaps in common. I haven't had sex for ages either. DH has a little problem in that department since the prostate cancer. Not that I mind. When the oncologist told us sex might be hard afterwards, I was secretly fist-pumping the air and saying (internally) bring on the surgeon's knife and a huge fat dose of radiation! Not that I let on to DH. Poor man was gutted. Absolutely gutted. As if they'd just told him he was getting both legs amputated.

And don't worry about what you said about Tessa in the email either. Some of the girls will probably think you've stirred up a hornet's nest, but I've always wondered if she slept with Brownley too and how the whole thing panned out. She seemed hell-bent on getting him, didn't she! Looking back, when I think about the underwear she'd bought for it and how certain she was that he was keen, I feel a bit sick. I've got daughters coming up to that age. Bloody hell, I can only hope they don't ever plan to do the deed with a hot teacher on school grounds (their sports teacher is a bit of hunk, so I'll be paying attention!)

Anyway, can't wait to catch up. See you at the reunion lovely lady ☺

Lots of love, Linda

CHAPTER SIXTEEN

EMMA

Emma jumped off the bed and grabbed the phone as Rosie's ringtone began blaring.

'Hello, sweetie, how are you?'

'Hi, Mum.'

'Are you alright, Rosie? I'm sorry about this morning. Dad should have asked before he brought that woman to your hockey game. I don't want to criticise your father darling, but it was really thoughtless of him.'

'What?'

'This morning… with Pia in the car when he picked you up—'

'Mum, what are you talking about? Grandma was in the car. I haven't even seen Pia. I told Dad if I had to see her on my weekends with him, I'd stop coming.'

'Oh, sweetie…' said Emma, and hot tears sprang into her eyes. *You go, my baby girl!* she thought.

'I'm just calling to say that Grandma wondered if I could stay at Dad's another night and she could drop me over on Monday morning early to get ready for school.'

'Is Grandma there for long?'

'Yeah. She's here for a few days, I think. She came to hockey this morning. It was really cool because I scored the winning goal and Grandma bought me a new outfit to celebrate!'

Emma felt the lump of anxiety in her chest starting to loosen, before it balled up and constricted again. She was glad it hadn't been Pia in the car this morning, but now Vivien was buying Rosie's affections and attaching monetary value to goal scoring. Any parenting expert would tell you that was a sure way to create a selfish, non-team player. Although it was lovely to hear the cheery note in Rosie's voice. Maybe parenting experts made exceptions for teenagers with idiot fathers.

Emma wondered where Pia had disappeared to for the weekend. Maybe they'd cancelled the weekend cottage bookings and Pia was staying in there. She hoped not. Despite Phillip and Pia deciding they should take over all the cottage bookings and cleaning, Phillip had agreed to give Emma the profits it generated for the next twelve months in addition to maintenance. She couldn't afford to lose bookings, just because Pia wanted to stay close to her new home.

'I guess you can stay again tomorrow night,' said Emma. 'If you really want to. But what about your homework?'

'That's okay, Mum. I can get it off the school drive from Dad's laptop. Grandma's going to help me with it.'

A wave of sadness made Emma feel weak. She sank onto the bed.

'Okay, darling. You have a wonderful time. I'll see you on Monday morning but ring if you need anything.'

She put down the phone and stared out the window at the gum trees, wondering how she was going to get through the weekend alone. A couple of white cockatoos flew out of a tree branch and landed on her fence. Their yellow crests shot up and flared like an open hand as they bent down and began gouging at the fence with jagged beaks. Emma launched herself off the bed and rapped her knuckles on the window. They looked up at her nonchalantly, their beady eyes staring with disdain.

'Go away, you pesky birds.' Emma flapped her hand at them, then fell back on the bed, suddenly exhausted. She needed to unpack boxes that had been cluttering up the hallway for weeks but she didn't have the energy. Maybe she'd ring Marlee. Tell her she'd been wrong about Pia being in the car. Tell her about Linda Perkins' email. But the gloom she'd felt since the failed shopping trip with Marlee seemed to nail her to the bed. She hated shopping. Those mirrors made her look enormous and pale. She thought about the last dress she'd tried on, a deep orange chiffon concoction with ruffles at the cuffs. The boutique owner had handed it through the crack in the changing room door just as Emma had given up on all the other dresses.

'Just put it on and come out and I'll give you my honest opinion,' Marlee said, when Emma complained about the style.

Emma zipped it up and looked at herself in dismay before she stepped out into the shop. Marlee and the boutique owner both had their arms crossed.

'Wow!' said Marlee, raising her eyebrows.

'Fabulous!' said the shop owner, her black designer outfit clinging elegantly to her tiny figure. 'Just divine.'

'I look like a lobster.'

'No you don't!' said Marlee.

'I absolutely do,' said Emma clasping her fingers into an imitation of pincers and letting the ruffles fall over her hands.

'You're a perfect catch then,' said Marlee.

'I'm a large seafood platter.'

'Look on the bright side,' said Marlee. 'Someone will pay a lot of money to crack you open and suck on your sweet bits.' They both laughed, as the boutique owner smiled uncertainly.

'Yeah, you're right. It's hideous. Let's go get some ginger tea at the Tea Pavilion,' said Marlee. 'The thought of seafood is making me nauseous.'

Now, as Emma smiled to herself at the thought, the phone began buzzing in her hand. To her surprise, Clementine's name flashed onto the screen.

'Hello?'

'Hi, Emma, it's Clem.'

'Hi…' Emma wasn't sure what else to say. The idea that Clementine might actually call her up again wasn't something she'd thought possible.

'I was wondering what you're doing tonight,' said Clementine.

'Oh. Well, I'm not doing anything really. I'm just at home on my own. Rosie is at her dad's place.'

'Excellent! Want to come see a band with me?'

'Tonight?' The idea made her feel giddy.

'Of course tonight. It's a Spanish band. They're here touring. A kind of mix of flamenco and a bit of rock. I heard them in Hanover once. They're quite big in Europe.'

'Alright,' said Emma. She hesitated. 'Clem – could I see if Marlee wants to come too? She might not be free, but it's the sort of thing I think she'd like.' Well, at least it was before she was feeling so sick. Still, Marlee would make her feel safer in Clementine's company. What if Clementine had expectations?

'Sure. How about I meet you guys at the pub. They're on at The Emperor. About eight?'

'Okay.' Emma got off the phone, her heart beating with excitement. When she'd said goodbye to Clementine last time, she'd felt awkward, not knowing what to say when the car had pulled to a stop out the front of the house. But Clementine had been breezy, as if the whole thing at the top of the mountain had never happened. It had been a relief that she'd made it so easy, but inexplicably Emma had also felt an adolescent sense of rejection. She couldn't stop thinking about the kiss. A couple of times the memory had caught her so unexpectedly, she found herself blushing. It gave her a secret thrill. Did she *really* do it? Then she would worry – did that mean she was a lesbian? It didn't make sense. She'd never even looked twice at a woman before that very moment in the car with Clementine. She was completely and utterly straight. Not even slightly bisexual.

But why had she liked the kiss so much? Perhaps it was because she hadn't been kissed for so long. Phillip hardly ever kissed her properly. She remembered how much she used to like kissing boys, then after she met Phillip and they'd been together for a few years, kissing seemed to have fallen away. No, that wasn't true. Emma had stopped letting Phillip kiss her. His kisses were only ever a signal that he wanted sex and they were so slobbery and insistent. Which left only sex. So primordial. All that grunting and shunting and panting – often it just seemed plain silly. But maybe kissing and sex wouldn't always be so disappointing. Maybe it was just how it was with Phillip.

She sighed, looking around at all the work she needed to do to set up the cottage. But the boxes weren't going anywhere. She picked up the phone and dialled Marlee's number, but it went to voicemail. She hung up and tapped out a text message, asking Marlee if she wanted to join her and Clementine at the pub.

CHAPTER SEVENTEEN

HARRIET

'Scarlett's arriving at three o'clock on Friday,' said Harriet as she pressed the button on her keys to unlock her car.

Ben was shoving a bag of garbage down into the bin behind the front fence. It was a small bag. He mustn't be eating at home. When he didn't answer, Harriet went on.

'I'll be in court. You'll need to pick her up.'

'Of course,' said Ben. 'I'll move a couple of things around. I can't wait to see her.'

He looked as if he wanted to say something else. Harriet waited.

'We need to do something about the house, Harriet. What if I organise a couple of real estate agents to come and do a valuation? It's time we thought about sorting things out.'

'Scarlett hardly needs the family home ripped out from underneath her this week, Ben. She hasn't even been told that we're separated! For goodness sake, you're not thinking straight. She needs somewhere to live when she starts university – the granny flat was supposed to be for *her*!' Harriet felt the unfairness of the situation folding in on her.

This house, and Scarlett in the granny flat, that was what they'd talked about, planned for. It was part of their future life together. Scarlett would study arts/law at University of Tasmania. She'd still be at home, but she'd have the independence of her own place in the granny flat. She could get work experience with Harriet. It was what they'd both imagined their family journey would be, until Ben decided at some indeterminate time that he wanted to travel a different road. One that had diverted from hers when she hadn't been paying attention. He was pulling all their plans apart over a tiny slip road that wasn't even signposted.

'Harriet, please.' He said it calmly, as if he were pacifying a toddler having a tantrum. How dare he look so superior?

She squared her shoulders, straightening her posture. 'Don't patronise me, Ben. I am perfectly aware that at some time in the future we will need to consider dividing our joint assets. I assume you don't want to live here alone, in which case I will buy you out. You can have the beach house and we can do a reconciliation of the rest. But I'd like to delay that discussion until we have given Scarlett a chance to accept this new… situation.'

Harriet opened her car door, then paused. She needed to keep things steady, just until she'd had a chance to let Scarlett settle back in. Plus, there was still a small chance that Ben would change his mind when Scarlett came home. Scarlett was like the glue in the family – something they could jointly focus on. A combined project that unified them.

'I imagine it might be nice for Scarlett if we all had dinner together on Friday evening. Is that alright with you? I know Clementine is free,' said Harriet.

'Of course. What about I book the Lake House for six o'clock? She's probably missed Tasmanian seafood. Even with jetlag she should still manage to stay awake for that.'

Harriet felt a blade of sorrow. She stamped it down.

'Fine.'

She got into the car and slammed the door. The Lake House. The place Ben had taken her when he was trying to convince her that she should keep the pregnancy, nineteen years ago. That the baby would be the making of them. It would change their lives for the better and cement their love for each other. How could he stand there and talk about selling their marital home to end their life together and then pretend he didn't remember the significance of that place? He must have suggested the Lake House on purpose. Just to spite her. Well, she would *not* be giving him the satisfaction of showing him that he could hurt her. She was fine. She was always fine. It was just practice. You got better at it the more you were hurt. It started out being quite difficult – when you first encompassed real pain and were shocked at what another human could do to you. When you found out that it was possible to want to rip off your own skin with disgust. But if you held tight and strong and absolutely rigid, if you became like an iron pillar, you could hold it up. And after a while, the weight of it started feeling like a part of you, until most days you didn't notice it too much. Some days you felt almost normal.

She backed out of the driveway. Friday was several days away. She would just do one day at a time. Today she was going to the gym then using the weekend quiet of the office to focus on writing a detailed advice for a new brief she'd received last week.

Harriet's phone rang. *Mary Andrews* flashed onto the dashboard screen and Harriet cringed. Her mother had perfect timing, as ever. She put the call on speaker.

'Hello, Mother.'

'Why haven't you been in to see me, Harriet? I've finished all those talking books. It's torture in this place with nothing to do.' Her mother's voice was slow and scratchy, but fundamentally the same – as unhappy and critical as it had ever been. The nursing home was not to her taste. The food was terrible. The staff were horrible. They even had men giving her showers. All of it was *completely* unacceptable. Harriet found herself in agreement with the last issue – there was something irksome about the idea of having a young man hand her mother the soap as he watched over the naked indignity of her ageing body. As if it wasn't bad enough that male doctors had spent so many generations dictating how women's bodies would be poked and prodded and fixed and stitched – now they were getting in their showers too.

'I'm busy, Mother. I have a career. One that you insisted on because you never had the opportunity, remember? I'll be in next week, as usual.'

Her mother sniffed. 'That girl came to see me yesterday. She's got black hair now. What happened to it?'

'I assume you're talking about Clementine, Mother. Your granddaughter. She dyed it.'

'Well, it looked better before. What sort of person cuts off nice blond hair like that? Anyway, she showed me some of her art on the iPad. It's terrible.'

Harriet wondered which particular works Clementine had been showing off. It probably didn't matter. Her mother would think all of it was terrible. There were no still-life pears or impressionist landscapes in Clementine's repertoire.

'That's not a nice thing to say about your own granddaughter's work, Mother. She's very famous these days. People pay a lot of money for her work.'

'Funny sort of work if you ask me. You paid a king's ransom for her to go to that ghastly school full of social climbers, and now look how she's repaid you. *Painting* for a living.'

Harriet was expected to say something that would validate her mother's disappointment at Clementine's existence. She was tired of the game. She looked in the rear vision mirror and changed lanes.

Her mother kept talking. 'Don't know how she possibly got so famous with those ugly things she paints. But I saw her on television *twice* last week. That's how I knew she was in Tasmania. The ladies here didn't believe she was my granddaughter, so I sent her a message on the Facebook to tell her to come in. Now they believe me.' Her mother sniffed again and paused, considering the social coup she'd pulled off. 'Not that she stayed very long. Said she had to go to a meeting with a man about some big art festival coming up. What was she on about?'

'I assume it's the Dark Mofo festival in June, Mother,' sighed Harriet. 'They put all sorts of subversive artworks around the city and throw in a few pagan rituals and so on.'

'What sort of rituals?'

'Oh, I don't know. A nude ocean swim at dawn. That sort of thing.'

'It's freezing in June. What idiot thought of that?'

'Who knows?' said Harriet, tiredly. 'I need to go, Mother.'

'Well I need some more boiled sweets next time you come in. And some good fruit. They only have apples and bananas in the bowls here, and they're old.'

'Alright.' Harriet felt a heavy exhaustion suddenly envelope her. And there was something else too – a bewildering mixture of sadness and surprise that her daughter and her mother had finally spent some time together without her having to orchestrate it. Her mother had had as little to do with Clementine as she possibly could since the day she was born. It was surprising that she'd gotten in touch with her at all.

Mary Andrews blamed Clementine, and her untimely birth, for Harriet's fall from grace at school. Harriet had been allowed to stay on at Denham House when it became obvious she was pregnant, but it had taken some lobbying. She was going to be close to her due date at graduation, and her mother had written scathing letters to the principal, threatening all sorts of bizarre actions if the school didn't let her finish. It had been a risky tactic, since Harriet had been the holder of a full scholarship, and her mother was a single and virtually penniless seamstress. And to be fair to the principal, on the face of it, it had been difficult to refute the school's claim that she had brought their reputation into disrepute by becoming pregnant, thus breaching the terms of her scholarship.

But Mary had a way with words and Harriet had also had the support of several teachers. It had helped that the headmaster had been a forward-thinking man who understood that in modern times, girls needed education more than ever and that Denham House may eventually benefit, if Harriet would promise to continue on to university and remember where she had been given her start. She was, after all, their brightest student in a decade. A 'once-in-a-generation' brain, as her English teacher had put it. In the end, they had let her stay. The headmaster had called her into his office and made her promise that she would continue to study hard and do something extraordinary with the education they had afforded her, so that she might redeem their good name. Harriet had been grateful.

But her mother had never gotten over the fact that she hadn't been awarded the dux of the school. The award was rightfully hers, given her near perfect results in all subjects. But having Harriet's name on the Honour Board for generations to come was one step too far for a school turning out bright young ladies for the next generation. It was 1975 after all, and the powers-that-be still expected purity along with all that shining brightness.

Harriet's swollen belly was a rude reminder to the conservative parent body, pockets lined discreetly with old money, that Harriet wasn't one of them. She was just a girl from the wrong side of the tracks whose education they had generously offered to support through their school endowment fund, and who had squandered a rare privilege. Silly little *slut*. They would enunciate the word carefully, the 't' as sharp as a pistol shot. It was testament to their good breeding, never mind that they themselves may originally have descended from convicts.

Still, they said to each other, *the situation was only to be expected. There was no father to be seen and the mother was a bra-burning shrew.*

A more objective observer, thought Harriet, might have described her background as one of 'genteel poverty'. Despite the overgrown garden and the cracked concrete balcony on their tiny, mould-filled bungalow that was constantly threatening to fall away from the house, inside the shelves were filled with books of poetry and plays by Shakespeare and classic novels by Tolstoy, Virginia Woolf and Miles Franklin. Her mother may have been bitter and unstable, but she was also fiercely intelligent and insistent that her daughter would receive the university education she herself had always coveted.

Harriet ended the call to her mother, promising she would bring grapes, kiwi fruit and new audiobooks next week. She had a headache. Her mother's calls brought one on every time.

CHAPTER EIGHTEEN

MARLEE

Marlee read Emma's text message. She felt the twinge of anxiety in her gut. Or maybe it was the morning sickness again – although inexplicably it seemed more prone to appearing in the afternoon. An evening at the pub with Clementine Andrews and Emma. Did she feel like going? Her brain was thick with exhaustion and having trouble taking hold of the idea. She pictured the idea floating on a lily leaf into the middle of a murky pond, beyond reach. What she really wanted was a drink. A crisp glass of Sauvignon Blanc with a hint of citrus and undertones of a sunny warm day when her life hadn't been so complicated. Her hand went to her stomach and rested there. Was it possible the baby would be alright? In the last few days she'd allowed herself to feel a tug of excitement every time she passed a person pushing a pram in the street. That could be *her* at Christmas time.

The pub, even if she did have to stick to drinking water, might stop her thinking about how she was going to manage to keep the baby and still keep her job working with Ben. He was hardly going to want a baby at his stage of life.

She picked up the phone and sent a return text.

The band sounds good. Pick me up?

*

As Emma drove them towards the city, Marlee kept putting her hand on her stomach, then taking it away as soon as she realised it was there. It seemed to be an instinctive thing, the hovering hand. She had another appointment with Anna-Beth in a couple of days and needed to make up her mind. She'd been rolling the idea of a termination around in her head. She wasn't exactly sure of the laws in Tasmania about abortion, but there was always a loophole for doctors to take into account the mother's mental state, wasn't there? She was definitely freaked out. There must be a diagnosable condition in there somewhere, however much Emma insisted she was perfect mother material.

Although, as the days had passed Marlee had started letting herself believe that the tests would come back and show that the baby was healthy. And now, when she looked at her naked reflection in the mirror and imagined her belly expanding, shards of excitement escaped from inside the tightly locked box that housed her heart. But the hope was laced with fear. A proper little human to grow and look after, guide and nurture. What if she turned out to be a hopeless parent? What if the baby grew up and did drugs or joined a cult that offered animal sacrifices to the devil? There were plenty of ways your kids could go off the rails if you didn't pay attention.

But along with a new baby, she'd need a new job. It wasn't like Ben had asked for this to happen. She knew it would be a disaster if she tried to work in the same place as the baby's father, whilst pretending he wasn't the baby's father. That was taking devious workplace politics a step too far.

And it wasn't fair to thrust fatherhood on him again without giving him a choice. She'd thought about telling him – but she wasn't convinced she was ready to hear his opinion about it just yet. He did have rights, after all. She wasn't sure how she felt herself. And it was her body, *her* life that was on the line. She'd never allowed herself to indulge the idea of having children before – why torture herself with something that she'd thought impossible? Especially because she didn't think she'd be a very good mother. Emma was much better suited to caring about things like screen-time and vegetables.

Marlee took her hand away from her stomach and picked up her hand bag as Emma pulled into a shadowy parking lot at the rear of an office building. As they neared the pub, the promising rumble of a good crowd spilled out onto the street. Marlee looked across to the lights of the wharves and noticed the boats bobbing prettily in the light of the full moon. She pulled open the door and they edged their way through the crowd to the bar.

'I don't know how we're supposed to find Clementine in this crowd.' Emma was frowning. 'I'll buy us a drink so we don't look out of place. What do you want?'

Marlee smiled. Emma looked so sweet and innocent in her mummy outfit of dark blue jeans and ballet flats with a dark green cardigan and tiny pink earrings. With her hair in a ponytail, she looked like she'd just stepped out of an ad for a cupcake packet mix.

'I'll have a lime and soda,' said Marlee.

'Right. Just when I finally get a social life you have to give up drinking,' said Emma, with a sudden grin.

The barman appeared in front of Emma. 'Umm, I'm not sure what we want. Maybe two lime and sodas please?' She turned back to Marlee.

'I'll have one to keep you company.'

The barman handed Emma the drinks and she passed one to Marlee. 'Let's go over there and see if we can find a table where it's not so noisy.' She pointed to the back of the pub where there were some scattered armchairs, fully occupied as far as Marlee could see.

'Hello!'

Clementine appeared at Marlee's shoulder. She was dressed in tight black pants and a rather fabulous red leather jacket over a black t-shirt. Her huge brown eyes were twinkling and she gave Emma a kiss on the cheek and then stood on tiptoe and gave Marlee one too.

Marlee looked up as a tall man emerged from the crowd at Clementine's side. She felt a disorienting flash of recognition. Jonathan Brownley turned towards her and his eyes widened briefly.

'Marleen. Hello.'

'Hello,' said Marlee, although she wasn't sure if the word had been voiced, or if it had remained in her head.

'Hello, Jonathan. I didn't know you were coming,' said Emma.

'Sorry to drag your boss along, Emma. I promise I won't let him spoil our fun. But it's just *so* not okay for a hot single guy to be at home checking emails on a Saturday night.' Clementine had a provocative gleam in her eye.

Marlee wondered what she was trying to achieve. She watched Jonathan lean down through the noise and say something to Emma. She smiled uncertainly. Then he turned and caught Marlee's eye again.

The wavy blond hair, the chiselled features, the muscular body in jeans and an open-neck shirt – twenty-five years seemed only to have enhanced his looks. Her breath felt shallow, ragged. She watched as Clementine tugged at his arm and gestured towards the bar, whispering something in his ear as he bent down once again. He tensed his face, as if he didn't understand what she was saying then shook his head. *No.* The nausea returned like an old arch-rival then. Marlee turned and pushed her way through the crowd towards the toilet, letting the sweat and energy and noise of the crowd and the music swallow her whole.

*

Emma watched Marlee disappear into the crowd. The way she'd just taken off, without warning, must mean she needed to be sick.

Pregnancy could be so awful. She turned back to Clementine and Jonathan.

'She hasn't been feeling well.'

Jonathan nodded then leaned down so he could be heard. 'How's Rosie getting along?'

'Good, thanks.' She looked towards Clementine, avoiding eye contact with Jonathan in case he could mind-read and guess at her traitorous thoughts about him and Tessa.

'What's he like as a boss, Emma?' asked Clementine, winking at Jonathan.

'Oh, good. Good.' Emma felt herself going red and she looked towards the rear of the pub, wondering when Marlee was coming back. When she turned her head back, Jonathan was looking at her intently. She felt her heart skipping. He was standing so close and was tall and intimidating in his jeans and a shirt that hugged all of his toned and muscled bits. Emma averted her eyes. It really wasn't a positive thing, to be so handsome and body perfect. It made people jumpy.

She caught Clementine's gaze then. She had a half smile on her lips, and Emma realised that the sick feeling in her stomach wasn't to do with Jon Brownley standing too close. It was Clementine, bringing him here, compounding her guilt and uncertainty over the whole Tessa thing on purpose. She wasn't used to being alone with Jonathan. She barely ever had cause to be in the same room as him at school, unless it was a whole staff meeting, and then she'd keep her head down and avoid drawing attention to herself.

Emma jumped as Jonathan leaned towards her and touched her arm.

'Do you know the band Clementine's brought us here for?'

'No, no. Clementine just suggested we come along.'

Jonathan nodded. 'I feel a bit out of place, to be honest. Give me a glass of red wine and a good murder mystery on the TV and I'm a pig in mud.'

Emma frowned.

'Not a murder mystery type yourself?' He smiled at Emma as if he was actually interested in the answer. She felt off balance.

'I am actually. The English ones anyway. *Inspector Lynley* and *Vera.*'

He smiled. 'Me too.'

Marlee suddenly appeared at her side out of nowhere. She leaned in to Emma and whispered, 'Sorry, I've gotta go. Not feeling too good.'

'I'll drive you home.'

'No, no you stay here. I'll get a cab.' Marlee gave them a quick, distracted wave and turned towards the door. Emma watched her tumbling russet red curls disappearing as she edged her way expertly through the crowd. She felt as if her lifeboat had just untethered itself and floated out to sea. Drips of sweat under her bra line began trickling down her stomach. She leaned down and took a careful sip of her drink, focussing on her straw. Jonathan began to speak again and just as he leaned down, a roar went up from the crowd and a crashing drum solo exploded from the stage in front of them. The electric guitar began, loud and long, and Emma had never been so happy in all her life to hear such a terrible noise.

CHAPTER NINETEEN

EMMA

Why was it assumed that Emma's job left time enough to cover everyone else's role when they were sick? She really didn't want to be anywhere near the headmaster at the moment, yet here she was, sitting outside his office door. She could barely look at him without feeling guilty. Saturday night had been excruciating. He was so friendly. So *nice*. How could she report him to police now? But how could she live with her conscience any more if she didn't? Voicing her suspicions had given them a form, so now they were ever-present, like an irksome neighbour who you tried to avoid, but who was always right there at the edge of your thoughts when you went out to check your mailbox.

She looked at the mail tray in front of her. Each document had been neatly marked in pencil at the top right-hand corner, noting where Tina, the headmaster's usual secretary, wanted it to be filed or sent to. She looked longingly at the bin and wondered if Tina would be back tomorrow.

She picked up the first document and flicked through it, looking up to ensure that Dr Brownley's office door was still closed. It was a completed application form from a prospective student. Vienna Loveday. Goodness. Where did people come up with these names? Perhaps Vienna's mother had lived in Austria. Or maybe the girl had been conceived there. Poor child. Imagine if that was it – living, breathing evidence that your parents had sex in an exotic place once, and for some reason assumed you'd like to be reminded of it for the rest of your life.

Emma rifled through the paperwork she'd already collected for the enrolments office and put Vienna's application in behind one for Arabella Longford-Spratt, and went back to the pile.

The next document was a letter to Dr Brownley informing him he'd been shortlisted for another national leadership in teaching award and that the winner would be judged next month. Emma read through it, wondering who had nominated him. Everyone seemed to worship at the altar of Jonathan Brownley. Apparently, he'd turned the school around since taking on the head's role five years earlier, when it had been floundering in the academic league tables. Now the waiting list was long again. You had to put your daughter's name down before she started primary school if you wanted a spot at the high school.

Phillip had once told her that Dr Brownley had to be more like a CEO of a multi-million-dollar company than an educator. He'd been trying to explain to Emma why the headmaster wouldn't be interested in introducing meditation into the curriculum. In Phillip's view, the fact that it was unlikely to have an impact on the bottom line of his business was a critical factor. Emma had been annoyed at his dismissal of her idea, but she'd also found herself thinking about the school in a different light. Five hundred and twenty students at nearly $30,000 a year – almost double that if they were boarders. It was a lot of money. Parents these days expected a return on their investment, according to Phillip.

She filed the letter and turned back to the desk and began flicking through the rest of the pile.

Emma jumped as Dr Brownley's door opened. He walked towards the filing cabinet where she was standing.

'Emma, thanks for filling in today.'

'Oh, sure.'

'I have Moira Ryan popping in to discuss something shortly. Would you mind letting her know that I need to reschedule unless she wants to wait for half an hour? She's not answering her extension and she's not great at checking her emails so she probably won't have got my message.'

'Sure. Of course.'

He held eye contact and Emma's heart began beating madly.

'I just need to duck down to the drama studio to introduce the senior girls' soiree for some guests,' he said.

She tried to breathe normally.

'Okay.'

'Are you alright, Emma?'

'I'm fine.'

'Really?'

'Absolutely.' Emma's hand trembled and she dropped the letter she'd been holding. They both dipped down to get it at the same time and she grabbed at it awkwardly.

'Sorry,' she mumbled.

She looked away and started fiddling with the papers on her desk, but felt his eyes on her.

'Right, well I'll be back soon.'

Emma let her breath out as the door closed. She really needed Tina to get better by tomorrow. It felt awful being near him. Traitorous. Everyone around here would hate her if she reported him. And she didn't have any hard evidence anyway. Not really. *It's my gut instinct, Officer. My friend Tessa said she'd bought this new lacy underwear and she was going to show it to him. Yes, that very afternoon! How silly that it slipped my mind.*

Tessa had been in love. She and Jonathan had seemed to share a secret musical language when they played together for the class. She was sure it wasn't just her hippocampus making false memories.

She stared at the filing pile blankly and wondered if she was going mad. Phillip had always told her she was too flighty. Maybe this was the sort of thing he meant.

A creaking 'click' made Emma jump again. A hunched figure, small and swathed in floral, with a wispy grey bun piled on top of her head, hobbled through the office door. Moira Ryan must have been nearly ninety by now, but if anyone had dared to ask her age, she would have fixed a charming smile on her wizened little face and changed the subject. She'd been a school institution for sixty-three years. Teacher. Librarian. House Mistress. Archive Manager. She'd done it all. If anyone needed to know something about the history of Denham House, Moira was their library.

'Hello, Moira,' said Emma.

'Hello, dear. I'm here to see Dr Brownley about a project I'm doing in the archives.'

'Oh Moira, I'm sorry but he's had to pop out but he said if you'd like to wait, you're welcome. He'll be about half an hour though.'

'What about I get us a cup of tea then, dear,' said Moira, heading towards the tiny recessed kitchen area adjacent to the headmaster's office. Emma stifled a smile as Moira began tidying the bench and then reached underneath to pull out a well-worn silver teapot. Moira's constant tea-sipping was part of her legend.

'That would be lovely,' said Emma, moving her half-full tea cup and packet of Tim Tams behind the filing tray. She picked up the rest of the filing pile and let the rising bellow of the kettle settle her nerves.

'How have you been, Moira?'

'Can't complain, dear. I have had a lovely time sorting through some old documents this week. From some of the classes during the 1920s. I'm putting together a retrospective for the school's 120th birthday.'

'Gosh, there must be some amazing stories and photographs,' said Emma.

'I'll get to your class soon, dear. The school uniform you girls wore was one of my favourites. I was so sad when they changed it in 1995.'

'Oh, you're making me feel ancient, Moira.'

'Piffle, Emma. It feels like yesterday. You're still young and beautiful.'

Emma felt herself redden. Then a thought struck her.

'Moira, do you remember much about when Tessa Terrano died?'

Moira fussed around at the tea bench a while longer, and Emma wondered if she had heard her. After a minute she walked towards Emma carrying two perfectly balanced mugs. Hunched over, her face fell squarely between the mugs, so that she was peering through them as if the teacups were a steering wheel and she was carefully driving them home. She lowered one onto Emma's desk.

'Well, what a question. Of course I do, Emma. I remember how very upset you were, having your lovely friend taken away so cruelly. But accidents happen. Life goes on.'

Emma felt a sadness in the words, but also a hint of evasion in the way Moira turned without looking at her. Moira was no fool. The old-lady act hid a shrewd operator for whom Denham House was husband, children and home.

'Did the police ever suspect that it wasn't just a fall?'

Moira took her cup of tea and shuffled across the room like an ageing hobbit. She took her time, settling into one of the chairs then looked up at Emma with twinkling eyes.

'There was talk, my dear, but it was only talk. She just fell. It was a shame the builder's fences weren't more secure. People conjured up stories because they couldn't work out why she would go inside the building zone. But it was just curiosity. Tessa was a curious sort of girl.'

'I've never really believed that. The trench was obvious – you could see it from outside the fenced area. I... I've always wondered if she was pushed. I've been thinking about it lately with our reunion coming up. I just think there was more to it.'

'Dragging up old pain will get you nowhere, Emma. That's in the past and that's where it should stay. Nobody around here coped well with that incident,' Moira's eyes flicked almost imperceptibly to the headmaster's office door, 'and nobody needs it dragged up again now.'

Emma caught a faint wind of a warning in her voice.

Moira picked up a copy of last month's Denham House Gazette and began flicking through the thick, glossy pages, closing the conversation like an iron gate.

Emma sighed. She put the letter into the filing cabinet in the appropriate folder, then shut the drawer too loudly and sank back into her seat.

She picked at her fingernail and wondered why Moira felt so sure about it being an accident, and why any sane person would continue down this path of madness when they had plenty of other issues to keep them busy. Like what was she going to have for dinner for example?

Now it was just the two of them it was hard to motivate herself to cook. She could defrost some bolognese sauce again. That would keep Rosie happy. Although all those carbs... she really should try to lose some weight before her school reunion. Not that she would go. She had nothing to wear and it would be too humiliating anyway after the email fiasco. Marlee's efforts to take her dress shopping for the reunion had been half-hearted due to her feeling so sick. They'd given up after the lobster dress. But she couldn't wear her blue floral dress – she'd worn it to every posh event she'd had for the last five years and she just didn't feel good in it any more. But that was the thing about stretchy dresses, there was no excuse to get rid of them because they always fitted you.

Phillip never seemed to notice what she wore, so she'd never worried about her weight fluctuation too much before. But even if it did still fit her, she didn't want to be the only lumpy, unglamorous one among the women who would be coming back to Hobart for the reunion. No doubt they'd all be wearing the latest fashions.

Moira looked up from the Gazette. 'How are you and Rosie getting along in that dear little cottage, Emma?'

Emma took a sip of tea while she thought about how to reply. 'It's okay. The heaters are ancient so I've been relying on the fireplace but I think they're going to renovate it in the Christmas holidays so hopefully they'll put in a heating unit that actually works.'

'Well it hasn't had much done to it over the years. When Dr Brownley lived there as a young lad, he probably had the very same complaints. A good spruce up is overdue I'd say.'

Emma froze, her teacup half way to her mouth. 'What did you say, Moira?'

'What do you mean, dear?'

'Dr Brownley, having the cottage…'

'Yes, he lived there for quite a time. I think he shared it with Mr Carruthers at some stage – the young photography and art teacher. Don't you remember? He didn't last long though. Didn't take to the traditions.'

'Oh.'

Emma wasn't about to get into the conversation about some of the school's eccentric traditions. She needed to think. She felt her mind swirling with the possibilities of Moira's revelation.

'Moira, when would he have lived in the cottage?'

Moira gave her a curious look and pursed her lips.

'I'm just interested in finding out the history of the cottage… since it's our new home,' urged Emma.

'Well, I guess he lived there when he first got here. It's not the top pick of the cottages, as you know. It's so small and a bit of a hike to the main buildings. So I think it was his very first few years at the school. They've always gotten the best teachers from around the place to come to the school by offering free accommodation as part of the package. But they tended to put the young teachers down that way, in either the Hellebore or the Tulip cottage.'

Emma felt a sick, cold comprehension dawning as the final piece of the faded, old jigsaw puzzle slotted neatly into place. *A naked photograph of Tessa taken in the week she died, found in the same cottage that Jon Brownley had lived in at that exact time.*

It wasn't coincidence, it was serious new evidence. Tessa's death would surely be re-opened if Emma took it to the police. Would they prosecute her for not coming forward earlier? Oh God, she couldn't go to jail. Marlee might know what to do. But she had to leave Marlee out of it. Marlee didn't need the extra stress right now.

She looked over at Moira, propped up in her chair like a tiny pillar of ancient history. An idea came to her. There might be an old file about Tessa's death. There *must* be one. It was a big thing in the life of the school. A huge catastrophe. There must have been lots of correspondence and statements taken and risk assessments performed. If she could find it, she could see what sort of investigation had been done, and she might be able to put her mind at rest about Dr Brownley. Maybe the police had already gone over his every movement.

'Moira, I'm doing some research for our school reunion. It's on in a couple of weeks. Do you have the key to the archives?' Emma felt her heart beat speed up a little, but she kept her gaze steady.

'Yes, dear.'

'Could I borrow it? I just need to get a few things from 1993.'

'What research are you doing, dear? Perhaps I can help.'

'No, it's fine. I just want to get the yearbook and photos of the major events that happened in our year. Thought I'd take the files back to the cottage tonight to see what I can come up with to give Leah. She's organising some memorabilia for everyone.'

'Alright, well pop in and see me later, dear. I'll take you through the archives and we can find what you need.'

'Thanks,' said Emma, turning back to her computer. Bugger. She stared bleakly at the screen. There was no way Moira would let her take the investigation file home. She'd have to sneak in when Moira wasn't there. She pictured herself slinking into the archives in an Angelina Jolie catsuit in the dead of night, then she shook the image from her head and adjusted the waistband of her pants. It wasn't a pretty thought.

CHAPTER TWENTY

EMMA

As Emma walked along the path to Moira's office, she wondered how Rosie was feeling. She'd seen her at lunch time, slumped on the grass under a tree with her eyes closed. She'd complained of a headache and of feeling sick. Emma was surprised she hadn't asked to go back to the cottage and lie down. She was probably enduring it because she had a double French class in the last two periods. It was Rosie's favourite subject and she excelled at it. Emma had hated languages at school and found Rosie's devotion to her French studies somewhat perplexing.

At the entry of the old cottage building that housed Moira's office, Emma peered through the screen door. Moira sat in an armchair in the corner of the room, her head drooped to one side. Intermittent gurgling snorts were coming from her half-open mouth. Emma wondered if she could find the key to the archives and get out the door again without waking her. She eased open the screen door and the loud squeak made Moira jump.

'Oh, Emma dear, you startled me. I must have dozed off. Don't tell anyone, will you, dear? They'll retire me if I'm not careful.' Her movements were slow, but as she pushed herself out of the chair, Emma noticed that her eyes gleamed with an iron intent.

'Of course not. I'm the same after lunch,' said Emma. 'Just wondering if I can get into the archives for those files for our class reunion?'

'Yes, now, let me get you the key.' Moira moved across to the desk and fumbled in the top drawer. She brought out a bunch of three keys on a ring and held them up. 'Would you like me to take you now, dear?'

'I can go on my own if you're busy.'

'Piffle. I'd love to help you.'

'That would be great,' said Emma flatly.

They set off across the grounds to a tiny old timber building surrounded by lavender bushes, which had once been the original schoolhouse. Now it was a kind of museum, although only open to those with special access privileges. Inside, old sepia-toned photographs of the school in its infancy lined the walls in dusty antique frames. She read the caption under the first photograph: *Miss Elliot, Miss Williams and students on a picnic at Wells Creek, 1897.* Two women in high-button-neck dresses and full skirts stood to the side of about a dozen teenage girls in similar outfits. In the background were picnic blankets and two horses tethered to a tree. Emma wondered how on earth they had traversed the rough Tasmanian bush in such unsuitable clothes.

'Over here, Emma,' said Moira. Down the far aisle, behind a row of old metal shelves, she was pointing to some boxes that were marked with the months and years that they related to. The sunlight streamed in from a small window and on the top shelf Emma could see that three of them were marked '1993'. Moira pulled a small stepladder from against the wall and motioned for Emma to carry it.

'I'll leave you here for a bit, dear. Just need to pop in and see Ms Given about some uniform orders.'

Emma couldn't believe her luck. 'Alright. Thanks, Moira'.

Emma dragged down the first box and in it she found documents from the Board of Education that looked like some sort of official register and copies of documents evidencing the registration of teachers. Underneath there was a yearbook and all sorts of correspondence that didn't look particularly interesting. She left it on the floor and pulled down a second box. There it was. Right on top.

Investigation into the Death of Tessa Terrano.

It was a thick hanging file, once belonging to a filing cabinet. She opened it. Dozens of documents were piled on top of each other and underneath were several photographs of the trench and the building site where Tessa had fallen. She flicked through the documents. There were letters to and from the building company about the failure of the fencing; insurance letters covering the school against potential liability in case the family took legal action and handwritten notes from various people. She stopped as she came to a typed document marked *Record of Investigation into Death.* It was an official looking paper marked with *Coroners Court* at the top. Emma scanned the page.

RECORD OF INVESTIGATION INTO DEATH
TESSA ESTELLA TERRANO
Report Date: 15 May, 1994

The deceased was an eighteen-year-old girl who attended Denham House School in Buckingham Road in Lenah Valley, Hobart, as a weekly boarding student. At approximately 4.51 p.m. on Thursday 25th November, 1993, the deceased was found at the bottom of a 3.5-metre-deep excavated trench that had been dug the previous day by an external building company, Telpinero & Linden, in preparation for pouring foundations for a new academic building at the school. The deceased was a senior student who attended the school and was just days from graduating. She was well-liked and a talented musician and singer. On the day in question the deceased was last seen at approximately 3.40 p.m. when she told other students

*in her after-school drama class celebration that she felt
unwell and was going to return to the school's boarding
house where she resided. Upon questioning from her teacher,
Ms Linda Telston, the deceased reported that she 'felt dizzy'
and somewhat 'foggy-headed' and thought she was 'coming
down with something'. Miss Telston suggested that she go to
the sick bay and 'check in' with the nursing sister on duty.
The deceased did not attend the sick bay, according to the
nurse on duty that day, Sister Peggy Drewry.*

*Subsequently, at approximately 4.45 p.m., the mother
of another senior student, a Ms Harriet Andrews, attended
at the school office to say that in the course of walking across
campus to fetch her daughter Clementine Andrews, who
she believed would be in the art room, she had seen a school
bag inside the high plastic barriers that formed the safety
fencing around the building site. Ms Andrews had noted
that at one point the barriers were slightly apart. Cognisant
of the 'keep out' signs, Ms Andrews then attended the office
and spoke with Miss Moira Ryan who was attending the
front office reception that day. She suggested that someone
should investigate why the bag was inside the barrier.
Approximately fifteen minutes later, Miss Ryan attended the
building site and went inside the barrier, where she noticed
the deceased body lying face up in the ditch. Miss Ryan
reported that the deceased's eyes appeared to be partially
open. Unable to render assistance due to the inaccessibility
of the deceased's location, Miss Ryan raised the alarm at
the office and called an ambulance. Ambulance and police
services attended the scene. The fire brigade also attended
due to the difficulty of reaching and rendering assistance
to the deceased. Miss Ryan reported that one teacher who
was walking near the office after she raised the alarm, Mr
Jonathan Brownley, risked his own safety by jumping into*

the hole to render assistance before the ambulance and fire brigade arrived. Mr Brownley attempted to resuscitate the student using CPR chest compressions. The deceased was, however, unresponsive and was later pronounced dead by ambulance officers at approximately 5.50 p.m.

Post mortem revealed a skull fracture and a serious neck injury, as per the medical examiner's report appended to this document, consistent with a fall from 3.5 metres. It appears that the deceased entered the prohibited area for some reason unknown, possibly out of curiosity. Due to a dizzy spell she may have suffered or due to reasons unknown, she fell and struck her head on one of the large rocks at the bottom of the hole. It was noted by police that her left shoelace was undone as were three of her shirt buttons beneath her tunic. There were no injuries on the deceased apart from those consistent with having been sustained in the fall. It was confirmed by the coroner that there were no indications on post-mortem that the deceased had engaged in any recent sexual activity. Her stomach contents revealed that she had not eaten on the day in question and this may have contributed to her reported feelings of dizziness. It was thought that the untied shoelace may have contributed to her tripping and falling. I am satisfied that a detailed police investigation has taken place into the deceased's death and that there are no suspicious circumstances.

Emma scanned the next paragraph, keeping one ear towards the door. It discussed inadequate fencing and made recommendations for future action and culpability of the building contractor. The words blurred. Only one thing stood out. Jon Brownley had been there, near the scene. He might have been with Marlee earlier, but he hadn't been with her when the body was found. She flicked over the pages. There was a draft statement by Moira Ryan for the Coroner, and some other documents to do with the court.

A post-it note with faded handwriting caught Marlee's eye. It was on the top of Moira's statement to the Coroner: *Michelle, this is a copy of the draft that I will fax to the police station. They are going to ring me about it tomorrow. Is this alright?*

Michelle… Emma wondered who she was. Then it came to her. Michelle Sharp. *Sharpy.* The headmistress of Denham House in 1993. A line at the bottom of the page of Moira's statement jumped out at her: *Mr Brownley was so upset he somehow got down into that hole and tried to give her CPR. It was a very deep trench. The fire brigade had to help him out as he couldn't get back up and he was very distressed when he was brought out.*

Emma was so caught up in reading the document, it took her a moment to register that a shadow had fallen across the boxes. A voice made her jump.

'Did you find what you wanted?' Moira was standing at the end of the aisle, blocking the light. Emma slammed the file shut but as she lifted it into the box, the Coroner's Report slipped out and landed face-up on the floorboards. Emma snatched it up and returned it to the file.

'Yes, thanks, Moira.'

She picked up the 1993 yearbook that was sitting on the top of the first box and held it aloft. 'Got it. Let me just put these away and I'll get out of your hair.'

Emma's heart was hammering. She climbed the stepladder and lifted the boxes back into place. When the final box was returned, she collapsed the stepladder and looked up. Moira's hands were clasped together and her eyes were alight with a peculiar, unblinking intensity. Then the old woman turned and motioned for Emma to walk ahead of her towards the door.

CHAPTER TWENTY-ONE

MARLEE

A taxi pulled up outside the winery and the driver wound down the window.

'Cab for Chadston?'

Ben nodded at him and opened the door for Marlee before walking around the cab to get in the other side.

'That went well.' Marlee smiled. She leaned forward and spoke to the driver. 'Salamanca Warehouse Apartments then on to Sandy Bay, please, driver.'

'Really well I thought. I'm looking forward to starting the project.' Ben grinned at her.

Marlee was pleased it was dark. His closeness was making her face warm and her heartbeat speed up.

'What was the wine like? You guys were drinking their awarded 2012 vintage the sommelier told me.'

'It was excellent. Your health kick is admirable in the face of such incredible plonk, Ms Maples.'

'Yeah, well, that's me. Admirable.'

'I would have joined you in a dry night but I couldn't let our biggest clients drink alone.' Ben's eyes twinkled at her.

'You have a spot of red wine on your shirt,' said Marlee, leaning towards him and touching his chest with her finger. The smell of Ben's aftershave gave her a warm, delicious tingle and she closed her eyes. Suddenly his lips were on hers, gently, then firmly. He brought his hand to her face then around into her hair, drew her towards him, their tongues meeting in an urgent frenzy. Marlee felt herself dissolving into him. Her hand traced the line of his chest, then his back. She pulled him closer, wondering if he would regret it this time. She knew she wouldn't.

Ben pulled back and looked at her seriously, his index finger resting under her chin. 'I've been wanting to do that every day since the first time it happened.' Then he leaned forward and kissed her again and every other thought was banished from Marlee's head.

Too quickly Marlee felt the car pull to a halt, and she realised they were at the waterfront beside the entry to her apartment. Ben looked at her longingly.

'My cousin is visiting from interstate. She's sleeping on the couch. And since the loft bedroom opens above the mezzanine… she'd hear every word we said.'

'I wasn't planning on saying much. I'd be as silent as a church mouse.'

'That sounds like no fun at all.' Marlee held his gaze.

'Driver, we might need to keep going to Sandy Bay, I think.' Ben raised his eyebrows in question.

Marlee let her hand graze over his crotch and grinned. 'That sounds like an excellent idea, Mr Chadston. The best you've had all day.'

*

Marlee pulled the corner of the blind aside and looked out onto the dew twinkling across the grass in the bright morning light. She could see straight up into the front window of Harriet Andrews' lounge room. She dropped it back into place, sat down at the kitchen table and drew the blanket up over her lap. She had eventually worked out how to turn on the heater in Ben's living room but it was still cold. She opened the issue of *Green* magazine that was lying on the table and began to flick through the pictures of beautiful modernist homes as she sipped her tea. She couldn't concentrate. Images of her love-making with Ben were playing like a soft porn video in her head – the sheen of his chest, the exquisite sensation of his lips on her nipples that were newly swollen by her pregnancy.

The thought of the baby jolted her back to reality. She still couldn't believe that her appointment with Anna-Beth the week before had gone so well.

'Great news, Marlee. Your CVS test has come back all clear. The baby looks perfect.'

Marlee had put her hand to her mouth and given a small squeak. 'Really?'

Anna-Beth gave her a warming smile. 'Yes, really. Are you feeling more settled about having the baby?'

'A little. Although on some days I still feel really unsure. It's a relief to know it looks healthy though.'

'How are you feeling generally?'

Marlee had sifted through the well of emotions. 'A bit terrified actually.'

'Would you like to know the sex? Sometimes a bit of knowledge can help with that.'

'Oh God! Really?'

'I can keep it secret if you prefer.'

'No, I want to know!'

'You're having a boy,' said Anna-Beth with a smile.

Tears began running down Marlee's face.

'Thank God for that!' she said, sobbing and laughing at the same time. 'Girls can get themselves into so much trouble.'

Since that thrilling moment last week, Marlee had felt the fractures in her heart piecing back together like a jigsaw. With each passing day she realised more clearly that her little baby boy was a gift. She couldn't believe she'd considered a termination. The idea now made her feel sick.

She had named the little boy Ned and in the bath the night before she'd whispered secrets to him. She felt a happiness taking hold, and now that the morning sickness had eased up, she felt physically better too. But there was no getting around the problem of how she was going to tell Ben. She didn't know what was going on between them. But after last night she thought it might be something special.

She looked down at her belly, covered by the t-shirt she'd found in the pile of clean washing in Ben's room. She'd thrown it over her head when she got out of bed. Her hand crept underneath it and rested on the firm, faint swell of the baby. Nobody else would notice yet, but she couldn't keep it a secret for too much longer. She needed to decide what to do. What if he didn't want it? What if he did?

She had closed the bedroom door to let Ben sleep on. But now she was stuck. Last night they'd had to tiptoe down the side of the house so as not to wake Harriet. But she couldn't risk walking out through Harriet's front garden in the daylight until Ben could go out and check that her car was gone. It wouldn't be right to flaunt Ben's sex life in front of Harriet – even if she had been a total cow the last time they'd met.

The door opened behind Marlee and she turned to see Ben coming out of the bedroom in his boxer shorts. His torso was lean and perfectly muscled.

He smiled at her and her stomach did a little flip. He leaned down into her neck and kissed it. 'Is that my favourite t-shirt you're wearing? Anything else under there?'

Marlee stood, lifting up the bottom of the t-shirt to show her knickers. 'My dress was far too uncomfortable for reading the papers in. Although…' she looked down at the magazine, 'no papers in yet. I had to stoop to a magazine.' She put her arms around his neck and pulled him into a kiss. His fingers dropped down her back and then inside her knickers as he pulled her close.

She could feel his erection pressing against her. He lifted her up, his biceps swelling briefly as he placed her gently on the kitchen bench top. Their heads were at the same height and she wrapped her legs around him. Maybe she didn't need to leave straight away. Another hour wouldn't matter. She'd text her cousin to move their coffee to a lunch date. A shot of pure lust ran through her as he dragged his finger down her arm. Marlee looked down at the slogan of his t-shirt that sat perkily across her breasts. *When I'm blue Papa Smurf makes me smile!*

'Hello, Papa Smurf,' whispered Marlee. 'I'm having very blue thoughts right now.'

'That t-shirt clashes with the rest of your outfit. I might need to take it off,' said Ben, as he lifted it up and put his mouth over her nipple. She leaned back, pulling his head in closer and groaned. He began kissing his way down her stomach.

The two sharp raps at the door were so quick, that before either of them had a chance to register what they were, there was a sound of a key in the lock and then a loud chime of inharmonious voices as the door swung open. A teenage girl in running gear stood in the centre of the room carrying a cake, aflame with candles. Fortunately, she didn't look towards the kitchen counter where Marlee had her legs locked around Ben. She dropped them and sat up straight as Ben swung around. Behind the girl, two other women walked in.

Happy birthday to you
Happy birthday to you
Happy…

The three of them looked across to the kitchen bench in unison, each with a different expression. A grin. A scowl. An open mouth. Ben grabbed at the blanket on the floor to cover the erect tent of his boxer shorts.

'A cake! Umm… great…' said Ben, wrapping the blanket around his waist like a towel as Marlee slid off the bench.

'Oh my God! Dad!' The girl put the cake down onto the table with a clatter and crossed her arms fiercely.

Well, hello, Scarlett, thought Marlee. The girl's bouncy, dark hair was pulled up into a high pony tail and the look of disgust on her elfin face made her look much younger than her eighteen years.

'Happy birthday, Ben. Morning, Marlee,' said Clementine. Her face was contorted with suppressed laughter.

Harriet stared icily at Marlee then walked back out the door.

Scarlett watched her mother leave. 'I can't believe you brought someone back *here*, Dad. That's disgusting!'

'Oh, leave it out, Scarlett,' said Clementine.

'Don't be such a bitch, Clementine!' Scarlett's face was mutinous. They watched as Clementine put a wrapped gift on the table. Then all four of them looked at the flaming cake next to it, now puddled with molten drops of wax from candles that had been alight too long. Clementine leaned over to the cake and blew them out.

'There, I did the honours for you, Ben. Might as well save the icing.'

'I can't believe you could ruin my birthday surprise so badly, Dad,' said Scarlett, her eyes shining.

'Oh, Scarlett… honey.'

Marlee wondered whether she should speak. What was the socially appropriate way to ask for an introduction when you were standing in your knickers? Neither Clementine or Ben seemed to notice that she was still there. She stepped forward slightly, angling to get around Ben in the direction of the bedroom.

'I, um, might just leave you to it.'

Scarlett recoiled and a look of revulsion flitted across her face.

'Gross! She's wearing the t-shirt I bought you in New York, Dad!'

She turned her head, so that her ponytail flipped across her slender back as she opened the door to leave.

'So much for the driving lesson you promised me this morning!' The door slammed behind her.

Marlee let out her breath.

Clementine shrugged her shoulders and ran her fingers through her hair. 'Anyone want some cake? I don't think Scarlett baked it, so it's probably edible.'

Marlee pulled down hard on the bottom of the t-shirt, hoping that she didn't look quite as pink as she felt. 'Umm, no thanks.' She turned to Ben. 'Sorry, I didn't realise it was your birthday.'

'I wouldn't be too concerned about it, Marlee,' said Clementine. 'From where I'm standing, it looks like you got him exactly what he wanted.' She laughed as she cut herself a huge piece of cream cake and started stuffing it in her mouth. 'Someone putting the kettle on?'

Nobody spoke. Clementine finished her mouthful and flopped onto the couch where she started flipping through the pages of the *Green* magazine. 'Anything of yours in here, Benzo?'

Ben ignored her and headed to the bedroom. Marlee followed.

'Well,' whispered Marlee. 'That was really awkward.'

Ben pulled on his jeans with his back to her.

'I'm really sorry about wearing the t-shirt, Ben.' Marlee wasn't feeling sorry, but it was something to say to fill the gaping silence.

'You'd better go, Marlee. I shouldn't have brought you back here. Scarlett shouldn't have seen us together.'

Marlee felt a jab of annoyance. 'She's an adult, Ben. I seriously—'

'Parenting is hard, Marlee. And it doesn't end just because she turned eighteen. Scarlett will always be my priority.'

'Always? I'm no expert on kids, but maybe it's not so bad that she sees you having a life too.'

'You're right,' said Ben. He sat down on the bed with a thud after zipping up his jeans. His head dropped into his hands. 'You're not an expert. I really need to go and make it up to her. I'll see you at work on Monday. And if you could just, well, not make it obvious when you leave through the garden.'

Marlee felt her chest constrict as he walked back out past Clementine to the front door. She called after him angrily. 'Sure, Ben, I'll just become invisible. No problem.'

He looked back at her and held her eyes for a few seconds. Then he shook his head and gently closed the door. Marlee pulled off the t-shirt and threw it on the floor, then pulled on her dress and zipped it up, tight across her belly. In the living area Clementine appeared to be engrossed in the magazine.

'Your sister's got Ben wrapped round her little finger,' said Marlee, flopping onto a chair.

'Yup. Don't worry about it.'

'Right. Sure.' Marlee stared out the far window into the neighbour's back garden, her hand sliding back and forth across her belly that protruded very slightly in the tight dress. The autumn leaves were brown and sparse on the trees now. When she turned back Clementine was watching her hand. Marlee snatched it away and felt herself flushing.

'What's going on between you and Ben?'

Clementine stared at her now, unflinching.

'Apart from him being such an arse-wipe just then?'

'The other night at the pub, Emma said you'd been feeling off-colour. Are you pregnant?'

Marlee put her elbows on the table and sunk her head into her hands. 'Shit.'

'You're pregnant by Ben?' Clementine's eyes were wide.

'Please don't tell him, Clementine. I wasn't sure about telling him before and I'm definitely not sure now that I know he's at Scarlett's beck and call and doesn't seem to give a toss about me.' Marlee looked up at Clementine's enormous velvet-brown eyes.

'Please, Clem?'

'Holy shit.' Clementine stared openly then she shook her head like a puppy, as if getting rid of excess water clinging to her coat after a swim. 'You'd have to be mad to push out a sprog at our age.'

'Gee, thanks,' said Marlee. 'And I haven't decided how to tell him yet. So just keep quiet about it.'

Clementine cut another hunk out of the cake. She pulled the slice out slowly, and cocked her head to look at it, as if the cake was a particularly interesting fossil she'd just unearthed. Then she shoved most of the piece into her mouth.

'Clementine?' said Marlee.

Clementine looked up as she chewed. 'Mum's the word,' she mumbled through her mouthful, then she stood up and hooted with laughter. 'God I'm funny!' Cake crumbs sprayed across the table and down the front of Marlee's dress, landing like ants in her cleavage.

Marlee gave her an icy glare.

'Seriously, Marlee,' said Clementine tapping the side of her button nose with unrestrained glee, '*Mum's* the word!'

CHAPTER TWENTY-TWO

HARRIET

'Scarlett, get up!' Harriet stood in the doorway of her daughter's bedroom, fuming. 'I told you I'd be back at ten to take you driving! If you want to pass the driving test you'd better be dressed and in the car in five minutes. I don't have all day.'

She walked over to the curtains and jerked them wide open. The sun's rays streamed across the bed and Scarlett screwed up her face and yelled, as if Harriet had thrown cold water on her face.

'Mum!'

Harriet walked out, leaving the door wide open. Scarlett had been home for two weeks now and she was getting sick of the excuses. Everyone else's children went out and got their licence at sixteen or seventeen. Ben had pandered too much to Scarlett, driving her everywhere and not insisting she face her fear of getting behind the wheel. Well, Harriet wasn't having it anymore. If Ben wasn't going to be around much longer it was time for Scarlett to bloody well grow up and take some responsibility.

In the car, twenty minutes later, Harriet watched Scarlett carefully adjusting the seat and the mirrors. Satisfied, she sat back. 'I've told Jonathan you're coming to see him this morning at the school to apologise. I need to drop something off to him, and you need to stop avoiding him. So let's head that way.'

'Great. That sounds like a riot.'

Harriet felt her chest tighten. Scarlett turned on the ignition and looked in the reversing camera as she backed out onto the street, a scowl fixed firmly on her face. The school was only ten minutes away, but it was probably all Scarlett was capable of managing without having eaten breakfast. And Harriet needed to be back in chambers by eleven. She'd come home specially to take Scarlett on a driving lesson, since she'd missed out on her lesson with Ben on Sunday, after the birthday cake incident. It wasn't that Ben hadn't wanted to take her. Scarlett had just refused to speak to him after seeing that half-dressed woman in his apartment. Harriet hadn't spoken to him either. The whole incident was tawdry. Humiliating. She had felt like he'd stabbed her through the heart when she'd walked in and seen Marleen Maples dressed in his t-shirt on Sunday morning. She had actually wanted to cry. It was the ending of their marriage, right there in front of her, in technicolour.

'Slow down up here, Scarlett, there are always drivers who fly around this roundabout not expecting traffic from this end.'

'Mum! I know!'

'Don't snap at me,' said Harriet. 'I'm trying to help you.'

'Which entrance to the school should I use?' Scarlett asked.

'Go to the staff carpark entrance. Jon is in his office for the next hour. I just got a text from him.'

Scarlett indicated and slowed down, far too early, then turned right and drove up the hill past the sandstone houses and ageing mansions of Sandy Bay, then skirted the city and headed towards Lenah Valley.

'Pedestrian. Stop!' called Harriet, more sharply than she'd intended. Her head jerked forward as Scarlett stamped on the brakes. The man was still twenty metres ahead of them.

'Mum! I saw him! Stop yelling at me! Dad's a much better teacher than you,' said Scarlett as she started inching forward again.

Harriet's heart was beating too fast. As they pulled into the school carpark five minutes later, she wondered why she hadn't just organised for more professional driving lessons. Five had seemed ample at the time. Profligate even. One every day last week, after Scarlett had gotten over her jetlag. Scarlett got out of the car and slammed the door.

'You need to be very contrite please, Scarlett. Jonathan's had his reputation tarnished, possibly irreparably over this whole gap year fiasco.'

'Thanks, Mum. You're so supportive. I haven't come out of it that well either you know. Anyway, it's such an overreaction by everyone.' Scarlett flicked her hair away from her face and stalked off ahead of Harriet up the pathway. She opened the door to the old administration building and walked through, leaving it to slam in Harriet's face.

In the office, Harriet kissed Jonathan, while Scarlett hung back. He came towards the door and gave her a hug.

'Great to see you home safe, Scarlett, even if it is a bit earlier than planned.'

'Yeah, well…' Scarlett looked sideways at Harriet.

My cue, thought Harriet. 'I just need to make a phone call. I'll leave you two alone for a few minutes.' She walked out into the office foyer. The secretary's desk was deserted. She sat down on the couch and pulled out her phone, checking the ten emails that had arrived since she'd checked an hour ago. She wondered if Scarlett would manage to apologise properly. Harriet couldn't carry the guilt alone forever. It was Scarlett's fault and she needed to face the consequences. Even if that did mean a dressing down from her favourite uncle.

Harriet sent three emails on her phone and then looked up. The office was hung with beautiful artwork, some by talented ex-students and others by collectable Australian artists who now made headlines around the world. An early work of Clementine's, depicting a Tasmanian forest, invoked a bleakness in Harriet that she couldn't easily explain. She looked away from it and wondered why Scarlett hadn't come out. She got up and walked noiselessly towards the office. Jonathan's door sat slightly ajar. She could hear snippets of conversation. She moved forward and leaned her ear against the door jam.

'Scarlett, we all do really dumb things when we're young. It's what you do afterwards that matters. You made a terrible decision. I was angry. But it's really what you do now that I care about. You need to put it behind you.'

'I would but one of the girls from my year keeps making comments and sending random snapchats about it and now everyone is talking about it, like I'm a druggie or something. It was just a couple of pills.'

'Anyone I know?' asked Jon.

'Elke Price, in my year. She always hated me.'

'Well, I'll see if I can have a word. I know her dad socially.'

'Thanks, Jon.'

'I assume you've written and apologised to the staff at the school?'

'No.'

Harriet watched through the crack as Scarlett crossed her arms.

'They were so rude to me. Didn't even let me say goodbye to my friends.'

'Well, it's something I suggest you have a think about. What about your parents? They've invested a lot in you, Scarlett. And not just money,' said Jonathan.

'I know. But I don't feel like apologising to Mum when she's being such a bitch to me. And Dad's got a new girlfriend. It's totally horrible. Everyone's just pissed off with each other. And Clementine's making everything worse. I can't wait 'til she leaves.'

'Scarlett, whatever it might look like, your family have your best interests at heart. Believe me. When I was your age, your mum was the same. An ogre. Always on my back. But you can take control back if you own up to your mistakes.'

Outside the door, Harriet bristled. An ogre? Well that was rich. Scarlett screws up and Jonathan calls *her* an ogre? After all these years of looking after him. Looking out for him. After all that she'd *done* for him.

The door was pulled open suddenly and Harriet stepped backwards, her face flaming.

'Bye Jon,' said Scarlett.

Harriet looked across to the ridiculously beautiful face of her baby brother and raised her eyebrows. He looked sheepish. Good. That was no way to speak about the big sister who had cared for him as if he were her own child.

'You're wrong you know, Jon,' said Harriet.

'In what, Hat?'

'I was only ever doing what a parent would do for you. Mum was never there. I was the only one there to love you. Sometimes it had to be tough love.'

'Harriet…'

'I know what happens when things get out of hand, Jon. When children aren't guided. Terrible things happen.'

Jonathan's face fell. 'Hattie, please. Stop. It's time to move forward.'

'Well that's easy for you to say. I'm doing my best, Jon,' said Harriet sadly, and she was surprised to find a tear brimming in her eye. She turned and walked through the empty reception office, not waiting to see if Scarlett was following.

'Goodbye, Hat.'

Harriet heard the words through a distant tunnel.

'Mum, wait!' Scarlett trotted after her. 'Do you want me to drive?'

Harriet wiped the tear away before Scarlett could see it.

'Not really,' said Harriet. 'I have a headache. I'll drop you home and then keep going. I have a meeting at work.'

As they headed back into Sandy Bay, Scarlett spoke into the heavy silence.

'I need to get to Jacqui's place later this arvo. Will you be around after your meeting?'

'Ask Clementine to drop you. I'm not a taxi service.'

'As if she'd do it, Mum. When is she going home anyway – I mean back to Europe?'

'I have no idea,' said Harriet as she indicated to turn into their street. 'She's staying for that winter solstice thing. The festival. So sometime after that I suppose.'

Harriet pulled into the driveway of the house a moment before Clementine's little orange car pulled in beside them. The car was a disgrace but Harriet wasn't about to be called a snob by voicing her thoughts.

Harriet opened her window. 'Clementine, Scarlett was just wondering how long you're here for.'

'Trying to get rid of me, Scarli? Well I've got my school reunion on the weekend. And Dark Mofo's starting. This year's festival line-up is awesome.'

Harriet sniffed. 'The debauched images all over town last year were bordering on obscene.'

'Oh Mumma, you're a duffer,' said Clementine.

Harriet cringed at her patronising tone.

'Anyway, I can't leave 'til we celebrate your birthday,' added Clementine.

'I'm not having a birthday party, Clementine, I told you already. Now, can you drop Scarlett somewhere later on?'

'No, sorry. I got invited out on a fancy boat. We're going on a cruise up the river to MONA. Some big swinging-dick art dealer. I probably won't be in any state. You know – later, after all the free booze.'

Harriet raised an eyebrow. Where had she gone wrong?

She turned to Scarlett. 'What time do you need to go out?'

'About five. We're going to plan Lilly's eighteenth party.'

'Alright,' Harried sighed. 'I'll be back at four-thirty to pick you up. Do *not* keep me waiting.'

She pressed the button to wind up the car window, but stopped as Clementine turned to Scarlett and spoke.

'Don't be late, little sis, or she'll cook your kidney and eat it with lima beans and a nice Verdelho.' Then Clementine made a grotesque sucking noise with her lips and moved her teeth up and down, in an excellent imitation of an evil rabbit.

Scarlett screwed up her face. 'What does that even mean? You are so *weird.*'

Then Harriet watched as Clementine dissolved into fits of laughter and Scarlett stormed up the stairs, let herself into the house and slammed the door.

As Harriet drove off down the street, quite inexplicably, she found herself laughing.

CHAPTER TWENTY-THREE

MARLEE

Seraphina. What sort of name was that? Marlee watched the blond bombshell who had walked into their meeting room an hour ago as she leaned over again to rest her hand on top of Ben's. He was laughing – she could hear it through the open door, then she caught it in his profile as he turned his head and looked directly at Seraphina. The woman lowered her eyes and leant forward even further, giving him an open view of her boobs that were spilling out over the top of a very tight, white t-shirt. Tanned, perky, huge. Clearly fake. Ben stood up, signalling the end of the meeting and Seraphina picked up her leather jacket from the back of the chair and shrugged herself into it, making sure Ben was watching. She leaned in and kissed both of his cheeks, her pink talons resting gently on his upper arms.

A new client. Loads of money. Would only have Ben – none of the other architects would do. That's what Lidia had told her. She could see Lidia sneaking glances at the boardroom every few minutes too. Poor Lidia.

Marlee watched as Ben walked Seraphina to the front door and waved goodbye. She closed her eyes. An image of Seraphina falling flat on her face and bursting one of her fake boobs popped into Marlee's head. It cheered her enormously.

Ben walked back across the room to her desk. 'Sorry that ran over time. Ready?'

'Sure.' Marlee closed down the document she was working on and looked back up at him. 'Looks like you met your Barbie after all,' she said, nodding towards the front door.

'She was lovely,' said Ben. 'A very switched on woman actually. Great project too.'

Marlee felt an unfamiliar surge of jealousy. Perky *and* smart. She picked up the large white roll of A3-sized plans on her desk, ready for their client meeting on site. Ben had hardly had time to look at the latest version, so she'd have to answer most of the questions. Richard Lekky was a difficult client and a perfectionist. She wasn't looking forward to the next few hours, partly because of Lekky but mostly because she was going to have to sit in the car with Ben for half an hour each way to and from the building site. They'd barely spoken since Sunday morning when he'd run off to placate Princess Scarlett after the birthday cake disaster. She hoped the awkwardness of the last two days hadn't been too obvious to the rest of the staff. When she hadn't been avoiding Ben, she'd spent most of each day tossing up the pros and cons of the two issues that had taken over her head – finding another job and how and when to tell him about the baby.

'Just give me two minutes.' She picked up her handbag and headed outside to the toilets, wondering if her summary of the latest round of changes to the plans could be stretched out to take up most of the car journey.

She hung her bag on the toilet door. As she sat on the toilet, she glanced down. A large bright red patch of blood stared back at her. For a moment her mind was blank, then she thought *why have I got my period when I'm pregnant?* Then – *the baby!* The fear was swift and shocking.

She sat frozen, fighting a rush of hot panic, as she wondered what to do. She rolled up some toilet paper and stuffed it in her knickers. Outside the bathrooms, in the cold, shaded courtyard she sat down on the garden wall and pulled out her phone. With shaky fingers, she swiped and scrolled and finally managed to dial Anna-Beth's surgery.

'Dr Rawson's rooms. Kiara speaking.'

'Hi, Kiara, It's Marlee Maples. I need to speak to Anna-Beth.'

'She's with a patient, Marlee. Is it urgent?'

'Um, yes, I think it might be. I'm bleeding and I'm really worried.'

'Can you remind me how many weeks pregnant you are, Marlee?'

'Fourteen tomorrow.'

'Okay, let me just see if I can put you through to Anna-Beth.'

Marlee waited. A cold gust of wind whipped into the gum tree above her, sending a single grey-green leaf floating and flipping down towards her feet. She shivered. She could feel her heart beating in her chest, pulsing the blood around her body, faster and faster. She wondered if she should be lying down to stop the bleeding, but the paved courtyard offered no options except a few faded timber chairs.

'Marlee, Anna-Beth has just said if you pop into the surgery now, she'll do a quick ultrasound to see what's happening.'

'Okay. Is that going to tell me if the baby's alright?'

'Well it's her usual procedure with a threatened miscarriage. You'll have to wait to talk to Anna-Beth I'm afraid.'

'Oh. Right.'

Marlee hung up. *Threatened miscarriage*. She really was losing the baby. Her vision was suddenly blurry.

The door from the office opened and Ben stood in the doorway, eyebrows raised. He looked pointedly at the phone in her hand.

'We're running late.'

'Right.' She stood up and then immediately sat down again.

'Are you alright?' He took a step towards her then stopped.

'No.' Marlee's eyes welled with hot tears. She looked down at her feet as she tried to control her emotions. Then she felt his hand on her shoulder, warm and comforting, bursting the dam of her tears. They rolled down her face, now hot and blotchy with fear.

'Marlee?' Ben squatted in front of her. His forehead was furrowed with concern. It was such an exact re-run of the last time she'd felt faint and sick at the art exhibition that usually she would have laughed, only now she could hear herself sobbing like a two-year-old.

'What is it?'

She couldn't get the words out. She couldn't tell him. But she couldn't keep going like this either.

'Marlee… Have you had some bad news? Are you sick?'

Marlee forced her hand across her eyes and took a deep breath. 'I'm pregnant.' A fresh bout of tears filled her eyes and began running down her face as she sniffed loudly. 'But I think I'm losing the baby.'

Ben stared.

'Can you please drop me at my doctor's surgery? I need to get an ultrasound.'

'Okay.' Ben's face was an unreadable mask. He stood absolutely still, as if a sudden movement might upset some sort of delicate balance.

She stood up and he reached forward and took her arm. She shrugged him off. The bridge between them was too raw and rickety. She walked ahead of him and opened the back door of the office and walked through the office with her eyes fixed on the front door. In the car park she heard the beep as Ben unlocked the door of his car and she got in. When he got into the driver's seat, she could feel him looking across at her. She gave him directions to Anna-Beth's rooms and they drove across the suburbs in silence. A few minutes later they pulled up beside a low-set brick building a street away from the hospital.

'I'll just wait here for you,' he said.

'No need. You'd better go to the meeting.'

'But, you… I mean… you might need something.'

'They'll be waiting for you.' She got out and slammed the door, not waiting for his reply.

Inside the cool, calm interior of the surgery, Anna-Beth ushered her in after a fifteen-minute wait.

'Right, Marlee, when did the bleeding start?'

'I noticed it less than an hour ago. Is the baby dying?' Marlee got up on the bed as directed and lowered her waistband.

'How much blood was there?'

'Well, my pants were stained – but not too much. It was maybe a teaspoon?'

Anna-Beth was pushing the ultrasound around on her lower abdomen, the slimy, pushing sensation now familiar.

'Any pain?'

'No.'

Marlee watched the screen. She couldn't see anything. Anna-Beth kept moving the doppler, staring at the screen as Marlee lay frozen, barely daring to breathe.

Then Anna-Beth spoke. 'He's there – see?' They both watched the rapid flashing light on the screen. After a minute she said, 'The baby's heartbeat is exactly right. He doesn't appear to be in distress. A small percentage of women experience minor bleeding in the second trimester, Marlee. What I recommend is getting some extra bed rest. Certainly, for the next day or so you should take it very easy. No exercise. And sitting or lying down whenever you can. If there's no further bleeding in a day or two just return to normal activities. Okay?'

'But… I have to work.'

'I'm assuming you've decided to keep the baby?

'Yes. Yes, I have.'

'Well then, you'll just need to take it easy to get you through the next couple of days and see what happens. Maybe work from home. This might be a warning that you're doing too much.'

Marlee felt a wash of relief as Anna-Beth handed her a paper towel to wipe the gel off her stomach. Then she thought of Ben – he'd be having trouble trying to explain the new concept to the client without her having brought him up to speed. She was glad. She felt angry with him for not being here with her, even though she hadn't asked him. She knew that her anger didn't make sense.

Marlee walked into the carpark, scrolling through her phone for a taxi number. Outside the door, Ben stood on the path typing something on his phone. He looked up and put the phone in his pocket, his face grim.

'Marlee. Are you alright? Is the baby alright?'

At the sight of him another well of mixed emotion rushed up and sat behind her eyes, threatening to spill out.

'Marlee – I'm so sorry.'

'Why?' she choked out the word.

'Well, the baby…' He ran both his hands through his hair. 'I just feel really bad, you know… I had no idea.'

Why were men so annoying in a crisis that involved women's business? He was obviously wondering if the baby was his, then worrying that he was going to have to stump up for child care for another eighteen years, until he was… She did a quick calculation: Clementine had said he was forty-eight, add eighteen. Sixty-six. God, really? *Sixty-six?* That was past retirement age. She felt a bit sick about it herself. Well if she lost the baby, he could head off towards his dotage with all his pennies intact and only Scarlett to spend it on. But unfortunately for him, she had no intention of losing this baby.

'The baby's fine. I have to put my feet up for a few days. I'm going to need the rest of the week off.'

'Oh, that's great – about the baby. And of course, take as much time as you need. Um – could you just maybe send me an email so I can see what direction you're going with the Lekky building?'

Marlee's heart twisted with such unexpected rage, she almost kicked him in the shins. How dare he think of work issues when she was trying to keep her baby alive. *Their baby.* She thought again of Seraphina, and all the women out there waiting for a guy like him to come along. There was no way he would want this baby.

He was waiting for her response, a deep crease running through the middle of his forehead. She really didn't want to get back in his car. She looked around hoping a taxi would magically appear down the street with its light on, waiting for her fare. But there was no avoiding it. She needed to get home quickly so she could lie down.

'Could you just drop me home? I'll send the email tonight.'

'Sure.' In the car he looked straight ahead. The silence made her self-conscious, as if they were a parody of a family going on a drive, except everything was upside down. She really didn't want to think about Ben, she had enough to worry about. She slumped back in the seat and closed her eyes, opening them only when he pulled up outside her apartment.

'Do you want me to get you anything at the chemist or… shops or anything at all?'

'No thanks.'

Ben got out and walked around the back of the car, but before he could open her door she was up and out of the car and had walked past him. She swiped her security card into her apartment foyer and let the glass door slam behind her, not looking back.

As she waited for the lift, she leaned her head on the wall and gave a silent order to little Ned to stay firmly inside his amniotic sac until she could lie down. The lift doors slid open and she pressed the button to the second floor. As the doors closed, she turned around and looked up. Ben was standing on the footpath watching her through the locked glass door. His hand was raised in a silent goodbye.

CHAPTER TWENTY-FOUR

HARRIET

Harriet peered over the top of her glasses as she heard a clatter, then the sound of a key tapping against the front door lock. After what sounded like several attempts, the key was inserted and the door opened. Clementine stood in the hall holding a large garden gnome under one arm and what looked like a half-eaten kebab in her hand. She wobbled slightly, then set the gnome down in the foyer. It was almost half her height. She looked up and spotted Harriet.

'Mumbles! You caught me. What are you doing still up?' Clementine slurred, leaning on the wall of the living room. She took a huge bite of her kebab without waiting for Harriet to reply.

'What is that?' asked Harriet, looking at the gnome.

'His name is Fred. Do you like him? I *love* him.' Flecks of food shot out of Clementine's mouth and landed on the floor. She turned the gnome around and Harriet recoiled in distaste. The gnome's trousers were pulled down and it was peering backwards over its shoulder displaying its bare bottom.

'Oh, Clem.'

'I stole him from a garden behind Mykonos when I stopped for food. Isn't that the best brown-eye you've seen for ages? I might even use him for sex. My first male lover.' Clementine looked briefly pensive. 'Well, maybe not the actual first.' She giggled to herself and walked into the kitchen.

Harriet let out a loud sigh and looked back at her computer screen. Just a couple more weeks. Then she was going. Isn't that what she'd said? She continued typing her advice.

Clementine walked back in with a beer in her hand and slumped down, putting her boots up onto the arms of the couch. Harriet flinched.

'How was the boat trip with the art dealer?' asked Harriet.

'Alright.'

'You didn't drive home, did you?'

'Of course not, Mumsy,' said Clementine. 'That's how I met Fred. Best idea to walk home I ever had. Well, wasn't my idea really. I ran into a couple of girls I knew at school down at Salamanca. Back for the reunion. They wouldn't give my keys back. Thought I'd had one too many.' Clementine tipped her head to one side and made a clownish face, widening her eyes in mock surprise.

Harriet laughed.

'Good to see the old school network is useful for something then,' said Harriet.

'Yup. All those lovely, lovely girls. You probably only sent me to Denham to keep me from meeting smelly boys with their nasty doodles. Except,' said Clementine throwing her arm out wide, 'you sent me into a den of temptation without even knowing it!'

Harriet sighed again.

'I don't remember you fancying anyone at school, Clem. You seemed to be far too tied up in your art.'

'Aah, but there you are wrong.' Clementine took a swig from her beer bottle. 'I was head over heels in love. For most of Year Twelve actually.'

'Were you?'

'Mmmm. With Tessa. Then she went and got herself killed like that. Very inconsiderate. I blame her for all the drugs that screwed up my twenties.'

'Oh.'

Clementine leaned back and poured the last drops of beer into her mouth, then put her eye up to the neck of the bottle and jiggled it. 'Emma Tasker reckons Tessa was at it with Jonno back then,' said Clementine, staring sadly at the empty bottle. 'That would explain why she wasn't up for a fumble with me I suppose – if *they* were doing it. Can't really see it, though. Can you? He's so straight.'

'Of course not, Clem. That's highly defamatory!'

'But she *was* in his cottage that afternoon. I saw her.'

'What?' Harriet felt a spiralling sense of alarm – similar to those awful times during a trial when her own witness began revealing new evidence on the stand that they hadn't run past her earlier. Like a train wreck happening before her eyes, knowing the fault for the crash would be all down to her, but that she was now powerless to stop it.

'In his bedroom. She broke in. I was smoking in the trees behind his house. I watched her go in through the window. Thought she was breaking in to change her exam paper actually.'

'What are you talking about, Clementine?'

'I saw Jon coming down the path to the front door too, not long after, so I put a stick in the window runner so she couldn't get back out. I was really pissed off with her.'

'Clementine, you mustn't repeat this. He would never have had an affair with a student. *Never.* This is ridiculous – to even be talking about it.' Harriet stood and closed her laptop. 'You mustn't speak of it again.' Harriet's heart was clattering.

She moved around the table, avoiding Clementine's glare. How was she supposed to get to sleep now? It was well past midnight. Her trainer was coming at 6 a.m. to start a new workout program. And she needed to be on form tomorrow to get on top of the Hensen trial. Curse Clementine and her ridiculous drunken talk. The sooner she returned to Prague, the better. She walked out of the lounge room and looked down at the gnome, a garish, creepy looking dwarf with a crooked smile.

'And get rid of that thing. Theft is a crime, Clementine. Return it or I'll report you.'

'Geez Mum, that'd look good in the papers. *Leading QC's daughter arrested for shenanigans with butt-naked garden gnome.*'

Harriet continued walking towards her bedroom, the sound of Clementine's raucous laughter reverberating down the hallway, bouncing off the walls and into her head like a violent storm.

CHAPTER TWENTY-FIVE

MARLEE

Marlee plucked idly at the strings of her guitar as she sat propped up against her bedrest. The boredom was making her fidget and itch, as if she had a rash. She couldn't concentrate on her work files either. She really wanted to go for a run. She looked down at her fingers and began playing random chords. She was rusty, but somewhere deep in her brain the synapses were connecting and guiding her fingers to form a tune. She'd given up guitar after high school, but her father had found the old instrument, out of tune and with a broken string, when he'd cleaned out the attic a few months earlier. It had sat for more than twenty years, forlorn and dusty, between boxes of her mother's clothes, an emblem of better times.

She was fine to get up and walk around now – go back to work even. There had been no further bleeding in the last couple of days, but she wasn't taking any chances with Ned's health. She had decided she would go to the reunion dinner tomorrow, though. She could sit down and take it easy at the restaurant, not that it would have been her first choice of social occasion, but for some reason the idea held a strange appeal. The other day she'd run into a few of her old school mates around town and they'd persuaded her to come.

The memory of her school days felt like an old movie she'd watched once and wasn't sure she'd take the time to watch again. But her old friends had been so insistent and now that she was pregnant, she kept having recurring thoughts about her mother and what she would have wanted Marlee to do. It was annoying that she couldn't drink though. Rehashing the experience with alcohol might have made it passably fun but who knows how these things went when you were sober?

She longed for a drink. For that first tiny rush of release when her frontal lobes let down their guard and her inhibitions escaped, swallowed by the wine.

Today was another rest day though. No exercise. And definitely no alcohol. Nothing to dim Ned's chances at growing into a real, fully formed human baby. The thought calmed her.

The apartment buzzer made her jump. She got off the bed slowly, looking briefly in the mirror at her crushed harem pants and tight white t-shirt, firm against the swell of her tender breasts. Her red curls tumbled, restless and messy over her shoulders. She knew how they felt.

She hurried down the stairs and pressed the intercom button, making the video camera spring into life. There was Ben, standing with his back to the door. He turned and looked into the screen.

'Marlee?'

'Yes.'

'Can I come up for a minute?'

'Why?'

He looked surprised, as if he hadn't expected to be questioned. As if he was sifting through appropriate responses for why he would be visiting a two-night-stand who might be pregnant with his baby and was currently using up her almost non-existent sick leave at his expense.

'I wanted to see you.'

'Why?'

'Marlee, can I just come up? Please?' He ran his fingers through his hair and stared into the intercom.

She pressed the buzzer then unlocked the door and walked across the room and plonked herself down on the couch. She put her feet up and stared out at the trees, half-bare of their leaves in readiness for the winter. She watched the cold drizzle running down the window pane. She'd always felt sorry for the trees – just when they needed their shaggy green coats the most, they fell off and left them exposed to the harsh, unforgiving elements. She shivered as the knock came at the door.

'Come in.' She sat back into the corner and tucked her legs up beneath her.

Ben stood in the middle of the kitchen looking at her. The two days of stubble on his face suited him.

'Hi,' said Ben.

'Hi.'

'I just wanted to check that you're alright.'

'I'm fine.' She turned back to the window, staring as the wind whipped through the trees. She wasn't about to come to his rescue. She stopped saving men from themselves years ago.

'That's good. That's… really good.'

'Do you need some input on the Lekky project?' she asked.

'Yes. No… I mean, only when you're better. That's not why I'm here.'

'I'll be back at work on Monday.'

'That's great.' He looked around at the mess on the kitchen table, the washing on the collapsible line, three bras slung carelessly over the end rails. 'Could I make us a cup of tea?'

Marlee looked back at him and tilted her head to one side. She wondered where this was going.

'If you want.'

He picked up the kettle and began to fill it. Then he stopped, his back to her, and spoke again. 'Marlee, is the baby mine?'

She felt a pang of sadness, overtaking the undercurrent of anger she'd felt towards him since the birthday cake incident. Then she felt a ripple of fear about her future if she told him the truth.

'Yes.'

He turned around and looked straight at her, holding her eyes, unblinking. 'Oh.'

And there it was. The bare truth. She didn't care now though. She could do this on her own. She didn't need a man to make her life complete, and neither did her baby.

But then Ben was walking towards her. He knelt down in front of her and broke into a huge smile. 'Wow, that's amazing.'

She felt the breath go out of her.

'That's really amazing,' he said again slowly.

The couch lifted beneath her a little as she sat up and twisted her legs out from under her then pulled her hair into a roll and placed it against her neck. A weight she didn't realise had been sitting across her shoulders seemed to trickle away like the drops of rain on the window pane behind her. Her smile was tentative at first. Then she grinned back at him and let out a laugh as unexpected as the sight of her baby's father kneeling in the middle of her kitchen holding the kettle.

He looked down at the floor, then stood up and placed the kettle carefully back on its base and flicked on the switch to make it boil.

'I know,' she said.

He stared at her, a smile threatening at the edge of his mouth. 'Do you think the baby will be alright?'

'Yeah, I think he'll be fine. It's his parents I'm worried about.'

Ben paused for a moment and looked thoughtful. 'Well, I wouldn't worry about his father. He's in very good spirits.

Marlee smiled.

'I'm sorry about what happened with Scarlett and Harriet in my flat. Harriet's not ready to accept that we've grown apart, and I know there's not much I can do about that, except try to avoid hurting her any more. But I made a mess of that day. I didn't tell you how I felt.'

'Well, I'm sure it's hard for both of you.'

He took a moment before he answered. 'I loved Harriet. She was so independent, so strong. I admired her intellect. I gave the marriage everything I had. But she never really knew how to love me back. Not properly. She tried, but I don't think she ever really knew what love looked like. She had… well, she had a difficult upbringing.'

'Ben, it's fine. You don't need to explain.'

'No, I want you to know. I'm not someone who walks away easily. I tried so hard to get her to trust me. To let down the barriers. But she couldn't. And it didn't help that she avoided the difficult conversations I tried to have every couple of years. I think she manages to prevent herself from thinking about things too deeply by working all the time. I suppose I should have known it wasn't sustainable, but I did love her, very much. Until I realised something had changed a couple of years ago. I realised that I didn't care anymore if she came home for dinner or not. I'd stopped noticing.'

'Ben, I'm not asking you to commit to me. I really don't even know what I want from you. And the situation's not ideal, with us working together.'

'I don't care about that, Marlee. I don't regret a moment of the time I've spent with you. Working with you is the best part of my day.' He smiled at her. 'And I hope you'll think about taking me on. I'm really capable you know. I can cook and clean and plenty of other things too. And despite what Scarlett might tell you, I'm not a bad dad, either.' He looked straight into her eyes, then opened the drawer under the kettle. 'And I make excellent cups of tea.'

She let out her breath. 'Well that's a relief. I hate bad cups of tea.'

'Empires have been built and lost over good tea. Tell me where the pot is and leave me to it.'

'It's tea bags around here.'

Ben sighed as he began opening drawers, hunting for the bags. 'I can see we're going to have to work hard at this relationship.'

Marlee smiled and felt the warm burn of tears pressing against her eyes again as she got up and walked past Ben towards the pantry. Hormones. It must be the hormones. Or the odd sensation of being cared for. But she liked it. She turned towards him offering two small teabags and he grasped her hand and bent forward and pulled her gently towards him, and in his kiss she felt desire, but also something warm and strong and kind. Something that felt like home.

CHAPTER TWENTY-SIX

MARLEEN

25 November 1993

Mr Brownley sat back from the piece of music he was marking, pencil poised like a dart. 'Come in, Marleen.'

Marleen avoided looking at him and went to the row of guitars lined up at the back of the music room and picked hers up off the stand. She sat down across from him in the chair, brushing her tunic down over her knees and flicking the colourful cape out from under her.

'Happy Birthday.'

'Thank you, Sir.' Marleen tugged at the piece of floral fabric that still sat bunched up under her thighs and balanced her guitar across her lap.

'It must be good to have the weight of all those exams off your shoulders.'

'Yes, it is.'

'You've done a wonderful job this year as Head Girl. I've been meaning to congratulate you.'

'Thank you, Sir.' She glanced at him and the plummeting sensation returned. He was so nice, so *gorgeous*. How was she going to warn him?

'Did you want to play "Days and Nights" through together and see how we go with it? Might be nice just to make it a fun lesson to wrap up the year.'

'Okay.' She watched his biceps as his arm curled around the guitar and his blond, slightly messy hair flopped down as he placed his fingers to form a D chord. Marleen started to pluck the opening chords, then strummed along with him, closing her eyes. She stopped playing and moved the capo along, then began tuning the guitar. 'Sorry… just give me a sec.'

'Sure.' He smiled at her and Marleen felt her palms getting sweaty. She knew if Tessa followed through with what she'd told Emma and Linda Perkins, things could go really badly for him. And for the school if anyone found out. He was such a great guy. He didn't deserve it. Tessa might have been his best music student and her friend, but she was also a bit crazy. Marleen reminded herself that as Head Girl she didn't have the luxury of standing by when she knew things were going to get out of control. Ms Sharp, the headmistress, was relying on her to make sure the school's reputation was kept unblemished. Frequently in their weekly meetings, she'd remind Marleen of her expectations. *You're part of my team, Marleen. You are my eyes and ears. I cannot run a successful school without knowing what the girls are thinking and doing. You have been chosen for this position because I like and trust you and equally because the girls like and trust you.*

Marleen knew she should just say something to him now. But what? *'I've heard Tessa might be waiting inside your cottage with some new lacy underwear because she's not leaving school a virgin and you're the one.'* Yeah, right. Tessa would tear strips off her. Not that Tessa had told Marleen about her seduction plan directly. She wasn't that dumb. But she'd told the others and Emma had told Marleen, sort of under duress, when she'd edged her way into their huddled conversation outside the library. She'd *made* them tell her. And now she was landed with the knowledge. If it went ahead and word of it got out – which she knew these things did when people were desperate for the gory details – Mr Brownley would get the sack. Or worse – Tessa's father would do something terrible to him. He might have been an influential property developer, but he was also a traditional Italian father with a scary reputation.

'Mr B, I wanted…' she stopped and closed her eyes, wondered how to phrase it. When she opened them he was still looking at her. 'I wondered if I could get a copy of that song you were telling me about last week. "Entirely True".'

'Sure. I've got it at home. I'll bring it up tomorrow for you.'

'Right. Thanks.'

She couldn't betray Tessa. What sort of friend would that make her? Not that they were close. But Marleen tried to be a friend to every girl in the school, no matter how hard that girl might make it. And Tessa was nearly eighteen. She was entitled to make her own decisions about her love life. She was leaving school this week. It wouldn't be that bad if she went through with it, not really. But a whisper of doubt was hissing at Marleen's conscience.

Then the words were out of her mouth before she knew they were coming. 'Mr B, what would happen if it was found out that a teacher had a fling with one of his students?'

Mr Brownley drew back, his honeyed features clouding into a frown. 'I wouldn't do that.'

'I know. But if you did?'

'Well, it depends on the circumstances. But I could go to jail.'

'No! Really? Even if they agreed to it and everything?'

'It's against the law, Marleen.' He sat up straighter in his chair and put his guitar down against the wall. Then he began rubbing one hand against the back of the other. 'Marleen, I hope I haven't given you the wrong impression. If I have, I'm really sorry.'

'What? No! I'm not saying anything like that!'

'Oh, good.'

'It was just hypothetical.'

He reddened and coughed into his hand. 'Right, well that's a relief.'

They sat for a moment in stilted silence, the wall clock ticking like an unexploded bomb. Then Mr Brownley picked up his guitar again and they began playing. Marlee made tons of mistakes, as the thoughts whizzed through her head. She couldn't let Tessa wreck his life. She'd tried to find her after lunch, but they didn't share any of the same classes and after the school bell rang, she wasn't near the lockers or in the boarding house common room or her bedroom. Marleen had to meet Mr Brownley for her guitar lesson without having spoken to Tessa about it. Was Tessa at his house already? Or maybe she'd sneak out of the boarding house later. But the girls had said it might happen after school.

'Let's wrap it up there, Marleen. Thanks for being such a great student this year. I really hope you get into the course you want at uni.'

'Thanks, I should be okay, I think. I've put architecture first, then engineering. I like the idea of designing something.'

'You'll be a star.' He smiled at her as she clicked the guitar case shut.

Outside the music centre she walked down the path, then paused and turned around. A large sycamore tree obscured her from the vision of anyone else coming out of the building. She waited, jiggling her foot impatiently as she listened to the hum of traffic along Ellery Way. After a few minutes he came out and walked to the left, taking the path towards the staff cottages. His was the last of them, furthest from the school, completely secluded. She'd been sent there once on an errand with another girl, to deliver something to him for Ms Sharp. What if Tessa was on the way to his cottage? Or there already?

She put her guitar case down carefully and stood, thinking quickly. She could just find an excuse, go after him, and if Tessa heard her voice and she was already in his cottage, she could duck out the back and he'd be none the wiser. Everyone would avoid embarrassment. Then afterwards she'd have a word with Tessa about why she needed to wait until after graduation. Tessa would just have to persuade her parents to let her spend a few days in Hobart after they graduated, then it would all be above board. She'd be a free agent and he'd be free to do whatever he wanted with her. Which was probably quite a lot. There was something simmering and sexual about Tessa. Even the girls could see it. And Mr Brownley was so good-looking and nice. Even Marleen couldn't deny it, and she was frequently accused of having her head in the clouds when it came to cute boys. It was obvious. Tessa and Mr B were bound to get together at some stage.

Marleen didn't want to think about that bit too much. She was a virgin herself. She'd been so busy with school captain duties and study this year she hadn't had time to think about anything more than a kiss with Liam Trudeaux after the school formal. She knew most of the other girls weren't as focussed on school as she was though. But their casual flings didn't interest Marleen. She was going to wait for love. And today, she was going to make Tessa wait too.

Marlee ran down the path after him. She could see him ahead through the trees. He'd come out of the thicket and was nearing his cottage. She needed to stop him before he got there – make a loud fuss, keep him talking outside, or make it seem like she was coming in so Tessa would get herself out. She ran faster, the trees thinning out and suddenly she was out of the shady grove and at the beginning of his long garden path, stones crunching under her feet. As she entered the clearing, a flash of movement to her left caught her attention. It was a brief glimpse – a small figure in blue, running from the back of the cottage, across the oval and in behind some trees. A girl heading in the direction of the school. Was it Tessa? She wasn't sure. It was someone in school uniform but the figure had moved too quickly for her to see. But it could only have been Tessa – this area was out of bounds, so nobody else would be down here. Her heart pounded a sick rhythm in her chest – relief mixed with adrenalin.

'Marleen?'

Mr Brownley had turned back towards her. She stopped and stared back at him, dumb. What should she say? He'd think she was stalking him after that comment in the lesson about being with a student. Think. *Think.*

'Sir, I just wondered if I could get a copy of that sheet music for "Entirely True" from you? I'd really like to play it for my mum tonight before she goes in for her next round of chemo. It's her favourite.'

Mr Brownley rubbed his hand over his chin then turned away from her and placed the key in the door.

'Yes, alright – but just wait outside okay. You can't come in. I won't be a tick.' He disappeared inside, letting the screen door bang, but leaving the main door wide open. Marleen walked closer, peering through the screen netting into the dim recesses of the tiny cottage. She let her eyes roam over the small dingy kitchenette, a battered old orange couch in the corner, the fireplace with a photo perched on the mantel – the figure of a girl staring out. A thought struck her then, disorienting and uneasy. She turned her head back to the mantelpiece to look again. Yes, she was right. The light was dim and it was across the other side of the room, but there could be no mistaking it – the girl in the photograph was naked.

CHAPTER TWENTY-SEVEN

EMMA

Emma sat bolt upright in bed, gasping, shedding the hands that had been pulling her down under hot liquid in a dark pool of murky sludge. The clock glowed through the dim light. 6.32 a.m. The warbling calls of birds drifted through the walls, calling in the dawn.

She looked across her bed. Rosie was huddled into a foetal position with the blankets pushed away. Emma leaned down and carefully pulled the doona up over her. Last night she had agreed to let Rosie snuggle up in the queen-size bed with her – a favourite childhood ritual every time Phillip was away at a conference or giving a talk at a university interstate.

Rosie had become quite sick after school yesterday, and Emma had tucked her into bed with her iPad and some paracetamol.

Emma slid back under the covers and thought about trying to get back to sleep, but it was impossible. Worries had already begun jostling for attention.

Last night she had called Marlee to check she'd been following doctor's orders and that there'd been no more bleeding. Then she had sat down and flicked through the 1993 yearbook, lingering over all the photographs of Tessa. She made a list of all the evidence that pointed to why Jonathan Brownley needed to be reported to the police. She wished she could talk to someone about it, but

Marlee had enough to worry about with the threatened miscarriage, and the possibility that she'd be having to find another job to support a baby on her own.

Emma lifted the list off the bedside table and squinted at it through the dim morning light.

- *Harriet Andrews – Jonathan's sister – on campus and reported the bag. She would not have had to pass that way from the carpark. Why really on campus at that time? <u>Lawyer.</u> For help if police came?*
- *JB was nearby. Was distressed, and jumped into the trench with T. An act? Remorse? In love?*
- *Naked hidden photo of T taken around time of death; found in cottage JB living in at the time.*
- *Some of T's shirt buttons not done up under her tunic. Everyone knew T was anal about the way she dressed. In a rush?*
- *JB and T's argument seen from window. T had admitted her plan to seduce him. T carried things through, whether taking up a dare, or a school work challenge.*

Emma remembered Tessa's single-mindedness clearly. She was always the one who lost most weight on their diets. Emma had suspected a few times during Year Twelve that Tessa was vomiting to lose the weight.

The thought struck Emma now that Tessa may have been bulimic. If that was true, she must have been more mixed up than Emma realised. It made her shift uncomfortably in the bed with the heaviness of it, as if all the wrongs of the past were now sitting on her shoulders. What had *really* happened to Tessa? She needed to go to the police to tell them what she knew about Jonathan Brownley – what she'd heard and seen. What they did with that information would be their decision, but she couldn't shoulder this burden any longer.

'Mum?' Rosie's voice was raspy with sleep.

'Yes, darling?'

'I feel bad. Really cold.' She shivered.

Emma leaned over and put her hand across Rosie's forehead.

'Goodness. You're boiling hot, darling. Not cold.' She turned on her bedside light and reached into her drawer and pulled out some paracetamol.

'Here take two of these, honey.'

Rosie didn't move. Emma hoisted herself up and walked around to the other side of the bed near the window. She pulled open the curtains to let the sun stream in.

'Oww. That hurts my eyes.' Rosie's voice was weak and she moved her hand to cover her face.

'Rosie—'

'My neck,' Rosie whimpered. 'Mum, I think I'm going to be sick.'

Emma felt a whisper of fear as she grabbed a towel from the end of the bed.

Rosie's skin looked sickly pale and her eyes lolled back in her head. She was slumped back against the bed and lay completely still. A vice-like pain gripped Emma's chest and she registered a dull throbbing under her ribs. Her panic pain. She needed to be calm, but something was very wrong.

'Honey, I need to take you to the doctor. Just sit up now.'

Emma reached down to help her but Rosie let out a feeble cry. 'My neck hurts so much, Mummy.'

Emma knew then. She needed an ambulance. She needed it now. 'We need to go to the hospital, darling.' Her heart pounded as she picked up the phone with a shaky hand and punched the numbers.

'You have dialled emergency triple zero. Which service do you require?'

*

Emma paced between the bedroom and the front door, straining her ears for the sounds of a siren or a vehicle approaching on the driveway. Just as she was heading back to the bedroom, she saw the ambulance come into view across the other side of the oval. It had missed her hidden driveway at the bend in the road near the willow tree. She had *told* the operator about slowing down at the willow tree. Stressed it. The ambulance drove silently towards the boarding houses, its blue and red lights throwing spinning patterns into the air. Panic began to stifle Emma's thoughts. Could she leave Rosie and go after it? Ring the operator again? Her phone was inside next to the bed. She ran out towards the ambulance. The school grounds were deserted, frost twinkling on the ground across the huge expanse of grass. The ambulance continued slowly away from her towards the main sandstone buildings.

She began waving her hands, 'Hey! Stop! Over here!' She ran to the bushes that marked the edge of her cottage boundary, a line that students were never supposed to cross. 'Shit.'

A rustling movement from the edge of the forest to her left made her jump. The headmaster appeared from nowhere.

'What's wrong, Emma?'

He was panting thick plumes of steam into the frosty morning, his layers of black running gear clinging to his muscular frame. For a moment Emma was confused. She looked back towards the ambulance.

'Rosie's sick, Jon. Really sick. I think it's meningitis.'

The headmaster followed her gaze as the ambulance continued to meander away from them towards the road's dead end at the staff carpark.

'I'll get it.' He took off, pushing through the bushes and sprinting across the oval as the ambulance followed the curve of the field around at the top. Relief washed over her as she ran back inside the house.

In the bedroom, Rosie had slumped further down the pillow. Emma leaned over and listened to her rapid, shallow breath.

'It's alright, darling. The ambulance is coming.'

Emma needed Phillip here. Anger swept through her like a flood, so that she could barely breathe. Her daughter needed *two* parents. He should *be* here. She picked up Rosie's hand and squeezed it. 'Dr Brownley's getting the ambulance, sweetie. Everything's fine.'

But the words felt brittle. She let her anger simmer, then flare. She needed to hold onto it. Nothing was fine. Nothing had been fine for as long as she could remember.

CHAPTER TWENTY-EIGHT

HARRIET

Harriet flicked the switch to turn off the light in the kitchen as she walked out, leaving Clementine in the dark. She took her cup of tea into the living room and picked up a magazine on the side table before she sat.

'You can't just shut down the conversation, Mother. It's my right to know. You of all people know that the rights of the child are always what matters in these things.'

She sighed as she looked up at Clementine, standing in the living room doorway. Clementine was meant to be at her reunion dinner. If Harriet could remember that the invitation on the fridge specifically said 7 for 7.30 p.m., why couldn't Clementine? It was fourteen minutes to seven and Clementine showed no sign of leaving.

'The rights of the child are of paramount importance only when the child is actually a child, Clementine. At forty-two you don't qualify. Why must you stir up trouble now? It's never interested you before.'

'Yes, exactly! I'm forty-two! And that's *not* true, Mum. I *was* interested before. I asked you who my father was when I was in high school and you refused to talk to me for a week! Why is it stirring up trouble? I don't even know what I'm bloody well stirring up. Just his name will do. *You* don't have to see him again.'

Clementine looked like an angry tree-frog. She was dressed in an outlandish bright green pantsuit that clung tightly to her tiny frame. She'd teamed it with dreadful thick purple boots and some startling white tassel earrings that hung like curtain ties to her shoulders. The suffragettes would turn in their graves.

'Well, I don't *want* to say his name, Clementine. It was a chapter from the past that should remain closed. He was not...' Harriet paused and looked down into the murky brown swirl of her tea, 'a nice man.'

'Jesus, Mum. There are plenty of arseholes out there. Just because they treated their girlfriend badly doesn't mean they don't get to know about their kids. You were only eighteen for heaven's sake! Maybe he changed.' Clementine plonked herself down on the white linen armchair and pulled the blue and white cushion out from behind her back. Her slouch caused a tiny muscle in Harriet's right eye to start twitching.

Clementine folded her arms across the cushion as if it could shield her from Harriet's glare.

'*I* may have been almost eighteen, Clementine, but he certainly wasn't. He was in his forties.' Harriet noticed Clementine's huge eyes widen, like a void that should not be crossed. Harriet could feel herself falling in. She pulled herself away before she hit rock bottom. She had to give her something.

'He was a teacher at my school.' Harriet felt the hot sting of tears at the edge of her eyes. She sniffed briefly and tensed her face, stifling the rush of shame and disgust.

'Mum?'

Clementine was looking at her with child-like confusion. *Oh God*. She did not want to have to do this.

She looked down at the carpet, remembered the day it had first happened, when she'd been called to the deputy headmaster's office, summonsed, she guessed, to explain her last exam results. That day in 1975 was still as clear and cold as ever in her mind. She'd been nervous as she waited, had glanced down at her shoes, then dipped down quickly, licking her finger and rubbing at a small mark on her right toe. They were shiny apart from that one small spot. She polished them every morning. She must have scuffed them on something. The mark almost disappeared. Still, her heart was hammering. The door remained resolutely closed. She was on time but she knew he would not appreciate her knocking. It was a well-known fact. She would just have to wait to find out if she was in trouble.

It wasn't that she'd *failed* the exams, exactly. But she'd done badly on her maths paper – only 79%. It was embarrassing. 'Thought you were meant to be the smart one, Harriet,' Sally Rolands had said the previous week in class, flicking Harriet's hand off her test page to see the result. Sally pushed her paper towards Harriet in a jubilant flourish, 'even I beat you and I hate maths!' The 81% circled in red on the top right of Sally's paper flashed at Harriet like a lighthouse warning beacon.

After the class, Mr Evans had taken her aside and asked what had happened. She'd had to explain she hadn't been feeling well for more than just the two weeks that she missed from school because of the severe flu she'd caught from her mother. She'd felt terrible, thick-headed and unable to concentrate for ages after, but it had been more than that. Her mother had ended up with pneumonia and been hospitalised so Harriet had been leaving school as soon as the bell rang to collect her little brother from school. They would get home to an empty house – she'd need to bathe and feed and read to Jonathan and then, after he was in bed, there was the washing and then finishing off her mother's sewing for clients who needed outfits by certain dates. Mary Andrews was a good seamstress, but she was narky and replaceable. Harriet knew they couldn't afford to lose the income. She would fall into bed at 1 or 2 a.m., having glanced at her maths revision briefly, but not having been able to go over it properly, to learn the difficult equations or memorise the strategies and steps. She'd done better than she'd hoped on her history paper – 83% – but nowhere close to the 99% she'd gotten the term before. Her other subjects had also suffered.

Now, she supposed, there would be consequences. The scholarship was dependant on 'obtaining the highest possible results that a student can achieve, taking into account her aptitude and circumstances.' She'd have to explain. She couldn't possibly lose the scholarship after all this time. Her mother would tear strips off her. It was unthinkable. All the years of relentless study; of being made to feel inferior inside and outside the classroom.

'Harry, you're such a drag! Never up for any fun – suppose you have to think about getting a good education so you can fend for yourself, because none of the St Marks boys would ever marry you, the way you go on.'

'Did you say you live in Swinburne? Who'd live there? Only criminals live on that side of the bridge.'

The bitching had settled down after the first couple of years, after she'd learned to shrug it off. She had her study, one or two friends and a strong relationship with a couple of the more progressive teachers. Her mother had no sympathy for her at all and some of the teachers thought she was lucky to be there in the first place. Complaining to anyone would only make it worse.

The office door opened abruptly, making Harriet jump. Mr Liddle looked over his glasses at her, his hair combed neatly from one side of his head to the other, covering his bald crown in an oily lie.

'Come in, Miss Andrews. Sit down over there.' He pointed to an orange couch on the back wall of the room. Harriet sat, eyes flicking down to her shoe to check the spot. A chair had been placed across from the couch. Mr Liddle took off his glasses and put them on his desk before moving to the chair opposite Harriet. He plucked at his trousers in a small, practiced motion as he sat.

'You value your scholarship, Miss Andrews.' Mr Liddle peered at her questioningly. She wasn't sure if it was a statement or a question though, and it was imperative that she take the right approach. On balance, he appeared to be waiting for an answer.

'Yes, Sir. Very much.'

'I thought so. It's just that your last exam results were well below what you are capable of and are not reflective of the gratitude you should be showing for the investment that this school is making in your education.'

He looked at her, Harriet imagined, like a displeased father might look at a child. She'd never had the experience of having a father. He had died when her mother was pregnant with her. Her brother Jonathan had been the product of a brief tryst with a married man that had left her mother even angrier at the world than she had been before. Their mother had taken her disappointment out on Jonathan since the day she brought him home from hospital, leaving Harriet in charge of dispensing the love.

'No, Sir. I was sick and I didn't keep up with my study plan. But I've gone back over all the work and I'm completely up to date now.'

'Yes, Mr Evans told me you'd been unwell. That's very unfortunate. How are you feeling now?' He leaned in, concern in the creases of his eyes. Harriet felt a small rush of gratitude. She was unused to being asked about her wellbeing.

'I'm much better, Sir. Thank you for asking. It was just a bad flu.'

'That's very good news. We can't have our best student falling behind. It would be a tragedy for everyone.'

Harriet watched his expression soften as he smiled. Maybe she had misjudged the reason she was here. He seemed genuinely concerned.

'Thank you, Sir.'

'It's just that with these less than exemplary results, Miss Andrews, I'm in a position where I have to advise the School Board on whether or not their generous patronage should be continued.' He paused, then took a bunched-up handkerchief out of his pocket and began blowing his nose vigorously, before wiping it down several times over his thick, neat moustache, and returning it to his pocket. 'Of course, I'm inclined to recommend that after all the investment we have made in your education to date, and given your obvious academic talent, it would be a shame to remove the scholarship,' he stood up then, quite unexpectedly, and sat down next to Harriet on the couch, 'but that would be dependent upon my confidence in your ability to cope. I fear you may need some extra encouragement.' He smiled at her, baring slightly yellow teeth.

He was leaning in, so that Harriet could see a tiny ball of snot caught up inside the bushy black hair of his left nostril. Harriet smiled back at him tentatively. It was awkward, sitting like this. She already knew she had to work hard to get her marks back up. She could cope. She unfolded her hands that had been sitting on her lap and put them on her knees, at the same time leaning back a little from him. Imperceptibly she hoped. She didn't want to offend him, but she'd never been very good at one-on-one chats with people she didn't know well. He was too close. It made her mouth dry and a nerve-like pain had started crawling over her chest like an army of bull ants.

'I can manage, Mr Liddle, I promise,' said Harriet, looking back up at his face.

His eyes looked strange, a little glazed. He didn't say anything, and Harriet began to wonder if the interview was finished. Then without any warning, Mr Liddle put his hand on her knee and slid it up her leg inside her tunic. Without thinking she clamped her legs together and threw herself backwards toward the other end of the couch, leaning backwards on her arms to get away from him.

Suddenly, Mr Liddle was on top of her. She could feel his hands pushing up her tunic and fumbling for the waistband of her tights, then with two violent tugs, he'd pulled them down.

'Be still, Miss Andrews,' he hissed at her. His face was red and he stood briefly and undid his pants, breathing heavily. 'You will be quiet and still or you will be out of this school before you can blink!'

Suddenly Harriet felt a terrible pressure as he pushed his hand into her breast to balance himself and knelt awkwardly between her thighs. The trousers around his ankles were hampering his balance. He was fumbling and pushing himself between her legs, sour breath in her face, long strands of oiled hair coming away from his bald patch and falling into her eyes as he pushed and heaved on top of her like a wild animal.

The pain was terrible, a screaming, stretching, ripping pain. His weight was crushing, unbearable. She smelt a sickly mixture of tobacco and sweat and fear.

Harriet couldn't breathe. He was breaking her apart. She felt a gagging noise rising in her throat. He was holding her chin and mouth hard in one hand and making small grunting sounds. She tried to move, but his weight felt like concrete. It seemed to go on and on. She felt herself float out of her body, away from the couch.

Then with an awful guttural moan, he suddenly stopped. His head lolled forward onto her shoulder, his body slumped in a dead weight, pinning her painfully underneath him. She froze back into herself. What was he doing? Was he dead? She forced herself to still her thoughts. No, he couldn't be. She could hear his ragged breathing. Perhaps he'd passed out. What if someone came in? What if they saw her with him like this? With a herculean effort, Harriet used all her strength to propel her body out from under him and towards the floor. Her legs were trapped and she scrambled on her hands to get away, wrenching her legs out from underneath him. She pushed herself along the floor, back towards the desk. Mr Liddle sat up on the couch suddenly, then stood and pulled his pants up, not looking at her. His breathing was loud and measured, as if he was trying to slow it down.

'Your appalling behaviour in here today will not be spoken about to anyone, Miss Andrews. This is just between us. I'm still prepared to support your scholarship at the School Board meeting if you continue to work hard. But you will report to me once every week until your results are back on track, so I can keep tabs on how you are progressing.' Mr Liddle finished buckling his belt and went to the mirror. He began smoothing his hair over his bald patch and then poking his hands in precise motions into his waistband, ensuring that his shirt was neatly tucked in.

Harriet pulled up her tights, biting her lip to stop her whimpering with the pain. She pulled herself up off the floor with wobbly legs, and backed towards the door. The pain in her groin area was terrible. She knew she was bleeding. She was breathing in shallow gasps. She registered vaguely that tears were sliding down her face. She didn't know what to do next. Was she supposed to say something?

'You look slovenly, Miss Andrews. Fix your hair in the mirror,' Mr Liddle walked around Harriet and back behind his desk. He picked up his glasses and put them back on his nose then started reading through some papers.

Harriet hobbled to the mirror. Her pigtail had come loose and strands of hair fell around her face. She wiped her eyes hard with the heel of her palm and straightened her tie. Her reflection looked pale, sick. She tasted bile, sour and threatening, at the back of her throat.

'Sir,' the word came out as a hoarse whisper, as if she still had the flu.

'Yes, Miss Andrews?'

'Can I go?'

'Please do. And stand up straight, girl. Your posture is terrible.'

He looked back down at his papers.

Harriet walked to the exit door at the back of the room, wincing with the pain.

'I'll see you next Tuesday, Miss Andrews. 2 p.m. will be satisfactory.'

Harriet remembered her response clearly. 'Yes, Sir.' That's what she'd said to him, after he'd violated her the first time, when he asked her to come back so he could do it again. Even now, more than forty years later, the words were etched in her brain.

'He raped me, Clementine.'

Harriet realised she'd spoken those words for the first time. It meant something, but she wasn't quite sure what. She re-focussed her eyes on the carpet. Clementine had left marks of dirt on the white wool. Usually it would have made her angry, but suddenly she didn't have the energy to care.

'Mum…' Clementine leaned forward in her chair. Her voice had taken a quiet, downward turn. 'That's awful. That's… terrible.'

'Yes, well. He's dead and I'm glad that you'll never meet him. He was a horrible, nasty, revolting man and now he is dead. And I'm glad.'

The silence settled around them, sucking up the air. Harriet forced herself to take a sip of her tea, accidentally making a small slurping sound. It was still hot.

'I can't believe you sent me to the same school that must have made your life hell, Mum.'

'Oh, don't be ridiculous, Clementine. It wasn't the school's fault. The headmaster was a lovely man. I owe everything I am to that school and the first-rate education they gave me. The man who fathered you was just a rotten apple. There are always one or two in any institution.'

'But, Mum… still.'

Harriet looked sadly at Clementine, and wondered how to explain it. 'Denham House was the best, Clem. And I wanted you to have the best.'

Clementine made a small sound of disbelief, looked down at her shoes, then up again at Harriet.

'When did he die, Mum?'

Harriet stared out the window towards the granny flat. Ben must not be home. There was no light coming from the granny flat window. The idea hit her with a sinking sadness. No light anywhere. So why was she suddenly having to light up this long-dead patch of darkness for Clementine? It wasn't fair. Except that she knew that it was. For Clementine, it mattered. It wouldn't stop mattering. For too long Harriet had feared this conversation. Now it was time to have it properly. To reveal all the nasty bits, the fallout, the peel-off-your-skin disgust that overtook her at unexpected moments and made her nauseous with repressed regret about what she'd become.

'He was killed in a hit-and-run accident when you were small. The culprit was never found.'

'Really? What happened?'

Harriet stayed absolutely still. She could still picture him. 'It was not far from where we lived. He remained on staff at Denham House after I left. I used to see him walking to get his newspaper in the mornings. He'd walk along Parish Drive to the shops and I would see him from the car on my way to work if I was going in early. I was working at a small firm near the school at the time. You'd just started in primary school and I was still studying part-time at night and working during the day. Every time I drove past I would see him and think *Why do you look so smug? You are a monster. One day, someone will discover what you've done.* But he would just walk along with his head held high, as if he wasn't the worst type of criminal there was. I couldn't bear it.'

Harriet looked up at Clementine, who was now perched on the edge of her armchair, leaning forward, the heel of her palms pushing into her knees. Harriet wondered if she needed to go to the toilet, but the thought floated past quickly.

'One day it suddenly occurred to me that I probably wasn't the only one. That if he'd done it to me, he'd probably done it to other girls. And perhaps all of them weren't nearly eighteen like me. Not as equipped to cope as I was. Perhaps some of them were in the younger grades. Still children.' Harriet felt a rush, as if she was coming up for air after holding her breath under water.

'It occurred to me that Derek Liddle was possibly not just a sex offender, but that he was perhaps also a paedophile.'

'Mum?' The fear in Clementine's voice crackled through the air.

Harriet landed with a thump, back into the living room. Clementine and her dirty boots were still there. 'Yes?'

'Mum, you… you didn't… Mum, did you…?'

Clementine's mouth was hanging open.

'Mum, was it *you* who ran him down?'

Harriet took a moment to register the words. Then she let out an explosive laugh, shattering the thin pane of desperation suspended between them.

'Clementine! Goodness me. You think I would run over that terrible man and leave him lying in pain, to die on the road like a dog?' Harriet looked at Clementine and surprised herself by laughing again, then suddenly tears were welling at the edges of her eyes and running unchecked down her face. She moved her gaze to the window again and looked out into the blackness. The next words slipped out quietly as she pondered the idea.

'Me? Run over Derek Liddle? Good grief.'

She wiped at her face briskly and looked back at Clementine's furrowed face.

'It wasn't me who killed your father, Clementine. But really and truly, it is such an *edifying* thought.'

CHAPTER TWENTY-NINE

EMMA

'I'm just waiting to find out now, Dad.' Emma stood in the hospital hallway with the phone hot on her ear, ignoring the laminated paper sign on the wall: *Please switch off your mobile phone.* Behind her, in reception, a large octagonal fish tank formed a central column in the room and sad-looking goldfish swam through straggly plastic plants. A basket of toys sat next to it on the floor and a small boy sat playing with oversized Lego. Emma turned away and looked through the glass wall that faced the empty courtyard. A large pile of mulch sat seemingly forgotten in one corner of the garden bed, not a single plant in sight.

Rosie had been on antibiotics for more than two days now. Emma had been given a dose too. But she was still waiting for a definitive diagnosis.

'Mrs Parsons?'

'Dad, I've got to go.' Emma shoved the phone into her handbag in a quick, guilty movement.

The consultant had a thick head of silver hair and smiled at her kindly. He drew her towards a small breakout area in the hallway.

'Rose's lumbar puncture results have come back. You'll be pleased to know it's not the more serious meningococcal disease. It's a virus. Viral meningitis is a much less serious form of the disease.'

'Oh,' said Emma. A rush of relief and exhaustion made tears well in her eyes. 'Thank you.'

'Dr Annaby will be along soon to run you through the test results and talk to you about treatment for the rest of her stay.'

Emma gave a small sigh of relief that she could talk to the junior doctor a bit later on. All the questions she'd saved up for this moment had suddenly flown out of her head and all she could think of now was, *Thank you. Thank you very much, Doctor. But I think I might need a little lie down right about now.*

*

The time on her phone was 4.06 p.m. Which was impossible. It was four o'clock ages ago. Maybe time warped inside the walls of a hospital. Emma watched Rosie's chest rise and fall in rhythmic motion. Rosie was in a pleasantly modern hospital room, in isolation, but she would be moved soon. A sign on the door warning all staff and visitors to *Wash hands for 15 seconds before and after entering the room*, would be moved on to the next child with a notifiable disease.

Emma wondered when Phillip would arrive. She'd called him on his mobile in London at the soil conference, in a panic after the doctors had sat her down and prepared her for all the possible scenarios when Rosie was first admitted. Meningococcal disease, which the doctors had originally feared, was potentially lethal. The alternative diagnoses of viral meningitis, or a strain of flu or various other infections, were much more likely they assured her, but there were precautions they needed to take.

It was nearly 11 p.m. in London when she'd called Phillip. He wasn't answering his phone. She left four frantic voicemails and texts, then updates as the doctors gave her information, so that by the time he checked his phone early the next morning and rang – flustered and contrite, in the late of Hobart's afternoon – it was just a few hours before his paper was due to be delivered to 250 eminent soil scientists from all over the world.

'I'll come now. I'll try to get the ten o'clock flight this morning. What are the doctors saying?'

'But your paper…' Emma had let the words slide away. The fear in his voice scared her even more. She could sense his anxiety about the lack of control over what was happening, and the word 'meningococcal' was frightening to anyone. Phillip was a scientist. He understood things. He wouldn't panic if he didn't need to. Plus, he would know the right questions to ask the doctors. She wanted him to come back. Now. Not after the paper was delivered.

'I can't stay here. The paper doesn't matter. I'll be home on the first flight I can get.'

He would be on the domestic leg of the journey between Melbourne and Hobart now, thirty-two hours after that call. She re-read the text she had sent for when he landed:

VIRAL MENINGITIS!!! Thank God!!! She's going to be okay.

Rosie was still sick, but she would be alright. She could go home sometime soon. Maybe even tomorrow.

Emma tucked her head towards her armpit and took a quick sniff. She didn't smell too bad. She hadn't let Marlee bring in fresh clothes – proximity to a child with suspected meningococcal disease, or the child's potentially infected mother was not the best idea for a pregnant woman in the early stages. Emma's father had bought her a few things, but not quite the things she needed. His basket had included homemade shortbread and a thermos of soup from Mrs Salinya next door, a soft blanket for Rosie and the old teddy bear from his spare room. Jon Brownley had come in on the second day, and had brought flowers, a delicious cappuccino and a *Beautiful Homes* magazine for her to read. She'd been speechless with gratitude. Then she'd sat in the quiet of the hospital room the day after, contemplating her conflicting emotions about his kindness.

Yesterday she'd ducked down to the chemist and bought deodorant, cleansing wipes and panty liners. Two and half days wearing the same knickers felt disgusting. She was desperate for a shower. Phillip's flight should be touching down soon and then she could nip home.

She sat and stared at her daughter's face. So sweet and sick. Her heart flipped whenever she thought about what the outcome could have been. Death seemed such a strange, distant, terrifying idea. For some reason Tessa's mother popped into her head. Mrs Terrano – glamorous and snobbish. If Tessa wasn't the daughter she had hoped for, Emma wasn't really the sort of friend she had in mind either. Long-legged grace, the easy confidence that came from at least a couple of generations of money, a beautiful complexion and the ability to entice men and keep them intrigued without giving them too much. They were the traits Mrs Terrano was looking for – an *It* girl who could attract the finest of boys from St Marks. Tessa fought with her mother constantly, not able or willing to be the perfect daughter. But for all her faults, Mrs Terrano still deserved to know why her daughter died. When Rosie was better, Emma would go to the police. She looked at Rosie's pale, sleeping face. She owed the truth to Tessa and her family, however kind the headmaster might be.

She dialled Marlee's number and walked to the far corner of the room, not wanting to wake Rosie. She needed to update her on Rosie's condition. She dialled, waited as it rang, looked out across the hospital grounds towards a children's playground. A mother was pushing her child on the swing. She thought of Marlee and her baby. The baby she'd never thought she could have.

Marlee's voicemail answered: *Hi, it's Marlee Maples. Can't speak right now. Leave me a message.*

As she opened her mouth to speak, the door opened and Phillip stood in the doorway. She ended the call.

Exhaustion and relief combined in a tumbling rush, and Emma threw her arms around him. A loud sob was out of her mouth before she could speak – grief, fear, gladness, her family all in one room again.

Phillip stroked her hair.

'It's okay. She's going to be okay. I spoke to the doctor on the way in.'

Emma let go of him and turned away but the tears wouldn't stop. She tried to stifle the sobs but they kept coming in loud hiccups.

'Oh, Em. I'm so sorry.'

She couldn't bear to look at him then.

Phillip walked across to the bed and perched on the edge, putting the back of his hand against Rosie's cheek as she slept.

'You gave me such a fright, munchkin.'

Rosie didn't stir.

'You're not the only one. I was so scared, Phil. I thought she was going to die.' Tears ran down her cheeks and slid down her collarbone.

'I know. I'm sorry you had to do this alone.'

'It's not just this, though, is it? I am alone. At night, when things go wrong. I hate it.'

'I know. I'm sorry.'

'Are you?'

'Emma, I've… I've split up with Pia. She's going back to Germany.'

Emma felt the breath go out of her. She leaned against the wall and slid onto the seat next to the window. She couldn't manage the enormity of it. It was too awful. He'd split up their family, broken their hearts, for a sordid fling that had lasted less than four months.

He looked across at her.

'I'm sorry, Emma.'

She couldn't think what she wanted to say. There *was* nothing to say. Maybe she didn't really love him anymore, but she'd loved him once and she thought it meant something – to be a family. It was as if every day she'd put up with being belittled by him, put down for her flights of fancy – they all amounted to nothing. She didn't want it to amount to nothing. Her ideas mattered too. *She* mattered.

'You ruined everything.'

'Things weren't that great between us.'

'They were fine.'

'Emma, you've always put your head in the sand – you run away from all the hard stuff.'

'No, I don't.' A wave of anger coursed through her. She wasn't the weak, helpless person he thought he knew. 'Jonathan Brownley killed Tessa Terrano. I have evidence. I'm going to the police'

He cocked his head to one side and frowned. It was out of place. Out of time. Everything was wrong.

He picked up Rosie's hand and stroked it, but she slept on, her veins full of medicine.

'What evidence, Em?'

'A photo. I found a naked photo of her hidden in our cottage. He used to live in it. And the Coroner's Report. It doesn't add up. I saw her that day Phil. They fought – I told you…'

Her words were rushed, as if she needed to prove them to him. It was something she could finally do right, not just for Tessa but for herself, and for Rosie, who deserved a mother who stood up for things that were wrong. A mother who didn't put her head in the sand.

'Yes.'

'What do you mean, "yes"?'

'I mean, I remember. And if that's what you saw, and there's new evidence, then you should go to the police. If you think it's the right thing to do. If the evidence stacks up.' His voice was quiet, measured.

'Will I get in trouble for not telling them what I knew?'

'I don't imagine so. You weren't interviewed back then. You'll just say that at the time you didn't think it had a bearing on the case. They won't be interested in prosecuting someone who was a frightened teenage witness who'd lost her friend. They'd only want the killer. If he is one.'

Killer. Emma let the word float between them. It sounded so strange. So far from what she knew of Jonathan Brownley. She looked down as her phone started buzzing. Marlee. She let it go to voicemail.

'I might go home and have a shower. The doctor is due back in an hour or so to check in on her. Will you be alright if I head off? Just for a bit.'

'Of course.'

The screen of her phone lit up again and it dinged with a calendar reminder, dragging her attention away from Phillip.

25-year-reunion dinner at Staghorn 7 p.m.

Phillip looked at her, raised his eyebrows in question.

'My school reunion dinner. It's tonight.' She gave a small sigh. 'Doesn't matter.'

'You should go. You were looking forward to it, weren't you?'

Emma didn't have the energy to tell him about the 'reply all' email she sent all those months ago, just before she found him in the cottage with Pia.

'Sort of.'

'Well, why don't you just go for an hour, have something decent to eat? Then you can get a good night's sleep at home. I'll be here. I won't leave.' He sounded like the old Phillip. The serious, kind man she'd fallen in love with. She tried to smile but there was a burning feeling behind her eyes.

'I think I'll just head home. Text me when she wakes up.'

Emma walked out of the hospital, the cold of the early evening hitting her through the thin jumper she'd pulled on three days ago. She hadn't brought a coat. The air was bracing, clearing out her thoughts. She walked towards the centre of town, wondering how she was going to get home. She'd arrived in the ambulance. She needed to get a taxi. Cars drove past, but none with taxi lights on top. She thought about Phillip's suggestion that she go to the reunion for a while. The idea of sitting at home without Rosie made her feel hollow with loneliness.

As she walked further down the road, Emma noticed the lights of the police station signage flickering into life. On the opposite side of the street two police cars were parked out the front in specially marked bays on the road, their chequered blue and white side panels brightening the dull, grey streetscape.

Her phone buzzed again. Marlee's name flashed. Then the ringing stopped before she could answer it. She clicked on the missed call and dialled Marlee's number back but it went to voicemail again. *Hi, it's Marlee Maples. Can't speak right now. Leave me a message.*

'Hi, Marl. Rosie's going to be okay. She's improved a bit. Phil is with her. I'm…' She looked up as a middle-aged policeman pushed open the front door of the station. He ran down the steps in a fluid motion and slid into his car. She watched him as he checked his phone, his profile strong and comforting. She felt an odd stillness descend. 'I'm… at the police station. I'm going to report Jon Brownley for killing Tessa.'

She ended the call and noticed her phone was almost out of charge. *Two per cent.* As she crossed the road, Emma thought of the story she was about to tell. She wondered how it was going to end.

CHAPTER THIRTY

MARLEE

Ben opened the car door for her and waited as she got in.

'It's not the 1950s. I can open my own door thank you very much.' But Marlee smiled.

'Sorry. It means absolutely nothing. Although I'm very good at it. It's one of my few talents.' He smiled back at her. 'I cook a mean chicken teriyaki too. And I like vacuuming. But that's about the extent of my hidden skills.'

Marlee let him close the door. They were still feeling their way around the idea that they were having a baby. Together. She was still floored that he had wanted to stay the night when she'd told him about it. They'd talked late into the night about what a future together might look like. She smiled as she thought about it and about what had come after that, when he kissed her and undressed her slowly. It still had a bizarre sheen of unreality to it – the idea that they could have a future, a ready-made family, without any real information about how things would work or who the other person really was. She didn't even know his middle name.

'Thanks for dropping me. I could have driven. There'll be no wine for me for a while.'

'I wanted to do it. I'll duck home and get some things. Text me when you're bored with rehashing all your schoolgirl stories and I'll pick you up. Doesn't matter if it's late.'

She smiled self-consciously as they drove towards the restaurant. Her phone began ringing then stopped. It was Emma. They'd been trying to get hold of each other all afternoon. A text had come through that Rosie was getting better and Marlee had felt a pall of anxiety lift. She adored her goddaughter and the possibility of losing her had been awful. Poor Emma, it must have been much, much worse for her. All alone at the hospital. Marlee felt guilty going to the reunion dinner without her.

But Emma probably wouldn't have come anyway, not after the email thing. She was too embarrassed about trashing Phillip in the email, and the speculation she'd caused about Tessa. Marlee felt a momentary tightening in her chest when she thought about that time. But she'd put an end to Emma's suspicions about Jon Brownley. Helped her to see that she must be imagining it. Now they all just needed to move on.

Poor Emma, who thought that she was the only one haunted by Tessa. Marlee had spent years working out which gin brand suited her best in an effort to wash away the ghosts of that day. But now she was having to manage without her mother's little helper. The irony of it. But she couldn't think about the past anymore, she had to focus on the future. Little Ned. She'd told Ben about his name and he'd been thrilled with it. Adopted it immediately, dropped it into their conversation a dozen times since.

A voicemail notification flashed onto the screen of her phone. She felt the warmth of Ben's hand on her thigh as she dialled in to listen to it.

Hi Marl. Rosie's going to be okay. She's improved a bit. Phil is with her. I'm… I'm at the police station. I'm going to report Jon Brownley for killing Tessa.

Marlee pulled the phone away from her ear and watched it shake in her hand. *No.* That couldn't be right.

'No.' She heard the word from a distance.

'What's wrong?' Ben pulled over to the side of the road in front of the restaurant. They'd reached Staghorn, the venue for the reunion dinner – a funky new modern Asian place that apparently did amazing cocktails, just down the road from Denham House.

'She's reporting Jon Brownley to the police. For killing Tessa.'

'What? Who?'

'Oh no.'

'What are you talking about, Marlee?'

Marlee saw the confusion in his eyes. 'A girl who died in our final year at Denham. She was killed after a fall. Emma's gone to the police saying Jon Brownley did it.'

'That's crazy. He's a great guy... he's Harriet's brother. Why would she say that now?'

Marlee stared at him. In her mind's eye she saw the naked photograph of Tessa, so young and lovely and confused.

'She found some new evidence.' Air. She needed air. She pulled the car door handle and got out onto the street, clutching at her colourful embroidered purse.

She turned back around and bent down, putting her head back into the car. 'I'd better go in. I'll ring you... if I hear anything.' She slammed the door shut and stood on the pavement, staring at the closed door, a wave of terror closing in. She saw the window coming down. Ben leaned across.

'Marlee, are you alright?'

'I...' His face was so earnest, so kind. She had to get away before he saw the black, hollow core of her. She raised her hand in a wave then turned and walked inside, her mind a whirl. At the door of the restaurant she stood still, felt the hot rash rising up her neck. The waitress came towards her. Marlee wanted to turn and run.

'How can I help you?'

'The Denham House Reunion?'

The waitress led her towards a private room at the back. Marlee followed her through and into a beautiful room strung with fairy lights and dotted with huge potted palms. About twenty women stood around in clusters, champagne glasses in hand, elegant outfits and vibrant clutch purses and diamonds sparkling. It was a mistake, to come. She turned back towards the entry.

'Marleen Maples!' Two women descended on her in a cloud of hugs and perfume. They stood back, assessing her outfit, her facial lines, her hair. She felt dizzy, sick. She kissed their cheeks in return, pulled out their names from some distant recess of her memory.

'Laura, Annabelle, hi…' She stared at them, willing some more words to come out, but her mind was blank. The music swirled around them. A Beatles song.

A voice broke through the music then, wild and loud like a carnival hustler. The women's stares shifted behind Marlee's shoulder.

'Well hellooooooo, ladies!' Clementine was grinning, her arms spread wide, as if she were embracing the elegance of the restaurant and all the seasoned, glamorous women who turned their heads to look at her. She looked like she was going to a St Patrick's Day fancy dress parade. Marlee watched the disbelief flitting across the women's faces as they tried to find the right words to greet this bizarre, famous apparition who they'd once known simply as the larrikin cool-kid who was constantly on detention.

'Holy shit! What a boot-scooter! Twenty-five years – it screws with your head, doesn't it?' Clementine smiled at Laura and Annabelle, then faltered when she looked at Marlee. She must have seen the panic in her eyes.

'Laura Leyton and Annabelle Dixon. You girls look the bomb! But listen here, ladybirds. My old mate Marleen and I have to have a quick chat about something. I just need her for two minutes. Okay?' Clementine pulled Marlee to the corner of the room and sat her on an armchair.

'Is that baby turning your guts upside down or have you just seen a ghost? Spill. Come on. You look awful.'

'Emma's gone to the police. With some sort of evidence that Jon Brownley killed Tessa.'

'What? Oh, *shit*. I told her that was rubbish. She had a bee in her bonnet about it, weeks ago. Jonno would never have pushed her into that ditch.'

'I know.'

Marleen watched the women across the room. They kept glancing over in their direction, sipping their champagne, air kissing newcomers. The music seemed to be sinking like molasses into her head.

'He didn't,' she said. 'He definitely didn't do it.' She sat perfectly still but she felt herself merging with the chair, decades of fatigue engulfing her. She grasped at the arms. 'I did it.'

Clementine became completely still. Then she narrowed her eyes and leaned in, her voice a fierce whisper. '*What* are you talking about?'

'I pushed her… I was—'

'No.'

'Clementine, you need to tell your mother.'

Clementine stared, her eyes glassy, mouth agape. The she let out a choking sound. 'And here's me thinking this night couldn't get any more screwed-up.'

'Please. Just ring your mother.'

'You think you'll need a lawyer? Or that Jon will?'

'I think she'll know what to do.' Marlee paused, then looked across to Laura and Annabelle who were eyeing them curiously over their champagne glasses. 'Please, Clem. She always knows what to do.'

CHAPTER THIRTY-ONE

HARRIET

25 November 1993

Harriet looked at her watch for a third time, then looked back through the windscreen, willing Clementine to appear. The carpark was empty, apart from a black sports car parked in the far corner and a new-looking blue Mercedes Benz that had driven in after her and parked, quite rudely, in the space in front of her, directly adjacent to the exit gate. A girl approached the Mercedes, backpack slung over one shoulder. She got into the front passenger seat and slammed the door.

Harriet watched as a shower of late-blooming jacaranda flowers floated down from the canopy between her car and the Mercedes like pretty, lavender-hued snowflakes. As she watched, the car reversed over them then turned towards the exit and drove off. A streak of brownish-purple flower corpses remained, clinging wetly to the gravel. It struck Harriet as portentous. Clementine was unlikely to come off much better if she didn't arrive within a minute or two.

They had a dentist's appointment to get to and Harriet abhorred lateness. Where *was* that girl? Perhaps she'd gone down to Jonathan's cottage. A movement in the corner of the carpark caught her eye. A young man seemed to appear from nowhere through the trees.

He'd come from the direction of old Alice Pemberton's house, a small dilapidated cottage that bordered the school grounds. Harriet watched as the boy settled himself lazily against the bonnet of the black car. He took a packet of cigarettes from his pocket and lit one. He was a good-looking boy, dark-haired and tall, and his shirt hugged the contours of his well-muscled chest, inviting attention. He turned and looked briefly in Harriet's direction and she felt a hum of recognition – even from this distance she couldn't mistake him. Tommy Terrano. Enzo Terrano's good-for-nothing son. Harriet recalled that he'd escaped a drug dealing charge a year ago when his father had hired a pompous QC from the chambers next door to Harriet's to defend him. The boy's sister was in Clementine's class. A mixed-up girl if ever there was one. Perhaps he was waiting for her.

The wind whipped up suddenly, lurching through the canopy of the forest that bordered the carpark. The leaves heaved in unison and Harriet shuddered as the gust of wind pushed through the slit in her car window and a tumbling rush of noise followed in its wake. Harriet wound up the window as a flurry of dust settled on the car bonnet. Annoyance surged in her chest. *Selfish bloody teenagers*. She'd have to go and look for her. She'd park at Jonathan's in case Clementine came down that way, although if Harriet wasn't mistaken, Clementine was probably caught up in the art room, oblivious to everything but the brush and paint and canvas. As she drove past the Terrano boy, another gusty squall of wind tugged at his hair, showing his square-jawed profile and a lovely olive complexion. Such a shame that the rotten apples came in such shiny packages. She hoped none of the Denham House girls were silly enough to get involved with him.

CHAPTER THIRTY-TWO

MARLEEN

25 November 1993

Marleen felt like an intruder – the photograph was obviously not meant to be seen by students. The girl's puffy dark hair framed the profile of her face. It was hard to see much from here, but it must be his girlfriend. Thank God she'd arrived in time to save Tessa from the embarrassment. None of them had suspected he had a girlfriend. She took a step backwards, confused and annoyed that she was spending her time down here saving Tessa from her own stupid actions instead of doing something useful or spending a few precious hours with her mother before she went back to hospital.

A sudden scream came from the back of the cottage – short and guttural. A man's scream. It hit Marleen like an electric shock and sent her reeling backwards. She stumbled back into the small pile of firewood next to the door, catching her ankle inside the edge of the wood box. She put her hands backwards to catch her fall as she twisted, but her ankle cracked painfully as she turned against the box to find the ground with her hands. She landed on her side with a shocking thud.

Marleen sat up and tested her wrist gently. Then she unlatched her sock from the splintery vice of the wood box. A hot, sharp pain in her ankle made her wince as she stood up and leaned on the doorframe.

'Mr Brownley? Are you alright?'

She waited, listening to her own breath coming out in gasps, as if she had just run a race. She tried to calm herself. The silence inside the cottage echoed and merged with the sound of the wind brushing through the trees behind her. The pain in her ankle was pushing into her thoughts, scattering her attention.

'Mr Brownley – should I come in? Sir?'

There was no reply. Marleen lifted her foot gingerly and tried to ignore her ankle. She opened the door, fully aware now of the reasons that he didn't want her in his cottage, why she mustn't be seen here. But something about the scream hadn't sounded right. She took two steps into the dim living room and stopped. She heard a voice, low and urgent. Then another, different voice – an angry whisper. She hobbled towards them, letting her good foot take the weight, pain shooting up her other leg with each step.

'Tessa, you cannot be here. This is completely out of line. I'm sorry if I gave you the wrong idea, but you have to go.'

'That's not what you really want though, Sir. Is it?' It was Tessa's voice.

'Tessa, come on – this is not something I intended. I take full responsibility if I misled you, but you have to leave. *Seriously.*'

Marleen's heart sank. She was too late. She sighed, searched her mind for what she should do next. She needed to get Tessa out of here so Mr Brownley wouldn't get the sack, or worse. She limped into the bedroom.

Tessa's mouth fell open. 'Marleen. What are *you* doing here?'

'Tessa, let's just go. Come on. This could get everyone into heaps of trouble.'

'It's nothing to do with you.'

'Yes, it is. Part of my job is to make sure we all graduate without getting into trouble. Please Tessa, just come.'

'Don't be such a pain in the arse, Marleen.'

Tessa bent down and shoved her feet into her shoes, then busied herself tying a lace. She looked up at Marleen and back at Mr Brownley, tears sliding down her face.

'You take everything from everyone, Marleen.' Then she mimicked a teacher, waggling her head from side to side. 'Marleen Maples is so clever. Marleen is so lovely. Why can't you be more like Marleen and put in a bit more effort? Marleen, Marleen, Saint friggin' *Marleen*. Now you'll be telling Sharpy about this and then she'll tell my dad.'

Marleen moved slowly across the room and put her hand on Tessa's shoulder as she fumbled with her shoelace.

'Please, Tess. I just want you to come out of this okay.'

Tessa pushed her hand away and let out a sob. 'Out of what? I didn't do anything.' She looked at Mr Brownley and pointed. 'He's the one who's been flirting with me. For all you know he told me to meet him here. Why should I be the one who gets in the shit for this? I'm sick of taking the fall for everyone. He's as bad as my brother, wanting me to lie to save his arse.'

Marleen looked across at Mr Brownley. For a moment he didn't look like a teacher. He just looked young and scared – she'd seen the same look on her own big brother's face when they'd been told about her mother's prognosis.

'Tessa, I didn't tell you that,' said Mr Brownley. He turned his head between Marleen and Tessa, as if he was in the den of a half-tamed lion and wasn't sure whether to stay or run.

'Tessa, let's go. Please don't say stuff like that. It could get him fired,' said Marleen gently.

'Really? Good! That's good then.' Tessa stumbled forward, her remaining undone shoelace catching as she pushed past Marleen. 'Maybe I need to be the one to tell Sharpy myself then. He thinks he's so hot. It's embarrassing the way he pervs at all of us.'

She bent down and picked up her school bag from the corner of the room and walked towards the cottage front door. 'Leave me alone, Marleen.'

Marleen heard the screen door bang and felt her heart pounding.

Mr Brownley looked at her, panic enhancing his beautiful features. 'Marleen, I promise I had nothing to do with this, but if she spins that story to Ms Sharp, I'll be out of here. Doesn't matter if it's not true. They'd have to investigate and I'd be stood down, pending the outcome. The mud will stick, Marleen. You need to talk some sense into her.'

Marleen sensed it acutely then. Her responsibility and her power, and the clinging dread that had arrived as she came to realise what it meant when she'd been voted Head Girl of the venerated institution that was Denham House. Duty hung around her neck, as heavy as the birthday cape.

'Please, Marleen?'

Marleen saw the hope in his face then. The desperate hope that she could be the one to fix this problem. To save his future. She felt her ankle throb painfully. She knew she'd have to find Tessa, but she was starting to feel sweaty and sick with the pain.

'We'd better catch up with her. I can't run though. I've hurt my ankle. Just run after her. Tell her you're sorry or something – anything to calm her down. I'll follow.'

He ran out the door and Marleen limped after him. From the doorway she watched Tessa disappearing towards the oval, Mr Brownley sprinting at a distance behind her. Marleen began a slow hobbling run. With every footstep, pain glittered at the edge of her vision as her left foot met the ground, and as she started across the oval, she wondered why the school captaincy had once seemed like such a desirable pot of gold.

She let the thought slide by, focussed her mind, blocking out the pain in her ankle until it was only a jarring stab. It was something Marleen had learned to do at night, when she was studying until one or two in the morning and her body was desperate for sleep and the pain in her back and neck threatened to cloud her concentration. She would focus on the discomfort and give it its due. Then she would dissolve inside it, move her attention, order her thoughts, slot the pain away.

As she neared the hedge, she noticed that the grounds on this side of the oval were eerily empty. School sports had finished for the year. And this part of the grounds was out of bounds due to the building works. As she hobbled past the old administration block, she saw Mr Brownley. He was near the hedge that obscured the building site beside the north gates. He caught sight of her and made two quick scooping motions with his arm. *Come on.* Then he walked on, out of sight.

As she rounded the end of the hedge, she saw him again and looked in the direction he was looking. Tessa was inside some safety fencing, leaning casually against a large wooden pallet of bricks right next to a huge hole in the ground. She looked up at Marleen briefly, then down again and resumed picking at one of her nails. Marleen walked over to Mr Brownley.

'What are you doing?'

'Nothing. She told me to stay out. I don't want this to get out of hand while she's near that hole. I should go and get another teacher.'

Marleen looked at the tiny gap in the fencing, where the panels had been moved slightly out of alignment. It must have been where Tessa had slid through. Marleen walked over to it, turned sideways and did the same. She walked towards Tessa leaving Mr Brownley alone a dozen metres away and out of earshot.

'Go away, Marleen.'

Marleen flinched at the shadow of the huge trench looming out from the earth next to her.

'Tessa, are you okay?'

'What are you, a psychiatrist?'

'Sorry. I just meant—'

Tessa looked up, then her eyes flicked sideways towards Mr Brownley. 'It's no big deal, you know.'

'I know, Tess.'

'I'm just so sick of guys thinking they know better than me. Thinking they can tell me what to do.'

Marleen nodded, unsure of how to respond.

'My brother reckons the police are going to interview me. He told them he was with me last Sunday when some drug deal went down that he was accused of being at. Wants me to say it couldn't have been him, 'cos he was with me. He's such a dickhead.'

'Oh, Tess.' Marleen saw the sadness and betrayal in Tessa's eyes.

Tessa crossed her arms and slumped back against the bricks again, defeated. 'If my dad hears about any of this stuff, I'll be so dead.'

'Tess, let's get out of here… go and talk somewhere else. I'll help you sort something with your brother. And I'll tell Mr B to go home too. I'll tell him to forget all about this.'

'Gee, thanks.' Tessa rolled her eyes.

'Come on. Please?'

The wind picked up, brisk and sharp, catching Marleen's hair, blowing the embroidered floral cape flat across her chest, then making it flap loudly.

Tessa reached out and plucked at the cape, seemed to consider the detail for a moment. She rubbed her thumb over an intricately patterned daisy stitched in golden-brown thread. She let her hand fall away. 'Great dress. You should be on the catwalk.'

'Thanks.' Marleen pulled her lips back in a small smile. She needed to win Tessa's trust, get her to see straight, see past her embarrassment, see the lighter side. 'You can borrow it if you like.'

'I'm right, thanks.'

'I wish I'd worn it to the formal now, actually.'

Marleen sensed a slight relaxation in Tessa's shoulders, a tilt towards levity, and she caught something forming in Tessa's eyes.

A tiny iris-shaped rebellion. A shiny pool of mirth, threatening to spill over and drown their carefully nurtured reverence for the quirky school traditions they'd accepted throughout their years at Denham House. The smug, archaic rituals and markers – the floral birthday cape; the colour-coded neck ties denoting status and achievements; the mandatory 'nudie run' to the slip house at midnight if you let in the final hockey goal by one of the Ellery Grammar girls, their sworn rivals in everything from equestrian sports to the St Marks boys.

Tessa's lips sucked against her teeth, as she tried hopelessly to smother a smile.

Marleen felt laughter bubbling up in her too. The years of striving to never put a foot out of line. The relentless study, keeping her from social events and family time, even while her mother was fading away before her eyes. She put her hand over her mouth. The absurdity of it. And now, here they were, standing inside a building site – Tessa humiliated, and Marleen with a sprained ankle in a ridiculous floral cape, holding a teacher outside the barrier to ransom. The scandalous, hilarious, unbelievable *cheek* of Tessa. To break into his house! The front!

Their eyes met and laughter burst from their mouths simultaneously, fizzing and spreading like spilled lemonade. They clutched at each other's arms, bent at the waists, loud snorting giggles erupting over and over – a maelstrom of relief. A shared understanding that they stood on the cusp of adulthood with all its dazzling promise, if only they could make it through these last few days of childhood.

Outside the barrier, Mr Brownley watched them, his puzzled face morphing into a frown.

'Girls, come out. It's dangerous in there.' The wind blew at his words, whipping them away towards the oval.

They looked at each other, a fresh burst of laughter catching Marleen in her chest. She was helpless to stop. Tessa swayed towards

Marleen, her back to the trench. She was bent double with the effort of laughing, shaking with it.

Eventually they caught their breath.

Marleen was panting, her hand across her chest. 'Come on, Tess. Let's just forget about it. We'll be out of here next week. He won't even remember you were there tomorrow. He's got too much marking to do.'

Tessa rubbed her hand across her eyes, then reached into her tunic pocket and pulled something out. A photograph. She looked at it briefly, then turned it towards Marleen.

'Except I left him one of these to remember me by. I got double prints.'

Tessa was reclining on a lounge. Her lips parted, dark hair spilling down in front of her naked shoulders. Her breasts sat pert and perfect in the centre of the picture.

'Oh.' Marlee looked up, wide-eyed. 'Right.' *The photo on the mantelpiece.*

Marleen thought quickly. He wouldn't have seen it yet. Maybe they could get it back.

She wondered whether she'd have to say anything about all this to Ms Sharp. She felt a sudden tiredness wash over her. Her ankle throbbed angrily as she lifted her foot off the ground, the flood of pain making her wince.

Tessa watched her and seemed to wither. Her face became child-like, imploring. As if she knew her consuming struggles could be solved by Marleen, who had today become an adult, after all. Marleen Maples, Head Girl, who could fix anything. Tessa's fingers turned slightly upwards, offering the photo, a gift that Marleen didn't want. She just wanted to go home. To her mother. She was so tired.

It was the hesitation that caused it. A brief, terrible moment where Marleen's hand stopped in mid-air, as she considered the kaleidoscope of possibilities flickering through her head – the same moment that Tessa decided, irretrievably, to let go of the problem and hand it over to Marleen. The wind, sensing the release of Tessa's fingers on the photograph, broke through the camellia branches like a thief, tossing the photograph up into the air.

Tessa let out a cry. Marleen's arm shot up and outwards to grab at the photograph, just a millisecond later. Except the photograph had flown away, across the other side of the fencing, and Marleen's hand caught Tessa's chest, hard and straight on. Tessa stumbled backwards. Then, just as she found her feet a metre from where Marleen stood, her left shoe found itself in a battle with the undone shoelace of her right shoe, so that when she tried to lift it to take one final steadying step at the edge of the trench, her foot didn't follow. Sick horror pushed Marleen forwards, her hands grasping as she watched Tessa's arms swinging once, twice, grappling with air. Then gravity and momentum took over and Tessa's terrified face was there, then it wasn't.

Marleen heard her own scream like a distant church bell – ringing and insistent. She fell to her knees. Mr Brownley was suddenly beside her. He knelt and peered into the depths of the hole.

'Tessa! Tessa – answer me!'

Marleen felt faint, fearful that she would topple forward. She put her shaking hands on the ground beside her and leaned in. She could see Tessa lying awkwardly, in the shadowy pit, staring back at them.

'Tessa! Are you alright?' Marleen knew as she said it, between her own jerky breaths, that the question was disingenuous. Tessa looked strange. Her neck was tilted to one side at an unnatural angle. As they watched, a trickle of blood slid down from one of her nostrils. It was shadowy down there though. Marleen couldn't be completely sure what she was seeing.

'Tessa, say something.' Marleen grasped at Mr Brownley's shirt sleeve. 'Sir, she's hurt… really…' Marleen was panting as the sick reality turned her mouth to a dry sludge. The words wouldn't come out. 'Sir… ambulance.'

Mr Brownley's eyes flicked back and forth.

'Right. Right…' He stood up, twisted, turned back. 'I'll go. Or maybe I should…' He was staring down into the hole. It was impossible to get down there.

'Sir, quick!' She shook his arm hard. He needed to run. *Run.* Marleen leaned over the edge of the hole again. 'Tess, we're getting an ambulance. They're coming.' Tessa's eyes stared back blankly.

Mr Brownley was looking into the hole, then around at the building site, dazed. His mouth hung open.

Marleen saw the panic rising in him, watched him slam his palms into his forehead. 'The *stupid* girl! There'll be no way out now. She's dead, can't you see?'

'Sir. Stop! Just get an ambulance. I've hurt my ankle. I can't run. You need to go!'

Suddenly, a figure was beside them. A small, well-dressed woman appeared from nowhere. Her face was taut with questions. Marleen's brain was spinning. *She knew her. How did she know her?*

'What's happened?'

The woman's tone was clipped and authoritative. She was so *familiar.*

Mr Brownley grabbed at the woman's arm.

'Oh God! I shouldn't have let this happen. What have I done? What are we going to do?'

Marleen followed the woman's profile as she leaned towards the hole and peered over, then she realised that neither Mr Brownley nor the woman were moving or speaking. She squeezed her fingernails into her palms and summoned every bit of remaining energy in her chest, forcing out words in a boiling rush of fear and dismay.

'You need to get an ambulance. Please! It was an accident. You need to get it *now*!'

CHAPTER THIRTY-THREE

HARRIET

'Mum, can you take me to Jen's house?'

Harriet looked up from her book at Scarlett. She was standing in front of the fireplace in full make-up, wearing an eye-wateringly short, pink satin dress. The neckline plunged dangerously towards her navel, leaving the view of her breasts almost entirely at the disposal of Hobart's male population. Female too, Harriet supposed. A loud sigh escaped her mouth. Her daughters were fortunate to have such a tolerant mother.

When Clementine had finally left for the reunion dinner after their talk, it had left Harriet feeling odd. Lighter. As if a part of her had disappeared into thin air along with her revelation about Derek Liddle and his unsolved death. She had felt pleased, even though Clementine had gone strangely quiet. Well, it wasn't a small thing to consider – the fact that your genetic lineage was not exactly as you might have wished it to be. Perhaps that's why Harriet had held back the secret from her all these years. The tarnish wasn't to be underestimated. And yet, suddenly it felt like it didn't matter. That he didn't matter. Clementine had always been here on her own terms. She was a good person, whoever her father might have been.

Harriet averted her eyes from the place where Scarlett's dress should have been and pushed her slippers back onto her feet.

'What's happening at Jen's house that calls for only half an outfit, Scarlett?'

'Mum! This is designer. It was expensive!'

'Well, more fool you.' She wondered if Ben had given her the money. Harriet gave Scarlett very little. In her experience, money was the cause of most problems. Sex caused quite a lot of the others.

'Can you take me or not, Mum?'

'*You* can take *me*, Scarlett. Evening driving hours – I'm sure you need some of those, don't you? Good experience.' Harriet closed her book and turned off the CD player reluctantly. Beethoven's Fifth Symphony, with its primal emotional energy and defiant key changes, was her favourite.

'Okay. I'll get my licence.' Scarlett stalked off down the hallway, teetering on absurdly high heels.

'Get some better shoes to drive in. And your L Plates are in the kitchen. Your father left them there on the weekend.'

Harriet walked to the closet and took out a jacket.

'Where are we going?' asked Harriet, after Scarlett had slid into the driver's seat and adjusted the mirrors.

'I think it's Tighe Street. You remember Mum – near the school. I don't know the number but I know the house so it doesn't matter.'

Scarlett pressed the button to start the BMW and flicked her eyes nervously between the reversing camera and the back windscreen. As they drove along quietly, Harriet relaxed a little. She was surprised at how she was enjoying this time with Scarlett. A small bell of happiness pealed inside her head as she watched her daughter perched on the seat, back ram-rod straight, arms clenched, eyes constantly checking. Scarlett was transforming before her eyes. Spreading her wings. A dazzling, nervous, semi-naked butterfly.

A buzz from her mobile phone made Harriet grope around in her handbag. She pulled out her phone. Three missed calls – strange. The phone hadn't sounded. There were two from Ben and one from Clementine.

'Scarli, let's just slow down up here for a minute and see if you can manage a parallel park up between those two cars.'

'What? Why? I hate parallel parking!'

'Exactly. You need to practise it. Come on, there's plenty of room between them. Two car spaces at least.'

Scarlett made a loud huffing sound in protest, then slowed the car.

'Just pull up parallel with the car in front, then reverse about a metre before turning the wheel. You know how it's done.'

'Why can't I just use the automatic parking function?'

'Because, Scarlett, not all cars have an automatic parking function. This is an expensive car. You won't always be in one of these!' Harriet slowed her breathing. 'Now, just reverse.'

A text message pinged. Then another. Harriet looked down at her phone. The first one was from Clementine.

Jon's in trouble. He's been reported to police as having killed Tessa Terrano. He'll need a lawyer. Pick up your phone.

Harriet felt a sick shot of terror.

She read the next one from Ben, her hand trembling.

Harriet, your brother will need legal counsel if what I've heard is true. Something about that girl's death at Denham years ago that he's been implicated in. You should call him. B.

Harriet observed the sensations of her fight or flight reactions, as the adrenalin coursed through her body. She understood the science of fear, and right now only small parts of her bodily responses would serve her. The adrenalin was making her blood pump more forcefully towards her muscles to make them move faster. She was shaking and edgy, alert. Her blood pressure was rising. Her instincts were ordering her body to act, quickly. But she needed her brain to be in control right now, not her body. She took a millisecond to speak sternly to the fright hormone as it pulsed through her. *Enough! That is enough. I am in control now.*

She looked at her daughter fumbling with the wheel, unaware that a chasm had opened up inside Harriet's head.

'Mum, I can't do it. I'm going to hit the curb.'

A beat. A moment too late. 'Yes, I see. Your angle's wrong.'

'What should I do? There's a car up my arse!'

'Drive on Scarlett. Drive to Jonathan's place. Quickly, it's not far. Something's happened.'

'What? No! I've got to go to Jen's. You can go after you drop me.'

A monstrous force was rising inside Harriet's chest. Taking her over. Threatening to drown out rational thought. It frightened her. All these years. The terrible, stupid death of the Terrano girl. The decades of living with the nightmares. Of protecting her brother. Protecting the Maples girl. And now that awful, clever girl was sleeping with the only man who ever loved her. But if Marleen Maples was brought down with this, Harriet and Jonathan would be too. There was no choice but to step in. She didn't have a choice. She needed to get to Jonathan. To protect him. To protect them all. To make sure the only words spoken to the police were the ones that told the story in the right way. Jonathan was precious. He had been gifted to her – his chubby hands, his beautiful blond curls – delivered to save her from the loneliness and the pain of growing up smart and poor and not so good at making friends. She couldn't break through the barriers, the disdain for her circumstances. The jealousy over her pretty face, her ability to synthesise a thousand conflicting thoughts into a coherent chain and deliver them back as a whole, beautiful concept. She was the stuck-up scholarship girl always on the fringe. Then pregnant. *Pregnant!* After all that investment they'd made in her education! An abomination. But she had something worth more than all of them and their fancy cars and houses – a precious jewel who gave her strength through the horrible days of her adolescence. Who snuggled into her lap and wiped away her tears on all the days that Derek Liddle had raped her, and once again on the day she realised she was carrying his bastard child. She had her beautiful, clever boy. Her brother. She was not about to let him down.

The car behind them began tooting.

'Drive! Now, Scarlett. Drive as fast as you can. I need to get to Jonathan's place.' Harriet looked at her daughter, a shiny pink deer caught in the headlights.

'I said *drive*, Scarlett! Now!'

CHAPTER THIRTY-FOUR

HARRIET

25 November 1993

'What's happened?' Harriet looked into the trench, then withdrew, shock widening her eyes.

Jonathan looked at her, panicked. 'Oh no! I shouldn't have let this happen. What have I done? What do we do?'

'You need to get an ambulance. Please! It was an accident. You need to get it *now*!' It was the head girl speaking to her. Marleen Maples. She was wearing a birthday cape that was flipping against her legs in the wind.

Harriet looked into the trench again, taking a moment to assess the situation. A girl was lying, unmoving, about three or four metres down. Harriet saw Marleen look briefly across the barriers towards the main school buildings in the distance. She had a wild look in her eyes.

'Mrs Andrews, I hurt my foot. *Please* can you go?'

Harriet looked down again into the hole. Something was very wrong. The girl's eyes were open. Her neck was crooked. It dawned on her then. Jonathan's words. The danger in them.

'What's happened, Jon?'

'Oh, Hattie! She was running to the office to tell them about being in my cottage. Saying I got her there for sex. Marleen tried to stop her – it was an accident. She knocked her… we were just trying to get her to tell the truth.'

Harriet felt the oxygen recede around her. She tried to take a slow breath as her brother's words sank like rocks into the pit of her stomach.

'Why was she in your cottage, Jon? The truth. I need the truth or I can't help.'

She watched Marleen Maples stand up, edgy with fear. The girl took two steps backwards, then sank to the ground with a groan, grasping her ankle, tears running down her face.

'Mrs Andrews, she might be alive. Please run. *Please* go now.'

Harriet ignored her and kept her eyes trained on her brother. 'Jonathan. Tell me.'

'She broke in. She wanted sex. I told her no. Maybe I led her on, Hattie, but I swear, if I did, I didn't know I was doing it. She got upset and said she was going to say we'd been together. Marleen was in my guitar lesson. She came down and found us. Then we followed her here and Tessa had a photograph, or something that blew away. They tried to get it but she fell.'

'What was in the photograph, Marleen?' asked Harriet.

'It was Tessa, naked. It was for Mr Brownley.'

Harriet felt Marleen slipping away, losing control of her emotions. She took a moment to gather her thoughts into order. Proffered sex, naked photograph, Jonathan's cottage, a dead girl.

'Marleen, an ambulance won't make any difference. Look at her. She would have fractured her skull on the rocks and her neck looks broken. The drop would be fatal with that kind of head impact.' Harriet looked across at the mountain of excavated dirt behind them, filled with odd-sized chunks of basalt.

Tears were flooding down Marleen's face. Harriet could see the panic rising up in her as she realised what she'd done.

Harriet closed her eyes, her face turning towards the oval. Then after a few moments she opened them again, the clarity of thought finally distilling itself into a precise picture of what must now happen.

'Marleen, you have a very bright future ahead of you. This was an accident. A *terrible* accident. But it was not of your doing. Not really. Tessa brought it on herself. She's dead and there is nothing to be done about that. I think it's best if you both say you knew nothing about this. An investigation would require you to give evidence about why you were in here with her. Where you had been earlier. What you had argued about. There will be dozens of questions. Hundreds. The answers you would give would be honest, but a shadow would be cast. Over you, and over my brother. It would tarnish your good names. Whispers would start. Why were you down by the cottage at all? What did you know? Were you having an *affair* with your teacher? Were you *jealous* of Tessa? Mr Brownley will also be under suspicion. His career would be finished. It has barely begun. Both of you have bright futures ahead of you. Now, I want you to listen to me. *Listen* very carefully.'

Harriet watched the head girl's face crumple as she began to lay out the plan. It was all down to Marleen now. Jonathan would do as she said. He'd always been an obedient boy. Completely trusting.

The memories flitted through Harriet's head as if they'd happened yesterday. In her mind's eye she could still see her brother's angelic five-year-old face hanging on her every word: 'Jonny, don't tell the teacher Mum's gone away, okay? If I'm held up after school and they see you on your own, just say you're waiting for your big sister because Mum's at an appointment. I promise I'll come and get you. I might be a bit late, that's all.'

Jonathan bit his bottom lip and nodded, his backpack jiggling against his shoulders and down to the back of his knees. 'You must promise, Jonny. If they find out there's no grown-up in the house, they'll split us up and put you in a horrible home with strangers. They won't let you take your books or Barney bear or anything. Okay? You wouldn't want that, would you?'

'No, Hattie.' He shook his curly head of hair and stared back at her with huge trusting eyes.

'Alright then. Soon I'll be eighteen and a proper adult anyway and it won't matter. Mum will be back though. Don't worry darling. She'll be back.' Harriet knelt down and tied his shoelace, feeling her baby twist and kick in her stomach, as she wondered why Jonny wouldn't try tying them himself. Surely you were meant to know how to do it at five? She remembered that she could do it by the first day of school. Their mother had insisted.

She just hoped Mum would be back soon. She'd been good lately. Since she'd gotten out of the hospital. More reliable. Less prone to taking off on a whim. But it still happened. She'd be sullen and edgy and leave Harriet a note to find in the morning, returning days later, pretending she didn't know what Harriet was complaining about. There was plenty of food in the cupboard (rarely the case) and no sewing jobs to be finished (Harriet had finished two skirts for Mrs Pulfreyman when she demanded they be ready on Thursday evening or she'd have her deposit back, thank you very much!).

Now, the wind whipped at Harriet's face, dragging her back from her memories. She watched the Maples girl. She was attractive in an unusual kind of way, with her long red hair and intense green eyes; and she was smart. The girl's doubts were written into her frown, making Harriet nervous about what she would do. But Harriet was not about to let that little Terrano slut bring down her baby brother.

Everyone knew Tessa Terrano was trouble. Her father was a bully. A dishonest, entitled multi-millionaire with a penchant for paying off women he treated badly. Harriet kept her ear to the ground around the courts. She'd picked up whispers of complaints that never made it onto paper. Hobart was a small place. Enzo Terrano's troubled, musically precocious daughter was probably lucky to be away from him. A spark of sympathy flared briefly for

Tessa, but Harriet extinguished it quickly. Tessa's home life was probably difficult, but whose wasn't? Falsely accusing a teacher of abuse was completely inexcusable. It was a slap in the face to those students who *had* been abused. A shallow, pernicious thing to do. She took another look inside the trench. The girl's vacant stare made her flinch with regret.

'Marleen, are you listening?' Harriet could see that the girl was grappling with a war between her conscience and the catastrophic possibilities Harriet was putting in front of her. Everyone knew Marleen was a straight shooter – clever, sensible, self-contained. Strong in the face of family adversity. Harriet needed to find a way in.

'I've heard your mother has only weeks to live, Marleen. She doesn't need her last days on this earth ruined by scandal, does she? You're a wonderful daughter and a great asset to Denham House. The school and your family both need you to stay strong in this.'

'Please, Mrs Andrews—' The words were followed by a suffocated sob. 'I need you to get her some help. Please!' Marleen had sunk to the ground and was holding her ankle.

'I'm going to get help now. Of course I am. But listen to me, Marleen. The truth will make no difference to the outcome for Tessa. So – you were not here. *Neither of you* were here. You must go, both of you. Now! You were in a guitar lesson. Do you hear me? Together.'

'In the music room,' said Jonathan.

'Yes, in the music room,' said Harriet. 'Marleen, did you hear that? Do you understand? You were nowhere near this building site. Now go!'

'Harriet, I don't know… I don't know if—' Jonathan stopped abruptly as Harriet turned to face him. Fear was etched across his face like a wound. This was his moment of reckoning, Harriet knew. The split second in time where his gilded journey ended and something more sinister came to take its place. Because nobody as beautiful as Jonathan, as intelligent and precious, could be handed it all for free. Harriet knew full well that that was just the way life worked. She must not falter now. What he needed now from her was tough love.

She clenched her teeth briefly and narrowed her eyes as she watched the Maples girl cup both hands over her face.

Jonathan put his arm on Marleen's shoulder, then he let it slide down and turned back towards her. 'Harriet, I don't think—'

'Don't think, Jonathan,' hissed Harriet. 'Just do it. *Do it now!*'

CHAPTER THIRTY-FIVE

HARRIET

Scarlett accelerated down the street, knuckles clenched white around the steering wheel.

'Left here,' said Harriet.

'Okay.'

'Go a bit faster. There's no traffic.'

'What's wrong, Mum?'

'Nothing. Just focus on the road. Go across Ellery Way. You'll avoid having to slow down at all the roundabouts on Johnson Street.'

'Alright, Mum! Keep your hair on.'

Scarlett stopped at the lights on Linden Road and Harriet punched in Jonathan's phone number. It rang out. She dialled it again but the result was the same.

'Blast him! Why isn't he picking up?' She knew it was unlikely the police would come out on a Saturday night to talk about such an old case. But without all the information, she couldn't be sure. *When had he been reported? What stage were the investigations at? Who had reported him?* Perhaps he'd gone down to the police station already, some sort of misplaced guilt guiding him now that the truth was catching up with them. Harriet shuddered as Scarlett began accelerating through the green light and down the hill towards the school. Jonathan had a large old family home on the prettiest part of the school campus. Headmaster's privilege.

She tried Ben's number.

'Harriet?'

Relief swamped her. 'What do you know about this investigation into Jon?'

'I... Nothing. Marlee mentioned it earlier. She was heading to her school reunion. She said her friend was with the police about Jonathan. She sounded worried for him. Something about a girl who died in their year at school. I presume it's the one you told me about when we first met.'

'I see.'

'She said her friend had been investigating things for a while now. She mentioned some evidence about Jon that had been dug up.'

'What evidence?'

'She didn't say.'

'Was that all?'

'Yes, that's all. Could it be true? It sounds crazy to think—'

Harriet ended the call, cutting off his final words. Scarlett moved forward through the intersection then slowed down at a pedestrian crossing as an old lady stepped onto the road.

'Mum, what investigation into Jon?'

'Just drive, Scarlett. That woman's far enough across now. *Go.*' Harriet made a shooing motion towards the old lady.

'Mum, you're being really weird.' Scarlett's voice was quivering.

The car in front of them slowed to a halt in front of a set of units and the passenger door opened underneath the streetlight.

'Go around that car, he's letting someone out on the street.'

Scarlett put on her indicator and pulled around the car, torturously slowly.

'Christ, Scarli, can you just go a bit faster! You're being childish. There's no bloody traffic.'

Harriet felt the car jerk forward as her daughter put her foot down. They were nearly there now. Just through the lights at Ellery

Way. It would all be fine when she got there to control things. To filter the flow of information to the police. Her heart hammered.

The school grounds started up ahead on the opposite corner, but the grounds were huge and Jonathan's house was a block further down. She glanced down at her phone again and redialled Jonathan's number and held it to her ear, letting it ring as she looked up at the traffic lights ahead.

'You'll make that orange light, Scarli. Go.'

Scarlett looked across at her, hesitation slowing her down.

'Mum, you're supposed to stop if you can.' But Scarlett must have caught something in Harriet's look and she kept going. The light hovered endlessly on orange as they approached the busy intersection of the main road. Then it turned red, just as Scarlett let her foot drop, a little too late, onto the accelerator. She didn't commit to it though. You have to *commit* to a decision to get through an orange light.

Harriet grasped her seat as the red light arrived, well before they'd nosed into the start of the intersection. Ahead she saw a bright green Ford Falcon with a thick black strip down the side of the car, waiting at the lights to go across in front of them. The driver was just a boy. He had his left arm out of the window resting on the car door, tapping the roof of the car in time to the thumping music that was coming directly out of his car speakers and into Harriet's brain like the howls of a rabid dog.

'Stop, Scarli.' But Harriet's words were strangled by the jolt of adrenalin that released itself into her system, as she recognised the pulsing rumble of the boy revving his engine, throbbing pools of testosterone belting down his leg, shooting through the rubber of his shoes and into the car accelerator, over and over, building and building to a powerful, pounding thrill. *ROAR. ROAR. ROAR.* Harriet's words wouldn't come out. Her voice was swallowed by the terror.

Scarlett was speeding up, but it was too late. *Far too late.* The boy was letting go of the brake. Letting the accelerator have its head.

His tyres screeched as he left behind a tail of black rubber marks on the road. They would have been such good, long ones too. Any other time. But this time they were cut short by the explosion, as his bonnet connected with Scarlett's door, the white metal of Harriet's BMW suddenly awash with bright green streaks of paint as the car door bucked and crumpled inwards. The screech of metal, the sound of glass shattering, a terrible hot cacophony that mixed inside Harriet's head with the petrol fumes and the sickly-sweet smell of Scarlett's blood as she and Harriet were pushed sideways and forwards and up and over in a tumbling crash.

With a violent jolt, they mounted the curb and slammed against the fence, crashing through and finally jerking to a stop as they were swallowed by the cypress hedge at the north gate entrance to Denham House.

Harriet felt a brutal *thwunk* as her head landed back against the headrest, then there was a jangling stillness. She forced her eyes open and words seemed to be spinning through her vision. She closed her eyes then opened them again. She realised the words were on a signboard they'd collected which was now jammed onto the windscreen by the dense hedge. Black lettering in swirling vintage font blared at her:

Denham House School for Young Ladies
Established 1898
Please Use Main Entry via Buckingham Road.

Harriet turned her head towards Scarlett and heard herself begin to scream.

CHAPTER THIRTY-SIX

HARRIET

25 November 1993

She watched them go. Each step an obvious effort for Marleen as she leaned on Jonathan's arm. Harriet wondered when she'd hurt her ankle. If it was during this debacle, she hoped Marleen had the wherewithal to come up with a believable explanation, preferably something implicating the music room steps. They'd been a hazard for decades.

They disappeared behind the hedge, leaving Harriet alone, at the edge of the hole, with a serious problem on her hands. She should hurry, but she needed to think. Just a minute to think through the whole thing clearly, so it sounded plausible. Why was she around this way? What made her come inside the barrier?

The bag, that was it. She came through the building barriers because she saw a bag inside them. It had worried her. She hurried back to the barrier and slipped through, picking up Tessa's bag from the ground where it sat outside. She slid back through, lifting it overhead as she did.

Now, where to place it so it was easily seen? She walked back over to the trench and placed it down carefully. The grass grew right to the edge, so footprints weren't obvious where they'd stood. Her court shoes had square heels. They hadn't pierced the grass, and if they were spotted, she could say she'd been here anyway. She had discovered the body, after all. She looked around carefully for other evidence that might place the others at the scene. There was none. She turned briefly back to the hole. Tessa's vacant eyes made her flinch, reminding her of the uproar that would soon break. In the following weeks and months, it would be raised in conversation countless times. People would feign great sadness, but secretly they'd be desperate to turn the details of the Terrano girl's strange death inside out over cups of coffee; to hear the reactions and details from a close insider. Harriet was a current mother, an old girl, the sister of a teacher, she discovered the body – there would be no escaping it.

The face of Sabina Terrano popped into her head, ageing and immaculate. Tessa's mother was an old girl too – like Harriet – except much older and covered with a thin skin of entitlement that sometimes grew on full fee-paying girls. Harriet could mix with that crowd easily enough, but she was never comfortable wallowing in their shared past. She'd spoken to Sabina only last week, at the leavers' assembly. Sabina had pulled away from Enzo, who was himself pulling irritably at his collar and tie, and she congratulated Clementine on winning the art prize. *Harriet must be so proud!* Harriet had been momentarily mute, then she remembered that Tessa was head chorister, and she'd given a beautiful, eerie rendition of the Lord's Prayer. Harriet had been pleased that she'd remembered to congratulate Sabina in return. Often she forgot to do things like that – compliments and so on. Poor Sabina would always have the memory of that song at least.

Harriet squatted and unzipped Tessa's backpack, checking for evidence of the photograph that Marleen had talked about, or other incriminating items. But there were only some books, a huge heavy pencil case and a hair ribbon. She flicked through the pages of the books. Nothing.

She dropped the bag in position and took one last look at Tessa. The hole reminded her of a grave, except it was larger. Much too large for poor Tessa's small, crumpled frame. Her left leg splayed at a strange angle, and Harriet wondered if it was broken. A sudden movement made Harriet draw back with a start. A brief, shocking, flutter of the fingers in Tessa's left hand. It was a tiny movement – almost unbelievable since the girl's eyes were open in a death stare – but Harriet didn't doubt that she'd seen it. She stood up, her thoughts racing. She knew a little about catastrophic head injuries. She'd done plenty of medical law and trauma cases. Perhaps the girl was in some sort of vegetative state. Perhaps there was still some brain function. Perhaps the girl... no, surely not. Various alternative prognoses presented themselves, and Harriet discarded each as they arrived. *Could she possibly regain consciousness?*

Harriet brought her hand to her mouth, slowly. She knew Jonathan would never have tried anything on with this girl. It wasn't his style. But what if there *had* been something? Something that she hadn't been told about? Or what if she'd been seen in his cottage and she woke up and made up some story about it. Gave evidence about what the inside of his bedroom looked like. If she had a grudge against him for some reason – poor marks on a test, or Jonathan's rejection of her – it would be easy to bring him down. A teary, articulate private school girl on the stand, imploring the judge and jury not to allow such a thing happen to anyone else. Even if Jonathan avoided a conviction, he'd never survive the scandal. No. Harriet couldn't take that chance. She walked towards the barrier and slipped out of the crack and into the grounds, then she stopped and thought. She needed to leave the girl a little longer, just to be sure.

She looked around, checked there was no one to see her, then she walked towards the main administration buildings, tracing the patterns of her thoughts. There was no room to doubt herself. Assuming the girl didn't wake, she could spin the situation.

After a few minutes, she reached the administration block and opened the office door. Old Moira Ryan sat behind the desk.

Surely she was past retirement age by now? She hadn't been all that young when Harriet had been at the school.

'Hello, Harriet.' Moira Ryan looked up from the desk that was covered in envelopes and folded letters. She smiled.

'Hello, Miss Ryan.'

'What can I do for you, dear?'

'Well, probably nothing. But I just thought I'd mention it. There's a school bag inside the construction site over near the cypress hedge at the north entrance gate. Thought it was a bit odd.'

'Mmm. Yes, that is strange, dear.'

'I didn't want to go in and retrieve it. There were Keep Out signs everywhere. Probably a leaving prank or something.'

'Alright. I'll pop over in a bit and have a look. Thank you, Harriet. How is Clementine feeling about her last days of incarceration?' Moira Ryan gave a small laugh. It made Harriet's stomach turn uncomfortably.

'Fine, I think. I'm just off to find her now. She was meant to meet me in the car park, but she's probably in the art room, so I'll check there first. That girl would forget her head if it wasn't screwed on.'

'Oh dear,' said Moira, smiling. 'They say artistic types haven't the same brains as the rest of us. Perhaps she's destined for great things.'

'Stranger things have happened I suppose,' said Harriet. She waved as she walked out. 'Goodbye, Miss Ryan.'

'Goodbye, Harriet. And don't you worry a jot. I'll go and hunt down that bag and its owner in a moment and sort her out quick smart.'

CHAPTER THIRTY-SEVEN

EMMA

Emma stepped out of the bathroom and picked up the blue floral dress. She turned it around on the hook. It was this or black pants and a cardigan. Definitely the dress. She wouldn't be up-to-date in the fashion stakes, but she felt unaccountably happy with it. She pulled it on over her head and the stretchy fabric hugged her hips in a way that looked strangely okay. The colour suited her. Picked up something in her eyes. She twirled in front of the mirror, then stopped and stared at herself. She felt brave. Impressed with herself.

As she'd stood on the pavement outside the police station earlier, her heart had been pummelling. She'd taken a few minutes to draw up her courage and as she'd stood staring at the entry doors to the police station through the dusky half-light, a woman in faded black jeans and a dirty white jumper with straggly long hair had stumbled out of them. She was followed by a giant of a man. His head was shaved and tattoos snaked up his neck and out the top of his black bomber jacket. The woman was thin and sick-looking and under the harsh fluorescent lights her skin was wrinkled and cratered with the tell-tale signs of cigarettes and drugs and booze. The man mumbled something to her. She whipped her head around towards him.

'Don't touch me, ya prick!'

Her words were slurred and she pushed the man away, stumbled on the steps, then righted herself with an indignant swipe as he tried to catch her. She walked straight down the stairs towards Emma, brushing up against her as she stumbled again towards the road. The smell of the alcohol smacked through Emma's thoughts, dissolving her righteous anger and confused emotions about Jon Brownley, and mixing them into a murky pool of guilt about the advantages she'd had in life – the loving home, the education, the money – not pots of it like some of the girls she'd grown up with, but she'd never gone without.

She deflated as a heavy sadness sank through her – for this woman and the thousands like her who waded through life lurching from one crisis to the next, because of addiction, or lack of opportunity or abuse. Somehow it didn't feel fair. She wondered if maybe the police had better things to do tonight than listen to her old story. More urgent problems to solve. Maybe she really should go to the reunion for a while and remind herself how lucky she was to live inside such a bubble of privilege. Maybe Tessa could wait for one more day. She would go home and appreciate what she had and find something to change into to celebrate with old friends.

Emma watched the couple walk off down the darkening street, one behind the other, the woman weaving unsteadily. A taxi pulled up on the pavement a little way down the street and the decision had been made. And now, here she was, about to brave the school reunion on her own.

She heard a distant wail of another siren, and hesitated as it became louder. It was the second one since she'd turned off the hairdryer. A different siren suddenly joined in, *Wee-Wah Wee-Wah Wee-Wah*. An ambulance on its way to some poor soul. Emma thought of Rosie in her hospital bed. She'd send a text to Phillip when her phone had charged to check how she was. The sounds got louder suddenly. Different sirens intermingling. Close by. Very close. She shivered. An accident in the boarding house? Someone in the neighbouring villas? She took a breath, tried to clear her mind, stop her thoughts spiralling. Mercifully, the sirens stopped.

She pulled on her shoes and got her cardigan out of the cupboard and looked in the mirror. She'd washed her hair and dried it and had managed to tame the blond mess into waves, like the hairdresser did sometimes. They sat nicely on her shoulders, some flicking out, some flicking under. She put her sapphire studs in her ears and added a splash of pink lipstick. Her eyes looked sparkling blue with this dress. The overall effect was… pleasing.

She pulled her phone off the charger and turned it on. There were four missed calls from Marlee and one from Clementine. Why would Marlee need her so badly? Perhaps she was together with Clementine at the reunion. They might be calling about her voicemail telling Marlee she was reporting Jonathan to police.

Emma shivered. The window must be open. It was so *cold*. She pulled back the curtains to check. Across the other side of the school grounds, flashing coloured lights whirled in circular motions, red and blue bursts of light breaking into the black sky. They were too close. Right by Ellery Way. She closed the curtains and pulled on her coat. She would walk to the reunion. She'd been cooped up in the hospital for too long. She'd call Marlee as she walked. It always made her feel safer walking at night if she had someone on the phone, protecting her from the shadows.

Outside her cottage the darkness hung like a thick, black blanket. She turned on the torch of her phone and scurried towards the main buildings, trying to keep to the pebbled paths. As she neared the office, new paths emerged out of the darkness, lit by the feeble security lights on the science block near the perimeter of the main buildings. Emma trod carefully as she cut through the music building slipway next to the library. She listened to the hum of traffic from the minor roads behind her. Ellery Way seemed strangely quiet. Turning off the phone torch, she wondered again about Marlee's calls.

She scrolled to find Marlee's number in her phone, then pressed it to call, finding comfort in the idea that Marlee must be there at the reunion before her. As she rounded the corner near the north gate, urgent voices, some low, some loud, surprised her. She cancelled the call and let her hand fall down to her side. Red and blue strobe lights were crashing through and over the hedge like an eerie tsunami, illuminating a glowing shape in the hedge that didn't seem to belong. Emma drew a sharp breath as she realised that the shape poking through the hedge was the corner of a car. She ran across the courtyard, and skirted the hedge, walking through to Ellery Way by the tradesman entrance.

'Stop there.' A policeman stood on the footpath, his hand raised towards her. 'Don't go any closer to the car. We have to close down this area. There's a girl trapped.'

Around him a slew of ambulances, police cars and emergency rescue trucks were parked at odd angles, lights strobing, blocking traffic going south. Further up, at the intersection a policeman stood in the centre diverting traffic onto the east-west flow of Canarvon Drive. Emma smelled petrol.

'What's happened?'

In the gloomy evening light, a green Falcon sat crookedly at the edge of the intersection, its mouth mangled. A boy stood next to it, shivering in his t-shirt, talking to a policewoman who was writing something down. Rescue crews dressed in fluorescent vests surrounded the white car that had been pushed through the hedge. A bright yellow 'L' plate on the car's back bumper flashed reflectively each time the light of the police car whooshed around. There were calls and shouts across the road, and Emma saw a man squatting at the mangled car door and heard him talking constantly to the occupant of the car.

On the road, a woman was being held up by a policeman as an ambulance officer tried to talk to her. As Emma watched she heard the woman wail then cry out. '*My girl – get her out! Out!*'

The woman was pulling away from both men, trying to get back towards the white car that had been half swallowed on the passenger side by the hedge. The rescue crews working on the driver's side door were ignoring her. Emma shivered.

'Are you a part of the school, love? I saw you come down the path.' The policeman was staring at her.

'I live there.'

'We'll need to contact someone in charge. The accident investigation crew are coming. We'll need to cordon off the school grounds here for a bit.'

Emma looked at him dumbly, panic emptying her mind. Her mouth felt parched.

'Er… yes, okay.' As she said it her eye was caught by a movement. Behind the white car, running up the footpath, she saw the tall figure of a man. She felt a twisted pang of relief as she recognised the headmaster. Dr Brownley stopped as a policeman approached him from the road. They spoke briefly as Dr Brownley surveyed the scene, looking for where he needed to go. Emma saw the young policeman motioning towards her, to the senior officer she was talking to. At the same moment, the screaming woman turned and saw the headmaster too.

'Jon!'

Dr Brownley turned to her, then he looked again at the mangled white car, his blond hair sweeping across the scene, reflecting the flashing lights like a blue and red halo.

'Harriet?' He reached out his arms and the woman slumped into his chest. He caught her tiny frame and bent into it, murmuring something Emma couldn't hear.

Emma turned to the policeman as she pointed towards Jonathan. Her heart was drumming a mad tune. Everything was off-kilter. The wailing woman turned her face and Emma recognised the precise, elegant profile of Harriet Andrews.

Clementine's mother.

Then a sick understanding filtered through her brain as she realised what that must mean about the L-plate driver they were trying to cut out of the car. *Scarlett.* She tried to speak, but nothing came out. She closed her eyes and tilting, tipping, images rolled out like a film. A hallucination. *The blond-haired man running below the window. Beckoning to someone behind him, then chasing after Tessa.*

Emma felt the energy draining from her. All these years she'd kept the secret of what she saw, had wondered what it meant. But she hadn't been there to see what had happened to Tessa. What did she really know about it? She hadn't spoken up when it counted, and now everything had moved on. Time had split in the moment she'd decided not to speak up about Tessa's plan, or about what she saw from the window, and history had been made by a million tiny decisions and actions that had occurred in the vacuum of her silence. A history that could never be altered. But here, now in the present, she had the power to make her words count.

Emma looked across to the crumpled bonnet of the green Falcon, then at the rescue worker holding the huge metal cutters. They both watched the other worker as he pulled, then stumbled backwards holding the side of the twisted wreckage of the BMW, the white door now a jagged wreck in his hands. *Let her live.*

Emma watched as Jonathan folded Harriet into the grasp of the ambulance officer, then walked across and spoke to the man who had pulled off the twisted door.

The police officer was still looking at Emma, strangely now, waiting for an answer. This was the moment with the police she'd thought she wanted. But maybe the truth she thought she knew wasn't hers for the telling.

She forced her tongue through the dry sludge of her mouth and pointed again.

'He's the man you want, Officer.'

'He's in charge?'

'He's... he's the headmaster.'

CHAPTER THIRTY-EIGHT

MARLEE

'Phillip says she went home. He wasn't sure if she was coming to the reunion or not. But she's not answering her phone.' Marlee dropped the phone in her lap and looked up at Clementine.

'Well there's not much we can do then, is there?' Clementine took a long slurp of her cocktail as the melodic notes of Adele piped through the speakers of the restaurant. 'Bloody hell, that's strong.' She winced then looked back at Marlee. 'Do you want to tell me what happened?'

'I can't…' Marlee faltered as two women peeled away from the main crowd and walked towards them. One of the women smiled, the smile not quite reaching her eyes.

'Well if it isn't Jemima Hooker,' said Clementine.

'Jemima Langdon-Traves now,' said the woman.

Marlee stood up.

'And Peta Elliot. You both look about twenty!' said Clementine, smiling at the other woman, who towered over her, thin, willowy and elegant in her stiletto boots and tight black pants.

'Thanks,' said Jemima, glancing at Marlee then back to Clementine.

Marlee knew she didn't make the muster. Clementine had told her she looked terrible.

'So Clementine, you're really famous now. Who would have thought?' said Jemima, letting her gaze run slowly over Clementine's green pantsuit. Clementine shrugged and took another sip of her cocktail.

'Love that English accent you've got going on,' said Clementine.

'Well, I've lived in London for years now. Couldn't live anywhere else. What about you, Clementine. Where are you based these days?' asked Jemima.

'Mum's spare bedroom at the moment.'

'Really?' Jemima turned up the corner of her mouth.

'Yeah. She's a good old stick, putting up with me.'

'I thought you lived abroad.' Jemima paused and glanced at Peta.

'Usually.'

'Well, I can recommend the Oriental Suite at the Henry Jones next time you're home. I'm sure you can afford it. My husband bought one of your pieces last year at auction for fifteen thousand pounds.'

Marlee squirmed and wondered again where Emma was.

'Good for him,' said Clementine. 'What piece?'

'Oh, I'm not sure of its name. He showed me a photo of it. Men with bleeding hands behind a razor wire fence. He's usually got a good eye for beautiful things, but this one was definitely an investment decision.' She smirked and rolled her eyes at Peta, who was nodding and sipping on her champagne.

'It sounds like *Resting in Refuge*. I did a series on the shit way that governments treat asylum seekers. Where did he hang it?' asked Clementine.

'Well, I wasn't about to let him have it in the house scaring the boys!' Jemima appeared to try to raise her eyebrows, but nothing on her forehead moved. She let out a laugh. 'It lives in one of the back rooms of his London office – away from prospective clients. Ha ha!'

'Sensible,' said Clementine. 'Wouldn't wanna upset those prospective clients. So, how old are your boys, Jem?'

'Nobody calls me that anymore.' She gave a tight smile then continued, 'Rupert is four and Freddie's nearly eight.'

'Great.' Clementine looked down into the depths of her cocktail glass.

'Gorgeous names, aren't they?' said Peta looking at Clementine and Marlee for agreement. Her hand landed on her chest, her perfectly manicured fingers looking oddly unbalanced by the weight of her diamonds. 'I really wanted to call my boy Rupert too, but my husband wanted Theo. He always gets his own way, but I was devastated!'

Jemima smiled graciously.

'Hmmm, well,' said Clementine. She sipped the last of the creamy cocktail and pulled the cherry from the bottom of the glass and held it up. 'I can highly recommend the Angel's Tit girls. Bloody fantastic.' She chewed vigorously on the cherry. 'So, Jem… your folks still living in Hobart? Looking after the boys tonight?'

'No. Definitely not! I left them at home. Too difficult to do the flight on my own with them. I have a great au pair though, back in London… an Australian girl actually. Very attentive.'

'Right,' said Clementine.

'Do you have children Clementine?' asked Peta.

'No way,' said Clementine, her eyes widening.

Marlee shifted from one foot to the other, wondering why she hadn't asked Ben to turn the car around and take her home.

'Well, you probably just haven't found the right man yet,' said Jemima.

Clementine narrowed her eyes, as if she was thinking about it, then furrowed her brow. 'That could be a reason. I guess.'

A waitress appeared at the edge of their group with a platter of tiny filo pastry cups filled with what looked like mushrooms. 'These look great,' said Marlee pouncing on one. She bit into it, the pastry mixing uneasily with her nausea at the thought of Emma with the police.

Clementine grabbed one too. 'Are they any good?' she asked the waitress with a grin.

The girl smiled and shook her head. 'Sorry, I haven't tried them.'

'I'm gluten free,' said Peta, shaking her head at the girl.

Jemima waived the plate away without looking at the waitress.

Marlee looked across the room as the door opened. Emma stood very still, in the doorway in her old grey overcoat.

Jemima followed Marlee's gaze. 'Oh my God – it's Emma Tasker! Did you girls read that email she accidentally sent round! It was hilarious. So *embarrassing*.' Jemima curled her top lip into a gleeful sneer. Then her eyes widened briefly as she looked at Marlee. 'That's right. It was written to you, Marleen! What a cock-up! Well, I'm surprised she's here, the way she was talking so rudely about her husband in it. And carrying on about Tessa's death, as though she knew something about it.'

Marlee stared at Jemima's flawless face and perfect pouty lips and felt a strange discomfort, as if she had just seen Jemima naked by accident. She couldn't think of anything to say.

Clementine squeezed Marlee's arm without looking at her. 'You know what, Jemima, I was just thinking, you're so trusting to leave your au pair at home alone with your husband. I hope she isn't *too* pretty, given that he's got such a good eye for beautiful things and all. You wouldn't want Freddie and Ronald walking in when the hired help was getting all *attentive* on Daddy, would you?' Clementine's girlish features were suddenly split wide open in a grin. 'That would make her a really bad investment decision.'

'It's Rupert,' said Jemima coldly. 'Not Ronald.'

'Roger, Rasputin, Ronald… whatever.' Clementine shrugged her shoulders. 'Come on, Marlee, let's have a cocktail with Emma. I'm gonna try the Wet Pussy next. Yummo! See ya ladies.' She threw her arm up in a lunatic wave.

Marlee felt their stares boring into her back. She felt lighter for a moment. But as they got closer, Marlee noticed something like fear in Emma's eyes. She looked sick.

'Em, is Rosie okay?'

'She will be. She's much better than yesterday. I walked here but… there was… ah…' Emma seemed to be avoiding looking at Clementine. Behind Emma's shoulder, Marlee noticed that most of the women in the room were watching them. Emma's face was a ghostly shade of white.

'That's great she's going to be okay.' She paused. 'I got your voicemail… about the police and Jon Brownley.'

'Oh.'

'Why did you report him, Emma?' asked Clementine. 'You're barking up the wrong tree.'

'There's been an accident,' said Emma. She finally looked at Clementine, her eyes bright, wet pools.

'What do you mean?' asked Marlee quickly.

Emma averted her eyes but spoke again to Clementine.

'Your mother, and I think your sister. A car crash.'

'Emma, Marleen, Clementine! How *amazing* is this restaurant?' The three of them stared at the vision in front of them – a huge woman had emerged from the front door in a large colourful kaftan, sparkling with gemstones. Her hair was short and a vibrant shade of reddish-pink.

'It's Lisa! Lisa Appleby! Leicester now, though. It's so good to see you, ladies! Clementine, you're so tiny! I'd forgotten that about you. You don't look this tiny on TV! Does she, Emma?' Lisa gave Emma's shoulder an exuberant shove, as she waited for agreement.

Nobody spoke. Lisa looked at each of them in turn, her smile slowly fading.

'Clementine's just had some bad news, Lisa. She needs to go.' Marlee took hold of Clementine's arm. 'We all need to go. Sorry, Lisa. Maybe we can catch up for coffee some time?' She turned without waiting for an answer, pulling Clementine, who'd become surprisingly quiet and docile.

Outside the restaurant, the cold air seemed to wake Clementine from her stupor.

'Where's the accident? Is it bad?' Clementine asked.

'Someone was trapped. I think it's Scarlett.' Emma pointed towards the school. 'This way. You can see the lights from here.'

Clementine's phone startled them, blaring a manic heavy metal song as it rang in her hand. She jabbed at the screen frantically, as she started walking towards the school.

'Mum. Are you okay? Is Scarlett okay?'

Emma and Marlee watched as she furrowed her brow, staring down the street.

'Okay, I'll come to the hospital. Mum, you need to stay calm. Stop that. You need to be calm for Scarlett. I'm coming.' She ended the call.

'Mum's not a crier. It must be bad.' Her voice was tight with worry. 'My car's over there if you want to come to the hospital.'

She pointed and walked across the road to the tiny orange Datsun. Emma and Marlee followed. Emma clambered into the back after Clementine pushed the driver's seat forward. Marlee ran around to the passenger seat. The car smelled like tobacco and rotting fruit.

Clementine took off without warning, speeding, swerving, spinning around corners. Marlee clenched her hands into tight fists as the road skated beneath them like a treacherous, icy lake. The silence inside the car was interrupted only by the high-pitched squeal of the engine. The atmosphere felt thick and surreal. As they drove through the darkened streets near the city centre, upturned crucifixes glowed an eerie red, signalling the beginning of the Dark Mofo festival. On the side of a building a huge semi-circular installation of garish pink lights screamed at Marlee through the darkness: 'FEAR EATS THE SOUL'. She knew it already. She wondered if she should tell Clementine to slow down. But her fate was sealed already. She would be going to prison for Tessa's death when the investigation re-opened. It was lucky that her baby had a good father. Emma would be a wonderful godmother. Ben would find a kind new partner, someone to raise little Ned with him. To love him, almost like a mother. Now that the reckoning had arrived Marlee felt strangely resigned to it.

Marlee looked back towards Emma. 'I know this might not be the right time to say this, but Jon Brownley didn't kill Tessa. He was on the other side of the barrier when she fell in the hole. I need to speak to the police, make sure they don't arrest him.' She looked down at the empty coke bottle rolling around on the floor and over her feet.

'What? How could you know—'

'I know, Em. I know, because it was me who pushed her.' Marlee looked back towards Emma. In the blue-black light, her face was a mask of confusion.

'What are you talking about?'

'I didn't mean to. My hand just… caught her. It was instinct.'

'What was?' said Emma.

'To grab the photo.'

'You're… you're not making sense.'

The car slowed down as Clementine turned into a bend.

'You mean it was nothing to do with Jon Brownley?' said Emma.

'No. It *was* to do with him. But I caused it… by accident.'

'But… then why would you not *tell* the police that, back then? All these years…' Emma let the sentence trail off.

'I know that! I wanted to tell someone. I was desperate to get the ambulance. But I couldn't. I'd broken my ankle, the pain was horrible. I *begged* them to go. You've got to believe me.'

'Them?'

'Clementine's mother. She found us there. She made us promise to keep quiet. She made us *swear*. She said it would be much

worse if we spoke up. I know now she was wrong, but I didn't…
I couldn't…' Marlee felt as if something inside her had cracked.
She felt the acid tears on her lashes, as a wave of raw angry longing
swept through her. An old yearning to live that day over, do things
differently, maybe warn someone, or leave Tessa and her plans
alone. Her body began to shudder, and sobs erupted, jagged and
loud. The car was filled with her grief for Tessa and for herself and
that awful, fractured moment as the photo slipped and blew away.

'Marlee? Marlee stop. I didn't report Jonathan to the police. I
changed my mind,' said Emma.

'What?' said Clementine.

Emma spoke louder. 'I said I didn't report Jonathan to the
police. Marlee stop crying. Please stop it. I didn't report him okay?
They're not going to find out.'

Clementine swerved out of the roundabout, and clipped the
edge of the gutter. 'Shit.'

'Slow down, Clementine! We don't need another accident
tonight,' Emma snapped.

'Alright, sorry.' Clementine put on her indicator for the first
time since they'd gotten into the car, as she turned and pulled
up inside the hospital carpark. She switched off the ignition and
turned to face Marlee. 'I need to go see if my sister's okay. But
I just need to know… you're saying that when you accidentally
knocked Tessa, Mum and Jon knew it and made you cover it up?'

'Well, I could have said something. They didn't force me exactly.'
Marlee's head throbbed. Her shirt felt damp.

'Yeah. Right. Except we both know my mother,' said Clementine.

'But why did they want it covered up?' asked Emma.

Marlee hung her head. A wave of nausea rose up as her headache
began shooting down behind her eyes.

'Because Tessa had been in Brownley's cottage and left a naked
photo of herself in there. Harriet thought he'd get in trouble. Tessa

was waiting to seduce him when I got there… threatened to say he'd lured her for sex.' Marlee let out her breath as the truth rolled off her tongue after all this time. Her shoulders sagged.

'So she *was* going to seduce him,' said Clementine. 'I really thought she was changing her exam results.'

Emma and Marlee swivelled their heads towards her in unison.

'I saw her break in. Locked her in there when I saw Jon coming down the path, then I ran off. I was late to meet Mum,' said Clementine, almost to herself. She shook her head, as if a fog was lifting. 'Girls, whatever you two decide, I'll go along with it. I'll support you, Marlee. Just do what you have to do and let me know. But I have to go to Mum now. She needs me. Scarlett needs me.'

Marlee watched her as she slammed the car door and jogged towards the glass entrance, the brightly lit sign above it announced *Accident & Emergency*. Clementine disappeared through the doors and they slid shut, blocking out the cold night.

Marlee felt Emma's stare. She closed her eyes. The last twenty-five years of their friendship, forged on her lie. But somehow it was a relief to have arrived at the truth. She waited in the darkness, listening to the wail of another distant siren. Then she felt Emma's hand on her arm, warm and gentle.

'This isn't good for the baby. You need to go home, get some rest. And I need to go up now and see Rosie.' Emma nodded towards the hospital.

'Okay.' Marlee hesitated for a moment. 'Would you mind if I come up with you? I know you probably don't want to even talk to me, but I'd like to see Rosie. And maybe we can find out if Scarlett's okay.' Marlee looked at Emma's kind, lovely face, her pretty blond hair, her old grey coat, not even stylish ten years ago when she'd bought it.

'Of course you can. Whatever happened, I know you'd only have been trying to help. It doesn't change who you are.'

'Yes, it does. It changes something in you. But I can't change it back now. I have to live with what I did – my decision to stay silent. Just like you'll have to decide, now that you know what happened. I can't tell you what to do with this.' She gave Emma's hand a squeeze.

Emma looked behind Marlee and pointed as a man ran through the carpark. Suddenly his face was lit by the bright, fluorescent lights of the ambulance parking bay. *Ben.*

'He's going to need you, Marl. And so is your baby. Come on. Let's go up.'

CHAPTER THIRTY-NINE

MARLEE

Marlee turned off the ignition and let the silent shadows settle around her. At the northern edge of the school grounds a wall of gum trees loomed over the broken bitumen in front of the last house on the road. She was surprised to see the witch's house was still standing. Paint was peeling off the weatherboards in great curling chunks. By the side of the path, a rusted skeleton of a long-forgotten child's pram was woven into long tussocks of grass. Cranky old Mrs Pemberton – the witch, as she'd always been called during their early school years – would be long dead by now.

Marlee yawned. She hadn't slept properly since the night of the accident. She needed to do something to sort out this mess. But her head was fuzzy, confused. The idea of reporting the whole thing to the police, lifting the silent weight of her guilt over Tessa's death after all these years, made her feel giddy with relief. But in the next breath, she'd be swamped by the heavy dread of anticipation. Did she have the right to ruin so many lives? Jonathan's and Harriet's – and by association Scarlett's and Ben's. Did she really want little Ned to know that his mother was a killer? How had she been so weak and easily led?

The baby made a fluttering movement and Marlee's hand dropped from the steering wheel onto the small swell of her belly. She rubbed at it, still staring out of the car at the sagging windows of the house, boarded up and broken. She wondered what would become of the old place. It looked completely abandoned. She supposed the school would soon snap it up if they hadn't already done so. They could bulldoze the house and build something fabulous on the block. It was prime adjoining real estate and the last annual appeal had been all about improving educational opportunities by extending the school campus to build another boarding house. They'd probably raised millions. Enough, anyway, for the last house at the end of the road with its wild acres to be swept into the coffers and under the cloak of privilege that shrouded Denham House.

She closed her eyes, the burden of the decision heavy and unpleasant. Her lashes felt like lead weights against her lower lids. She felt the fluttering movement again in her stomach, and she knew then what she needed to do. *Had to do.* There had been no excuse for keeping silent all these years, whatever Clementine might say about Harriet and her iron-fisted tactics. She needed to do the right thing. For her younger self, and for Tessa, and all those lost years of replaying that moment in her head when the photograph had flipped away and she had reached out to grab it. A pure moment of instinct that had punctuated two childhoods like a full stop.

This morning she'd woken up next to Ben for the first time since the morning of Scarlett's accident. He'd been staying at the hospital all week, taking only snatched naps in the granny flat during the day. But that couldn't go on indefinitely. The warmth of him as he stroked her face this morning had made her feel safe. As if she could face whatever were to come.

He hadn't asked her about Tessa's death yet, although she knew Clementine had talked to him about it. And Marlee hadn't volunteered anything about it either. It was as if they were both holding their breath until they knew what would happen with Scarlett. It felt to Marlee as if their new relationship sat on the edge of a narrow precipice – not so big that it couldn't be jumped over, if only she could navigate to the right crossing point.

Now, finally, Marlee could see where that was. She turned on the ignition and swung the car around, leaving the crumbling witch's relic behind her. She ignored the pull of the willow tree at Emma's driveway and drove around the block and along the road until she came to a concealed entrance. This one was marked by a large maple tree, the remnants of some fading autumn leaves still clinging to its branches in the grey winter light. She turned in, noticing the gnarled old trees, bare and forlorn, that formed a piteous welcome line along the length of the driveway. How pretty they must be in autumn. She pulled to a stop in front of an imposing double-storey house made from convict-hewn sandstone and opened the car door before she had a chance to reconsider. She shivered as a freezing gust of wind rustled through the gum trees ahead of her. Then she took a deep breath, thinking about what she would say.

'Hello.'

The voice startled her. Jon Brownley was sitting on a faded timber garden bench behind a bare bed of leafless, hard-pruned rose bushes. He wore jeans and a navy woollen jumper and his blond hair was swept back off his face. When he stood and walked towards her, she felt her breath stop. He was still so unbearably beautiful.

'Hello, Mr Brownley. Sorry… Doctor Brownley.'

'Surely you can call me Jon by now?'

'Jon…' She frowned, chewed on the idea of it, closed her car door. Then she let out a small sigh. 'It doesn't feel right.'

'Mmmm. Sometimes we're stuck with our history.' He gave her a sad smile.

'Do you think I could come in. I need to talk to you.'

'Of course.'

He pushed open the front door and beckoned her into the dim hallway. The high ceilings and old stone walls announced an elegant history. A lush Persian rug, red-patterned and intricate, ran the length of it. The walls were lined with photographic prints, black and white images of forests, mountains and beaches, ethereal and spooky, bright and sharp-edged, blurry and moody. There were twenty or more in huge chunky black frames placed at thoughtful intervals – a gallery of good taste that seemed to stretch on forever as she followed him through.

He ushered her into a surprisingly light and cosy kitchen at the rear of the house and motioned to the worn timber table.

'Would you like a coffee? Tea?'

'No. Thank you.' Marlee watched him flick the kettle on anyway. She looked around at the tidy bench surfaces, a neat bookshelf in the corner, a photograph of a boy and a young woman holding a toddler in a silver frame next to the television. It had been so many years since she'd sat alone in a room with him. The tarnish of their lie began to rub at her, thick and dirty. She felt the old panic rising in her chest.

She nodded at the photograph. 'Is that your mother?'

Jonathan followed her gaze. 'No. It's Harriet. I was eight. That's Clementine on her hip.'

She nodded.

'I need to tell the police what happened, with Tessa. I can't live with it anymore.'

Jonathan nodded slowly, as if he'd been expecting it. But he didn't speak.

'I know I'm not the only one, that it's not just my decision. It affects you and Harriet and your family. I don't want to bring any more trouble your way. Not after what's happened to Scarlett.' She stopped, looked out the kitchen window as the afternoon light caught the top of the trees, filtering through their bare branches.

'I'm going to tell the police it was just me who was there. You did nothing anyway. I was the one who did it.'

Jonathan gave her a piercing look. He turned as the boiling of the kettle reached a rumbling crescendo then clicked off. He pulled out a cup and a tea bag, poured the water, dunked it; small swift motions, repetitive and familiar. He walked to the fridge, opened it for the milk then turned to her unexpectedly as he held it open.

'Marleen, if you're going to tell the truth, it needs to be the actual truth.' The look he gave her was paternal, all-knowing.

She let out a choking laugh. It was like history repeating itself – him telling her how it needed to be. The easy confidence he wore like a birth-right; his power around this place; the privilege of being the one who didn't push her in – all rolled into a huge egotistical assumption that he knew best. How dare he?

'I'll be doing you a favour, *Jon*. You're not the one who killed her.'

He gave a short, strangled exhalation. Disbelief or maybe amusement.

'Marleen, I've run this school long enough to know when I'm only getting half a story. I assume the police get pretty good at that too. They'll see straight through it. They'll wonder why on earth you didn't just report an accident straight away and if you can't explain that, they'll have to assume there was some sort of malice involved. You'll be facing a murder charge before you can blink. What other possible motive would you have had for not raising the alarm?'

'No, I don't… I don't think so.'

'Yes, Marleen. There are loose ends. I spoke to Emma at the hospital the other night. She told me she saw me that afternoon from the art room arguing with Tessa. If the police pursue you, you'll be making her live with a lie too, if you try to keep me out of this. And there might be others who come forward. Those who didn't speak up then, but will now.'

'I need to take responsibility – don't you get it? Tessa's parents deserve to know what really happened.'

'Do they?' He closed the fridge and poured the milk into his tea.

'What do you mean? Of course they should damn well know the truth.'

'Leaving aside that it wouldn't actually *be* the truth you'll be spinning in this scenario for police, Tessa's parents saw the coroner's report when it came out. She hadn't eaten for more than twenty-four hours. She'd reported feeling dizzy in class and was supposed to go to see Sister at sick bay. They assumed she'd deviated out of the way for some unknown reason. They accepted the coroner's verdict that she just became dizzy and fell in. Do you really want them to know that she was pushed? Because the whole story of how it came to happen *will* come out Marleen, and when it does, the fact that it was an accident won't matter anymore. They won't see it like that. Not when we concealed it, and not when they hear about what she'd been up to. They'll fight back. The only thing they'll see is that you're trying to besmirch the good memory of their daughter by dragging up a sleazy story about her breaking into a staff member's house so she could have sex with him. How do you think that will sound to them? Do you think that's the sort of truth they'll want the world to hear?'

'I… maybe…'

'They won't accept it. They'll fight back, Marleen. They will. Enzo Terrano isn't someone you want to take on, even at his age. It will be all over the media. All over the world. Is that what you really want for Tessa's parents in their old age? Is that what you want for Tessa?'

Marlee put her head in her hands. She wanted to cry, scream, scratch the words out of his perfect mouth, but she could hardly breathe. After a while she looked up. He was staring out the window.

'So you're telling me I have to carry this god-awful secret forever, because telling the truth is worse? *Jesus Christ.*'

'I'm just saying, if you tell the truth, Marleen, it has to be the whole truth.'

'And nothing but the truth?' Marlee let out a hollow laugh. She felt her reserves crumbling. She was suddenly back on her eighteenth birthday, Harriet Andrews berating her, pulling her away from the ghastly sight of Tessa down in the hole, telling her she had to protect her parents from the truth so her mother could die in peace. She already knew the price of playing God with the truth.

'I was only there trying to help *you*. And to help Tessa. I was just trying to get us all through that stupid bloody last week. Next thing I know I have a huge, terrible secret that I never asked for. I wanted to shout it out, to tell anyone who'd listen, but I couldn't. The silence tore me apart. I spent the next years drinking myself stupid and getting into the bed of any poor sod who'd have me just so I could hold onto someone in the dark.'

Then as soon as it had come, Marlee's anger was fading. Tears she'd held in for years began pouring down her face.

Marlee looked out the window, remembering that terrible time, feeling so alone. The months when her father was so hollowed out by the grief of losing her mother that he couldn't even remember to buy food. She stood up and put her hands on the edge of the table.

'I couldn't even grieve my own mother properly when she died that Christmas because I was so screwed up about this. I had nothing left in me except fear. But that's gone now. I don't think I can keep quiet anymore.'

'Then don't. But don't think about keeping me or Harriet out of it. Tell it how it happened.'

'You'll lose your job,' said Marlee.

He tipped his head to one side. 'I've resigned already. I told the Board I'd stay for as long as it takes to find a suitable replacement.'

'What? Why?'

'I'm sick of not making a difference, Marleen. I'm a teacher. I want to teach.'

She gave a bitter laugh. 'Everyone talks about you like you're the bloody Messiah.'

He made a strangled sound. 'As you well know, I'm not. These girls don't need me. Whether I'm here or not, they'll have the same opportunities, every privilege money can buy.'

'What will you do?'

'Who knows? I might do some volunteer teaching. There's plenty out there.'

'How noble.' But her cynicism felt ugly and cheap. She could see that he meant it.

Jonathan sat down opposite her and took a sip of his tea.

'It is what it is.' He sighed. 'Do what you have to do, Marleen, and don't worry about Harriet either. She could do a plea bargain with the devil and still come out smelling of roses. The Bar Association will probably strike her off for perverting the course of justice, but she'll find something else to do.' He smiled at her then, and she forced herself to look properly at him. His eyes were sad and tired, like a priest who'd heard one too many confessions. He seemed to be waiting for an answer.

'Believe me, Harriet isn't my major concern. But since I'm carrying Scarlett's baby brother, I suppose I should also care about Scarlett's mother.' Marlee watched his face as the words settled between them. 'I guess Harriet's part of my family now.'

'What? You... I mean, you and Ben?'

'Yes.'

'That makes things... *Jesus.*' He stared down at the table for another long moment. 'Marleen, you need to understand, Harriet, she... she was protecting me. She raised me like her son. I guess she saw how it would all play out, that it would all be over for me if rumours spread about Tessa in my cottage. She's not a bad person.'

Marlee sighed.

'If it was your child, your boy, maybe you'd have done the same thing,' he said.

'I doubt it. But I don't suppose I'll ever have to find out.'

Marlee stared past Jonathan and out the window again. Her furious, jumbled thinking began to slow down. Clink, clink, clink. The thoughts were falling into place, finding order, just as they did when she was working on a complex design. She gave a loud sigh.

'Emma thinks I shouldn't go to the police either. Maybe you're both right. Maybe there's some other way to pay for what I did.' Marlee wondered if her words had any meaning. They felt light and false, but true at the same time.

'Marleen, the only thing you did wrong was listening to Harriet and me. I'm ashamed of what we did to you. I was your teacher and I let you down badly. I should have taken control of things much earlier. I failed. Much more than Harriet even.'

'We all failed, Mr Brownley. All of us. I failed Tessa most of all.'

'Tessa failed *you*, Marleen. You did nothing wrong. Look at me, Marleen…'

Marlee looked up into the deep blue of his eyes and let herself be drawn into the swirling sadness.

'You did *nothing* wrong.' Then he stood and turned his back to her and looked out onto the manicured garden, clipped to perfection by the team of gardeners. He sighed and turned back from the window, picked up the photo on the sideboard, then spoke as if to himself.

'Nothing we can fix now anyway.'

EPILOGUE

Twenty Months Later

Marlee slumped on the edge of the bed and looked at herself in the full-length mirror. The make-up was working. It hid the bags under her eyes, gave her a veneer of glamour. The black dress hid the thickening of her waist that now seemed permanent too. She wondered how it was possible to be so tired and still be a fully functioning person, walking around in the world without supervision, or a warning on her forehead that said, 'do not operate heavy machinery'. But it was only tiredness. She'd managed worse.

In the early days after Ned was born, she had wondered how she would ever keep the black fog from swallowing her. She would look down at her perfect sleeping son in his cot and in her mind he would morph into Tessa, in that hole, and she would remember how her mouth had gone dry, how every cell in her body had wanted to scream and run for help, and the images made her want to claw her way out of her own head. She was sometimes afraid to touch him. But the antidepressants had helped. And the psychologist's strategies to keep her spiralling thoughts in check. A daily run was also her saviour – and Ben. Always steady, listening, understanding. She'd told him everything after she had spoken to Jonathan that day, and he'd been silent for a long time. He was angry at what had happened to her, at what Harriet had done. But he seemed to slot the anger away as time wore on. He agreed with

Jonathan, that opening up the truth would be fruitless, but he also knew that carrying the burden of silence would be a lifelong sentence for all of them.

She looked across at the photo on the bedside table: her, Ben and Ned at Piper's Rocks. A happy, imperfect little family. Marlee allowed herself approximately thirty seconds to acknowledge the sadness in her heart, before reminding herself of her good fortune, then she pushed herself off the bed, slipped on her heels and walked out into the lounge room to tidy up.

As she walked down the hall, she heard the door open and turned to see Scarlett walking into the house with a large bag on her shoulder, Ben close behind. Scarlett's limp was less pronounced now. The scars on her cheek were fading too. One eyelid hung slightly lower than the other, but it was barely noticeable. In the days following her accident, she'd suffered through seven rounds of surgery, losing her spleen in the process. After her condition had stabilised, they'd mostly worried about the concussion. She'd been unconscious and put into an induced coma while her life-threatening internal injuries had been dealt with. Thankfully there were no obvious ongoing signs of brain damage, although she tired easily.

Marlee moved quickly across the room taking Scarlett's bag and drawing her into a hug.

'Hi, Scarlett. Thanks for doing this.'

'That's okay. It'll be fun.'

Marlee laughed as they walked through to the kitchen. 'That's not guaranteed. I'll run you through everything in a minute, but do you want a cuppa or something to eat first?'

'I'm okay. I just had something with Mum. She's always trying to make me eat something healthy these days.'

Marlee caught a fleeting plea in her eyes.

'How is she?'

'Driving me mental. She really needs to go back to work. I told her to try something different if she's finished with law.'

Marlee smiled and looked around. 'Where's your dad got to, I wonder?'

'We're here, aren't we, mate!' Ben walked in from the bedroom and lifted the baby up over his head, making him gurgle and chuckle. His chubby legs jerked back and forth with excitement. Ben put him into Scarlett's arms. 'Be good for your sister, matey. She doesn't deserve to be pooed on or cried at. Got it?'

'Hello, Ned,' said Scarlett. She gave him a kiss on the top of his head, then put him onto his feet and held him by his hands. 'I hear you took some steps the other day, mister,' she said. 'Wanna show me?' She took him to the edge of the couch, and right on cue he walked along it, babbling and looking back at her. His sister got slowly onto her knees and followed him around. 'I'm gonna getcha!' She lunged forward, making him giggle as he pulled himself to the other end, before falling back on his padded bottom and scuttling across the floor on all fours to his mother.

Marlee scooped him up and kissed him. 'You two are going to have a blast. There's dinner on the bench for him Scarlett and two bottles of formula in the fridge, just in case. We should be back before ten-thirty though.' She looked across at Ben, raising her eyebrows.

'Don't be daft, woman. We won't be a minute before midnight. We're bound to win the *Best Renovation and Extension* category. Maybe *Best Design* too. Did you see Tussock Hill House featured in *Modern Arch* magazine this month Scarlett? Marlee did most of that.'

'Yep. Sure did, Dad. You showed me. Twice.'

'We *will* be partying after the awards Marleen Maples, and there *will* be champagne and dancing. Maybe on the tables.' Ben took Marlee's hand and looked across at Scarlett. 'Scarli, I've made up the spare bed. We'll be back by midnight. Ring if he doesn't settle or you're worried. The awards are on at Billycart Creek Winery, so we won't be far. There are a few new books in Ned's cot to read too, if that's okay?'

'Sure. No problem, Dad,' said Scarlett, taking Ned from Marlee, who had left lipstick marks on his chubby cheeks and forehead.

'Wave to Mum and Dad, Neddy.' The little boy leaned out of her arms towards Ben and Marlee and watched them go. As the door closed his face crumpled and he let out a huge wail.

'Awwww, Neddy,' said Scarlett, jiggling him up and down. 'Don't cry. Let's go and watch *The Bachelorette*. You can have a TV dinner. Who wants to read stupid books in your cot when you can hang out with me?'

*

Emma sat at the reception desk of the guest house, pleased that she'd insisted on Stefan having a few hours off for his mother's birthday lunch. He'd been so devoted to her in the last year. He deserved the break. She needed to write a new manual anyway, and this shift would give her time to fit that in between guest check-ins. She picked up the print out of the guest list and wondered idly if Rosie had found something for lunch in the kitchen. She scrunched her eyes shut, trying to picture if there was bread in the freezer inside their cosy manager's apartment at the rear of the building.

'Mum, I'm going down to the docks now, okay?' Rosie had walked in the back door of the reception area, dressed in a midriff top and skimpy cut-off denim shorts that made her coltish legs look outlandishly long. The upper curve of her hip bones peeked over the waistband. Her hair had been carefully straightened and Emma noticed lip gloss and a hint of mascara.

'Okay. Have you eaten something?'

'Yeah. I had the leftover pasta.'

'Well, make sure you're back before three, okay? I'll drop you to Dad when I finish this shift.' Emma smiled. 'You can always bring Hugo back here you know, darling.'

'*Mum.*' Rosie rolled her eyes. 'I'm not bringing him back here to subject him to your pearls of wisdom. Seriously.'

Emma laughed. She'd only met Hugo twice, but she had liked him enormously. He was chatty and funny and seemed to adore Rosie. Emma had been nervous when Rosie had started at the local high school, sick to her stomach with worry that the teaching standards would be poor, or that the other children wouldn't accept Rosie, or that something fundamental would be missing from her daughter's high school education after she left the cossetted bubble of Denham House. But it had been Rosie's decision in the end. The high school had been piloting a French immersion program for students during years eight, nine and ten. All the classes except English and Maths would be taught completely in the French language and Rosie was desperate to be included in it. French was her favourite subject and she had been topping her class at Denham House by miles.

And so far, Rosie seemed quite happy with the change, and Hugo, one of her fellow French immersion students, seemed very happy to take her under his wing. Emma still saw Snapchat messages pinging up regularly on Rosie's phone from her old schoolmates at Denham House, so she knew Rosie was retaining her old friendships too. There was something comforting about that. Rosie seemed to be able to move easily between different social circles, and to mix them in together now and then. It was a gift.

'What are you talking about?' asked Emma, mock frowning. 'My advice is always excellent. Hugo would be lucky to be subjected to it.'

Rosie screwed up her face good-naturedly and walked across reception to the exit door.

'Rosie…' Emma waited until she turned back to look at her, 'I'll only say this once. If he's not a good kisser, you should seriously consider whether he's worth the effort.'

'Eeeww! Mum! That's just so… *wrong.*'

They both burst into laughter.

Emma watched Rosie walk down the street towards Salamanca Place. If she was honest, she was still nervous about Rosie being with such a mixed crowd every day, but she was also happy that Rosie would now be able to make these male friendships so readily during her teen years. Perhaps she wouldn't make the mistake Emma had made when she left the all-girl confines of Denham House – marrying the first young man to turn her head.

Emma was still smiling when an elderly couple walked in the doors.

'Hi there, we're Ian and Louella Payne from Pennsylvania, just checkin' in.' The small bald man smiled a huge toothy grin at Emma and swiped an imaginary hair from his shiny head.

'Hello, Mr Payne, Mrs Payne. I'm Emma. I'm the manager here at Bellicose Bay Retreat. Welcome to Hobart.'

Emma smiled at them both as she pushed the guest card across the bench top towards him. She noticed they were holding hands. How nice to be in love at their age. Perhaps one day that would be her. The idea struck her as amusing, and she found herself laughing out loud.

'What are you laughing at, honey?' smiled Mrs Payne.

'Oh nothing. It's nice to have such happy people around me, that's all,' she said. A blossom of contentment nestled into Emma's heart as she watched them filling in the guest registration card.

After she directed them to their room, she thought about the couple that would be checking in at the cottage, at Phillip's house. A returning couple from Queensland. Emma had resumed running the guest bookings at the cottage after Pia had left. It was part of a loose arrangement she had worked out with Phillip, and they had agreed that she should do it for as long as it worked. If he decided to remarry, and move someone into the house, things might have to change, and lately, that thought didn't even bother her too much. But for now, the cottage was a solid extra source of income to top up the maintenance he paid for Rosie. She had to drop Rosie out there on weekends anyway, so it was generally no trouble to oversee the cleaning and maintenance and make sure the lawns around it were kept tidy. The rest she managed online.

Through the front window Emma watched the retreating figure of her daughter, so gangly and adorable. Rosie had the world at her feet. But then, mused Emma, smiling to herself, perhaps she wasn't the only one.

*

Harriet closed her eyes and let the music wash over her. The tempo and volume rose like a cresting wave, and she sailed across it, smooth and free. She opened her eyes. In the front row of the orchestra, the cellist with the shaved head rocked and receded dramatically in his chair, following the flying movements of his bow. The line of his jaw reminded Harriet of Jonathan and a sudden sadness wrapped itself around her. She closed her eyes again. What was it the psychologist in the mindfulness meditation class was always saying? *Sit with the feeling. Notice it. Examine the way it makes your body feel.* She unclenched her shoulders and let the music wash over her once again – Smetana's Overture to the Bartered Bride – fast, suspenseful and beautiful, the winsome oboe melody a lovely contrast, capturing her soul with the purity of its grace. She felt that for Jonathan too, *grace*. Through the orange, grey light of her closed eyelids she pictured him when he'd returned last month from the school in Uganda, backlit by the sun in the doorway, tall and beautiful. Standing next to Simon. A documentary film maker.

The oboe stopped and the violins burst through the concert hall, bustling with the story of the bohemian festivities, furious lovely movements she could picture, even with her eyes closed. She'd liked Simon. She let the heavy jumble of emotions sit across her chest. She'd known as soon as she'd seen Simon step out of the car that he was the reason that Jonathan looked so happy. He'd been charming too, wanting to find out all about Harriet and her work, and how she coped with the stress of the courtroom. And he'd been delightful with the baby. *Ned.* Scarlett's little brother. Scarlett had been desperate to bring the little boy home for the special lunch to meet his surrogate Uncle Jonathan.

The lump of anxiety lodged itself again in the pit of Harriet's stomach. She let it sit as the music built to a beautiful crescendo. Well, he *was* a lovely little baby, she had to admit that. *Marleen Maples' baby.* Harriet sighed as the music stopped and the applause erupted around her. Marleen deserved happiness. It was just a pity she was finding it with Harriet's husband. Harriet's big toe was pushing down hard into the pointed toe of her shoe. She reduced the pressure and raised her hands to join with the clapping. *Ex-husband.* Ben had moved on, and she supposed it was time that she did too. And she had something in mind that might help her do it. Clementine had sent a link to a job in one of her recent emails, which had otherwise been filled with news about her new show in Luxembourg and the new girlfriend who Clementine planned to bring home to Hobart at Christmas time. When she'd read that, an image had popped into Harriet's head of a proud mother hen, clucking to everyone about her daughter bringing home her heart's desire to meet the family. Then she realised that she *was* a proud mother hen, and the idea had felt strange and soothing.

The clapping subsided and Harriet picked up her handbag. She thought about the copy of the employment contract that was waiting at home for her, ready to be signed. CEO of a charity that worked with underprivileged teenagers in high schools. The pay was terrible, but what did that matter? Education, staying in school, that was the key. The schools that the organisation worked with were mostly over the bridge, dotted around the poorer parts of Hobart. Harriet let the rising melodic strains of the cellos land softly in her head, like a revelation. Yes, it was the new direction she'd been waiting for. She knew what was needed now. It was time to go back over the bridge. Time to go home.

A LETTER FROM SARAH

Thank you very much for reading *Good Little Liars*. Investing your precious time in a book is no small thing, so I really hope you enjoyed spending time with Emma, Marlee, Harriet and kooky Clementine as much as I did during the writing of this book. I was sad to leave them!

If you'd like to keep up to date with my latest releases, you can sign up at the following link. Your email address will never be shared and you can unsubscribe at any time:

www.bookouture.com/sarah-clutton

If you enjoyed the book I'd be grateful if you could write a short public review, so that other readers can have the benefit of your recommendation and might consider choosing my book. It really makes a difference. I'd also love to hear any feedback you have, as it brings the characters back to life for me in the very best way: through new eyes. You can get in touch via my Facebook page, Twitter or Goodreads.

Happy reading and keep in touch!
Sarah

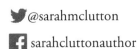

@sarahmclutton

sarahcluttonauthor

ACKNOWLEDGEMENTS

I'm fortunate to come from a very large, fabulous and creative family, many of whom have been incredibly supportive during the writing of my first novel. For your help and encouragement, a huge thanks to my gorgeous and proud mum, Helen Clutton, and my younger sister Kate Clutton; my aunts, Ruth Stendrup, Margie Sadler and Jan Sadler; my cousins, Emily Frewin, Milly Arnell and Missy Bennett; my eagle-eyed niece, Meg Jenkins and my surrogate sister-in-law Ann Brooks – each of you has given invaluable feedback on at least one of the many drafts of this book. I'm particularly grateful to my ever-supportive big sister Sam Jenkins, who is unshakeably devoted to the idea that I have some talent. Thank you, Sammy for your endless interest and your professional expertise in unpicking my characters and their psychological frailties.

Matt and Missy Bennett, thank you for the comfy bed, gourmet meals and background information on Hobart and boarding school life during my research trip, and Duncan and Sally Sadler, thank you for a beach house worthy of my best edits.

To my brilliant medico mates, Dr Stephen Barnett and fellow writer Dr Katie Pullinger, thank you for straightening out the details relating to illness and death. Any remaining errors are mine, and probably due to the fact that most of what you said went straight over my head.

Grant Tucker and Karen Abey – how lucky that my family have friends! Thank you for your input on the Tasmanian legal system.

A huge thank you to the clever and indomitable Cathie Tasker at the Australian Writers' Centre, and to all my classmates in the wonderful Write Your Novel course: in particular Sarah Jones-Nygren and Paula Silveira for their excellent full-text critiques, but also to June, Sal, Jess, Marisa and Gezza for your critiques and ongoing virtual support. For your expert, detailed, early structural edit, a big thank you to Alexandra Nahlous. You made everything much tighter.

To commercial fiction author extraordinaire Fiona McIntosh, thank you for believing in my writing and awarding me the Dymocks Fiona McIntosh Commercial Fiction Scholarship in 2018. I had an absolute blast during my week in Adelaide with you and Nathan, and your tips on writing synopses are now tattooed on my brain (also the story about underpants).

I am immensely grateful to my super-duper talented and enthusiastic editor, Emily Gowers. Your editorial insights are phenomenal and the way you have championed my writing is very touching. And to the rest of the team at Bookouture, thank you, thank you! So far the ride has been rollicking.

To my three beautiful children, Henry, Grace and Georgina, thank you for cheering me on and for being such big-hearted individuals. And a special hug for Miss Georgie for checking on my writerly progress every single day. You are the queen of the word count and the keeper of secret endings.

To all of you who read *Good Little Liars* and made it through to this page, I hope I didn't let you down. Thank you for investing your precious time in my story and I'd really love to hear what you thought.

To all the Clementines out there who speak up when they see injustice, thank you. Keep going!

Finally, to my extraordinary husband Justin. Your love and unwavering belief that I can do anything are gifts that I don't take for granted.

Printed in Great Britain
by Amazon